THE
HOLLOW
MEN

THE
HOLLOW
MEN

ROB McCARTHY

PEGASUS CRIME

NEW YORK LONDON

THE HOLLOW MEN

Pegasus Books Ltd
148 West 37th Street, 13th Floor
New York, NY 10018

First Pegasus Books hardcover edition December 2016

ISBN: 978-1-68177-249-3

10 9 8 7 6 5 4 3 2 1

Printed in the United States of America
Distributed by W. W. Norton & Company, Inc.

Sunday, 20 January

The hearing is the last sense to go, and the first to come back. That was why doctors and nurses still spoke to coma patients even when brain scans showed no activity, and why the sound of his ringing phone interrupted Harry Kent's dreams even when the low winter sun filtering into his living room hadn't. The dream had been a vague one, mercifully peaceful, a series of vignettes interspersed with blackness. Purple skies and mountainsides full of lavender; a young woman, skin as pale as bone, hair dyed pink, trying to speak to him despite the plastic tube he was placing into her throat.

Harry woke up and saw his phone vibrating on the glass coffee table, but couldn't get to it in time. He reached over and picked it up, squinting to make out the number. It was a mobile he didn't recognise. He glanced at the time. Quarter to seven in the evening. Outside, it was already dark, and had been for hours. He returned the call and got a question from the voice that answered.

'Dr Kent? This is Dr Kent, yeah? The police surgeon?'

In the background he could hear chaotic shouting, engines. The voice was female, direct, well spoken.

'Speaking,' Harry said.

'This is DI Noble with Southwark CID. Frances Noble. Call me Frankie.'

'Harry.'

'So, Harry. We have a bit of a situation developing and we'd like your input.'

Harry could hear a vehicle pulling up behind Noble. He stood up from the armchair he'd fallen asleep in and rubbed his forehead. The membranes in his brain were pulsating with every heartbeat, bringing a fresh headache with each strike. 'What kind of situation?'

'You'll be briefed when you get here. But we need a doctor, right now.'

'Which station?'

'At a scene on Wyndham Road. We've closed off a section of the Camberwell Road just after the junction with Albany Road. There's a strip of shops and takeaways. Know the place?'

It was half an hour's walk from Harry's apartment, the other side of the Elephant & Castle roundabout. Five minutes by car.

'Yeah,' he said. 'If someone's hurt, you should call an ambulance.'

'We already have one standing by,' said Noble. 'No one's been injured yet.'

Yet. A knot turning in his stomach, Harry stumbled into the kitchen. The apartment had been his for only four weeks, and a lot of his life was still in boxes in the hallway.

'I can be there in fifteen,' he said, breaking into a cough halfway through.

'Great,' said Noble. 'Are you alright?'

'Yeah, I'm fine. I was on call last night, finished at nine this morning. You woke me up.'

'We could be here some time. I can ring someone else if you want, but the on-call FME is all the way down in Woolwich. I saw your address was nearby and I thought I'd take my chances.'

FME was his official title, Force Medical Examiner, but that sounded far too official and American for most people's liking. Even if the old term, police surgeon, was a misnomer, given that Harry never performed surgery on his patients.

'It's OK, I'll be there,' he said. 'But don't hesitate to use those paramedics if things develop before I arrive.'

'Sure,' said Noble, and hung up.

He didn't have time to shower, so pulled on a clean shirt, jumper and trousers, thick socks for his steel-toed boots and took a shot of mouthwash. Washed his face with his hands in his bathroom sink. He didn't look too tired, which was good, and now his hair was shorter it was easier to control.

Harry reached into the cabinet above the sink and rummaged until he found the prescription bottle in the back corner. It had an orange-and-white label, announcing its contents as aspirin, 300mg, to be taken as needed. The label was peeling at the top corner where Harry had stuck it to the bottle – the previous one had been turquoise and in a different font, and had read dexamphetamine, 10mg. Not to exceed the stated dose.

He put one of the amphetamines into his palm and swallowed it with water. Every hospital had its speed addicts among the registrars and senior house officers but Harry was careful – never more than one a day, and never more than two days in a row, even if he did fall asleep standing up in the lifts. Over the past week, he'd been the registrar on call for the ICU for three nights running. He picked up his medical bag from the hallway, checking that everything was in place, and retrieved the drugs pack he kept in a locked safe in his bedroom. In the hallway, he stopped to put on a woollen fleece.

Harry headed out of his flat and onto the landing. The view northward was impressive: the Docklands, the Eye, the City, St Paul's. From the roof terrace, two floors above his sixth-floor apartment, it was even better. It was why he'd bought it. The tower block on Borough Road had only existed for a few years, replacing what had previously been a council estate of over a thousand people. Those families had been shipped out to Croydon, their homes destroyed to make way for a posh new block of poky professional flats, each costing more than most of the previous inhabitants would make in their lifetimes.

The lift arrived at the ground and Harry walked to his car, the red-and-orange medical bag hoisted over his shoulder. He was thinking about DI Noble and her 'developing situation'. No one could be seriously hurt: not all police surgeons were trained in emergency medicine; many were GPs or psychiatrists. An anaesthetist by training, Harry was a relatively rare specimen. The vast majority of his police work involved taking forensic samples, or deciding whether substance abusers or the mentally ill were fit to be interviewed or detained. As he approached the car, he mentally flipped a coin. It was a little early for the junkies to surface, so he prepared himself for one of the tortured personalities the city might decide to throw at him.

By the time he was out of the car park, he had forgotten the dream.

The police had cordoned off Camberwell Road and the diversion was running riot with the evening traffic, sent north up Albany Road to join the Old Kent Road towards Peckham. The road was blocked by police cars parked facing one another and a line of blue-and-white tape. A second cordon inside went around the square of concrete that was Wyndham Court, leading onto a nondescript estate, the row of shops and takeaways Noble had mentioned blocked by larger police vans. Four uniformed officers stood at the outer cordon, two of them armed.

Harry's stomach tightened again as he wound down his window. Police with guns at the cordons meant firearms involved at the scene, even in this part of town. Nightmare visions of a schizophrenic man waving a shotgun flooded into his consciousness. Whatever this situation was, from the sheer amount of police vehicles present it would evidently not be as simple as Harry had been hoping.

'Road's closed, mate,' the officer at the cordon mouthed. His white breath spiralled in the air and hit Harry's windscreen.

Harry reached out of his window and presented his ID card.

'Dr Kent? You the police surgeon?'

'No,' Harry said. 'I'm the police dentist. DI Noble's six-monthly check-up is due.'

The officer shook his head and pointed over to his left.

'Park up here. I'll walk you in,' he said, before turning to a colleague. 'Sandy, log Dr Kent in. 19.16.'

Harry parked on a double yellow and locked the car, retrieving his bag from the passenger seat. Even with half the Met watching, it was still Walworth. He ducked under the tape, his medical bag bouncing on his back as he walked towards Wyndham Road. A line of patrol cars and vans had formed a semicircle around the shopfronts, a fried chicken takeaway separating an internet café from an Islamic cultural centre. A group of three people were standing behind a large police command unit at the apex of the horseshoe, its side labelled TERRITORIAL SUPPORT GROUP in stencilled letters.

The only woman was not in uniform, her black leather jacket reflecting the floodlights surrounding the group.

'Guv, this is Dr Kent,' the officer escorting him said.

Noble extended her hand. 'Thanks for getting here so quickly. This is, er, rather rapidly getting quite hairy. I'm Silver Command.'

She stepped to one side to introduce the two men standing to her right. The officer in plain clothes was black, six foot four at least, and dressed in the tracksuit bottoms, blue camouflage hoodie and glossy gilet that was the uniform of the estates surrounding them. The other man was in tactical gear: a blue insulated jumpsuit beneath full body armour, complete with bulletproof helmet, visor and sidearm. 'This is DS Wilson, he's with me from CID. And Inspector Quinn, with Trojan. He's Bronze Command.'

The police used the same Bronze-Silver-Gold system for major incidents as the NHS, so Harry was vaguely familiar with it. As the team leader with Trojan, the Met's specialist firearms unit, Quinn was on the front line, in charge of whatever was going on behind the blockade of police vehicles, while Noble managed the scene and dictated strategy. Gold Command would be the chief superintendent at the borough headquarters, pacing anxiously around the office and watching video feeds. Harry nodded at both of the men and shook their gloved hands.

'OK,' he said. 'So what's going on?'

The TSG van's side shutters had been pulled up to reveal a camera image displayed on a flat screen; Wilson moved to allow Harry to see it. It showed the takeaway's façade, peeling blue paintwork above plate glass windows, behind which were four tables and a counter. A youth in a coat too big for him was sitting at the rear table, on which sat an empty box of chicken, three Coke cans and a small black gun. The other people were arranged in a huddle at one side of the room, all standing: two builders in orange high-vis, two men wearing Chicken Hut polo shirts, a family with a young daughter, a hipster with tight jeans and a knitted cardigan.

'This is Solomon Idris,' said Noble. 'That's a provisional ID, DS Wilson and his team are working on confirming it as we speak. He's been holding those people hostage for about an hour now.'

Noble's explanation was concise and clear, but it left Harry cold. 'I don't know what you expect of me,' he said. 'I'm not a psychologist. If you want me to profile him, or negotiate, I can't do that.'

She laughed. 'Believe it or not, Dr Kent, we have our own specialist officers trained for just that.'

'Where are they?' Harry said.

Noble shook her head. 'The ones attached to South-East

London are all at a European police conference in Antwerp. I think there's someone on their way from the Yard, but this is hardly high priority.'

Harry had some sympathy with them. A kid with a gun in a fried chicken takeaway, he thought. It wasn't a Middle Eastern embassy siege.

'So what happened?' he asked. 'Is he trying to rob the place?'

'Not as far as we can tell,' she replied. 'We've managed to get the CCTV feed. He ordered and paid, sat down and started eating. Then he just pulled out the gun, fired into the air and told everyone not to move. He let three schoolkids who were there go and told them to call the police. And here we are.'

There was a chime from inside DS Wilson's gilet, and he reached in to retrieve a BlackBerry, opening up an email. From his expression, Harry guessed it was something useful.

'Mo, what have we got?'

'His record,' Wilson said, waving the screen around.

'Anything interesting?' said Noble.

'Solomon Idris, seventeen years old, address on the Albany estate,' Wilson summarised. 'Got previous for possession of a bladed weapon, ABH, robbery. Used to be affiliated, Wooly OC, but he got himself shanked in 2010 and since then nothing. Looks like he's gone straight.'

Everyone listened intently to Wilson, who spoke quickly, but with an almost mournful tone in his voice, like a disappointed parent. Noble was working a piece of chewing gum from one side of her mouth to the other furiously. Harry would bet that it was the nicotine-rich variety, and the chewing was an addict's release.

'Some kind of vendetta?' Quinn suggested.

'After almost two years on the straight?' said Noble. 'Unlikely.'

She turned back to Harry.

'Anyway,' she continued, 'he's made a few demands. He wants to speak to a lawyer, and he wants to make a statement and have it broadcast on BBC News.'

'Are you meeting them?' Harry asked.

'We've got some legal aid bod coming over from the Yard. We're still working on Huw Edwards.'

Quinn put his hand to his earpiece and went running off

towards the back of the van. Harry noticed two bored-looking paramedics with cardboard cups of tea, sitting in the front of the ambulance and waiting for someone to get shot. He stepped forward, his breath dancing in the cold air.

'With all due respect,' he said, looking between Noble and Wilson, 'I still don't see what I'm doing here.'

'He's sick,' Noble said. 'Solomon.'

'What, you mean mentally ill? You want a psych assessment?'

'No. Well, not as far as we know. The kid's physically sick. He's been coughing his lungs up, maybe once every few minutes, for about half an hour now. That's why you're here. Also looks like he's having trouble breathing. We've negotiated a deal. Three of the hostages will be released in exchange for medical attention.'

Harry leaned in closer, as though if he could hear her better she'd make more sense. He put his palm up, then regretted it. Outside his fleece pocket his hand burned cold. 'Sorry? You want me to go into the takeaway with Idris and treat him, am I right?'

Noble nodded and started to explain. 'Look, we really think—'

'And all this time he's still armed, yeah?'

Inspector Quinn returned from behind the van and put a hand on Harry's forearm, squeezing just too tightly to be considered reassuring. 'Look, I know that sounds scary, but trust me. I've got sixteen officers deployed, four round the back covering the fire exit, six at the front, all eyes on the target.' He pointed up at the council flats that looked down onto the takeaway. 'Two sharpshooters up there. At all times at least one of them has a crosshair right on the subject. The other four guys are a walk-in team. They'll take you right up to the door. Believe me, this guy makes even a fraction of a move for that weapon and my boys will take him out before you even start to shit your pants.'

Quinn laughed and Harry didn't. 'I'm glad you're not negotiating,' he said.

'So am I, mate.'

'You'll do it then?' The voice was DI Noble's, blunt, to the point.

Harry hadn't finished nodding before someone tapped him on the shoulder. He turned around. DS Wilson was holding up a

Kevlar vest. 'Let's get this on under your fleece, then,' he said. 'Wouldn't want you to get chilly, now, would we?'

Harry sat on the step of the van trying not to shiver. Inspector Quinn was next to him, addressing the four armed officers gathered in front. They were battle-ready, two with MP5 carbines slung across their chests, the others with heavy metal shields and handguns, hard-man bravado visible on their faces. Harry took one look and knew each was as nervous as he was.

'OK,' Quinn said. He was holding a whiteboard tablet on which he'd sketched a map of the storefronts. 'Charlie One and Charlie Two will advance up the street and wait behind the concrete bench here. Once they're in position, Charlie Three and Charlie Four will escort Dr Kent up to the same position. From there, I want radio confirmation of eyes on target before Dr Kent approaches the front door. If at any point you lose your shot, radio in.'

Grunts of understanding from the four officers. Harry's heart was starting to race. A familiar feeling was coming back to him, one that he hadn't missed. But it had been different when he'd been in the field – he'd been a cog in a machine, whether in the safety of the hospital at Bastion, behind dozens of security circles, or darting out of the back ramp of a helicopter with a platoon of Royal Marines to take the heat for him. There, he'd had a mission, something he could focus on to ignore the flying bullets. The kid in front of him with three limbs blown off and half of his circulating volume soaked into the dust.

Here, though, it was just him and a seventeen-year-old boy with a gun. The one who was really in charge of the situation, whatever the Met said.

'Radio check,' Quinn ordered. Harry had been given his own earpiece and collar mike. He heard the armed officers' call signs one by one as they checked their communications. He was trying to reassure himself that they had his back. It wasn't working. He felt an itch under his right arm, and took a deep breath of freezing air.

'And you, Doc.'

'Check.'

'OK,' Quinn said. 'Move up, stand by.'

The two armed officers took their positions between two police vans, one of the gaps in the armoured horseshoe protecting the officers from the siege in the takeaway. The media were starting to arrive at the far cordon, and Harry could hear a helicopter somewhere in the night. Quinn leaned out and nodded to Noble and Wilson, who were still standing by the command vehicle. Harry followed his gaze and made eye contact with Noble for a brief second. She nodded and smiled. At that moment he realised where he'd seen her face before, and felt a twist in the pit of his stomach. Putting the memory away, he watched her raise a black satellite phone and start talking.

'Hi, Solomon. It's Frankie again. How are you?'

I can't imagine how he is, Harry thought. Coming to terms with the prospect of his life ending in a fried chicken takeaway.

'Is our deal still on? Good, that's great to hear. OK, this is what we're gonna do. You're gonna see some of our officers in front of the shop. But don't worry now, they're just there to make sure Dr Kent gets in safe and to collect the other people when they come out.'

The other people. Harry guessed the book didn't let her say the word 'hostage'.

'OK, I understand, Solomon. He'll be with you shortly. Thanks for cooperating.'

Noble turned and nodded to Quinn, who put his hand over his earpiece.

'Charlie One and Two, move to position,' he said.

'Copy.'

Harry watched the two officers walk round the corner, the one with the shield leading, his handgun poking out behind it, trained on the figure behind the panel glass.

'In position.'

'Charlie Three and Four standing by.'

Quinn looked across at Harry and pointed to the two Trojan officers crouched either side of him, checking their weapons.

'Good luck, mate.'

Harry filled his lungs with crisp, empty air and stood up, taking his position between the two policemen.

'In your own time, Charlie Three.'

They emerged from behind the van and Harry felt every muscle in his body tense involuntarily. The first two guys were now crouched behind a concrete bench, aiming towards the figure at the far table. Harry looked up at the logo next to the flickering Chicken Hut sign, the smiling cockerel, and wondered how thick the glass beneath it was, whether it would cause the bullets to ricochet.

They reached the benches and the second pair of officers took up positions either side of him.

'This is as far as we go,' one of them said.

'Excellent.'

Harry held the strap of his medical bag, the orange fluorescent stripe reflecting the takeaway's lights. The internet café and cultural centre were closed, blinds down, their owners and staff no doubt evacuated earlier. His right armpit was itching again. He stood up, fixed his eyes on the blue strobes reflected in the takeaway's front window and began to move. As he walked towards the light, he thought about what a good target the fluorescent strap across his chest was.

'Romeo One Rifle, no shot.'

The voice was a new one, one of the marksmen somewhere on the tower block behind him. Rifle bullets were twice as long and travelled twice as fast as those in the officers' carbines, or Solomon Idris's revolver. If the sharpshooters missed, they could easily slice through Harry and then a hostage.

Quinn's voice: 'Rifle Two, check in.'

'Romeo Two Rifle, I have a shot. Standing by.'

Harry wrapped his hand around the metal handle of the door and pushed it in. A bell rang to announce his arrival. He took four steps forward so he was standing right in the middle of the shop.

Solomon Idris was sitting far from the door, his back propped up against the wall, one arm on the counter. Tracklines shaved into his hair, hands in the long front pocket of his hoodie, beads of sweat on his forehead, red, spider's webs of blood on the whites of his eyes. The grainy camera image and the baggy hoodie had managed to disguise just how thin he was. DS Wilson had said that Idris was seventeen, but to Harry he seemed far older – his face was sunken, the cheeks sucked inward, close to the bones, and his eyes looked out with a stare Harry had seen before, an old man's stare in young men who had seen things beyond their years. His figure shone in a halo of glowing meal deals, chicken buckets and side orders.

Harry looked around and buried an almost uncontrollable desire to burst out laughing. Here he was, less than an hour after waking up in an empty flat, the scaffold of his mind held up by speed, standing in a fried chicken shop with an armed teenager. A chill ran through him, despite all the layers he had on, and he saw that the hostages were all shivering too.

The mobile phone on the desk next to the gun rang and Harry tried to conceal that it had made him jump. Idris reached down with a delicate, measured movement and picked it up.

Harry imagined Noble's voice on the other end of the phone, firm but caring, like a schoolteacher. Idris's face didn't change and he said nothing. He hung up the phone and turned his gaze to Harry.

'Take off the vest.'

No sooner was the command out of Idris's mouth than he collapsed into a fit of visceral coughing, his body jerking with every spasm.

Harry's eyes moved down to the gun on the table. A pocket-sized revolver, one of the thousands of street guns that circulated around the city. It looked small-calibre, not one of the magnum varieties which could cut through Kevlar like it was paper. At this range, Harry's vest would stop the bullet.

Idris nodded at one of the hostages, the young girl with her parents. 'Take it off, bruv, or I waste the girl.'

Her father let out a whimper, and Harry released the Velcro strap keeping the vest in place, sliding his arms out of the fleece and laying it and the vest on the ground. He decided that under no circumstances would he give the vest to Idris. Two layers of clothing down, the cold bit Harry's skin even harder.

Silence and cold air filled the restaurant and somewhere outside a distant siren stopped. Harry didn't know what to say. The kid broke the deadlock.

'Is you hungry?'

At the mere mention of the word, Harry's stomach did a full turn. Night shifts meant working from 8.30 in the morning to

8.30 at night, and handing over at the morning meeting usually went on until 9.30. His last meal had been a toasted sandwich from the hospital's twenty-four-hour café somewhere around one a.m., eighteen hours ago.

'Yeah, actually, I am,' said Harry. 'Starving.'

Idris gestured towards the two Chicken Hut employees, their polo shirts the same colour as the blue plasters on their fingers, who jerked to their feet.

'Boss, make man some chicken,' he ordered, before turning to Harry: 'What you want?'

'I'm fine,' said Harry.

'Nah you isn't!' Idris said, coughing again. 'You's hungry. That's what they there for, innit? That's what they get paid to do, yeah? Just like you's a doctor. You make people better. Or you s'posed to, innit? They make us chicken.'

'Honestly, I'm fine,' said Harry. 'But thanks for the offer, mate.'

Idris shrugged his shoulders and settled back into his chair. The smell of grease and spices hung in the restaurant, and Harry's hunger worsened. The paradox of simultaneous hunger and zero appetite whatsoever was an all too familiar one to him.

Noble's voice sounded in his ear. 'Tell him we had a deal, Harry.'

Harry took a deep breath in.

'You made a deal with Frankie about letting the other people go,' he said.

Idris looked at him through the bloodshot eyes that had evidently seen too much, rolled his head from side to side and burst into another fit of coughing. Harry could see the sternocleidomastoid muscles above his collarbones jerking as his lungs spasmed.

'Fair,' Idris said once the coughs subsided. He pointed to the family gathered in the near corner of the shop and then threw his hand towards the door. 'Go,' he said, and pulled a napkin to his mouth and coughed into it. Harry watched it fall, noting red spots surrounding the smiling cockerel on his white background. The family ran into the arms of the Trojan officers waiting at the door, who shepherded them to safety, a chorus of boots on concrete.

As the officers melted back into the darkness, Harry felt more alone than he had in a long time. He tried to remember the sharp-shooters behind him in the tower block, their crosshairs over the man, or rather the boy, in front of him. He looked at Solomon Idris and thought that he must be feeling pretty lonely, too. Probably lonelier than he had ever been before.

Over half the patients at Bastion had been enemy combatants, insurgents responsible for the deaths and injuries of his comrades, men willing to kill for an ideology that included shooting young girls in the head for demanding an education. Your patient has an inalienable right to life, he told himself now, as he had then. The teenager in front of him hadn't done anything nearly as bad as most of the people he'd treated over there. Victims of birth: just like growing up in a theocracy where Westerners had destroyed your livelihood and culture made you an insurgent, if you grew up poor in a concrete mausoleum in North Peckham, life inside a gang was the only security you could ever hope for.

'Can I call you Solomon?' said Harry.

Idris grunted and nodded. More coughing.

'I'm Harry. Can I place my bag down on this table?' He got an imperceptible nod in reply. 'What seems to be the problem?'

'Can't breathe. Got bare pain in my chest.'

'How long have you been coughing?' said Harry.

'Weeks, man.'

Harry reached into his medical bag and watched Idris wrap his fingers around the gun, releasing it when Harry withdrew his hand with a stethoscope entwined in it. How many gunshot wounds had he seen in his career? Six or seven in two years in London. Maybe a hundred in nine months at Bastion. Nothing quite as destructive as a bullet, its complete disregard for organ, bone or tissue, tearing through everything with equal malice.

'You normally fit and well?'

'Yeah.'

'Any health conditions? Asthma? Diabetes?'

'No.'

Harry tapped the diaphragm of his stethoscope to check it was set round the right way.

'Travelled anywhere recently?'

Idris rolled his bloodshot eyes over to meet Harry's.

'Solomon, I don't work for the police. I'm a doctor. Anything you tell me falls under doctor–patient confidentiality, and I'll only pass it on to the police in the event that not informing them would risk placing you or someone else in danger.'

Idris shook his head and laughed, but it quickly degenerated into coughing. Wet particles of saliva bounced off the table and onto Harry's sleeve. He reached into the bag and put on gloves and a surgical mask. Once Idris was finished he indicated the two Chicken Hut workers, the builders, and the student in the cardigan.

'Bruv, I's sittin here with a piece and these five bitches. I think you could get away with sayin I's dangerous.'

Harry smiled. Idris didn't react.

'Maybe I could,' Harry said. 'But telling me if you've been abroad won't change my mind. It might help me help you, though.'

Idris nodded. Harry watched the neck muscles he used whenever he breathed.

'Fair. I been in Nottingham a bit. I ain't never left England.'

Harry said nothing and felt the weight of fear in his chest. Or maybe it was guilt. At Solomon Idris's age, Harry had never left the country either. It was one of the things that had been most noticeable, that had embarrassed him most, when he'd arrived at medical school, his peers all fresh from gap years in Phuket or Paraguay or Paris, or from the family safari in Kenya. If things had been different, could he have been here? Surrounded by the filth, a gun in his hand, contemplating the prospect of his last meal being a box of chicken?

He ignored the feeling and put the diaphragm of his stethoscope just below Idris's left collarbone.

'Take a deep breath in.'

He did so. Harry heard crackled, muffled whispers of life. He looked down, saw the gun again, and imagined the bullet in his own chest. He wondered what would kill him if Idris decided to use it. Sometimes gunshot victims died before they had time to bleed to death: their lungs collapsed and the pressure in their chests built up until it crushed their hearts, or the great vessels leaked into the airways and they drowned in their own blood.

'Have you lost any weight recently?'

'Yeah.'

'Since when?'

'A couple months. But I ain't been eatin, not much anyway.'

Idris erupted into the worst coughing fit so far, and Harry jumped backwards, pulling his stethoscope back over his neck. Idris bent double and retched, and Harry reached into his pack for a clinical waste bag, holding it at Idris's chin so the teenager could cough into it. When the fit was finished, he leant over and inspected the sputum, but there was nothing in the bag despite the fact that the teenager's lungs were audibly full of crap. Maybe there were cysts, or he was too weak to cough it up. Christ, Harry thought.

'How long have you been feeling like this?'

'About a week. Thought it was a cold, innit.'

From the muffled breath sounds and the distress he was in, it was more than a mere chest cold. Harry suspected a serious pneumonia, maybe even tuberculosis, and when he spotted a greyness in the nail beds of Idris's fingers, he went into his bag for a pulse oximeter. He had almost forgotten that he was in the midst of a police siege, because all this was routine. A sick patient, who needed a differential diagnosis and stabilisation. Ignoring the smell of fried chicken and the radio static in his ear, the sterile yellow light was the same as A&E at night.

Harry held up the oximeter and pushed it open.

'Can I slide this onto one of your fingers, please?'

'What is it?'

'It measures how much oxygen is in your blood.'

'No needles?'

Idris's other hand closed around the gun's handle, and Harry tensed again. Although it was a natural reflex, it was actually the worst thing to do. The bullet would do less damage if his muscles were relaxed when it hit him. The kid looked as terrified as Harry felt, although that was little comfort.

'No needles.'

Idris released the gun. Another irony, Harry thought. A teenager who'd taken a knife blade to the thigh nervous about a needle-prick. The reading flashed up. Eighty-seven. Ninety-five and above was normal: Idris's levels were life-threatening.

'Solomon, listen to me—'

Idris grabbed the bag and coughed into it.

'I need to go and get an oxygen cylinder for you to breathe

from. Your oxygen levels are so low you're in danger of damaging your brain.'

'Go get it.'

Idris picked up his gun and gestured. Harry pictured the sharp-shooters behind him breathing in and quickly out again, so their bodies would be totally still when they applied the modicum of final pressure to triggers they were already squeezing. His earpiece burst into life. It was Noble, her voice striking the reality of the situation back into him like a cold wind.

'Harry, stay where you are,' she said. 'We can use this as leverage to get the hostages out.'

Idris broke into another coughing fit, sending blood-streaked saliva into the clinical waste bag. Harry watched the muscles in his neck and shoulders contracting, every breath drawing a pained grimace, a new struggle for air.

He turned around and headed to the door.

As Harry walked out of the shop, sleet hit him in the face. He stepped up to a run until he passed the concrete bench, where two Trojan officers emerged from the shadows and took him by the arms, practically dragging him to cover.

'Give it a rest!' he said through clenched teeth. 'He's not gonna shoot me in the back, is he?'

'You don't know that, do you?'

Noble, Quinn and Wilson were waiting behind the police van, and it was Noble who accosted him first. Harry headed past them towards the ambulance, instructing one of the paramedics to open it up.

'Dr Kent!'

Harry turned to face Noble. Her calm exterior was gone, and the redness in her face indicated a mixture of cold and frustrated rage. He guessed that the friendly first names of their introduction were out of the window.

'Is your earpiece working?' she said. 'You did hear me tell you to stay put, didn't you?'

Harry pulled off the dirty gloves and mask and threw them into the clinical waste bag the paramedic was holding in front of him.

'I did,' he said. 'But that boy in there is seriously ill, Inspector. He needs to be admitted to hospital or he could be in real danger.'

'I get that,' said Noble. 'But if he starts shooting then those innocent people in there are in danger, as are my officers and as are you. You can't just work against us, alright?'

'OK,' Harry said, raising his palms. 'I'm sorry. I shouldn't have disobeyed you. But don't you forget, I'm a doctor, not a police officer. My first responsibility is to my patient and I won't let his health be used as a bargaining chip.'

'And my first responsibility is getting all five hostages out of there alive, so I'm afraid your patient's health is not high on my list!'

Harry said nothing. One of the paramedics passed him an oxygen cylinder and he took it by the handle.

'How serious is it?' Quinn asked.

'Without proper medical attention, he might not last more than a few hours. Maybe not even that. He's heading into respiratory failure.'

'Just hypothetically,' Quinn said, 'if we went in there, is he still capable of pulling the trigger?'

'I can't answer that; I don't know. He's incredibly weak. I doubt he's capable of running more than a few metres before collapsing. In this state, he isn't much of a threat.'

As he said the words, Harry realised they were false. It didn't require much strength to lift a gun and pull a trigger: that's why people used them. Firearms were great equalisers.

Noble shot Quinn a crystalline look. 'That's staying hypothetical, Inspector,' she said. 'We're not going in unless he makes a move. I am not going to let the Met shoot dead a young kid on my watch. This is my fucking patch, and I do not want it turning into Tottenham in summertime, understood?'

'Absolutely.'

'Good. You ready, Dr Kent?'

Harry nodded. As I'll ever be, he thought. Ready to walk back into a place armed police had been forbidden to go, with his only protection lying on the tiled floor. He heard the sound of the helicopter overhead and for a second was back in the mountains. He felt the same fear, the same taste of adrenaline, as he had in the field. Discounted it, put it down to the amphetamine he'd taken.

Noble's voice destroyed the memory.

'Inspector Quinn, have your men walk Dr Kent back in.'

Harry went back into the restaurant and the bell rang again. Both of the takeaway employees looked up towards the door, creatures of habit.

Idris was clutching the clinical waste bag and looked even worse. Those lungs had to be seriously diseased, he thought, for him to have deteriorated in the short time Harry'd been outside. Seventeen was too young for cancer, even though Idris had said he'd lost weight. If it was indeed pneumonia, then it had already progressed to the stage where his lung function was significantly impaired if he was running sats of eighty-seven. A lung abscess was possible, as was TB, even though Idris had denied going anywhere exotic. But these days, London was exotic enough.

'When's the lawyer coming?' Idris demanded.

Harry got out a non-rebreather mask from the oxygen cylinder's bag and connected it to the valve, turning the gas supply on.

'I don't know,' he said, passing it to the teenager. Idris tossed it back to him.

'You first, bitch.'

Harry laughed. Of course kids of Idris's age distrusted the police, but that level of paranoia was something new. He wondered if the fear in Idris's eyes was something else, whether he was psychotic. As a young black man, he ticked most of the risk factors for schizophrenia. But those diagnoses could wait until they had him physically stable. Harry put the mask to his face and took a few deep breaths of the oxygen, then connected a sterile one to the cylinder and passed it over to Idris, who sealed it over his face and took long, laboured breaths. Each time he looked scared it would be his last.

'If you need to cough again, take the mask off and cough into the bag.'

Idris nodded placidly. They sat in silence again while Harry checked the reading on the pulse oximeter. Eighty-nine, little change. His pulse was elevated too, a hundred and eighteen. He turned up the oxygen to four litres.

'Fuck's sake!'

The voice was from one of the five hostages, the fat, greasy man with the smiling cockerel on his polo shirt. Harry closed his eyes and felt his heart thump in his chest. One thing he'd learnt growing up in Lewisham, which had been reinforced by the military: keep your fucking head down.

Idris looked round slowly, like it was taking all of his physical effort.

'Yeah?'

'You gonna let me turn the heating back on? Or you gonna freeze us all to death?'

Harry had noticed the cold when he'd first entered the room, but then he'd forgotten it. Maybe it was the stress, the adrenaline warming his core. But he felt it now, biting at his skin, easily as icy as it was outside.

'Too hot,' was all Idris said.

Harry took Idris's wrist, the one not resting on the gun, and felt his brow with his other hand. He was sweating profusely, the skin warm to the touch. Systemic fever. The infection in his chest was spreading. He could have septicaemia already.

'Solomon,' he said. 'Listen to me.'

Idris coughed and looked up. His words were muffled by the mask, but Harry had heard the question so many times he could lip-read them without effort.

'Allow it, mate. Am I gonna die?'

He said it with the nonchalance you might expect from someone on the street asking if it was going to rain later. Harry gave his stock reply. 'Not if I can help it.'

Idris pulled off the mask and coughed violently into the bag, the plastic shaking as each expulsion of bloody mist hit it.

'Solomon, we can help you, OK? But you have to let these people go.'

Harry winced inwardly, as if Idris was about to raise the gun and shoot him for sounding patronising.

'I think you've got a serious lung infection. I can give you some fluids and drugs to bring the fever down, and the oxygen will help you breathe better. But only for a while. It might buy you an hour or two. You need to get to a hospital now, or you'll be in big trouble. So let these people go, get in an ambulance with me, and don't give them the satisfaction.'

Idris looked up at him. Harry watched him actually considering what he'd said, seeming to weigh everything up. Was that what this was, suicide-by-cop? If that was the plan, maybe Idris was working out if he didn't need to provoke them into shooting him. It might be easier to simply fade away, let the disease take him.

'I want the drip,' said Idris. 'But no hospitals.'

'OK. Are you allergic to anything?'

'Penicillin.'

Brilliant, Harry thought. That ruled out most of the drugs he'd want to start with, and all but one of the antibiotics he carried with him. He reached into his bag and pulled out a cannula, a tourniquet, a sharps bin and a packet of saline. Tied the tourniquet around Idris's arm, started searching for a vein in his elbow. The sweat on his skin, and the shock from the infection, made them hide, so Harry went down to the wrist and found a bulging one on the dorsal surface of his hand. He rested the drip on top of his bag, twisting the valve and letting the fluid start running into Idris's system. He watched the teenager wince as he taped the cannula to his arm.

No hospitals. There was only a limit to what he could do here. Examine him, provide initial care. He didn't carry any antibiotics powerful enough to treat the infection which Idris could safely receive, just oxygen and fluids. And he really needed to get an X-ray. Maybe if he could get Idris talking, get him to trust him, then he would agree to come with him. He tried to pick his words, to sound friendly, approachable.

'What's this about, Solomon?'

The words were out of his mouth before he had time to regret it. It wasn't his job to get this kid out of here, it was DI Noble's – wherever she was, and whatever she was doing. Which at the moment looked like nothing.

The reply came through another bout of coughing.

'Keisha.'

'Who's Keisha?'

Idris erupted into coughing, his head jerking as if he was head-butting the orange bag. When he was finished he wiped his eyes and looked up at Harry. That look was there again. The one that said the teenager had seen things he shouldn't have. How many seventeen-year-old boys can look people in the eye and say they've come close to dying?

'You don't give a shit, bruv.'

'You give a shit, don't you?' said Harry. 'You wouldn't be doing this otherwise.'

'Fuck you.'

Were those tears in his eyes? Tears from the fever, the shortness of breath, or at his situation? He might have a gun, not to mention a criminal history most adults would shirk at, but here he looked vulnerable.

'What happened to Keisha?'

'She died. They fucking killed her. Killed her and you feds didn't give a shit.'

The crap in Idris's throat punctuated his speech, each word like a silenced gunshot. The words ran through Harry's mind like the raindrops down the shop window, some meeting up and merging along the way.

'Who killed her, Solomon?'

'Not talking to you. These ends, you don't talk to the feds. You talk to the feds and mandem get you.'

'I'm not with the police, Solomon,' said Harry, aware that he sounded as desperate as he was. 'I'm a doctor. I don't work for them. I don't do what they say. Let me get you to the hospital, and we can talk about Keisha while we're getting you better.'

'Gonna talk about Keisha when the lawyer comes. Gonna tell him and the BBC.'

Idris descended into coughing, the longest and most violent episode yet, now so short of breath he could barely form sentences. His head came slowly back up from the bag, and he replaced the mask. He raised a hand, palm open, and even that movement looked like it took most of his effort.

'Unless you let us treat you, you might not make it that long,' Harry said. It was on the dramatic side, but he wasn't sure if Noble and the other police officers had any intention of granting the requests. He went through various scenarios in his head: he could take blood and have the police courier it to the hospital for tests. The messenger could return with broad-spectrum antibiotics usable with a penicillin allergy. He could start intravenous paracetamol to bring down the fever. But even that might not buy Idris more than a few hours.

Not good enough. Pulse elevated, pyrexic, respiratory rate up, blood pressure holding for now, but Harry had that hunch, that gut feeling, that told him it would crash at any minute. Patients like this were the ones he got called to on the wards because the nurses and the junior doctors were worried about them.

'When we get to hospital, we might have to sedate you so we can take control of your breathing and give you more oxygen,' Harry continued. 'We really don't have a lot of time here.'

He thought about it. He had sedative drugs in his bag. Midazolam, ketamine, morphine. Would Idris buy it if he said it was an antibiotic for the infection, but gave him a bit of midazolam, enough to knock him out and let the police come in safely? Maybe not when he'd first come in, Harry thought, but now the teenager trusted him, it was possible.

Possible, but morally abhorrent. He's your patient, and you do what's best for him. That's the first commandment, the unbreakable law. Noble's looking out for the hostages, the 'other people'. Nobody else is looking out for the kid with the gun and the haunted eyes.

'Talk to me about Keisha. I'll tell your lawyer, I'll tell whoever you want.'

'Feds didn't give a shit then. They won't now.'

Harry leant forward.

'I don't think—'

The gunshot was loud, cutting through the cold air, somewhere to Harry's left. His earpiece exploded into life.

'Shots fired!'

Harry's eyes flashed down to the gun on the table, to Idris's hand, which reached towards it, the clinical waste bag dropping into his lap.

'GO! GO! GO!'

Feet crashing onto concrete, Harry diving for Idris, screams from the hostages, the bell of the opening takeaway door. Idris ducking sideways, hand sluggish, finger groping for the trigger, Harry rolling onto his back, men in black in the doorway.

'DON'T SHOO—'

Crack. Splitting windows and rolling off the walls.

'—T HIM!'

Nothing but ringing in Harry's ears.

'He's down!'

Police flooded into the restaurant, some with guns raised, others grabbing the hostages and dragging them out into the night. Idris was on the floor, awkwardly propped between the counter and the table, blocked from Harry's view by his medical bag. He felt hands on his shoulders, pulling him up.

'Doc, you hit? Are you OK?'

He patted himself down, waiting for the adrenaline to subside, for the pain of the wound to strike, but nothing came. A tight agony spread from his chest to his right flank, and he felt alive, his vision heightened, his ears ringing. This was a feeling he knew. This was the fear and rage of war, in a chicken shop on the Camberwell Road.

Harry pulled himself to his feet.

'I'm fine. Get the medics in here, now!' he said.

A low moan from behind the table. A pair of Trojan officers who'd come in the back were patting Idris down, checking him for weapons. Harry grabbed the table between him and the teenager and threw it to one side, a leg snapping off as it hit the wall. He tapped the officer closest to him on the shoulder.

'Let me through.'

Quinn was there now, his voice calm, the eye of the storm.

'Dr Kent, we need to get you out of here.'

Harry ignored him and knelt down. Idris was still conscious and moaning loudly, his eyes flickering between the various people crowded over his body. Harry cut off the hoodie with shears from his medical kit. He could see the entry wound, over to the left of Solomon Idris's torso, underneath the curve of the ribcage. Probably too low to have hit the heart. Hopefully. But there was something hit, it was leaking blood, crimson against the white floor tiles.

'Clothes off!' Harry shouted. 'Cut his clothes off!' He patted Idris down, checking for other wounds. Found blood on the left wrist but it was just where the cannula had been pulled out as he

25

fell. He reached underneath and felt for an exit wound, but there wasn't one.

'Stay still! Stay fucking still!'

The shouting was one of the Trojan officers, weapon still trained on Idris's chest.

'Gun's clear!' said Quinn.

Idris was thrashing on the floor, a combination of shock and fear. Like this, Harry could do nothing – couldn't place another IV line, couldn't keep him on oxygen, couldn't dress his wounds.

'Get pressure on that wound and hold him down!' he barked.

He reached over into his medical pack, putting the anaesthetic kit on the table in front of him and biting open the packaging of an intramuscular needle. He kept preloaded syringes with standard doses of anaesthetics ready to save time.

'Scene is secure, get the medics in here!' Quinn said into his collar mike. He was holding a clear plastic bag with the gun inside. Four Trojan officers were holding Idris to the ground as he struggled and thrashed, their weapons slung over their backs. One, wearing only a sidearm and with a green cross on his helmet, had managed to get gloved hands and a white dressing over the teenager's shoulder.

'Trigger-happy pricks,' Harry muttered, attaching the needle to a preloaded syringe. Working out the dosage in his head. Sixty-kilogram teenager, ketamine in the muscle, call it seven hundred to be on the safe side.

'He fired first,' Quinn said.

'Save it for the inquest,' Harry said.

He knelt down by Idris's thrashing body and aimed the needle at the large deltoid muscle over the teenager's good arm. Went in and was met by a pained moan, before the thrashing slowly subsided. Noise drifted in from outside as the ambulance pulled up, and the Trojan officers began to retreat, letting the paramedics through.

'Jesus Christ, is he dead?'

The officer who'd fired the shot was young, maybe just twenty. The way he was shaking told Harry everything he needed to know about how he was handling the situation. Quinn grabbed him by the arm and led him towards the back exit, away from the massing crowd.

'The doctor's sedated him, Greg. Let's go.'

Harry lifted the dressing off the wound to inspect it further – it was still bleeding, but not catastrophically. Looked venous, not arterial. There was always the risk of a major structure being damaged internally, but nothing he could do about that now. The area where Idris had been hit was rich with large blood vessels and vital organs: spleen; kidney; gut. All of them could exsanguinate if they were hit. If they managed to save the kid's life, it would be on the operating table.

Harry considered working on him there, securing another line, intubating him on the floor of the Chicken Hut, transferring him to the hospital once he was stable, but with the Ruskin no more than five minutes away on blue lights it wasn't worth the delay – every second he spent at the scene was another one Idris was losing blood without replacement. Just like Helmand, he thought. Get the casualty out of the hot zone and run for their life.

'You're the police doctor?' one paramedic said.

'I'm an ICU registrar, too,' Harry said. 'Can we scoop him onto the trolley?'

He was waiting for the paramedic to take over, but she simply nodded and ran back towards the ambulance, leaving her partner waiting there. Harry stepped into the void.

'Get a line in, as quick as you can.'

The paramedic knelt by Idris's exposed arm and started searching for veins, and Harry replaced the pulse oximeter on the teenager's finger. Got his stethoscope to examine the chest, and was relieved to still hear breath sounds, albeit dull, on the left side, even lower down, right near the wound. There was no way to tell if the dullness was due to infection or an internal bleed.

'Sats are eighty-one.'

Still heading down. Harry reached over to the oxygen cylinder and picked it up, switching it to maximum flow, fifteen litres a minute, as the female paramedic returned with an orthopaedic scoop stretcher, which she broke in half. Harry placed it at one side of their patient, the paramedic mirroring him, and they joined the halves at the head and feet and arranged themselves either side of the scoop.

'Ready, steady, lift.'

They carried Idris out of the takeaway like pall-bearers at a funeral. Got him onto the trolley and onto the lift at the back of the ambulance. The police medic looked up at Harry, his hands still pressing on the wound in Idris's chest, while the male paramedic ran to the front door and started up the ambulance, blue lights on, so they could leave the moment the lift was up. They rolled Idris into the back of the ambulance on the trolley, and locked the doors.

Blasted sirens as the street lights, snow and concrete flew past through tinted windows.

'Got the line in,' the paramedic shouted. 'Want the fluids?'

Harry looked up at the vital signs monitor. No blood pressure recorded yet, so he wrapped his fingers around Idris's wrist and squeezed. A faint, fast pulse rebounded against the bloodied, sticky material of his gloves.

'He's got a radial, let's hold off for now,' said Harry. 'Can we get a pre-alert in, make sure Resus knows we're coming.'

The voice from the paramedic driving the ambulance squawked over his colleague's radio. 'This is call sign Papa 2-4-2, we have a Code Red trauma call. Seventeen-year-old male with a gunshot abdomen, unrecordable blood pressure. ETA three minutes.'

Truncating the tragedy of everything Harry had seen in the last half-hour into a couple of sentences transmitted over the radio. His fingers were still wrapped around Solomon Idris's wrist, feeling the pulse slowly weaken.

'Solomon! Can you hear me, Solomon? Squeeze my hand!'

Just a shiver, a hint of movement, even with the ketamine in his system. What else can we do for him? There were plastic tubes in his nose and mouth providing a temporary airway; he was on high-flow oxygen to optimise his ventilation; there were big peripheral lines in place, ready for a massive transfusion. Only blood and surgery could help him now, and antibiotics and ventilation to sort out his chest. Harry could think of a few surgeons good enough to help Solomon Idris, and every one at the Ruskin fitted that description.

'Solomon! Talk to me!'

Pulse still there at the wrist, vital signs monitor reading an ECG trace. Blood pressure crashing now, just like Harry knew it would. Eighty over sixty-five.

'Get me a grey cannula, please, I'm putting in another line!' he barked as the ambulance blared its horn, cutting through another red light.

As his gloved, bloodstained fingers squeezed Solomon Idris's wrist more tightly, Harry felt the pulse disappear.

In a typical shift, a staff member at the Accident & Emergency department of the John Ruskin University Hospital can expect to watch one person die. On nights where the young men of Camberwell are feeling particularly virile, it isn't unusual for six or seven teenagers to come in, wounded, bleeding and hopeless. Often with a moment's notice, a team would assemble, like the one waiting in Resus now, gathered in the three minutes between the pre-alert and the ambulance's arrival. A trauma consultant, team leader, at the foot of the bed, checklists and algorithms on a clipboard in front of her; surgeons, anaesthetists, nurses, junior doctors, radiographers. The porter was running to the blood bank for the emergency blood, O-negative, the universal donor type. There could be a hundred years of medical training between the team combined, but the man who could run for blood trumped them all. Tonight's porter was Wallace, a semi-professional foot-baller who'd been working at the Ruskin for six years. His personal best, from bedside to blood bank and back again with four units of O-neg, was two minutes and thirty-six seconds.

'He's going into six!' the charge nurse shouted as the paramedics wheeled Idris through the door.

Harry pushed the trolley into Resus and immediately recognised three of the faces. The first was the team leader, Bernadette Kinirons, who watched over her team from behind wire-rimmed glasses, dark grey scrubs accentuating her mottled skin. Another was George Traubert, a senior consultant anaesthetist, and Harry's educational supervisor. Traubert was in a blue scrub top but below that were cream chinos and Italian shoes, the uniform of someone who'd been ready to go home when the call had come in. The third face was tucked away in a corner of the resuscitation bay, disguised behind a green plastic apron and gloves and rectangular Armani glasses. James Lahiri had been his best friend in medical school, and gone with him to Afghanistan and back again, but they didn't speak any more. Day to day, Lahiri was a GP in Camberwell, but three or four times a month he worked locum shifts in A&E. Plenty of GPs did, especially the younger ones, to keep their skills up, for a bit of a challenge.

Sod's law said he was working tonight.

'Harry!' Traubert exclaimed. Lahiri looked up, the expression on his face frustrated surprise.

'Do we have blood?' Harry barked.

'On its way,' Kinirons replied, as if scolding Harry for ever doubting the team. 'Are we going to get a handover?'

Harry nodded and took his place at the foot of the bed next to her as the nurses and junior doctors helped the paramedics slide the unconscious seventeen-year-old from the ambulance trolley to the bed. He found himself subconsciously assessing the team: Kinirons was rock solid, the surgical registrar he didn't recognise, and then there was Lahiri. Even if Lahiri's presence was unfortunate, there was no one he'd rather work with. On the other hand Dr Traubert was an academic at heart, and only ventured into A&E if the rota was in a dire state; the on-call anaesthetists must all have been busy with emergencies elsewhere, otherwise he wouldn't have been there.

'OK,' Harry said, beginning the handover. 'This is Solomon, he's seventeen. About fifteen minutes ago he was shot by a low-velocity weapon. There is an entry wound in the left upper quadrant, just beneath the costal margin, no identifiable exit wound, no other obvious injuries. He has a background of suspected atypical pneumonia and baseline saturations around eighty-seven before being injured. Currently, he has no radial pulse, a central pulse of one-thirty, a respiratory rate of twenty-eight, and sats of eighty-two on fifteen litres of O_2. I've put in airway adjuncts, he's had two hundred of saline before he got shot but none since, seven hundred of IM ketamine for sedation, and he's got a line in. He's allergic to penicillin, and he's got no known medical history.'

Everyone present recognised the description of a young man holding on to life by a thread, entering severe shock. The team each moved into their assigned task like a pit stop crew. Traubert straight to the head, checking the plastic airways Harry had placed in Idris's mouth and nose. Lahiri and the surgical registrar assessed his breathing and circulation. Kinirons stepped back, looking at the big picture.

'Did you say you gave him saline *before* he got shot?' she asked.

'Long story,' said Harry. 'I'm a police surgeon with the Met. He'd taken hostages, I was treating him, and then the police shot him.'

He looked across to see Kinirons staring at the ground, shaking her head. The doctors around Idris shouted out their findings, and Harry was back in the room.

'We need to intubate!'

'I don't have any breath sounds on the left.'

'Ultrasound shows fluid in the abdomen!'

Of course it does, Harry thought. He's been shot there, and he's going to bleed to death unless we get him on the table and a surgeon opens him up and stops it. Harry looked around the resuscitation bed and realised there was no senior surgeon present – one must surely be on their way. No breath sounds in the left chest, which was worrying. Kinirons barked an order, then a question.

'James, make sure it's not a pneumothorax. Have we a blood pressure yet?'

One of the nurses shouted a reply. 'Eighty over fifty.'

Wallace the porter came crashing through the doors to Resus at a sprint, sweat dripping through his polo shirt, the insulated freezer bag of blood bouncing in his hand.

'Are the blood warmers set up?' said Kinirons.

'Yes!'

'We should have another line in, please,' Kinirons continued. 'Get O-neg going through his right arm in the meantime. Get the BP up. Then we'll intubate and straight to CT.'

One of the A&E nurses hung up the first bag of blood on a drip-stand and ran it through the fluid warmer, connecting it up to the line the paramedic had placed in the ambulance; the other crouched by Idris's other arm and started searching for veins. Harry realised he was pacing relentlessly.

'Use me,' he said. 'We need to get access, I can help.'

'You're right,' said Kinirons. 'Wash your hands, and go get yourself an apron on.'

Harry returned to the resus bay with a plastic apron and fresh gloves, only to feel his heart sink at what he saw. The blood bag, the bridge between Solomon Idris and life, was up and running in, but the line had tissued – the blood was running into the soft tissue of Idris's elbow instead of into his veins and thence to his heart, where it was needed.

'That line's blown!'

'We know!' Kinirons said. 'Dr Traubert's working on another one.'

Anaesthetists were the experts at placing lines, and Traubert had the most experience of anyone in the room, but Harry immediately knelt down on the opposite side of the patient to his supervisor and began searching the other arm. Without a good IV line, there was no way to get blood into Idris, and it would keep leaking out of the hole inside his abdomen, and he would die. It was as simple as that.

'I've got nothing here,' Harry said. All the veins in the usual places – the back of the hand, the inner surface of the elbow, the forearm – had collapsed. These are the moments you live for, Harry told himself. The moments you were trained to overcome. Get a neck vein, or a scalp one. Use the ultrasound machine to guide you in. Find a way, any way. In these moments, the chaos in his head would eventually stop and he would know the right course of action in an instant.

He knew. Turned to one of the A&E nurses.

'Can you get me the IO drill, please,' he called. Looked down at Traubert, waiting for confirmation from his consultant. Instead, what he saw was Traubert leaning over Idris's ankle, scalpel in hand, methodically dissecting the fascia away as he searched for the great saphenous vein. It was a procedure so outdated Harry had only ever seen it in textbooks.

'No need, Harry, I'm almost done here.'

George fucking Traubert, Harry thought. Even if he managed to get the vein, at Idris's ankle the line would be miles away from his heart and brain, where the blood was needed. Harry's plan was the right one, even if it was more brutal. The nurse handed him the drill, a device that would place a needle straight into the medulla of Idris's bone, through which they could infuse the blood that would save his life. Directly from the humerus into the great vessels, and the rest of his circulation.

'I'm doing it, Dr Traubert,' Harry said. Placed the drill against Idris's arm, heard the buzz as he squeezed the trigger, felt the change in resistance as the needle screwed through flesh, then hard bone, then the soft marrow where it locked in place.

'We're in,' Harry said. 'Get the blood up.'

Before he'd even said it, a familiar figure was behind him. Lahiri screwed in the connecting line to the bag of blood, and Harry stepped back, watching the viscous, red liquid start to flow into Solomon Idris's arm, into his lifeless body, with its grey, pallid fingers, and motionless, bloodshot eyes. They didn't have the look any more, the thousand-yard stare replaced by one of drug-induced indifference.

Harry looked up at Lahiri and their eyes briefly locked before his old friend turned away. It had been months since they'd seen each other. At least it was in a situation without much room for small talk. It felt bizarre, a bit like turning up to work after a drunken one-night stand at the Christmas party.

'Can we do the same on the other side?' Kinirons barked while Lahiri squeezed the blood bag as hard as he could. With good pressure, a unit could be run in within two minutes. Traubert stood up, seeming almost perplexed at what had happened.

'Dr Kent, have you forgotten who—' he started.

Harry handed him the bone drill.

'We need a line in the other side,' he said. You can bollock me later, he thought.

Traubert looked between the device and Harry, the mess he'd made at Idris's ankle and the teenager's lifeless face. Behind him, two Trojan officers arrived in Resus, guns low.

'Um, you do it. You do it, Harry.'

Harry cursed under his breath as he bolted around the bed to the other side, fitted a new needle onto the drill and repeated the procedure in the other arm. As if in the distance, Kinirons was shouting out orders.

'Get an aspirate from that line, and send it for urgent crossmatch, then hang up another unit, alright? James, let's get a blood gas as well, please. A unit of FFP once the first bag of blood's run through, yeah? Can we give him one gram of tranexamic acid and get ready to RSI. And where the hell is the surgeon?'

'Abe's on his way down,' said the surgical registrar. Abe Gunther was an old-school trauma surgeon with a pox-scarred face, but he was one of the best in the country, and had pulled at least a hundred bullets out of bodies in twenty years at the Ruskin. If anyone could save Solomon Idris, Mr Gunther could. Harry took a step back, satisfied that they were now replacing the blood Idris had lost as fast as possible. Usually on a trauma call, Harry's job was to wait at the head, ensure the patient had an airway, and put them under an anaesthetic if surgery was deemed necessary. As he stepped out of the bay, Gunther arrived, heralded by the sound of his rubber-soled Nikes on the floor. The surgeon was the shortest of the team by far.

'Plan?' was all he said.

Harry glanced over at the vital signs monitor. There was a blood pressure recorded, seventy-five over forty. It wasn't good, but it was better than nothing. The first transfusion, almost done, was ready to be replaced.

'Get him stable enough, intubate, then to CT,' said Kinirons. 'And then to theatre.'

Stable was a nice word to use, Harry thought. In situations like this it meant that the patient wasn't at risk of instantly dying, which was something they couldn't achieve here until they stopped the blood loss, turned off the tap. In the bay, Lahiri had commandeered the ultrasound probe from the surgical registrar and was running it over Idris's bloodied chest, looking for a collapsed lung.

'He's got a left-sided pneumonia,' Harry called.

Lahiri turned back. 'If you say so,' he said. 'I can't hear anything over his left chest, but it doesn't look like a pneumothorax. Pneumonia would fit.'

'Let me get in there,' Gunther shouted. He moved in and began directing the ultrasound probe across Idris's belly. Lahiri stepped backwards, out of the bay, taking a place between Harry and Kinirons. As he moved, he looked at Harry again.

'Just like old times, eh?' he said.

It was. He and Lahiri had made a good team. There was at least one squaddie walking around who wouldn't have been without them, and a good few more who were wheeling. Locals Harry had put under while Lahiri operated, the two of them alone inside a forward operating base, fighting to keep some poor Afghan bastard alive until the helicopter could get them out. When we were inseparable, Harry thought, brothers-in-arms. Before Harry had fucked everything up.

One of the A&E clerks arrived. 'Do we have a name yet?' she said.

'Idris,' said Harry. 'Solomon Idris.'

'Yeah, there's blood in the belly,' said Abe Gunther. 'He's pretty damn unstable, isn't he? Not sure CT's a good idea. I'd say put him under and go straight to theatre.'

'Fuck,' said Lahiri. Out loud, and he didn't swear much, so Harry knew something was wrong.

'What is it?' said Harry, heart pounding. Eyes running over the vital signs monitor, double-checking that nothing had changed.

'He's one of mine,' said Lahiri.

Lahiri wasn't like most GPs. His practice wasn't far from the Ruskin, the other side of Camberwell Green. It covered some of the most deprived streets in the country, let alone London, and while it saw its fair share of toddlers with ear infections, it was known for registering gang members and previous victims of youth violence.

'I'm sorry,' said Harry, though he wasn't sure who he was saying it to. Maybe it was to Idris, sorry that he hadn't been able to stop what had felt inevitable from the moment he'd walked into that chicken shop.

'OK, we go to theatre,' said Kinirons. 'Dr Traubert, are you happy with that? Let's have the six crossmatched units sent there and the rest of the O-neg, along with some FFP and cryo. Get some O_2 ready for intubation.'

'He needs volume,' said Gunther. 'I'm not happy taking him to theatre with only the IOs in place. I'd like a central line.'

'Sure,' said Kinirons. 'James?'

Lahiri nodded and swung round to Idris's neck, ready to pass a cannula straight into his jugular vein. It would get the blood into him faster than the ports they'd drilled in his bones would.

'We'll intubate once the pressure's up to eighty,' said Kinirons. 'George?'

It was the final stage between Idris and the operating table where Abe Gunther could save his life: passing a breathing tube into his lungs so they could ventilate him during the surgery. After five agonising minutes, Lahiri had the central line sorted and a nurse hooked up Idris's fourth unit of blood, his blood pressure up to ninety. Stable enough for them to have a crack at the tube. Harry would do it in a heartbeat, if Traubert looked like he was going to fuck it up.

'OK,' Traubert said, heading up to Idris's head. 'Harry, can you sort the pre-ox, please. And I'll need some ketamine and rocuronium, thank you.'

Harry headed up to join Traubert, placing a high-flow oxygen mask onto Idris's throat while Traubert prepared the intubation equipment and injected the anaesthetic drugs, one to place Idris into a medically induced coma, the other to paralyse every muscle in his body. That one took a minute to work, so Harry looked at his watch the instant Traubert injected it, memorising the position of the second hand. He watched as Traubert prepared the laryngoscope he'd use to sweep away Idris's tongue and locate the vocal cords, through which he'd slide the breathing tube.

'That's sixty,' Harry said once the second hand was back around.

'Thanks,' said Traubert, stooping over and looking down into Idris's mouth. There was silence in the resus bay now, all eyes on the blood pressure and saturations monitor. Given that they'd just paralysed him, Idris could no longer breathe on his own, and they had perhaps five minutes to intubate him before his brain became starved of oxygen. After thirty seconds adjusting the position of the laryngoscope, Traubert asked for the tube and Harry gave it to him.

'Dammit,' Traubert said. 'Give me a bougie.'

Someone passed him a thin plastic stylet, and Traubert tried again, poking it forward, trying to find Idris's trachea. Harry looked across at the saturations monitor, and down at his watch. They'd been trying for a minute and a half.

'Ninety seconds,' he said out loud, hoping Traubert would

realise, pull out, and let Harry squeeze some more oxygen into Idris's system.

'Hang on, I've almost got it,' Traubert said. The silence was oppressive now, beads of sweat forming on Traubert's forehead. Harry hadn't taken a look himself, but anatomically, Idris shouldn't have been a particularly difficult intubation. Traubert might be a bloody good teacher and researcher, he thought, but his rustiness was beginning to show. Harry set two minutes as a cut-off in his mind. If it took him longer than that, he would step in. They'd worked too hard to save him to let it all be lost by an out-of-practice administrator.

He never got the chance to interrupt, because Dr Kinirons did it first.

'George, it's been too long, withdraw and bag.'

Harry was there in an instant, fixing the mask over Idris's face, squeezing the oxygen bag. The saturations were down in the mid-eighties, and Idris was still paralysed. In an elective case, they'd wake him up and try another method, but without surgery to stop the bleeding, he would die.

'Can we get the fibre-optic scope down from theatre?' Traubert suggested, wiping his brow with his sleeve.

'That'll take ten minutes,' Kinirons said, 'Do you want to try, Dr Kent?'

Harry nodded. In a minute or so of bagging, the sats had climbed slowly, eighty-nine now. He crouched down, pulled the tongue back with the scope, could see the apex of the vocal cords, not all of them, but he got a better view by lowering his back a bit. Fucking Traubert, he thought as he passed the bougie in, then slid the tube down, inflating the cuff that would keep it in place: he'd heard rumours of how useless the consultant was around the hospital, but this was the first time he had witnessed it first-hand. A nurse connected the tube to the oxygen supply and began squeezing the bag that had now become Solomon Idris's ventilator.

'We in?' said Kinirons.

'Excellent work!' Traubert said, patting Harry on the back with a sweaty palm.

'Check the capno.'

. Harry looked up at the monitor, read the vital signs: low blood pressure, but higher than it had been, fast pulse, a good waveform on capnography. Solomon Idris was probably as stable as he would ever be with a hole in his abdomen. Harry looked across at Lahiri, who wore a familiar expression, one of pained exhaustion. He'd done everything he could for Idris, but now his patient's life was in the hands of someone else, or worse, pure insentient luck. Harry knew how that felt. Gunther had already run ahead to prepare theatre.

'Everyone happy to go?' Kinirons said.

A chorus of yeses spilt from the group. Traubert turned to Harry and said, 'I want you with me in theatre, if you can?'

Harry nodded furiously. He wasn't about to let Idris out of his sight.

'So let's go,' Kinirons said, and the brakes came òff the trolley, the blood bags transferred from drip-stands onto extendable arms attached to the bed. They rushed out of the bay, everyone grabbing a bit of the trolley, Lahiri sprinting ahead to hold the doors.

As they went through, Harry brushed past Lahiri, who whispered low enough so Harry could hear him but no one else, 'Don't you fuck this up, Harry. You owe me that.'

Harry ignored him. None of that shit mattered now. It mattered outside, and maybe eventually they'd get around to sorting it out, but right now, only one thing mattered. And, just as Harry had decided that, they were in the anaesthetic room, and sliding their patient across, and Harry was running into the scrub room to get changed.

Just as quickly as chaos had arrived in A&E, it left. Resus Six was a mess: empty packaging and syringes strewn all over the floor, the shadows of the team who'd just inhabited it. Slowly it faded again to quiet noise, another episode added to the horrors that the cubicle had witnessed. A nurse counted the empty blood bags, scrawling them into the records. Bernie Kinirons hunched over the central desk, scrawling down a log of all the efforts they had undertaken. The nurses knelt down on the floor, picking up scalpel blades, opened packages, used needles, sliding them into sharps bins.

Minutes later, a cleaner arrived, her mop slowly reducing Solomon Idris's blood to pink foam.

It took Gunther thirty minutes to find the bullet. During that time, Solomon Idris had come closer to the grave than most people ever recovered from, blissfully unaware. Seventeen years old, and for the second time the Ruskin's doctors and nurses had saved his life.

'Lucky guy,' Gunther said as they wheeled Idris out of theatre, towards the CT scanner.

'How so?' said Harry. Only a surgeon like Gunther, who'd cut his teeth in the trauma theatres of Cape Town, could ever refer to someone in Idris's situation as lucky.

'Two inches higher and that bullet would have hit his heart,' came the reply. 'Three inches to the right his aorta. Either of them he'd be dead for sure.'

The operation had been an exploratory laparotomy, slicing the belly north to south, retracting the skin and the rectus muscles to find the blood and plug the leak. When Gunther had opened it, there had been a lot, and thankfully the surgical registrar had been there to assist him in suctioning it out so they could see what was going on. The bullet had nicked one of the gastrosplenic arteries on its way in, which they'd been able to clip with relative ease, but the main issue was Idris's spleen. In the end, Gunther had taken the shotgun approach and clipped every artery he could find in the tight network around the spleen, before unclamping them one-by-one until he found the bleeders. The tap was off. The bleeding had stopped.

At Harry's end, it had been plain sailing. They'd managed to establish a trauma line, a long, wide-bore tube, in one of Idris's neck veins, and after that keeping him under sedation was second nature, and now he was at least stable. As Harry looked down at the anaesthetised teenager, he considered the irony. The likely reason that Idris had survived an injury which would kill most people was his youth, the ability of his body to compensate for devastating blood loss, shut down the periphery and protect his vital organs. Idris had been saved by his innate desire to live, even though he might have walked into that Chicken Hut wishing only to die.

Gunther had already left when they got through the scanner, to try to get some sleep in case another emergency case arrived. Idris had been on the table for just over an hour, and was far from fixed: there was a rectangle of transparent film over his abdomen, instead of a closed scar. Surgery at this point was about damage control, stopping the bleeding so they could get the patient into Harry's realm: the intensive care unit. They would send him back to theatre once he was fully stabilised, probably in the next twenty-four hours, to have the damaged arteries repaired and the incisions sewn up. Harry looked up at the vital signs monitor. He was happy with everything apart from the oxygen saturations, which were still hovering around ninety-one.

The damn oxygen, he thought. That chest infection. It could well kill Idris anyway. The bacteria Harry suspected were colonising his patient's lungs didn't care that he'd been shot that evening.

Traubert had left them as they finished up with the CT scan, satisfied that Harry could manage the transfer to the ICU without any help. Not that the consultant had been much help in A&E, Harry thought but didn't say.

'Good job, Harry,' Traubert had said as he left, muttering something about not getting home until late now, and missing a dinner reservation.

Upstairs in the ICU, Harry looked at Solomon Idris's CT scan, ran one hand through his hair and swore under his breath. The nurses were transferring Idris over to the life support machines by his bed, and a Trojan officer had arrived to guard him through the night: standard protocol in shooting cases, even when it was the police who had done the shooting. Marek Rashid, the duty ICU consultant, arrived. They both stood at the central computer station in the unit, looking at the images coming onto the system in real time.

The good news was that the bleeding had stopped.

The bad news was that Idris's chest looked like shit.

'You say you thought this young man had a fairly advanced pneumonia, yes?' Dr Rashid was thinking out loud. 'I'd say you were right about that.'

The radiologist's report stated 'widespread pulmonary infiltrates', which in layman's terms meant that there were large cysts and collections of thick, infected tissue throughout the lower zones of Solomon Idris's chest. On the chest X-ray that had been taken – merely to help confirm the placement of the tubes Harry had inserted – the severity of Idris's illness was obvious. There was more white than black across the lung fields. But it was diffuse, all over the chest, rather than concentrated in one lobe like a normal pneumonia would be. The most obvious diagnosis jumped out at Harry, and he looked up at Rashid, waiting for him to say it.

'Pneumocystis,' Rashid said. 'We'll confirm it with cultures, but I'll bet you ten quid that's PCP. Remind me why you didn't get a chest X-ray done down in Casualty?'

Rashid was fairly strict for a consultant, but he didn't bullshit you and didn't expect any back, so Harry liked him. The consultants were on call for three days at a time, and not all of them would have come in when the night registrar could see the patient for them. Marek was one of the good ones.

'Because he was bleeding to death,' Harry said.

Rashid briefly regarded Harry from behind his glasses, before nodding acceptance at this excuse and turning back to the computer screen.

'The question is, what does it mean?'

Harry knew that the question was rhetorical. Pneumocystis was an organism too weak to cause disease in otherwise healthy people – it was an opportunist, jumping in to attack a vulnerable immune system. Idris hadn't had chemotherapy recently, nor was he on long-term steroids. That left only one other reason a seemingly healthy young man would get infected with a pneumocystis pneumonia. It was commonly seen as the first presentation of AIDS.

'I didn't think about that. He's young for it, bloody young. I'll order an HIV test now,' Harry said. 'And an urgent CD4 and differential white count. And I'll arrange a bronch for sputum cultures.'

'You put him on antibiotics?' Rashid said.

Harry took a few breaths of the sterile air of the ICU and felt his heart rate drop somewhat. He'd changed into the maroon scrubs that everyone on the unit wore, from the top doctors like Rashid to the physiotherapists. The ward had a restless quiet about it. Even at night, the nurses moved around performing their duties in solemn silence, punching codes through doors, pushing out their right hands like automatons to receive a dollop of disinfectant gel.

'Sorry,' he said. 'He's penicillin allergic, so he got doxy and gent.'

'OK,' said Rashid. 'We'll prescribe him some anti-fungals to cover the pneumocystis. I'll get on the phone and wake up the microbiologists, let them earn that on-call money.'

'I can do it,' Harry offered.

'No way, my friend,' said Rashid. 'You look awful. I heard what happened to you tonight. You should get yourself to bed. I'll go see what the situation with relatives is like.'

Harry yawned. At night, the ICU had its lights dimmed, an attempt to maintain a relatively normal circadian cycle for the patients, most of whom were in medically induced comas. It meant Harry was struggling to stay awake. He could hear whimpers and groans from one end of the unit and shivered: some patients, driven mad by the simultaneous sensory deprivation and stimulation, entered a state called intensive care psychosis, where even the hardiest of sedative drugs couldn't drive the demons away.

'Make sure you follow this one up, Harry,' Rashid said. 'He'll be good for your portfolio. Not that you wouldn't, mind you.'

The reminder was worthless, as Rashid clearly knew. To Harry's mind, there were two sub-species of medics. There were doctors that went home at closing time, played golf, went to the pub, watched TV with their families and forgot everything that had happened that day. They were somehow able to roll everything they'd seen into a vault deep inside their consciences and forget about it until their next shift. Others went home, but rang wards and texted colleagues and didn't rest until they knew the outcome of that one patient they'd seen that day who'd troubled them. Those in the first camp, like Marek Rashid and George Traubert, were for the most part stable, happy people. Doctors like Harry and James Lahiri were firmly in the second.

He headed over to Idris's bed, where the nurses were finishing the handover. The kid looked dead, a tube in his mouth, one in his chest, a line in his neck, and the lines Harry had drilled into his arms in A&E all still in place. A bag of blood up with fluid and antibiotics either side, a catheter collecting urine, a monitoring line in his radial artery. Clinging to life, both physically and metaphorically.

Harry heard someone clear their throat behind him, thought it sounded familiar, and put it together in his head just before he finished turning and saw the face.

James Lahiri looked like shit, too. Bloodshot eyes, one half of his pale blue shirt untucked, a small stain, probably blood, over the left-side pocket, where the eartubes of the stethoscope hung around his neck rested. A paper bag from the hospital's twenty-four-hour coffee shop was crumpled in one hand.

'Lunch break,' he explained. 'You got five minutes?'

Harry grinned. 'I'm not working, remember?'

Lahiri looked like he was trying to smile and said, 'You always manage to get into trouble.'

'Come on, then,' said Harry. They headed into the doctors' office at one end of the ward. Harry folded his arms and stood with his back against the wall, briefly thought about his locker in the room opposite and the bottle of amphetamines inside it, and then remembered he wasn't actually at work and he didn't need to stay awake all night. Lahiri shut the door behind him and collapsed into a swivel chair. It was the first time they'd been alone in a room together for almost a year. Harry tried to stop himself from breathing too loudly, and then decided just to speak.

'How are you doing?' he said. 'Still enjoy spending your Sunday nights in A&E?'

Lahiri pulled a can of Coke from the bag, opened it and took a big gulp.

'Look, Harry. You don't give a toss how I am and I don't give a toss how you are, so let's not play friends, OK? I'm here cause one of my patients got shot, and I want to know if he's going to live, and I reckon you might be one of the only people in this hospital who'll give me a straight answer.'

Harry tried his best not to bite. The resuscitation of a young, male gunshot victim, with Harry there in front of him, would have brought back uncomfortable associations for Lahiri, just as

43

Lahiri's presence had done for him. He tried to keep that in mind. Of course, that wasn't the reason for the venom, but Harry liked to pretend that it was.

'He's been admitted for five minutes,' he said. 'He's still alive now. He might not be tomorrow morning. Christ, James, you know how this works.'

Lahiri shook his head and sighed. He knew that Harry couldn't even begin to guess how Idris would do, and he knew that Harry knew that, too.

Harry looked at his old friend and decided to try and get something other than an awkward silence out of the conversation.

'When you say he was your patient, do you mean you were his GP? Or was he just enrolled in your pilot scheme thing?'

Lahiri's GP surgery ran a unique scheme for former gang members. The ethos was a modern one, treating gang violence like a disease and managing it as you would any other. Reducing the risk factors, focusing on prevention. The high-risk cases were identified by youth workers in A&E, referred to Lahiri and the team for follow-up appointments. Most of them got therapy, some got medication to calm them down. As Harry understood it, right now nobody had a clue whether it reduced reoffending or not. All he knew was that it evidently hadn't done much good for Solomon Idris.

'He was my patient,' Lahiri repeated. 'I was his GP.'

'When was the last time you saw him?' Harry said.

'Last year. December, I think.'

'Was he OK?'

'Physically, you mean?'

Harry nodded.

'Yeah,' said Lahiri. 'He was fine.'

'Is he HIV-positive?' said Harry.

Lahiri pulled a sandwich from the paper bag but stopped before taking a bite. 'Not to my knowledge. What makes you say that?'

'He was sick before he got shot,' said Harry. 'Really sick. It looked like pneumonia, and I thought it would be community-acquired. But the radiology came back, and it looks a hell of a lot like PCP.'

'Jesus,' said Lahiri, chewing on his sandwich and apparently concentrating hard on staring at the ceiling. 'At seventeen?'

Seventeen was young for the disease to have progressed so far, unless he'd been infected in childhood, which ought to have showed up on his medical records, or he was one of the individuals particularly susceptible to the virus. It seemed Solomon Idris had been unlucky: a recurring theme.

'Fucking police,' Harry said. 'He was bad enough before they shot him.'

'I'm sure they were just doing their job,' said Lahiri. Harry thought he looked a bit like a father, disappointed because one of his sons was in trouble again.

'No,' Harry said. 'They fucked up. He'd taken hostages in a fried chicken place, they had it surrounded. There was some loud bang from outside, the police thought he'd opened fire and they took him out.'

Lahiri scoffed and finally looked up at Harry. 'What, you were there, were you?'

'I was, actually.'

Lahiri paused again, bread stuck between his teeth.

'You're shitting me?'

'I'm serious,' said Harry. 'I'm a police surgeon now.'

Lahiri smirked, shaking his head.

'Harry Kent, urban youth, all cops are bastards, works for the police?'

Harry nodded. Granted, his upbringing had included a couple of run-ins with the Met which had evolved into a chip on the shoulder he'd carried through university, and perhaps vocalised once or twice after a couple of pints. But he had his reasons for doing the work, and they went beyond the fairly generous pay. And he had no intention of discussing them with Lahiri.

'You were there when they shot him?' Lahiri said.

Harry felt the tension begin to build in his chest. The shrinks called it rising anxiety, a symptom of a couple of disorders Harry was sure he didn't have.

'Yeah,' he said. 'They'd sent me in to treat him. He was sitting there, talking to me. Next thing I know, there's a gunshot from outside the shop, the place is full of coppers, the first one in the door drops him, and he's on the floor bleeding out.'

'Christ,' Lahiri whispered. 'Are you OK?'

Harry picked up on the subtext of that one and tried to ignore it. James Lahiri knew exactly what situations like that one felt like, and worse. Harry's nightmare had been over in seconds. Two coppers through the door, one shot, a kid with a bullet in his abdomen. Lahiri had gone through a few ordeals like that, one of which had involved putting two tubes into Harry's chest. For a brief second Harry saw Solomon Idris's eyes, staring back at him from behind a vinyl-topped table in the freezing-cold Chicken Hut.

'I'm fine,' he said.

Neither of them spoke for about a minute. Lahiri finished his sandwich. Harry went to the computer and checked if Idris's bloods were back yet. Fuck this, he thought. Lahiri had come up, broken their unspoken detente, just to sit in a room and say nothing and eat a sandwich. The air hung heavy, leaden.

'Sol,' said Lahiri.

Harry looked up. Lahiri's mouth was opening and closing as he stumbled for the words. The man looked shattered. It was a fearful thought that he had four or five hours left to work before his shift in A&E ended. Harry wondered whether he had a clinic tomorrow, too.

'I feel like I've failed,' Lahiri said. 'We were doing so well. The whole point of the programme is to stop these things from happening.'

Harry shrugged, and Lahiri shook his head, threw his lunch bag into the bin and opened the door. Harry followed him out, and they walked, heads bowed, along the central corridor of the ICU, with the noises, chimes and ventilator cycles emerging from the silence.

'Do me a favour, yeah?' Lahiri said as they reached the T-junction that led to the ward exit. 'Let me know if anything changes, OK? Would you do that for me?'

'Sure,' said Harry.

Lahiri nodded.

'Thank you.'

He began to turn away before Harry spoke.

'James,' he said. 'It was good to, umm. Well, I mean – it was good to work with you again. Just like the old days.'

Lahiri's eyes closed and he looked tired.

46

'Fuck off, Harry,' he said under his breath, and walked away.

That shouldn't have been a surprise, but it still hurt. Just like the old days, he thought. Just as some of their patients couldn't be fixed, despite everyone's best efforts, some relationships were broken beyond repair, too. Of course Lahiri had to have been working tonight.

But that didn't matter, and this did. Harry looked down at Solomon Idris, his lips blue, naked under only a blanket, lines and tubes, blood starting to crust over his skin. Listened to a barely functioning chest, but a strong heart. Shone a light into eyes fixed with a hypnotised stare, and remembered the look they'd had when he'd first seen them. Wondered what they'd seen, and heard Idris's voice. *They killed Keisha, and the feds didn't give a shit.* Harry wondered if the police would give a shit about Solomon, either. Even if he made it out of hospital, he would be inside for a long time, long enough to destroy any recovery his shitty life had threatened to make.

Harry realised he was almost falling asleep when he heard someone repeating his name.

'Sorry,' he said. It was Angela Valdez, the ICU's nurse-in-charge.

'Solomon Idris's family are here,' said Valdez. 'The police liaison officer told them it probably isn't a good idea for them to see him until the morning, what with his condition. But Rashid was hoping—'

'I'll do it,' said Harry. 'Relatives' room?'

Valdez nodded.

'You coming, too?' Harry said.

'If you'll have me.'

Harry nodded his assent, went back to the console to remind himself of the notes – his standard ritual before talking to relatives – and then shook his head.

'How do you take your coffee, Harry?' Valdez asked.

'Strong and white,' said Harry. 'Give me three of the little Kenco cups. Christ, Angie, you're a godsend.'

He finished reading the notes and realised that he still didn't have a fucking clue what he was going to say to Solomon's relatives. The complicated stuff, the HIV infection, the pneumonia, could wait until the morning. We stopped the bleeding, but he's still critical. Hope for the best, but prepare for the worst. If in doubt, fall back on the clichés.

Valdez returned with coffee and Harry thanked her again.

'So what's the deal with you and James Lahiri, then?' Valdez said. Evidently their parting words hadn't been quiet enough to escape nearby ears.

'He's an old friend of mine,' Harry said. 'We lived together in medical school, and then we served together in the forces.'

'Yeah, I knew that. Everyone knows that. But there's a deal with you two, isn't there? Frosty, not talking, none of the usual doctor banter. Everyone's been talking about it.'

Harry turned away and sipped his coffee, burning his lips. Valdez was a serious woman, probably one of the best critical care nurses Harry had ever worked with. But she was still a nurse, and nurses gossiped, after all.

'You really want to know?' he said. He hadn't ever pictured having this conversation at twenty to one on a Monday morning.

'Not if you don't want to tell,' said Valdez. 'But I did get you that coffee just now.'

Harry laughed.

'Well, I guess none of it matters any more,' he said. 'Long story short, I slept with his wife.'

These days, he could say it without even reacting. Valdez looked up at Harry, her face a mixture of disgust and confusion.

'Sorry I asked,' she said.

Harry sat down in the relatives' room with Valdez, joining the three people already there. The police family liaison officer was easy to spot, a motherly-looking woman in a knitted jumper, who could easily have been a social worker or one of the volunteers who read to elderly inpatients long since abandoned by their own families. The woman whom Harry took to be Solomon Idris's mother was wearing a winter coat from a charity shop, given that half of the price sticker that said 'Cancer Research UK' was still stuck on the lapel. Idris's younger brother, the resemblance striking, had his hands in the pockets of his puffa jacket and was staring at the floor.

They were separated by a mahogany table, two boxes of tissues, and a jar of dying flowers.

Harry addressed the mother. 'I'm Dr Kent. I'm one of the intensive care doctors. And this is Angela. She's the nurse in charge of this unit.'

No one said anything. Harry knew what the book said to do. At 1.15 in the morning in a windowless room in South London, ask the mother who for the second, maybe third time in as many years is preparing for the loss of her teenage son an open, non-confrontational question.

'What would you like me to call you, Mrs Idris?'

'Joy.'

Unlike Solomon, whose accent had been straight off the SE5 estates he'd grown up on, Joy Idris still retained the broad vowels and happy intonation of West Africa, which along with her name doubled the weight of the irony Harry was fighting to hold off.

'OK, Joy. What do you know already?'

'That Solomon got shot. The police shot my son. And he needed an operation.'

A tragedy in three acts. Joy Idris sat in one of the chairs, the most comfortable in the hospital, ramrod straight, her hands folded over one knee, like a woman giving evidence in court. No tears yet dropping from her misted-over eyes.

'Where is he now?' she asked.

'He's here in the surgical intensive care unit,' said Harry. 'In bed number eighteen. There's a nurse who's going to be looking after him personally, and Angela will introduce you to her after we've had this conversation.'

'Will he die this time?'

The last two words hit Harry's chest and the pain came again.

'Solomon is in a critical condition. We have all the resources here we could possibly need to get him better. You should absolutely hope for the best, but you may also need to prepare for the worst. He'll go for another operation tomorrow, and after that we'll know more. I'm sorry.'

'They told me that last time, and he survived,' said Joy. 'God took him through. And God will take him through again.'

Harry saw the police liaison officer shift uncomfortably on her seat. He got the impression that she'd been dealing with the religion for most of the evening. It was easy to judge, but in Harry's experience people who had nothing turned to faith far more readily than those in more comfortable surroundings.

'Are you Dr Kent?' said Joy.

'I am.'

Valdez looked across at him, and Harry returned her subtle glance of confusion with one of his own.

'Then you were the doctor who talked to him on Camberwell Road.'

'Yes. That was me.'

'I don't know if I should thank you or curse you,' said Joy.

Harry said nothing.

'Can we see him now?' said Joy.

'I don't have any problem with that,' said Harry. 'But you should be aware that it's going to look very frightening. Your son still has a surgical opening in his tummy, which looks far worse than it is.'

Valdez cut in. 'I'll take you there. But as Dr Kent said, it's quite scary. Solomon won't be able to talk to you, because he's on very strong drugs that put him to sleep. And there's a machine breathing for him. But you can hold his hand and speak to him if you want. I'd suggest that at the start, maybe you go by yourself, and then your other son can join you after a few minutes.'

'Junior,' said Joy. 'His name is Junior.'

Junior Idris was still staring at the floor. Harry kept his eyes on the boy, hands in his coat pockets, moving around. Couldn't be older than fourteen. Either playing with a phone or something, or just fidgeting around.

'Have you got any other questions?' said Harry. There were details about the operation that could wait, and he had no intention of broaching the topic of Solomon's HIV status in the wee hours of the morning. The likelihood was that Solomon was HIV-positive, by one means or another, but nothing in his medical records suggested any doctor had ever seen him about it. Discreet enquiries could be made in the morning, not just before his mother was about to see him in a hospital bed, with a tube in his mouth and a plastic window in his abdomen.

'He's a good boy,' said Joy Idris. 'He's an angel.'

And then Junior Idris started to move, first a silent retch, at which the police liaison officer jumped back, expecting vomit to hit the floor. When it didn't, Junior jerked again and then extended back his head in a long howl, one which pierced the skin and went deep into Harry's chest, where it echoed around the space inside. Then the tears came and the boy was held by his mother. When the police liaison tried to offer a tissue, Joy Idris batted her away with a flailing arm, screaming insults as her son sobbed against her shoulder.

'Get away from my son, you devil! Don't you dare touch him! You people tried to murder my son! I hope you burn, you devil! You burn! Burn, you devil!'

When Joy stopped screaming, Valdez picked up one of the tissue boxes and offered it forward.

'Take your time, Joy,' she said. 'We have as much time as you need.'

When they left the relatives' room, Valdez led Joy and Junior Idris towards Solomon's bed in the ICU, and Harry headed for the exit. The police liaison officer was shaking her head at her mobile phone and scratching at her neck when she turned around and came up to him.

'Someone to see you, Dr Kent,' she said.

The someone was waiting outside the ward for him. He was small and barrel chested, dressed in a suit at least one size too small for him and a beige trenchcoat that cut around his waist, and as he shook hands with Harry, he came so close they almost touched cheeks.

'Marcus Fairweather. I head up a team from the Directorate of Professional Standards.'

Metspeak for internal affairs.

'You guys investigating yourselves again?' Harry said.

Fairweather didn't smile. 'There's an IPCC team at the scene right now. We're conducting a joint investigation into what happened earlier today. I'm just here to arrange a time for you to come and speak to us. Would tomorrow morning be OK? We're using the incident room at Walworth – you know it?'

'What time? I have to be at work for half-eight.'

'Shall we say seven, then?' said Fairweather, coming closer again, as though he had no concept of personal space. He handed Harry a business card, which gave his title as detective chief inspector. Harry placed Fairweather's age as early to mid-thirties, around the same as himself, and wondered what was responsible for the man in front of him holding a rank usually held by officers at least ten years his senior. Maybe he was one of the fast-track graduates, maybe he had a unique combination of ambition and political acumen. If Harry was feeling particularly cynical, though, he might suggest that placing DCI Fairweather in charge of professional standards meant the Met could put a young black man on the press conference lectern to explain how they'd shot another young black man. Harry had only spent six months with the police, but little would surprise him any more.

'Hope you have a safe journey home, Doctor,' said Fairweather. 'And I'd like to thank you on behalf of the service for your courage today.'

Definitely press conferences, Harry decided. 'And I'd like to thank the service for shooting my patient in the abdomen. It made my job a whole lot easier.'

Harry turned on his heel before Fairweather could hit him with another soundbite. He thought about home but knew the course his evening would take: A3 down to the south edge of Richmond Park, then all the way to Kingston-upon-Thames.

'Dr Kent!'

Fairweather's voice cut through the corridor like a monitor alarm. Harry turned. The detective bore a smug grin, dangling a set of keys from an outstretched hand.

'I'm assuming the black Audi at the scene is your car, Dr Kent. Want a lift?'

Harry walked up to Fairweather and snatched the keys from his grasp, throwing them into the pocket of his scrubs. The detective stepped forward, invading Harry's bubble by just an inch too far.

'Thank you,' said Harry. 'I'll take a cab.'

Harry didn't take a cab, he walked. It was only about twenty minutes, and the cold night air woke him up a bit. He felt exhausted, but awake. This happened when he came off night shifts, the body clock simply disintegrated.

When Harry got back to Wyndham Road, the cordoned area was surrounded by police officers, some still toting guns, older detectives in suits and technicians in white zip-up jumpsuits. There was a small crowd, ten or twelve young men hanging around one of the police vans, shouting and filming things on their phones, but no real threat of disorder. He snuck in and spotted DI Noble, a white forensic jumpsuit over her leather jacket, accompanying a crime-scene analyst with the sourest face Harry had ever seen on a police officer. Fortunately, he managed to get out unnoticed.

The roads south-west were clear and empty, the shitty weather – it was now pounding with rain – making them quiet even for the late hour. On Kennington Park Road, he passed the twenty-four-hour McDonald's and a sudden hunger pang gripped him, reminding him that he hadn't eaten all day. He parked and went up to the kiosk, returning with a brown paper bag and a large coffee in a plastic cup, which he balanced on the passenger seat. He ate in the car park, his mind wandering around the caverns of a dying teenager's self-hatred and a vague recollection of a dream about the girl with pink hair, trying to speak to him. Searched for something inoffensive on his iPod, and found Bruce Springsteen's *Nebraska*. Good driving music, especially at night.

Skirting the southern edge of Richmond Park, the grey area between the city and suburbia, Harry felt a hard jolt and braked sharply. He had driven the route so many times he could do it on autopilot, and at this time the roads were empty enough anyway, so maybe he hadn't really been concentrating. He put his hazards on and looked behind him. There was enough of a straight that whoever was behind would see him and overtake.

Harry got out of the car, the rain bouncing off his shoulders and running down his face, the cold making his hair stand on end.

He had killed a fox. Its bushy orange tail was protruding from his front right wheel arch, viscera and blood spread over the road and the undercarriage of the car. The head and thorax were left intact on the tarmac. Harry looked down at its eyes and saw them unseeing, lost. He had seen that look in people so many times it had lost its impact, but somehow it was different in an animal. He thought of Solomon Idris's eyes in the Chicken Hut, how they had looked through his own. They had been lost, too, but in a different way, as if the teenager had decided everything was lost already.

Harry kicked what was left of the corpse away into a ditch at the side of the road. As he eased the bushy tail from the wheel arch, a modified hatchback with rear spoiler sped around the corner and swerved theatrically to avoid his car. He got a loud horn blast for his trouble and watched its tail-lights disappear into the darkness, blurred by the rain.

Harry looked down at the tail he was holding, threw it into the ditch, shivered and got back into the car.

The receptionist always changed at Marigold House. Despite Harry's twice-weekly visits, usually at night or other unsociable hours, he had never to his knowledge seen the same one. Today's was black, young, male, with dreadlocked hair.

'Oh, hello,' said the receptionist, looking up from his iPhone. He was playing a game where a gorilla was chasing an avatar through a temple.

'Hi,' said Harry.

'You're here for Room Nine, aren't you?'

'You remember me?'

'Nah, mate. I've heard about you. The midnight visitor. The man who never sleeps. Legend is you stayed up with him one night for eight hours, then went straight to work.'

Harry said nothing. The receptionist laughed.

'Hope you ain't a doctor like he was.'

'Is,' Harry said. 'He's still a doctor.'

'Oh, of course. Sorry.' The receptionist put on his sympathetic face and went back to running away from the gorilla.

Harry knew the way to the first floor, Room Nine, with his eyes closed. He watched every corner for fear of hitting another fox.

He opened the door without knocking first, and upped the dimmer switch slightly so the light in the room was enough to make out the face of the man in the bed. Peter Tammas stirred and looked across. He moved his head slowly but definitely, as if everything was planned with military style and took great precision to execute. His eyes flickered, with the scared look of a child whose bedroom door opens in the night.

'Harry?'

The voice, hoarse and measured, sounded almost rushed. Having lost the ability to breathe to the bullet which had transected his spinal cord, Tammas could speak only when his mechanical ventilator wasn't pumping.

'Evening, boss,' Harry said. He pulled up a chair and poured a glass of water from a jug on the bedside table.

'Aren't you. Working. Tomorrow?'

'Short day. Nine to five.'

'Go home. Harry. Anyway I. Need my sleep. I've got. A squash match. Tomorrow.'

Harry laughed and drank some water. The ventilator pulsed, moving Tammas's chest as it did. He looked at his friend and saw Solomon Idris, the same muscle wastage despite Tammas's daily physiotherapy. Lieutenant-Colonel Peter Tammas had been a legend, a twenty-year veteran of Northern Ireland, Bosnia, Sierra Leone, Iraq, Afghanistan and the army rugby team, who could carry a man on his back without breaking a sweat. Now, in winter, he looked frail.

'Good day?'

'Had better,' said Harry.

'You look. Like shit.'

'Thanks, boss. You're the second consultant who's told me that today.'

'Do you need. That shrink?'

Harry shook his head. 'I haven't seen a shrink in two years.'

'Do you want. A fucking. Medal?'

Tammas made a sound that was a little like a rattle. Harry decided he was trying to laugh while breathing in.

'Do you still. Take those pills?'

'Not much. Once a week or so, just when I need it.'

Ironically, he'd started taking amphetamines because of his trouble sleeping. He'd started feeling tired at work, about six months ago. Registrars' rotas were often unkind, switches between night shifts and long days without time to reset the body clock, and he'd had one incident where he'd slept through his bleeper. One of the nurses had heard it going off and opened up the doctors' office to wake him. Thankfully, the page had only been for a chest drain that had fallen out, but Harry had decided it was better to use a few chemicals to stay awake than risk a patient dying or coming to harm because he was asleep.

Tammas was quiet for a while. 'Don't worry. Harry. I believe. You.' Another rattle. 'Just wondering.'

Harry closed his eyes and was back in the fried chicken restaurant, with cold air blowing in from outside and a sick teenager with a gun on the table. The pain and pressure under his right arm. He felt briefly sick and when he opened his eyes he wondered how long he'd been silent. Maybe a few minutes. Tammas had been waiting, the ventilator wheezing in even beats, twelve times a minute.

'What happened. Today?'

'I got a call-out from the police. There was a kid in a takeaway restaurant, he'd taken hostages. He had pneumonia and was coughing his guts up. They wanted to trade three of the hostages for me.'

'I forget you're a. Police surgeon.' Another rattle-laugh. 'What a joke. Harry Kent. A surgeon.'

Tammas had trained as a surgeon, and naturally viewed all other specialities with disdain. Anaesthetists especially.

'Yeah. Turns out it's one of the teenagers from Lahiri's practice. One of his kids.'

'That poisoned. Chalice,' said Tammas. 'I told him. Not to get. Involved with. That. Noble work. Perhaps but. It'll always end in. Tears. Just leave. It to the. Social workers.'

'Yeah,' said Harry. 'Kid was seventeen. Probably HIV-positive. Just walked into the place with a gun, took hostages, demanded the BBC and a lawyer. Said he was doing it all for some girl called Keisha.'

Harry let the words ring in the room. Tammas turned his head awkwardly, as if asking Harry what comment or opinion he was being asked to offer.

'What happened?' he asked.

'The coppers shot him.' Harry leant forward, bringing a

trembling hand up to his forehead. 'Just fucking shot him. Right there in front of me.'

'For an unarmed. Police force. They shoot a lot. Of people.'

Harry shook his head, giving a sarcastic laugh. Tammas turned his eyes back to the ceiling. Harry stood up and moved over to the desk in the far corner, kicking the chair, feeling an awful rage come up inside him. There was something new on the windowsill of Tammas's room. An iPod dock with speakers either side.

'When'd you get this?'

'James brought it. He says he loaded. It with all my. Favourites.'

Typical Lahiri, Harry thought. He often wondered how regularly Lahiri had trod the same path as him, down to Marigold House, up into this room. Without the same guilt, though. With the shame replaced by a shining fucking halo.

'Do you want me to put something on?'

'It's two. O'clock. In the fucking. Morning, Harry. I've got. Neighbours.'

'Fair enough.'

'What. Happened to. The kid?'

'He's alive, just,' Harry said. 'He's in ICU. He's got what looks like a PCP pneumonia, but damage control went well, and we'll have to see what happens when they open him up tomorrow. It could go either way. But for now he's fighting.'

'Well done.'

'Lahiri was there. He was working in A&E tonight. There for the trauma call.'

'Ha. Just like. The old days. Then.'

'Yeah.' Harry went back to the chair and sat down. 'He said that. Then I said that, and he told me to fuck off. It was weird. He came up to the ICU to check on this kid, and just sat there in front of me. Had a bit of a moment, like he expected me to break down, confess my sins.'

The altered pitch of the ventilator and the rolling of Tammas's head told Harry he was about to be interrupted.

'Because. He saved your. Life. And look how. You. Repaid him.'

'Yeah,' said Harry. 'First time I've had to speak to him properly since he got back.'

'You two. Don't speak?'

'You know what happened, boss. Of course we don't speak.'

'I don't. Understand. How can you not. At least. Have caught up?'

Tammas looked vulnerable, painfully vulnerable, like the father to estranged sons. He rolled his head back so he was looking at the ceiling.

'Boss, he came back from the Ghan three weeks after saving both our bastard lives and seeing us flown back in comas. He was at home, what, a month, and then he's on a plane back out there, and then he returns to find out that I'd been shagging Alice all the time he'd been gone.'

'Bloody shame. You two were. A good. Team. You must have. Your work. Cut out to. Avoid him.'

'He's only in A&E two nights a month.'

Harry felt acid burning on the back of his throat and picked up the glass of water to take a drink.

'Brave man,' said Tammas.

Harry slammed the tumbler down on the table by Tammas's head and was briefly disappointed that it didn't smash. 'Don't wind me up, you son of a bitch! I know he's a fucking brave man, boss, all anyone ever goes on about is how fucking brave he is! What a fucking hero, dragging me to the chopper under fire, saving all those people's lives. James fucking brave fucking Lahiri!'

It was pretty low, Harry thought, as he heard his curses echo back to him, to transfer the responsibility for what he'd done onto his friend for having the audacity to be such a good man. Of course James had flaws, as all men did, but none that could have deserved the betrayal Harry had committed. Tammas knew this, of course, and had chastised Harry for such thoughts on multiple occasions, but now he said nothing, just breathed in perfect time. One of the night nurses peeped in through the window of Tammas's door, saw that it was Harry in with him making the racket and walked away.

'He was. Lucky, too.'

Harry looked up. 'What?'

'The attack. He was lucky. That's all. Lucky. That he needed. A piss. And you. Didn't. He found. Us and treated. Us and did his. Job. Because he. Needed a. Piss. If you'd had a. Full bladder. It would be. You. With the medals. And him. Coming to. See me three. Nights a week. And trying to. Break my. Furniture.'

'And going back?' Harry said.

'You can't. Blame him. For that. He enjoyed the. Military life. Wanted to. Make a difference. I'm sure what. Happened. Fucked him. Up. As bad as. It fucked us.' Tammas rattled again.

'Doesn't change a thing, though, does it?' said Harry. 'So we both got back, fucked up. What does he do? He goes back to Helmand. What do I do? I go back to work and start shagging his wife.'

'It's funny what. People think a hero. Is. A man was. Visiting his daughter. Car crash. Drunk driver. Waist down. Very sad. I heard them. Talking about me. In the corridor. As soon as he. Heard those words. Helmand Province. Neck down. He's in here. Telling me what a. Hero I am. How proud I. Should be. Fucking. Self-righteous. Wanker.'

Harry nodded. Tammas had managed to guide the conversation away from Harry's self-pity, a dance at which he had by now become expert.

'Bet they do the. Same to you. The women, you know. When they see. All the scars.'

What women? Harry thought. There's been no one since Alice. And she knew all about the scars. Lahiri had told her everything. Of course he had, Harry thought, she was his fucking wife, wasn't she?

'I don't know, boss. I know I'm not a hero. Not like he is.' Harry got up. 'I should leave,' he said.

'Sometimes I. Worry about. You, Harry.'

'Why?'

''Cause you're. Hollow.'

Harry had been looking at a painting of mountains and birds from somewhere up in Scotland, on the far wall. It was a fine thing for a quadriplegic to look at for most of his life. He turned to Tammas.

'T.S. Eliot,' said Tammas. 'Wrote about. Hollow men. Lost souls. To violent. Causes. I worry. That you're one. Of them. I think he. Meant that. We all are. Born. Hollow. We each have a. Deep.' He paused, to think, to gain energy. 'Hollow inside us. And we all have to. Find something. Which can fill it.'

Harry touched the place on his chest where the bullet had entered, and felt the wind go through it and out where it had exited, an inch or so to the left of his own spinal cord. That felt like a hollow sometimes. It was what had hurt in the fried chicken shop.

'What do you fill yours with?' he said.

'Ha. Good question. Used to be God. You know they put. My breathing tube. Right where my. Crucifix. Used to sit. Ha. Ha. Not any more. Now it's. A machine. I have a machine. For everything else. Lungs. Voice.'

Tammas turned and looked Harry straight in the eyes.

'Might as well. Run my. Soul, too.'

Monday, 21 January

'Hello, you must be Dr Kent. Bit early, is it? I'd have thought an early start would be bread-and-butter for a junior doctor.'

The detective showing Harry through to the bigger offices on the upper floors of Walworth police station was bouncing from one wall to the next as they navigated the maze of corridors. Most of the police station was quiet at this time of the morning. They'd come in opposite the custody suite and even that wasn't busy, the desk sergeant munching a bacon roll and reading the *Express,* nodding to them as they passed. They eventually arrived at a relatively pleasant-looking interview room, one with a window at least.

'Sit down, Doc, make yerself comfortable,' the detective said. 'Anything I can get for you? Coffee? Milk? Sugar?'

Harry said yes to all four questions and the detective pulled out a BlackBerry and texted someone, before heading over to a recorder on the table and starting to set it up, inserting a fresh cassette and rewinding it. Even as he did that, he was still bouncing, shifting his weight from one foot to the other. Either the man was over-caffeinated, or he was taking similar medication to the circular white pill which had woken Harry up after four hours' sleep. And in much higher doses.

'Innit funny how we still use these old piles of shit, eh?' the detective said. 'What would they think if we was typing up statements on typewriters, or using a blackboard for investigations? Don't suppose you can say blackboard these days, eh, Doc? Probably racist, innit? Remind me, I'll ask Fairweather when he gets in 'ere.'

The detective finished with the cassette recorder and sat down opposite Harry. He was about to speak again when the door opened, and a PCSO came in carrying two polystyrene cups of coffee.

'Oh, Brenda, you're a star! Pop 'em down on the table, why don't you?'

Harry picked up the coffee. It warmed his hands.

'Cheers,' he said. 'I'm sorry, remind me what you said your name was again?'

'I probably didn't, I'm terrible at that,' the detective said, taking a big slurp of coffee, burning himself and then spilling some on his suit and skinny red tie as he replaced the cup. 'Fuck! Fuck me! Sorry, Doc, excuse the language.' He stood back up, brushing down the front of his suit. 'It's DC Kepler. Tony Kepler. I'm normally local here – CID, Homicide & Serious, Sapphire, I've been around. My old beat used to be the Albany estate. I'm trying to do some time in Professional Standards now, the missus wants us to get an extension, she's got our second on its way, reckons it's time I got myself promoted.'

The Albany estate, Harry thought. Solomon Idris had lived his whole life there. Harry read Kepler easily after that. He was old-school police, coming to work to collar yobs and lock them up, didn't give a shit about targets or local government initiatives, and looked with suspicion on any senior officer with a university degree.

The new-school police walked in the door as Harry sipped at his coffee. Marcus Fairweather took off his coat to reveal a much nicer suit than Kepler's, the perks of a chief inspector's salary. Came up close to Harry, too close, and shook his hand.

'Good to see you again, Dr Kent,' Fairweather said, his dulcet voice a contrast to Kepler's rough edges. 'And thank you for coming in at such unsociable hours.'

'No problem,' said Harry.

'We'll crack on so I don't delay you any further,' Fairweather continued, 'Sorry about the recording, but the IPCC will be going over everything we do here with a fine-tooth comb, and I'd hate for them to get their knickers in a twist and demand to interview you for themselves.'

'Me too,' said Harry.

Kepler reached over and flicked on the cassette recorder.

'It is 07.13 on Monday, 21 January 2013. This is interview code Waldron Six, subject Dr Harry Kent, force medical examiner for Inner South-East region. Present are DCI Marcus Fairweather and DC Tony Kepler.'

Operation Waldron was the task force set up to investigate Idris's shooting. As far as Harry could tell, it was being led by Fairweather in reality, but officially it was an 'independent inquiry' under the Independent Police Complaints Commission. Harry took a sip of coffee.

'So, Dr Kent, I'm aware you've got other commitments, but if we could take things slowly . . .'

Fairweather gave Harry the unmistakable feeling that he had been caught smoking in the school toilets again and was explaining it to the headmaster. They took half an hour as Harry described being called at home, being briefed by Noble at the scene, and the process of deciding to send him in. He recounted as best he could the exact words of everyone there, watching the two detectives as he spoke. Fairweather smiled and nodded, leaning forward, his fingers interlinked; Harry saw in him the mannerisms of a shrink, and wondered if he'd been right about his fast-track theory, if the DCI was some kind of sidetracked psychologist. Kepler had a legal pad on the desk and was furiously noting down everything Harry said. Harry watched his pen dart around, putting quotation marks around the quotes, circles around pairs of numbers and capital letters that indicated the police officers. He caught at least one absent-minded doodle.

What if Idris dies? That had been the question in his head on the drive back from Marigold House, and on the way to the station that morning. He wondered which of the circled capital letters Fairweather was selecting as the fall guy: Noble, Quinn, the kid from Trojan who'd fired the shots?

'So Solomon was breathing through the oxygen mask?'

Harry found it interesting that Fairweather used Idris's first name. It stank of politics, but maybe he was being cynical. Maybe the detective had kids himself.

'Yeah.'

'And you were talking?'

'Yes.'

'What about?'

'He said he was doing it all for someone called Keisha. That they had killed her, and the police didn't care.'

'Keisha?' said Fairweather. 'Did he give you any more details?'

'No. He wanted to talk to the lawyer about her, not to me. He thought I was one of you. I got the impression he didn't much care for the police.'

'How did he seem?'

Harry thought back to the shivering teenager, hand curling around the barrel of the gun, chicken bones in a box on the table.

'Like a man at the end of the road. He had a look in his eyes, like he had no way out.'

Harry recalled Tammas's words from the night before. *We each have a deep hollow inside us.* The hollow inside Solomon Idris had appeared right there and then, and everything that had previously filled it had spilled out onto the floor.

'What happened next?'

'I tried to get him to tell me the story, but he insisted on waiting. And I was trying to persuade him to let me take him to hospital.'

'Had he agreed?'

'Almost. But then there was that shot from outside. I threw myself to the floor. Trojan charged in, and the first one through the door shot him.'

DC Kepler spoke for the first time in the interview.

'Hang on there, Doc – you heard a gunshot. How did you know it was from outside?'

Harry turned and made a point of delivering his answer straight to Fairweather.

'Because there was only one gun in that room and I was looking at it. And it didn't go off.'

'So where were you when the police officers entered the shop?' Kepler said.

'On the floor.'

Fairweather resumed the questioning.

'Did you say anything?'

The memories came back, as did the pain on the right side of his chest. He took a deep breath.

'I shouted something. Something like, *Don't shoot him!*'

Fairweather nodded and Kepler wrote, and added quotation marks and a capital letter with a circle. Harry couldn't quite make out which letter he'd been assigned.

'W22, the officer who first entered the building, reported you shouting, *Shoot him!*' Fairweather said. His glare was unrelenting now, the headmaster facing his student. Harry wasn't even a full-time employee of the Met; he could be replaced by practically any

66

other doctor with a bit of spare time and the ability to take blood. Of course he'd make a great scapegoat.

'That wasn't a question,' he said.

'I know,' said Fairweather. 'We're not in court.'

Harry shook his head, and eventually stopped resisting the reply.

'I definitely didn't say that. I said, *Don't shoot him!* because I knew that Idris hadn't fired the gun and didn't pose a threat. I'd also like it on the record that the officer fired almost simultaneously with me speaking, so he did not fire after hearing what I said, but either just before or as I said it.'

'Which was it – before or simultaneously?' Fairweather said.

'I can't remember,' Harry said. 'What are you saying, this guy's story is that he burst in, I yelled *Shoot him*, so he goes and drops the poor bastard on my orders? Bullshit.'

The silence in the room was disrupted only by the humming of the tape recorder. Fairweather exhaled and smiled and leant backwards. The therapist had returned.

'Dr Kent, I understand this has been an emotional incident, but we'd appreciate it if you'd keep your language clean. I should inform you that there were other officers who reported you saying *Don't shoot!* or something similar.'

Harry made eye contact with Fairweather and held it for too long.

'When you entered the restaurant for the second time,' Fairweather continued, 'where did you put the oxygen cylinder?'

'On the table with my medical bag.'

'Where was that in relation to the gun?'

'It was in front of it. Between the front door and the gun.'

'So could it have occluded the view of the gun from someone standing at the front of the room?'

Fairweather smiled. Harry thought hard.

'Possibly,' he said.

He clenched his fists under the table. He could see the scenario building. The oxygen cylinder blocking the officer's line of sight, him shouting at the man to shoot. A reasonable police officer would have pulled the trigger, and that was all they needed to prove.

'After the shooting, what did you do?'

Harry detailed the medical attention he had given Idris, everything up to the point at which they loaded him into the ambulance. He remembered asking Quinn why the police had opened fire and Quinn saying that Idris had fired first, and one of the Trojan officers asking whether Idris was dead. Fairweather didn't push him further on either of those. Kepler shuffled together his papers, and Harry began to relax.

'One final thing,' said Fairweather, stopping Kepler from switching off the recorder. 'How did you feel about DI Noble's decision to send you in to negotiate?'

'She was the Silver Commander. I was acting on her directions.'

'Some of the officers present have indicated that you were initially uncomfortable with the idea.'

Harry leant forward and raised his voice a little. 'If I hadn't been comfortable with it, I wouldn't have gone in.'

'Do you think it was the right decision?' said Fairweather.

Fuck you, Harry thought. At least when the bastard had been trying to scapegoat him, he'd been subtle about it.

'It got three hostages released,' said Harry. 'So, yes. But I'm not trained to make decisions like that. I have no authority to comment.'

'Thanks, Dr Kent. Interview concluded, 08.06.'

Kepler reached across and flicked off the recorder. Harry drained his coffee cup, by now long cold.

'So,' he said. 'What happened?'

Kepler looked over at Fairweather, who nodded slightly.

'We examined the gun recovered at the scene,' Kepler said. 'It was an old revolver, a converted starting pistol. Ballistics said if Idris had pulled the trigger, there's a fifty-fifty chance nothing would have happened. The only weapon we recovered that had been fired was the MP5 assigned to W22, the officer who shot Solomon.'

Fairweather looked particularly uncomfortable and shifted position on his chair.

'So what about the gunshot?' Harry asked. 'The one which caused you lot to charge in? A mystery?'

'Well, the Evidence Recovery Unit did a sweep of the area,' Kepler continued. 'There's an alleyway on the Wyndham Court housing estate that runs right alongside the Chicken Hut. We found firearms residue and a shell casing there, and a nine-milli-metre bullet was found inside a recycling bin.'

'A police bullet?'

'No,' Fairweather cut in. 'It was a full-metal jacket round. Trojan use hollow-points. Ballistics are having a good look at it as we speak.'

'Wow,' Harry said. 'That's convenient for you.'

It meant someone had fired a shot in the alleyway behind the buildings, which had been deserted at the time. There were two scenarios in his head: the ridiculous coincidence that another crime involving gunfire had been happening at the same time as the crisis in the restaurant, or that someone had deliberately discharged a gun in the hope that it would provoke the police into shooting Idris.

'Dr Kent,' Fairweather said, leaning forward. 'I can assure you there has been no planting of evidence. Our team is following up several leads, and a suspect was seen running away from Wyndham Road while the police were securing the restaurant. Trust me on this, we're going to find out what happened.'

He got to his feet.

'Detective Constable Kepler will show you out.'

DI Noble was leaning against the rear wall of the police station, opposite Harry's car, one hand pulling her chequered coat close to keep the warmth in, the other holding a cigarette.

'Dirty habit,' Harry said.

'You've been spending too much time with Fairweather,' said Noble. 'Honestly, that fucker gets into your head. You don't strike me as one of the clean-living brigade.'

'You've pegged me,' said Harry, palms up. 'Were you waiting for me?'

'I saw the car, twigged you were here. And I heard rumours that Fairweather and our friends from Professional Standards had you in their sights.'

Harry shook his head. 'I can't believe it. You guys mess up, a kid gets shot, and I'm the first guy they go for.'

'Don't underestimate him,' Noble said. 'As far as scapegoats go, you're perfect. New to the game, no supporting faction in the

Met, not attached to internal politics. No one's gonna stick up for you for sentimental reasons.'

She stubbed the cigarette out with the tip of her boot. Black Doc Martens, Harry observed.

'No offence,' she said.

Harry felt the fury rising, tempted to burst back into the station, find the detective chief inspector and slam his bald, shiny head into a wall.

'Do you know what he told me? When Trojan came in the door, apparently I yelled for them to shoot Idris. That's what's been said, anyway.'

'Ignore him; he's a bastard,' Noble said. 'He's just riding the trends, and at the moment the trend is that half the Met is either racist or selling everything they know to Rupert Murdoch. And if Fairweather's hunting bent coppers, then his career will keep on rising until someone realises that he's so fucking crooked himself that he sleeps on a spiral staircase. But by then he'll be too high up, too well connected to get rid of.'

Harry leaned in closer to her, lowering his voice.

'Well, you should watch out yourself, too,' he said. 'Fairweather also heard that I appeared uncomfortable with your strategy, apparently. It might not just be me they're stitching up.'

'Fuck's sake,' Noble muttered. Her cigarette end still glowed orange on the tarmac, and she put a zealous amount of effort into grinding it out. 'Thanks for the heads-up.'

'No problem.'

'Was Tony Kepler in there with him?' said Noble.

Harry nodded.

'Kepler's a safe pair of hands,' Noble said. 'We go way back; we were DCs together. He'll give me a decent warning if he reckons Fairweather's coming after me. Which wouldn't be unlikely. We've got history.'

'Really?'

'Yeah. Those pricks have nailed me once already. I used to work in the Central Task Force, up at the Yard. Me and my husband Jack – he was the lead officer – we ran undercover teams all over the city. After Jack died, I took over his job. Acting DCI, of course, 'cause there's no money these days to promote anyone.

First big case we had went nasty, we had to let some bad people go on a technicality. They brought in Fairweather's lot to sort out the mess. He got me suspended and wanted me kicked out, too, said I'd "overestimated my capabilities" and the whole fuck-up was my fault. The tribunal said he was full of shit, but they had to make an example of someone, so here I am working CID in fucking Peck'nam.'

She pronounced the 'nam' like Vietnam, an idiom which had started with the gang members on the local sink estates and been quickly adopted by the coppers going after them. He absorbed the history and said nothing, wondering how many DCIs called Jack had died in the past couple of years, now completely sure that he'd met Noble before the inner cordon on Camberwell Road. If she remembered him, she wasn't letting on. It had to be an unpleasant lifestyle, constantly watching your back to see if your own organisation was going to start ripping your career apart. The NHS did it, too, but in a somewhat more insipid, palatable way. Harry'd only been with the police for six months, but even so, he'd come to appreciate its dysfunction. An organisation where the whole was far less than the sum of its parts.

'So, why were you waiting for me?' he said.

'Are you going to see Idris now?' said Noble. ''Cause I'd like to come with you.'

'Sure.'

'There's no chance of him waking up this morning, is there?'

He might not wake up at all, Harry thought but didn't say. 'No way. The operation we did last night was only so we could stop the bleeding and stabilise him. He'll go for definitive surgery today, or possibly tomorrow. There's not even a chance of us waking him up until after that. It could be weeks.'

He unlocked his car and opened the passenger door. 'I take it you want a lift?' he said.

'Well, the weather's shit, isn't it?'

She smiled and got in. Harry pulled out onto Walworth Road and headed south, towards the hospital. The morning congestion had eased slightly.

'You still on the case, then?' he asked, switching off the radio.

'Yeah. Even though it seems pretty clear cut, we've got to get it all together so we can hand it over to the CPS, and they can charge Idris. If he makes it. Mo's looking at the gun, too, see if we can trace how he got hold of it.'

Harry accelerated past a broken-down 68 bus, the passengers spilling out onto the pavement, asking directions. The surroundings were familiar, but it took Harry a moment to realise they were coming up to Wyndham Road. The Chicken Hut was still closed off with crime-scene tape.

'Keisha. He said he was doing it all for Keisha,' Harry said. 'Do you have any idea who that might have been?'

'Didn't take us long to find her,' said Noble. 'Keisha Best, eighteen years old. Lived in the tower block next to Idris's on the Albany estate.'

'She's dead, right?'

'As of 14 November last year. Threw herself in front of a train at Peckham Rye station.'

'Fucking hell,' said Harry. His stomach twisted again, Solomon Idris's words ringing in his head. *They killed her, and you feds didn't give a shit.* At medical school, he'd learned about copycat suicides – people who were depressed were more likely to end their own lives if someone close to them had recently done so, or if there had been a high-profile suicide covered in the media. The more Harry mulled them over, the more Solomon Idris's actions at the Chicken Hut looked like a suicide attempt by proxy.

'You looking into it?' said Harry.

Noble rubbed her temples as she answered.

'I'll have a look over the file. But Fairweather and the Yard don't give a flying fanny what was going on in that kid's life. He's in for it, no one else got hurt, job done. Nothing to investigate.'

An eighteen-year-old girl throws herself in front of a train, and a seventeen-year-old boy attempts suicide-by-cop, and there's nothing to investigate. Only in this city, Harry thought. But he detected a deep resentment in Noble's tone, and at least that might give him an option later.

'Well, apart from us,' he said.

They arrived at the hospital and Harry managed to find a place in the staff car park, not too far from the East Wing, the block that hosted the acute wards and theatres where Harry spent most of his time. They got out of the car, and he noticed Noble scratching at her wrist. More than ten minutes since her last smoke, he reasoned.

'Mind?' Noble said.

'Go for it.'

'You intrigue me, Harry.' She lit up and Harry shepherded her into a corner of the car park close to a fire exit, one of the hospital staff's illegal smoking corners.

'How so?' Harry said.

'I can't work out why a high-flying doctor like you decided to start working for us in your spare time. Especially since, as you showed both yesterday and this morning, you hate the police with every fibre of your existence.'

Harry laughed. 'That's a bit of an exaggeration.'

'I can tell,' Noble said. 'Where'd you grow up? Local?'

'Bermondsey, then New Cross,' Harry admitted. 'I'm a Millwall fan and all, I guess that means I have to hate the filth.'

Noble laughed. 'Cheers for warning me about Fairweather,' she said. 'You didn't have to do that. If it got back to him, you could lose your job. Or your contract, or whatever it is.'

Harry shrugged his shoulders. 'Dunno. And don't call me high flying. Most of the people who were in my year at med school are GPs or consultants now.'

'So why aren't you?'

'Well, the army paid for my degree, so I had to work for them for five years. While everyone else was doing research and ticking boxes.'

'Really,' Noble said. 'Get to see the world?'

'Not really. Mostly jumping around the UK. They sent me to Birmingham and Frimley for the first and second years, then a few postings to Canada, and then I was a general duties officer for two years. They let me out but I stayed on as a reservist, working at the Ruskin, doing A&E, anaesthetics, ICU. Then my unit got rotated out to Afghanistan, so I was called up and went out there.'

'Bloody hell. What was that like?'

'An experience. Hairy at times.' Harry expected the pain in his side but it didn't come.

'Still doesn't explain why you decided to be one of our resident stethoscopes,' Noble said.

Harry looked at his watch. He started at nine, so they had time. 'I can show you, if you'd like,' he said.

Noble fixed him with a wary stare, the smoke mixing with her breath and the drizzle, floating off into the sky. 'OK, then.'

They headed into the main hospital building, moving through busy corridors. Harry called a lift and pushed the button for the sixth floor in the North Wing, which contained the majority of the hospital's long-stay wards.

'This isn't the way to the ICU,' Noble said. 'Where are we going?'

'Roll up your sleeves and take your watch off.'

'Harry, where are we?'

'Tennyson Ward,' said Harry. 'It's the neurological rehab unit.'

The doors opened and he headed for the nurses' station, Noble following reticently. Both of them worked alcohol gel between their hands, the steps a rehearsed muscle memory for Harry, requiring Noble's attention as she tried to imitate him. The ward was quiet, more homely. Every patient had their own room, and the nurses almost looked out of place in their blue tabards.

'Ah, the elusive Dr Kent,' a quiet, measured voice said.

It belonged to a thin, wiry man with a comb-over and perfectly circular glasses, several pink folders of patient notes under one arm. He was dressed in a white cotton shirt and tan chinos, his bow tie pastel blue.

'This is Professor Niebaum,' Harry said. 'He's the ward's head consultant.'

'And to whom do I have the pleasure of speaking?' Niebaum asked.

'I'm Frances Noble. Detective Inspector, Southwark CID.'

Harry could tell from the stuttering that Noble was nervous, and that he had successfully removed her from her comfort zone. He felt a small stab of pride.

'Ah!' Niebaum said, smiling. 'It's fantastic that you're here! Let me take you through.'

Noble was about to speak but Harry cut her off. 'DI Noble is at the hospital investigating a different matter, actually,' he explained. 'But we had some spare time and I thought I'd bring her up here.'

Niebaum was already walking towards one of the side rooms off the ward, and Harry instinctively fell into step behind him.

'One of the physios is in with Zara at the moment, so it's probably best if she isn't disturbed. Sorry, Harry,' said the neurologist, before turning to Noble. 'I don't usually turn him away. If it wasn't for Harry's visits, I don't think we'd be making any progress at all.'

Niebaum's phone started ringing, and he dashed to the nurses' station to take the call.

'Who's Zara?' Noble asked. Her body language was passive-aggressive, hands on hips, legs braced. They were standing outside the side room, and Harry craned his neck to look through the door's small window. He could see the shocking pink of her hair contrasting with the off-white bedding, the grey hospital gown. Two physiotherapists in white polos were going through the exercises used to maintain her muscle tone while she remained in a coma.

'Her,' Harry explained. 'Zara's her name. Well, it's not; we don't know her name, but it's what we call her. She's in the system as Female, Unknown.'

'She's unidentified?' Noble said. 'How's that possible?'

'She's in a minimally conscious state. She was found unconscious with no identification on her, and she's never regained enough cognitive function to respond to us, even if she does know who she is.'

'A vegetative state?'

'Close,' said Harry. 'Slightly better. She can follow simple commands, like moving her eyes from one side to the other. But she can't process information. And we can't communicate with her, so we're not really sure to what extent she's aware of her surroundings.'

'Why Zara?'

'She was wearing a pair of denim shorts from Zara when they found her,' Harry said. 'It stuck. It was the only identifiable feature on her. It's a little more dignified than Unknown Female.'

'What happened to her?' Noble said.

'August before last. The riots.'

Noble looked up, slackjawed.

'She's been here since 2011?'

'Yup,' said Harry. 'I still remember it. The Monday evening. I'd been working a double shift in A&E – completely illegal, but fuck it. The hospital could barely cope, we were seeing so many injured. Some paramedics found her in an alleyway near Clapham Junction, rushed her in here. She'd been kicked in the ribs, hit on the head with something blunt. She had these little pinprick wounds on her chest, the kind you get if you're lying on gravel and someone stamps on you. Whoever did it tried to strangle her, too, but didn't succeed. When she came in, the hyoid bone was broken. That's the—'

'The bone across the front of the throat,' Noble interrupted. 'I know. I worked Homicide & Serious for two years.'

'I had to do an emergency tracheotomy in A&E,' Harry said. 'She spent twelve weeks in intensive care. During that time it became clear that things hadn't been perfect before she was attacked. She had needle tracks in her elbows, but none of the usual complications of long-term drug use. She was severely anaemic, had a vitamin D deficiency, her immune system was barely functioning. We analysed her hair and it suggested a history of benzodiazepine use and severe malnourishment. We spoke to some of the people who deal with child abuse, refugees and the like, and they say the results are in keeping with someone who was kept against their will for some time before she was attacked.'

'Some time? How long?'

'At least a month, according to them,' said Harry. 'Maybe longer, even.'

'Fucking hell.'

A passing nurse frowned at the language and Noble muttered an apology.

'She's stable now, medically speaking,' Harry continued. 'And there's little brain damage visible on the scans. But she's been here more than eighteen months now, no improvement. You lot were interested at the start, but the case got shuffled around. No one's come forward to claim her. Homicide & Serious poked around for a few weeks, so did Missing Persons, but since last year she's had no one visiting her. Apart from me.'

'You mean no one's currently working the case?' Noble asked, sounding surprised.

'Not actively,' said Harry. 'I've been told that it's the remit of the riot crimes unit, but as far as I can tell that's all being wrapped up.'

Noble said nothing.

'There's got to be a family somewhere,' he continued. 'Someone who cares about her, who needs to know where she is.'

He remembered the first time he had seen her, a memory as clear as almost any of his life. She had no identity, save for her shocking pink hair and the T-shirt she had been wearing, a grimy off-white crewneck with the slogan 'What the f*** are you staring at?', each asterisk a different colour. The initial investigators had found that it was a relatively popular one, sold on the Internet and at several London markets. Likewise the bracelet she had on: a simple bronze chain, with a one-pence coin hanging from it, a hole drilled through the middle. Generic, possibly home-made, nothing that assisted them in identifying her. Every time the colour in her hair started to fade, Harry arranged for it to be redyed. Just to preserve what semblance of individuality remained.

'You've got nothing else for an ID?' Noble said, incredulous.

'Nope,' said Harry. 'Nada.'

'Dentistry? DNA analysis? Bone isotopes?'

Harry shrugged. 'We sent DNA. No match on the UK register. Met wouldn't fund the smart stuff.'

'Will she get better?'

'Probably not. In some similar cases, there have been reported recoveries after months, even years. Niebaum's a world expert in minimally conscious states. But probably not, no.'

A short silence. A nurse headed past, comforting a crying relative.

'Why do you keep visiting her?' Noble asked.

'No one else does. Also, Niebaum thinks that she responds better to me than to any of the other staff. Sometimes she displays spontaneous eye movements, patterns of blinking and rotation that might be an attempt at communication. I think it's just coincidence, but he wants me to keep coming.'

Noble said nothing. The two physiotherapists left the room, discussing whether to go for a coffee or not, leaving the girl with the pink hair lying on her side, still attached to the monitors.

'Bloody hell!' Noble exclaimed. 'She's only a kid!'

'Between twenty and twenty-three,' said Harry. 'At least, that's what the experts think. But if she had been severely malnourished, she could be older.'

'Jesus.'

Harry took a deep breath in and spoke quietly. 'I just think she deserves more than this existence. She's not a vegetable. She's capable of some interactions with her environment, and she deserves to have her family here with her. And I can't find out who she is by myself.'

'So that's why you're working with the Met?' Noble said. 'You're hoping you just stumble on this girl's identity?'

'Well, no one else is looking for her,' Harry said, turning out of the room. 'And she didn't just appear by magic, half dead in Clapham, did she? Somebody in this city knows who she is, and I'm not going to find them sitting around in this hospital.'

Noble looked at him the way she might have done at one of those people who ring up the police claiming to have solved the identity of Jack the Ripper. Harry considered a variety of responses, from pleas for help to condemnations that she, like the others, was only interested in the glamorous cases, the ones with press conferences at the end and promotions a few weeks afterwards.

Instead he just said, 'Let's go downstairs.'

Back in the ICU, Dr Rashid was surrounded by a crowd of junior doctors and medical students as he strode from bed to bed. He was recounting Idris's history as a perfect example of the type of patient that intensive care doctors were particularly suited to treating. Critically ill, a combination of medical and surgical problems, several interacting systems which all needed to be controlled. Rashid noticed Harry and walked over to him.

'You're late, Harry. Ward round's at nine, sharp. I guess I'll let you off, given recent events.'

Harry mumbled some thanks.

'I'll carry on with the round. Maria's the long-day reg, so you two sort out the tasks that need doing. Central lines out, beds twelve and nineteen need a trachy, we think, and we have a transfer in from Canterbury at about lunchtime.'

Harry added the tasks to the mental list in his head. Rashid appeared to be done, but then noticed Noble standing behind Harry.

'Who's that?'

'She's a detective,' said Harry. 'She's investigating the shooting.'

Rashid nodded. The ward round had moved away to the next patient, and Harry turned, hoping to catch a glimpse of Idris.

Bed eighteen was empty.

'Where's he gone?'

A transfer out so early in the day would be for only two reasons – either he'd been rushed back to theatre for some emergency procedure, or he was in the mortuary.

'Calm down,' Rashid said, touching Harry on the arm. 'We moved him to the side room. Police request, so the guard could keep an eye on visitors.'

Bay ten was an isolation room, with just one set of doors as opposed to the cubicle set-up of the other ICU beds. As Harry looked over, the copper on duty was making conversation with Noble. To protect Idris from infection, he wasn't allowed inside the room itself.

'Maria will fill you in,' said Rashid, before leaving to rejoin the ward round. Harry looked around for the other registrar, who had the unpleasant job of working eight until eight as opposed to Harry's kinder nine to five. When he finished turning, a short, tanned woman was waiting. It wasn't unusual for Harry never to have met the junior registrars, who were often rotating from a different training programme, such as A&E or general medicine.

'Maria Saltis.'

'Harry Kent. Did we get a Micro opinion on bed ten, Solomon Idris?' Harry asked.

Saltis brought it up on the computer screen. 'Yeah, based on the X-ray they said treat for PCP, and cover for a secondary bacterial as well. We've started co-trimoxazole.'

'Do you mind if we quickly go and see him before we go through the list?' Harry said. 'I'm not sure if Dr Rashid told you, but I brought Idris in last night. And there's a police officer who wants to see him, too.'

Saltis appeared hesitant, and Harry clocked why. She was a

new registrar on a new rotation, and with the consultant on the unit she didn't want to be seen as taking liberties.

'Start without me, and give me all the crap jobs, then,' Harry said. 'I'll be ten minutes, I promise.'

Saltis smiled and nodded.

'OK, then.'

Harry thanked her and headed towards the side room where Idris was. Outside the room, the plainclothes cop on guard duty leant against the wall, a pistol on his belt. Noble caught Harry's eyes as he headed into the isolation room.

'Can I come in, too?' she said.

'Roll your sleeves up, wash your hands in that sink and put gloves and an apron on,' Harry said, pointing at a roll of plastic aprons attached to the wall.

'Mornin', Dr Kent,' said a voice from inside the room. Each ICU patient had their own assigned nurse, and Idris's was Gladys Lane. Despite a number of frustrated conversations, Gladys insisted on calling him Dr Kent.

'How is he?' Harry said, stepping into the room. Idris looked tired – as the ventilator kept breathing for him, his chest expanded beyond what it normally would, the skin stretching across his ribs and making him look even emptier than he was. As he watched Idris breathe, Harry briefly wished he could read minds.

'Been OK in the mornin'. His saturations dropped down at about six-thirty so they had to put his oxygen back up.'

'What's he on now?'

'Point six,' said Lane.

'Is that bad?' said Noble, who had entered the side room behind him.

'It means he needs to breathe sixty per cent oxygen,' said Harry. 'You and I make do with twenty-one per cent. So it's not brilliant.'

He hunched over the computer screen in one corner of the room and started scrolling through all of the results. Idris's blood gases had improved steadily throughout the night, and his kidney function appeared good, which was reassuring. The rest of the blood work was as expected. He was anaemic, but that was because he had almost bled to death. His platelets were on the low side, too, but Harry looked up at the drip-stand and saw that there was a bag of them running in now. Whoever the night registrar had been, he or she had done a good job.

'Try and drop him down to point five on the ventilator,' Harry said. 'His last gas was good.'

'As you wish,' said Lane, moving over to the machine to make the change.

'So what's the deal?' said Noble.

'He hasn't got worse,' Harry said. 'He's stable now. Which I was worried he'd never be, after the state he was in.'

'That's good, right?'

Harry nodded. 'But as you can see, the surgeons still need to get in there and fix the problem. His spleen needs a definitive repair. Might even need to be removed.'

He pointed down and Noble followed his gaze, looking at the plastic covering, about the size of an A4 paper sheet, which sat between peeled-back skin edges over the centre of Solomon Idris's abdomen, stapled crudely in the four corners and covered with a transparent dressing. Beneath it, the dark pink shapes of Idris's abdominal organs pulsed and twisted, reminders that the teenager connected to the tubes and wires was still alive, not just an exhibit in a human museum.

'That'll happen today?' said Noble.

'Probably. The sooner the better,' said Harry. 'I'd be happy for him to go today, and I'm sure the anaesthetists will be too. We don't like leaving patients with their bellies open.'

'So when do you think he'll be waking up?' Noble said.

'I can't answer that question,' Harry said. 'He's in a serious condition. Not today, by any means, and not tomorrow, either. And that's assuming he wakes up at all.'

'But we're looking at days?' Noble said.

'That's the best-case scenario,' Harry said. 'It could well be a week or two, here in the ICU, if there are complications. And I've known cases like this where it's been longer.'

'Right.' Noble sighed. 'We're not going to get to sit down with him for two weeks, is that what you're telling me?'

'I don't want to keep him asleep any more than necessary. And believe me, I want to find out what's going on with this kid just as much as you do. But if he needs to be under for two weeks, or a month, then so be it.'

Noble backed away, shaking her head.

'I'm sorry, Harry, I didn't mean to—'

'Forget it,' Harry said. He started scrolling down to see if the tests Rashid had ordered in the early hours of the morning were back yet.

'Well, you haven't wasted a trip,' he said, tapping the computer screen with the end of his pen. Noble leaned forward to read the results and Harry moved out of the way. Tapped the part where it said: MICROBIOLOGY RESULT AVAILABLE – URGENT SEROLOGY (HIV-1): ANTIBODIES DETECTED.

'He's HIV-positive?' said Noble.

'Yes, he is,' said Harry. 'And all the evidence points to him having no idea. And he might be able to hear us, so keep your voice down.'

'What kind of evidence?'

'Well,' Harry said, 'the organism causing his pneumonia is called *pneumocystis,* and we only ever see it in patients with a poorly functioning immune system. When people get infected with HIV, it kills their white blood cells, particularly a type called CD4, and eventually they get these opportunistic infections. We call them AIDS-defining illnesses.'

'And he's got one of them?' Noble said.

'Exactly,' said Harry, flicking to another page on the screen. 'Solomon's CD4 count is low. Which, combined with his youth, suggests to me that he's not been undergoing any HIV treatment, and this is the first presentation of the illness.'

Noble took in the information and sucked air in through her teeth.

'Christ,' she said.

'Yeah, he must be especially vulnerable to have developed an infection so soon, but even then he was probably infected two or three years ago. We'll start him on therapy,' said Harry. 'What with our catchment area, we see more HIV than most other hospitals in the country. Our guys are good. And there's this.'

Harry switched to the main screen for Solomon Idris, where it showed all his hospital visits, which totalled three: the present one,

July 2011, and March 2009. Harry brought up the 2009 record, which was summarised by a brief report from a doctor who'd treated Idris in A&E for a cracked rib and superficial cuts and bruises, gained in a gang brawl.

'What a start in life,' Noble said.

'Here's the interesting part,' Harry said, reading out the last sentences of the A&E doctor's report. 'Patient reports that the injuries were gained as part of a gang initiation and refuses to give consent for police involvement. Saviour Project referral accepted.'

'2009, he'd have been fourteen,' said Noble. 'Jesus.'

The Saviour Project was the scheme run out of Lahiri's GP surgery, over in Camberwell. Harry opened his mouth to comment, but was interrupted by a knock on the door, which Gladys Lane rushed past them to open.

'Dr Kent, the surgical team are here to see the patient,' she said. Harry and Noble made their excuses, threw their gloves and aprons into one of the clinical waste bins, and moved to leave, replaced by Abe Gunther and the rest of his team. Gunther nodded solemnly to Harry as he entered.

'How is he?' the surgeon asked.

'Stable,' said Harry. 'His platelets are running low but there's a bag going in now. And the serology's back. He's HIV-positive.'

'That's confirmed, is it?'

Harry nodded.

'We'll go back in this afternoon to repair his vasculature,' Gunther said. 'But his spleen took a tough hit. We might have to take it out. I'll do my best to avoid it, but sometimes there's no choice.'

Most people could live without a spleen, but if you had HIV it was much harder. Harry looked at the floor and shrugged his shoulders.

'Let's just get him out of the woods, and we can let the immunologists worry about the future.'

'Very good,' Gunther said, and finished washing his hands. Harry left the isolation room and joined Noble, who was checking her phone in the corridor.

'Anything else I can help with?' he said.

'Not that I can think of,' she replied, sliding her phone back into

83

her dark jeans. 'I encounter so many people like this. Every single thing I find out about them just tells me their lives were even shittier.'

The copper who'd been assigned guard duty for Idris emerged from the stairwell opposite them, holding two cups of coffee.

'How many of those do you drink a day?' Harry asked.

'Twelve,' she said. 'Jack used to say that a detective was a machine for converting caffeine into paperwork. Can I ask you a straight question, and you give me no bullshit?'

'Sure,' said Harry. He had a bad feeling about where this was going.

'Is Idris going to live?'

'I don't know. He's young. He's got that going for him. But when people with severe systemic illness get critically injured, and have to undergo multiple operations . . . it doesn't usually end well, that's all I'm saying.'

'Well, I'm sure you'll do your best,' Noble said, sipping her coffee and briskly changing the subject. 'Would you like to know who I just spoke to on the phone?'

'Fairweather?' Harry guessed.

'No, thankfully,' said Noble. 'The duty inspector who went to Peckham Rye station on 14 November and watched Keisha Best being scraped off the tracks. It was a straight suicide, apparently. CCTV and a dozen witness saw her waiting on the platform for half an hour, smoking a joint to calm her nerves, and then just climbing down onto the track and standing in front of the 5.38 to Dartford. A right tragedy, he said.'

Harry nodded. The phrasing struck a chord inside him – he suspected Noble was quoting, and that it bothered her, too. She'd not simply jumped in front of the train, but climbed down onto the track and stood waiting for it to hit her. That took a certain something. Perhaps the same something he'd seen in Solomon Idris's eyes.

'Right, let me know if anything changes,' Noble said. 'You've got my number. I've got a day's work to be getting on with.'

'You're leaving?'

'It's a Monday morning, I've got to sift through all the crap

CID has been given over the weekend.' Noble gestured towards the ward. 'And our mate's not going anywhere, is he?'

He understood where she was coming from: the Met had their man, comatose under police guard, and nobody cared about what had driven him to do what he'd done. He was a criminal, a nobody from the estates, who probably would have ended up in prison eventually even if he hadn't started waving his gun about.

'And anyway, it looks like you've got a visitor,' Noble said, before she turned and left. He moved to return to the ward round, grunting, angry, before he spotted the visitor that Noble had referred to. He was leaning against the wall, and looked serene. There was an NHS ID badge on a lanyard around his neck, but Harry couldn't make out the writing.

'Harry Kent?' the man said.

He wore a chequered shirt, at least an eighteen-inch collar, and a dark burgundy tie that exploded out of his neck fat, disguised by a full, black beard flecked with white and grey. Harry approached him and nodded.

'I'm Duncan Whitacre. I'm a GP over at Burgess Park.'

Harry nodded. He knew the practice – it was the one Lahiri worked at. In common with many inner-city surgeries, it had several partners, but Harry got the impression that Whitacre was fairly senior. He'd heard the name quite a bit. Youth work. Making a difference.

'Harry Kent.'

'Ah. You know James.'

Harry took a deep breath. Nothing Whitacre had said implied any particular preconception. So he just nodded.

'I believe one of my patients is here. Solomon Idris.'

Once again, it wasn't a question.

'Yeah. The surgeons are with him right now. It's a bit of a circus, as you can imagine.'

Whitacre nodded slowly.

'How is he?'

Harry started shuffling slowly down the ICU's main corridor as he explained Idris's condition. He stopped outside a quiet, empty bay, where a technician was fiddling with a haemofiltration machine.

'So it's a real possibility he won't make it?' Whitacre said.

'I'm afraid so,' said Harry. Whitacre looked solemn again and focused on the machine. Behind them, Abe Gunther and the surgical team retired to view some images on a computer.

'We can—' Harry began.

'No bother,' said Whitacre.

'Can I ask you a few things, while you're here?'

Whitacre nodded.

'He's HIV-positive, and James didn't know,' Harry said. 'Did you treat him for that? You wouldn't have any idea of the story there?'

'I treated him, yes,' said Whitacre. 'But as part of the Saviour Project, not as his GP.'

'You run the Saviour Project, do you?'

'Yes. I helped set it up.'

'Where'd you get the name?' Harry said. He had always wondered, but had never got around to asking.

'It's an acronym,' said Whitacre. 'Southwark Against Violence and Unrest. Started off as a charity based here in A&E. And we still do a lot of that. Assemblies in schools and the like. But we took it formal and got it NHS-funded. The whole philosophy is that we treat youth violence like any other disease. If you have someone come in with a mini-stroke, you reduce their risk factors. You refer them to their GP who puts them on statins, anti-hypertensives, you screen for arrhythmias. You have someone come in who's had ten Stellas and fallen into the road, you make sure their GP gives them a chat about alcohol intake. It's the same story.'

'How does it work?'

'We have a team of youth workers located in A&E who screen for any gang-related injuries. If it's minor, we see them then and there in the department. Anything serious, we take the name and go to see them on the ward once they're better. If they're between twelve and nineteen and they're from Lambeth or Southwark they get referred to me. And my team works with them, four introductory sessions at the very least, to try and get them out of the wretched lifestyles many of them are leading. We're just in the process of publishing data, but I can tell you, this project changes lives. And it probably saves them, too.'

Whitacre spoke with heady words and impassioned eyes. His accent was a mirror of Harry's own, dropped H's and consonants, but mellowed out by years of the medical establishment. Harry suspected he was local, definitely a Londoner.

'Who mentored Idris?' Harry asked.

'I did, at first,' said Whitacre. 'I do all the preliminary interviews, along with the youth workers. Me and one of the shrinks from the Maudsley developed a screening questionnaire. But later it was James. We've got five or six registrars attached to the project, and they do a lot of the longer-term patients.'

Lahiri. Harry pictured him, broken-eyed in the ICU on his midnight lunch break. Idris had got himself shot, and Lahiri probably saw that as a personal failure. Maybe it was, Harry thought. He had no idea.

'Are the family around?' Whitacre said.

'They were, this morning,' said Harry. 'Joy and the brother, Junior.'

'That's another tragedy. The mother has ME, the poor woman, but the bastards won't give her disability benefit. She can barely work, but she does.'

Harry didn't ask about the boys' father because he knew what the response would be. Whitacre's phone rang loudly and he apologised, before checking it and killing the call. Searching in his pocket, Whitacre found a business card and handed it over.

'Any change in his condition, I'd appreciate a call,' he said. 'And likewise, if there's anything else you need.'

Harry thanked him, and Whitacre moved over to Idris's room, arching his head through the doorway to take a peek before shaking his head and moving to the exit. Harry wondered whether he should have asked more questions, about Keisha Best, but by then he was gone. Perhaps Noble was right, anyway. In the hospital, under police guard, Idris was safe. What had motivated him to do what he'd done could wait until he was better, and Harry should concentrate on making that happen as soon as possible. He slunk back toward the ward round, catching Dr Saltis typing into one of the bedside computers.

'Sorry about that, Maria. What do you need me to do?'

Saltis was already speaking rapidly, the stress of the day

evidently already getting to her. 'Beds two and six need tracheotomies placing. Bed six has a BMI of thirty-eight so she might be tricky – I've called ENT to let them know. And fourteen needs a central line, but none of them are urgent.'

'What are their names?' Harry said.

'Oh,' Saltis said, fumbling for the list, 'Mr Archer in two, Mrs Singathawaran in six. And Mrs Kufeji in fourteen.'

'OK,' said Harry. 'Who have we got waiting for us?'

The referrals from A&E and the wards were usually seen by the registrars first, who would then sort the wheat from the chaff and feed back to the consultants. Saltis flipped the list over to read off the list of patients she'd scrawled since the morning had begun.

'Brenda Collingwood's a seventy-three-year-old woman in Resus, COPD. Wraclav Kaminski, fifty-four, over on Owens ward, he's a GI bleeder, encephalopathic.'

'We'll take one each?' Harry suggested. Saltis nodded, said she'd head over to Owens, and he could take the woman in A&E. As he headed out of the unit, he noticed Duncan Whitacre at the central computer station, deep in conversation with Abe Gunther, a worried look across his face, and remembered his words. *This project changes lives, and it probably saves them, too.* It was a shame that the benefits hadn't extended to Solomon Idris, Harry thought as he worked alcohol gel into his hands, the doors closing behind him.

Brenda Collingwood should have quit smoking forty years before she did, and she wished she had, but it was hard when you'd been hooked early. Her Alfie had gone through sixty a day since he'd been a lad, and it hadn't done him any harm, until the stroke which had effectively widowed her four years ago. At first, she'd tried to care for him herself, but now she had three carers a day, all of them foreign, not that she minded, but Alfie would've done had he been able to talk. She'd worked behind the bar of the Kings Arms on Penge Common for forty of her seventy-three years, where Alfie had been the landlord, until his illness, when they'd sold up and bought a bungalow. Their only son, Eddie, was on his way over from Essex, having been told his mother was very ill in hospital. Brenda wasn't worried about herself, but she was worried about Alfie and the garden and Geraldine, the ninety-two-year-old demented woman in the house next to her who she checked on every evening to make sure she hadn't left the gas on.

Harry knew none of that, but he knew Mrs Collingwood was pretty damn sick from her posture, upright on the bed, too weak to prop herself forward, recruiting all of her upper-body muscles in the battle for each breath. The notes said she'd been diagnosed with COPD last year, the combination of emphysema and bronchitis having built up over fifty-five years of tobacco-induced damage. Now it was winter, and it only took a mild infection to bring an already fragile body to the brink of death.

'Have you got the latest gas?' Harry asked Dr Maitland, the on-call medical registrar who'd asked the ICU team to come and see Mrs Collingwood. Normally the high-dependency unit would have come down to take the referral, but HDU was full, and so Maitland had called Harry.

'CO_2 was nine point five; we'll get another one done in five minutes,' Maitland said, passing Harry the readout so he could see for himself. He'd worked with Dr Maitland several times before, and liked her. The on-take medical registrar had probably the hardest job in a hospital, with responsibility for seeing and admitting all medical patients who came through the front door. On a busy day that could be as many as thirty in a twelve-hour shift.

In the case of Brenda Collingwood, Harry couldn't fault Maitland's management. She'd had intravenous antibiotics started to battle the infection that was the cause of her respiratory failure, and once it had become apparent that Mrs Collingwood's condition had deteriorated further still, she'd called ICU and asked A&E to set her up on a non-invasive ventilator. The machine was connected up to a wide mask strapped tightly to her face, using alternating air pressure to help force air in and out of her lungs. It was a horrible feeling, and Harry could see that Mrs Collingwood was in considerable distress, but the machine was keeping her alive.

Harry went up to her, told her she was doing well and he knew how uncomfortable it was, but she had to keep going. Mrs Collingwood nodded quietly and kept fighting to breathe. Harry listened to her chest and felt her pulse. Then he looked at Maitland and nodded towards outside the cubicle.

'I think you're right,' Harry said. 'She needs to be in a critical care bed.'

Maitland nodded. There wasn't really any disputing that. The problem, as usual, was beds. The HDU, which was the ideal place for their patient, was full; the ICU was split in two, ten beds for medical patients, like Mrs Collingwood, and ten for surgical and trauma cases, like Solomon Idris. The ten beds set up for medical patients were all occupied, and there were only two free on the surgical side. To an outsider, it was probably amusing: centuries of medical advancement, and yet a spell of cold weather still brought the system to its knees.

'I'll do my best,' Harry said. 'Can you do another gas while I go and ring my boss?'

He was hoping that things would improve, but he knew that was wishful thinking. He stepped up to the central station in Resus, looking across at bed six, where yesterday they'd resuscitated Solomon Idris. Now it was occupied by a man in overalls with a painful-looking injury to his arm.

Harry called the surgical ICU and reached Dr Rashid quickly enough.

'Make me happy, Harry.'

'I might not do that, I'm afraid,' Harry said. 'I've got a Mrs Brenda Collingwood down here, seventy-three-year-old with an infective exacerbation of COPD, she's haemodynamically stable, gas shows Type II failure, A&E have established her on BiPAP and referred to medics, but she's running a pH of around seven point two five and she really needs to be upstairs.'

In this case, upstairs meant in a critical care bed, with monitors and nurses checking every five or ten minutes, and access to ventilators or dialysis if they became necessary.

'I'm sure she does, but that bleeder from Owens ward is having a TIPSS and then he's coming to us. If I take her that's our last bed gone.'

Harry swore silently and hoped no one had seen. Getting a patient into the last available ICU bed in a hospital was harder than getting into medical school, and with good reason. If a trauma call or a cardiac arrest came in, they'd have nowhere to put them. If the crisis persisted, they'd have to shut down operating theatres and use them as beds instead, which cost the trust thousands of pounds a day in cancelled operations.

'I'd put her in HDU if they had a bed, but the med reg has checked and none of their patients are anywhere close to discharge.'

'Ha,' said Rashid. 'Two or three on the medical side are well enough to step down, but there's no room in HDU to take them, and they're not ready for the wards yet.'

Harry sat hunched over the phone, listening to the static and ward noise on the other end and the frantic sounds of Mrs Collingwood trying to breathe, waiting for Rashid to make a decision. 'I'm not keen to block our last bed,' said Rashid. 'She won't die if we leave it another half-hour, will she?'

Harry looked over through the half-pulled curtain at Mrs Collingwood, who seemed more relaxed, not fighting the mask any more. A&E had a nurse with her constantly, which was good.

'Probably not, no.'

After that, Rashid said the words Harry had been dreading.

'OK. Call Dr Traubert, it's his decision.'

'OK, boss. Thanks.'

Harry cursed again and felt his stomach twist as he called the switchboard and asked to be put through to Traubert. After he'd usurped Traubert yesterday in A&E, he'd hoped not to have to encounter him for a couple of weeks, to let the dust settle.

'George Traubert.'

Harry exhaled, told him the situation.

'Didn't think you'd be at work today,' Traubert said. Harry could picture him, working in his spartan office, the events of last night probably nowhere near the forefront of his mind. 'Where are you? A&E?'

'Yeah, Resus,' said Harry.

'I'll be down in five minutes.'

Harry had spent quite some time with George Traubert – he was his educational supervisor, and they'd met for appraisals, how-are-you-getting-on meetings and the like. But he'd hardly had the chance to see what he was like with patients. If Harry had seen one extreme with Solomon Idris, he was seeing the other one now. Genial, professional Dr Traubert sat on the edge of Mrs Collingwood's bed, gently clasping her hand, asking how she was feeling and explaining what was going on.

'The thing is, Mrs Collingwood,' he said, nodding gently, 'we need to make sure you're in the right place. We're doing all we can to make you better.'

Mrs Collingwood nodded solemnly, still too weak to speak. Harry tapped his foot against the linoleum flooring, waiting for Traubert to hurry up and make a decision. Though he was primarily an anaesthetist, Traubert had wound up as the hospital's Clinical Services Director for Critical & Emergency Care, responsible for A&E, the anaesthetics department and the intensive care and high-dependency units. As well as sitting on the board and reporting to the Medical Director, it was his job to sort out the kinds of problems which arose when the hospital ran out of intensive care beds. Such bureaucracy, in addition to his academic activities, meant he spent much less time actually seeing patients, with the consequences they had seen last night.

'I'll be back soon,' Traubert said, patting Mrs Collingwood on the hand again. He reviewed the chart before joining Harry at the end of the bed.

'She's tolerating the BiPAP,' he said. 'I don't think she'll need intubating. We could admit her to Lawrence Ward.'

Lawrence was the respiratory unit, and the nurses ought to be able to manage the ventilator there, but that wasn't Harry's concern. Mrs Collingwood needed continuous monitoring, not the hourly checks common on the acute wards.

'What if she goes off?' Harry protested. 'They're busy as hell up on Lawrence. If she deteriorates up there, it might not be picked up until too late.'

'I know, but we've got one bed left on the surgical side now,' Traubert said. 'We get a single trauma call and we're stuffed.'

Harry felt his face begin to redden, realised he was still angry at Traubert for the previous night, tried to separate that out and think rationally, but it didn't work.

'You said she's improving. She'll be on the unit for a day, no more, and we can move her into HDU as soon as a bed is available. If it was my mother . . .'

Traubert looked at him with dark eyes set into his tanned skin, and Harry waited for the cutting remark, the reminder that he was a registrar and when he was qualified enough to run four hospital departments, he could make comments like that. But it didn't come.

'Good point, Harry. Ring ICU and tell them she's coming up. I'll talk to theatres about opening up some beds in Recovery and get onto HDU about prioritising discharges.'

Harry went and made the phone calls, and when he came back, Traubert was back on the edge of the bed, explaining.

'. . . to our intensive care unit. I know that sounds scary, but it just means we can keep an eye on you a bit better. The nurses are fantastic, so you'll be in good hands. OK?'

He patted her hand a final time and stood up. With great difficulty, Mrs Collingwood raised her arms, lifted her mask off and rasped.

'Thank. You. Doctor.'

'Not at all,' said Traubert, replacing the mask. 'Now keep this on, we'll soon have you better.'

Traubert came out of the bay and started washing his hands. The porters would be down in five minutes, and the A&E junior doctors could watch her until then. He finished rolling his sleeves back down – unlike yesterday, he was dressed in suit trousers and a pinstriped shirt with ice-white collar, silk tie tucked between the third and fourth buttons. He turned to Harry and said, 'Heading back upstairs?'

Harry nodded, then regretted it.

'I'll walk with you,' Traubert said. 'I wanted to have a bit of a chat anyway.'

I know exactly why, Harry thought. He had already decided to eat his words and apologise, live to fight another day, even though he'd been in the right.

'How is the young man doing?' Traubert asked as they headed towards the East Wing stairwell.

'He's stable. I expect the surgeons will go back in today, hopefully won't have to take all of his spleen.'

'Thank God,' Traubert said, grimacing. 'Good work on your part, from what I've heard.'

Traubert held open the stairwell door for him, and as Harry passed through he caught a whiff of cologne. At work, he thought. Now they were alone, in the quiet of the stairwell, but Traubert lowered his voice anyway, stepping across two of the stairs, leaving Harry no place to go.

'The thing I wanted to say was,' Traubert said, inhaling deeply, 'that I'm very sorry about last night. I let you, and the rest of the team, down. I let the patient down. And you did very well under difficult circumstances. You were unafraid to challenge the hierarchy because you felt that the patient's safety was compromised, and that was the right thing to do.'

Harry said nothing. He knew first-hand that all doctors were human, and those who made mistakes were often hard-working, decent people. But there was something, residual anger perhaps, that stopped him from speaking.

'I didn't see many shootings in Switzerland,' Traubert said, smiling so hard Harry got the impression he was trying to force one in return. Traubert had worked in Toronto before moving to London, and there must have been a fair few shootings there, but Harry bit his tongue. That would have been a while ago, perhaps when venous cutdowns were still done.

'All I'm trying to say is, I don't hold anything against you, OK? Is there anything you want to say? I'd appreciate any feedback.'

Harry looked Traubert in the eye and saw sincerity that could even be described as genuine.

'With all due respect, Dr Traubert,' he said, 'I might not be there next time. And if the rest of us hadn't been there, Solomon Idris might not have made it to theatre. Your registrars won't always be around to cover for you.'

'More's the pity,' Traubert said. 'You guys get better every year. I've booked myself on the next ATLS course anyway, to refresh my memory. It's in March. Thank you again, Harry. You were fantastic down there, in your element.'

Harry immediately regretted his words. Traubert was charming, international, popular, cosmopolitan, the very epitome of the modern consultant in everything but medical acumen. It was only through his mastery of hospital politics that he held his senior position, and the sooner the stupid bastard ended up behind a desk as a glorified accountant, the better. It was a wonderful irony that the best way to get people like Traubert away from the wards, where they could do damage, was to promote them even farther up the hierarchy they clung to. He might even turn into a useful friend in a high place. God knows Harry needed them.

'Just doing my job,' Harry said. They had started climbing again.

'Ah yes, the police work,' said Traubert. 'How is that going?'

'It's going great,' Harry said, aware of how unconvincing he sounded. 'Yesterday was a bad day.'

'I see,' said Traubert. 'Do you know if the police have any leads about what made him do what he did?'

'I don't think so,' said Harry. 'They think it might be gang-related.'

'I see,' said Traubert. By now they had arrived at the crossroads at the centre of the ICU block: to the left were the medical beds, to the right the surgical beds, and ahead the consultants' offices. Traubert patted him on the back with a heavy hand. 'I'll let you get back to work, then. We'll have another mentoring meeting some time next week.'

Harry smiled, unsure what to reply, but was saved by the piercing chime of his bleep on his belt.

'I'd better—'

'Of course!' Traubert said, already pacing away towards his office, the biggest of the lot. 'Have a good day, Harry.'

The rest of the morning passed with routine jobs and procedures, and by half past twelve, Harry had enough time free to grab lunch. He sat down in the junior doctors' office, pulling open the cardboard wrapping on a sandwich from the Sainsbury's in the main hospital atrium.

He'd done his best to put Idris out of his mind: the porters had turned up an hour or so ago to take the kid to theatre, and when he'd come back, the anaesthetist had said it'd all gone to plan. The surgeons had removed a portion of the spleen and used endovascular stents to repair the larger damaged blood vessels. He munched on the sandwich and remembered the feeling of hunger from the chicken shop, heard Idris's voice again, his breath spiralling out over the vinyl tables. *They killed Keisha, and the feds didn't give a shit.*

At his computer, Harry brought up the patient records system, found the main search engine and typed Keisha Best's name in. The Ruskin was the closest hospital to Peckham Rye. Unsurprisingly, the admission was to the mortuary.

14/11/2012. Admitting clinician: Dr Megan Wynn-Jones.

Harry was in luck. Wynn-Jones was on the staff at the Ruskin, and also on the Home Office list. He'd learned in six and a half months with the police that when a suspicious death occurred, standard procedure was to summon whichever certified Home Office pathologist was on duty for the region, and then take the body to the closest suitably equipped hospital for the post-mortem examination. Out of hours this usually took a while as the pathologist had to come in from home. Often, Harry would be called to certify death in situations that initially appeared non-suspicious, only for the duty CID inspector to arrive, spot something which seemed out of place, and suggest that forensics get involved. He'd not yet encountered Dr Wynn-Jones, though he'd heard her name mentioned once or twice.

Wynn-Jones picked up the phone when Harry dialled her extension. He pictured a mousy-looking middle-aged woman, hunched over a microscope with a white coat and a cup of tea.

'Hi. My name's Dr Kent, I'm one of the FMEs for Inner South-East.'

'This is a hospital extension you're calling from?' said Wynn-Jones.

'Yeah, sorry,' said Harry. 'I'm an ICU reg here in my day job.'

'Ah, right. How can I help?'

'Do you remember someone called Keisha Best?' said Harry. 'You're down as admitting her for a post-mortem on 14 November last year.'

'The suicide at Peckham Rye?' said Wynn-Jones. 'Yes. Very sad. There wasn't much of her left.'

The rush-hour trains from Victoria through to Kent didn't stop at the smaller stations like Peckham Rye, so they'd come through at at least seventy. Energy delivered equals mass times velocity squared, equals not a lot left.

'A straightforward suicide?' said Harry, thinking of what Noble had told him earlier.

'A suicide,' said Wynn-Jones. 'But not straightforward, no.'

Harry felt his stomach twist again. He reached over and pushed the office door shut.

'Did the police investigate it?'

'To some degree. Why do you ask?'

'The name's come up in a case I'm involved with,' said Harry. 'What made you say it wasn't straightforward?'

'We found quite a few things wrong with Keisha Best,' said Wynn-Jones, her own voice now quietened too. 'CID couldn't come up with anything tangible, though.'

'Can we talk about this later?' said Harry.

'Sure. I finish at four, pending any drastic emergencies, but I have some academic work I ought to stay late for. What about a coffee? You can bring a large cappuccino from AMT down to my office, it's by the cell path lab.'

Harry laughed. He knew many consultants who'd trade caffeine for second opinions.

'OK, that's very—'

He heard thumping on his office door and called, 'Come in!'

It was Dr Saltis, sweat on her face.

Her expression told him everything he needed to know.

'What is it?' he said, getting to his feet.

'Bed ten.'

Idris. Harry started running.

Hands washed, gloves on, apron on, *hurry the fuck up, he's crashing.* Harry squinted to make out the readings on Idris's vital signs monitor. Heart rate was fast, very fast. Blood pressure dropping, systolic in the low seventies.

'What's going on?' Harry demanded.

Vicky Faraway, the F2 junior doctor on the surgical ICU, was standing by the bed, listening to Idris's chest. Harry stepped beside her and saw the issues immediately. Idris's face, neck and hands were swelling up, his lips beginning to protrude from his face like a grotesque mask. It was an emergency Harry had seen once or twice before, full-blown anaphylactic shock, nothing to do with the infection in his lungs nor the damage to his abdomen. Until proved otherwise, it was an allergic reaction.

'Get his oxygen up to a hundred per cent, now!'

Faraway ran around to the ventilator to change the settings while Gladys Lane got a crash trolley to the end of the bed. There were drugs that could reverse it, but some of them had to go in centrally, rather than through the peripheral lines. Harry leant up to the central line running into the jugular vein in Idris's neck and shouted for drugs.

'IV adrenaline, fifty micrograms,' he barked. 'Change the Hartmann's bag and give two-fifty.'

Faraway started drawing up the drugs, powerful stimulants which would increase the blood pressure and oxygen delivery to Idris's brain and kidneys, which was all Harry cared about. He didn't need to worry too much about airway swelling, because the breathing tube would protect against that. Allergic reactions seldom killed people on the wards, but in ICU patients like Idris, the normal reserves of the human body to fight off such an insult were already depleted.

Faraway finished drawing up the adrenaline and passed it to Harry, who injected it into the jugular line.

'Is he on any new antibiotics?' Harry said.

'Co-amox. Started just now,' Lane replied.

'Stop the infusions!' Harry ordered. 'That's the cause; he's allergic to penicillin.'

Before he had even finished speaking, Lane was disconnecting the two antibiotic infusions from the ports in Idris's wrist, hanging the bags back up on the dripstands. Harry looked up at the vital signs monitor, waiting to see what Idris's blood pressure was doing. Eighty over sixty, not brilliant. The daytime ICU charge nurse, Aoife Kelly, had arrived as well, and was setting up the fluids.

'Another two-fifty of Hartmann's, please,' Harry ordered. The adrenaline he'd given was a huge dose, but the problem was the swelling in his tissues stopping the blood getting through. That could happen in his hands and feet and Idris would survive, maybe after an amputation or two. In his brain or his kidneys, it would kill him.

Somewhere along the line, someone had fucked up, but that didn't matter now. What mattered was making sure it didn't kill the poor kid. They waited. Five minutes was the deadline for the adrenaline to work, and Harry was ready the moment it elapsed.

'Another fifty of adrenaline, please,' Harry ordered. Faraway drew up the dosage, her hands shaking, and injected it.

'Do you want another bag of Hartmann's in?' Kelly said.

'Please,' said Harry. He looked up at Idris's face. The swelling hadn't come down, but it hadn't got worse, either, which was the normal state of affairs. In the interim, Saltis had run with a blood sample to the gas analyser and returned with the result.

'O_2 is nine point six, CO_2 is four point five, pH is seven thirty-one, lactate of four and a half, bicarb of twenty.'

The picture was confirmed. Thankfully, Idris's oxygen levels were still holding up, despite his lower saturations. He was in shock, even with all the oxygen being pumped into his lungs and the fluid charging around his system. Blood pressure was up at ninety, the adrenaline beginning to take effect.

'Harry, look at the ECG,' said Saltis, as an alarm sounded on the monitor. Idris's heart, weak and fast already, had hit a hundred and ninety beats a minute, dangerously high. The trace was saddle-shaped too, meaning the heart muscle was deprived of oxygen, the complexes of the trace so close together they were overlapping. Idris's heart was beating so fast it could no longer pump blood. Harry dug his fingers into Idris's neck, searching for a pulse that was so faint he couldn't even be sure he felt it.

'He's in VT. Get me the pads, please! Has somebody called Rashid?'

Harry looked up at the monitor. Blood pressure was perishingly low. Then Solomon Idris went grey and died, and the numbers disappeared.

'CPR, now!'

Aoife Kelly, leaning over, hands on Idris's sternum, breaking ribs.

'Do you want amiodarone?' Saltis said.

Harry opened up the defibrillator pads that Gladys Lane had

thrust in front of him, sticking them onto Idris's chest, looking up at the monitor, checking the rhythm.

'No, we'll shock him. Sync shock, two hundred.'

A loud whine as the defibrillator started charging, and a chime as it finished.

'Stand clear!

Saltis recoiled away from Idris's chest, and Harry stepped back, finger on the button.

'Clear!'

Idris's body jerked weakly, his muscles flexing as the electricity pulsed through him. Harry interlocked his hands, ready to start CPR if the shock didn't work, when the trace returned to the vital signs monitor, normal sinus rhythm, one hundred and ten beats a minute. Harry's heart sank back down into his chest. The drugs Idris had needed to save him from the allergic reaction had sent his heart into overdrive and nearly killed him. His blood pressure was still in his boots.

'OK,' said Harry. 'Let's get an infusion ready, and we'll need chlorphenamine and hydrocortisone. And it might be wise to start some vasopressin, too.'

Dr Rashid burst into the room, his brow sweaty.

'Got here as soon as I could,' the consultant said, tying his apron around his back. 'What's going on?'

'Full-blown anaphylaxis,' said Harry. 'Had to give him two rounds of adrenaline. He went into VT, systolic dropped to fifty, then he lost his output. We shocked him once and now he's back in sinus tachy, BP's up to eighty.'

'Where's his allergy band?' said Rashid.

'What allergy band?' said Faraway.

Harry looked down at Idris's wrist. Patients with drug allergies had red ID wristbands instead of the normal white ones to remind people to check when they gave drugs. Idris's was gone. There was meant to be a red sign, too, at the head of the bed, but there wasn't.

'Is he allergic to penicillins?' Faraway said.

'Yes,' growled Harry. 'Yes, he fucking is.'

Faraway's face went white as a sheet.

'I prescribed him the co-amox,' she said. 'The AM plan said

give him micro prophylaxis. I didn't realise! It wasn't in his notes! I checked, I swear!'

Harry glared at Faraway, all the morning's anger and contempt packed into his expression, his disregard for this fuckwit a year and a half out of medical school who'd come close to killing Solomon Idris with mere laziness.

'Doctors' office. Now. I'll deal with you later,' Rashid said, before turning to Harry: 'Have we set up that infusion? Let's get the hydrocortisone up as well, and then we'll recheck everything. Another ABG as soon as we can, please.'

Harry went to prepare the infusion while Saltis drew up the steroids, and Rashid checked the ventilator settings. In silence, Faraway turned and shuffled towards the office.

'Dr Rashid, I promise, if I'd made a mistake I'd admit it!'

An hour after Idris had almost died, Dr Faraway's protestations were starting to strain her voice, and Harry was trying his best to keep his eyes on the floor, rather than show her how angry he was. They stood in the ICU doctors' office, the door locked, a Do Not Disturb card over the door handle. Rashid was on the swivel chair by the computer, Harry perched on the desk. After a good forty-five minutes of graft, Idris was stable, and Aoife Kelly was under strict instructions to fetch the consultant if he went off again.

'You told me to sort out prophylactic antibiotics for all of the patients who needed it. Micro opinion had said to start broad-spectrum for bed ten to cover for secondary bacterial pneumonia. I checked his allergy status on the system, there were none, and so—'

'You're sure you checked?' interrupted Harry.

'Absolutely sure. And he didn't have a sign. I looked! And I looked for an allergy band, and he didn't have one!'

Harry looked at her, his sense of fury beginning to fade. Idris's wristband should have been red, and that wasn't her fault. But there was no way that Faraway would have missed the allergy if she'd checked the computer system. The Ruskin was a university hospital in London, and as such the junior doctors' jobs were highly competitive. You had to be good to get in. Faraway had been in the top decile of her class at Edinburgh. Harry had worked with her only for the six weeks or so since she'd been attached to the ICU. Viewed her as no superstar, but diligent, good at her job.

But even decent doctors sometimes made mistakes.

'Bring up the records!' said Faraway.

Rashid sighed. Harry could tell he hadn't wanted to do that, to humiliate Faraway by showing her how wrong she'd been. He'd been hoping she would admit to an oversight, a lapse of concentration, then at least they could move forward. Harry watched as Rashid selected Idris, Solomon from the list of patients on the surgical ICU, clicked 'patient information', and scrolled down to the allergies part.

'What the . . .'

Harry didn't even finish his sentence. It was staring back at him from the form on the screen, in the old-fashioned type the patient records system used.

THIS PATIENT HAS NO KNOWN DRUG ALLERGIES.

'That's impossible,' said Harry. 'I handed over in A&E. They would have written that down! And it would already have been on the system from either 2009 or 2011.'

Rashid refreshed the page, perhaps thinking that it would change. Double-checked the date of birth, that this was the right Solomon Idris. His nine-digit hospital number. The very same.

'I told you I checked,' Faraway muttered.

'We don't doubt that you did,' said Rashid. 'Go get me Aoife, if she's free.'

Faraway unlocked the door and started off into the main ICU corridor. Harry watched the door close behind her, and turned back to Rashid.

'What the hell's going on here?' said Rashid.

'I've got no idea,' said Harry. 'But I don't like it one bit. We ought to let Patient Safety know.'

Any event as serious as this one would have to be investigated by the hospital's Patient Safety Directorate, whose managers were probably the most feared of all of the trust administrators. Rashid groaned wearily and picked up the phone.

'I'll call them now,' he said. 'They'll want to speak to us all, so why don't you go and check on Idris, then gather the troops.'

Harry stood up from the desk.

'Sure thing.'

Later, in the coffee shop by the hospital's main entrance, he called Noble.

'Hello?'

'It's Dr Kent.'

'Can this wait, Harry? I'm right in the middle of something here.'

'We need to meet,' said Harry. 'There have been developments with Solomon Idris. Something happened. He almost died this morning.'

'OK. I'm stuck at a scene at the Coral on Peckham High Street, so if you could meet me up here that'd be great. I should be free by seven, alright? I'll keep you posted.'

She hung up before Harry could reply. He would have called her sooner, but Patient Safety had kept them all for two hours, taking statements, putting the stories together, trying to figure out what had happened. Idris was on the mend, but the anaphylactic reaction had given his circulation a bit of a bash, and he'd been put on a careful programme of fluid replacement.

What they knew was that at some point the allergy had disappeared from Idris's medical records. Possibly it had happened between his previous admissions and Sunday night, but even so it should have been added when Harry had turned up with him in A&E. Something had gone seriously wrong. The managers from Patient Safety had seemed most worried about some kind of glitch in the electronic records system deleting patient allergies at random, which could have wide-ranging consequences. Harry was worried about something equally serious, but much less random.

It could have been an accident, he told himself. If it hadn't been, then Christ knows what that meant. Before he had left the ICU, though, he had showed the police officer on guard how to wash his hands and don an apron and gloves, and given him a chair right next to Idris's bed.

Cappuccinos in hand, Harry headed downstairs and found the cellular pathology lab with no difficulty, just along the corridor from the mortuary. It was one of the international constants of hospital design that the dead have no right to be up above ground with the sick, and are temporarily buried along with those who work on them. As he passed the mortuary, one of the assistants was clipping an identification tag around the toe of a recently deceased elderly lady. The assistant, herself of reasonably advanced years, made the sign of the cross as she zipped up the polythene bag. Harry looked across at the cadaver, noted a red spot on the dark-skinned forehead, and wondered whether she would have wished to be blessed in such a manner, but decided to let it pass.

Dr Wynn-Jones was not the mousy middle-aged woman that he had expected. A ponytail of blond hair draped down over a tight maroon sweater, and she couldn't have been older than her late thirties. Not bad at all for a consultant histopathologist who'd also managed to get on the Home Office register.

'Hi,' said Harry. 'I wasn't sure if you wanted chocolate sprinkles.'

'I'm impressed,' said Wynn-Jones. 'I was wondering where you've been, I've been done for an hour.'

She finished sending the email she'd been working on then turned her attention to Harry, picking up the coffee and sipping from it.

'Four o'clock finishes,' he said, shaking his head. 'I should have gone into pathology.'

'Quarter past four every day, I go straight to the sunbed to make up for all the Vitamin D I miss out on down here,' said Wynn-Jones. 'And I've done my share of late-night call-outs. This Saturday gone, actually, three in the morning down in bloody Swanley, of all places. Hedge fund manager decided to suffocate his wife and sit in the car with a couple of disposable barbeques.'

Before Harry could even begin to process what she'd said, and regret his off-the-cuff remark, Wynn-Jones had reached into her desk drawer and pulled out a bound laminated report.

'I thought I'd bring up the file,' she said. 'Jog my memory. Remind me again why you're interested in this poor soul?'

Harry briefly explained what had happened with Idris in the Chicken Hut, leaving out most of the graphic details but saying that Idris had claimed it had all been for Keisha. *They killed her, and the feds didn't give a shit.*

'Any idea who "they" might be?' said Wynn-Jones.

Harry shook his head.

'Not First Capital Connect, then? Because the cause of death was fairly obvious. Most jumpers get hit side-on, but Keisha . . .'

Wynn-Jones stopped, and Harry thought he'd seen a lump form in her throat. A lot of medics used gallows humour as a psychological coping mechanism, but every now and again things pierced the armour. It had happened enough times to Harry himself that he could spot it easily in someone else.

'Keisha was standing up, facing the train when it struck her. The impact threw her about eight feet into the air and she landed head first on the opposite track. She would have died immediately. Broke her neck, caved her skull in. The worst internal injuries I've seen in many a day. But it all fits with the picture, the witness accounts, the CCTV. It would have taken some gall.'

Harry thought again about the parallel with Idris's actions the previous evening.

'She would have had a chance to save herself,' Wynn-Jones continued. 'When she was standing, facing the train. She stood there for a good few seconds.'

Harry nodded. If Solomon Idris had gone into the Chicken Hut intending to die, then his conviction evidently hadn't been as strong as Keisha Best's. He didn't know what to make of that.

'You said earlier that it wasn't a straightforward suicide, though,' he said after a while.

Wynn-Jones nodded and started leafing through the report.

'We did a routine toxicology screen. Vitreous, blood and hair samples. Nothing apart from alcohol and cannabis in the blood and vitreous.'

'But the hair?'

'Long-term cannabis usage, as well as benzodiazepines and ketamine. Traces of crack, too, and GHB. No evidence of inject-ing drug use, though, and that's interesting.'

'How so?' said Harry.

Wynn-Jones flicked the report over to some of the later pages and tapped a table of results with her fingers.

'Keisha was HIV-positive,' she said.

'So's Solomon Idris,' said Harry. 'He's got a PCP pneumonia at the moment, in fact. Poor kid.'

'Keisha Best's viral load was about four hundred thousand,' said Wynn-Jones. 'But her CD4 count was still quite high. I'm no immunologist, but it suggests she'd been recently infected.'

'What's recently?' said Harry.

'A matter of weeks or months, rather than years.'

So Idris and Keisha Best had been either romantically or sexually involved, unless they'd both acquired HIV independently, which seemed like a massive coincidence. Both had been recreational drug users, but there was no evidence that they had ever injected.

'So Keisha's disease was early-stage,' said Harry, after thinking for a while. 'And Solomon's is fairly advanced. That would make me think that she got it from him.'

'Perhaps,' said Wynn-Jones. 'After the initial infection, she wouldn't yet be at the stage where she'd have symptoms. Maybe she didn't even know about it. Or maybe she found out, and that was when . . .'

Wynn-Jones didn't finish the sentence, but merely shook her head again. Every time she did it, her ponytail bounced from shoulder to shoulder, and her sweater rubbed against her skin. She was for sure the most attractive pathologist Harry had ever met, but he wasn't looking. He was picturing a young woman climbing down onto a railway track.

'So she was an HIV-positive long-term drug user,' Harry said. 'That's still not much to write home about in a seventeen-year-old girl from North Peckham.'

'But this is,' said Wynn-Jones. She slid over the post-mortem report, open to the sixth page, where it described the weight of all the organs removed from Keisha Best's shattered body in the mortuary of the Ruskin on the night she had died, and any notable characteristics. Such as the presence of a small, totally benign stone in her gall bladder. Or the fact that the lower part of the bowel was 'not present in the body cavity on examination, likely due to traumatic removal at the scene'.

'Sorry, what am I looking at?' Harry said. He was scanning over the organs. The stomach was unremarkable, and had contents including 'tomato, cheese and a dough-like material' as well as a noted smell of unabsorbed alcohol. Keisha Best's last meal, a pizza washed down with vodka.

Wynn-Jones tapped the last item on the list removed at the post-mortem. Harry read. Keisha's uterus had weighed in at 150g, above the normal range. Wynn-Jones's notes suggested that the reader see page ten, and the subsection 'Hormone Analysis'.

Harry looked up at the pathologist.

'She was pregnant?' he said.

'No,' said Wynn-Jones. 'But she had been. Recently. From the histology, I'd say she'd been at least twenty weeks gone. Could have been as many as twenty-six.'

'And she miscarried?' said Harry.

Wynn-Jones shook her head and shuffled in her seat.

'Well, maybe she did,' she said. 'But we analysed her Beta-HCG levels. If you're pregnant and it fails, for whatever reason, your Beta-HCG keeps rising for a bit and then falls, gradually. We put her levels on the curve and it looked like the pregnancy ended between four days and two weeks before she died.'

'The pregnancy ended? Not, she miscarried?' said Harry.

Wynn-Jones sat up. 'Sorry?'

Harry looked across at her. She was too young to have kids of Keisha Best's age, so that wasn't why it was affecting her. Maybe she was pregnant herself, or recently had been. Or maybe it just troubled her that an eighteen-year-old girl could lose a baby and throw herself under a train. No, Harry corrected himself. Climb down to the railway tracks and stand in front of one.

'You said the pregnancy ended. You didn't say she miscarried.'

'Well, that's because I'm not sure that she did,' said Wynn-Jones.

Harry leant forward. He wanted to sound empathic, rather than accusatory.

'Do you think she had an abortion?' he said.

Wynn-Jones spent a few seconds looking down at the wastepaper bin beneath her desk, then slowly rolled her head up and nodded.

'I think so. But I don't have any proof, any proof at all. If she was twenty, twenty-two weeks gone, then that's past the threshold where you can safely use the abortion pill. I did tests for the usual termination drugs anyway, but they clear out of the system after forty-eight hours. They wouldn't show up after that. And if it was a surgical abortion, the evidence was destroyed when the train hit her.'

Harry leant back, leafing through the rest of the post-mortem report.

'So it's not clear?'

'The last time Keisha Best went to see a doctor, as far as all the records show, was in 2008, when she was thirteen. Ear infection. She didn't go when she got pregnant, and when she either miscarried or had a termination, she didn't go through her GP, or through the Ruskin. And I checked the other local A&Es, too, Lewisham, Tommy's, George's, as well as every GP and pharmacy in Lambeth, Southwark & Lewisham. No one saw her.'

'If she did get a termination, it wouldn't necessarily show up on her medical record,' said Harry. 'She could've gone to one of the anonymous clinics. Marie Stopes, the Havens?'

'Not anonymous,' said Wynn-Jones. 'You can't get an abortion without giving your name. Especially not at twenty-two weeks. She could have been past the limit, even. And we checked around the clinics. Me and one of the Sapphire detectives, you know, from the sex crimes unit. Nothing. They'd release the records after a death. We had a coroner's order.'

Harry sat back and looked at the woman across from him. The calm, clinical demeanour that Wynn-Jones had possessed when Harry arrived had evaporated, and her cheeks flushed red with an infectious rage. His head was like a thunderstorm, thoughts bursting through the clouds, and he forced himself to stick to questions rather than trying to lead her to his own conclusions.

'And what do you make of all that?'

'Ever worked in Obs & Gynae?' Wynn-Jones said. 'Bet you're military, aren't you?'

Harry was struck silent, his surprise at being read so easily turning to indignation. He got the impression that he wasn't the first person to underestimate the young pathologist sitting across the desk from him. He nodded quietly.

'Then you probably haven't treated a pregnant woman in years,' Wynn-Jones lectured, a lock of hair falling over her forehead. 'Let me explain. If you lose a baby at twenty weeks, even if you never knew you were pregnant, you'll bloody well notice. Keisha would have had significant bleeding, maybe even a stillborn delivery.'

Harry listened, chastened for his ignorance, until he worked out where she was going with her thoughts.

'And she would have come into hospital,' said Harry. 'Which we know there's no record of.'

Wynn-Jones nodded, and they were silent for a while. Outside, two of the morticians were locking up and heading home, laughing about something, and the sound felt out of place.

'So what do you think happened, then? She got an illegal termination?'

'I think that's one explanation,' the pathologist said. 'There are two possibilities here. Firstly, that for some reason Keisha induced her own miscarriage, but she didn't want to come into hospital. Even though I can't fathom why anyone, even in the most desperate of circumstances, would do that.'

'How?'

'There are plenty of ways,' Wynn-Jones said. 'Read any medical journal from the 1950s. Pessaries, drugs. All she would have needed to do is Google it.'

Harry nodded, the gravity of what he was finding out starting to strike him. Twenty weeks didn't sound like a lot, but that was the lower bound that Wynn-Jones had set for the length of time Keisha Best had been pregnant. The upper bound had been twenty-four, and it wasn't unheard of for babies born at twenty-four weeks to survive into adulthood.

'I think that's the better of the two possible scenarios,' Wynn-Jones said. It didn't take Harry long to work out what the worse one entailed.

'Jesus.'

Wynn-Jones nodded. 'I think it's very possible that somebody who didn't want Keisha's pregnancy to be known about decided to take matters into their own hands. I've had a case like that before. A man threw his pregnant daughter down the stairs.'

Harry leant forward, his voice hushed. In the time since they'd been speaking, the giggling morticians had departed, and the pathology lab was now a silent, dark place.

'Was there any evidence of anything like that?' he said. 'On the post-mortem?'

'Not on the post-mortem,' Wynn-Jones said. 'But there was the matter of what the police found in her bedroom. A blister pack in the bin under her desk, one which had compartments for two pills. Now, I don't know about you, Dr Kent, but I can't think of too many prescription medications which only require two doses.'

Harry felt increasingly uncomfortable. After the first sip that she'd taken, Wynn-Jones hadn't touched her coffee. Harry could tell that Keisha Best's death had troubled her greatly, but that she'd compartmentalised it since, put it in a box, which Harry had opened with his phone call that afternoon.

'The morning-after pill?' Harry suggested. 'But it failed, and she miscarried anyway?'

'That's exactly what DC Kepler said,' Wynn-Jones muttered.

'Kepler?' said Harry.

'Yes, do you know him?' Wynn-Jones said. 'Seemed like a nice bloke, but he gave me the usual spiel about investigative resources when he was saying that they weren't prepared to spend time on it. But I don't believe for one minute that was the morning-after pill. She must have emptied that bin in her room fairly regularly and she'd been pregnant for at least twenty weeks.'

'Would it work?' Harry said. 'The abortion pill, at twenty weeks?'

'It would,' Wynn-Jones said. 'But like I said, it would be unpleasant. She should've wanted to come to hospital.'

'But she didn't,' said Harry.

'No. And a week or so later, she throws herself under a train,' said Wynn-Jones, her eyes rolling down so she was looking at the floor. 'And that, Dr Kent, is why in my opinion this wasn't a straightforward suicide. It might just be my imagination running wild, and I don't have anything concrete, but it just isn't right. The Met lost interest about two days after I cut Keisha up, so if you can get anything out of it, then I owe you one. If there's anything else you need, I'm here.'

Harry opened his mouth to say something, but Wynn-Jones slid a copy of the post-mortem report over the desk towards him. He realised that what she'd said told him a lot about Solomon Idris.

They killed Keisha. And the feds didn't give a shit.

Harry got up, picking up the report. He wondered if Idris had lost a child as well as a lover, or if he'd even known about the baby. Assuming that it was his, of course.

'OK,' he said. 'And you're sure you checked all the records, and that she hadn't been to any kind of GP or hospital since 2008?'

'No,' said Wynn-Jones, finally sipping the coffee Harry had bought her, only to realise it was cold and throw it into the bin.

'I'll do everything I can,' he said weakly. 'I think you're on to something.'

Wynn-Jones slouched back in her chair, looked up, and brushed her hair out of her face again.

'I called DC Kepler, a week after Keisha died,' she said. 'I wanted to know why the police weren't launching a full investigation. You know what he said? He told me that there was no evidence a crime had been committed.'

She leant forward and pointed at the report in front of her, still open at the page where it listed the organs. Heart, 293g, unremarkable, no ischaemic changes. Brain, only 468g present for examination owing to massive traumatic injury and distribution at the scene. He followed her finger to where she was tapping. Uterus, *gravida 1, para 0*. A former home for a former future child.

'Twenty weeks, Dr Kent. How the hell can that not be a crime?'

It had taken Harry most of the walk upstairs from the pathology department back to the ICU to make the decision, and he enacted it by calling the number on the business card Duncan Whitacre had left him.

'Burgess Park Practice.'

'Dr Lahiri, please. It's the Ruskin,' Harry lied.

'He's with a patient at the moment. Can I put you on hold?'

Harry held, leaning against the wall in the stairwell. A sweat-drenched student leapt past him, taking the stairs three at a time. The medical school's sports teams made their members run up to each one of the hospital's three ten-floor wings in turn and back down again. In Harry's day, it had been a simple race to the top of the thirty-three-storey tower at Guy's, with the last to finish being punished with a quarter-pint of London Dry Gin. In their first years, he and Lahiri had both been on the football team, and Harry recalled spraining his ankle on the penultimate floor and Lahiri carrying him to the top, only to be rewarded with an unpleasantly generous measure of the spirit.

'Hello?'

'It's Harry.'

'Is there a problem?'

'There might be,' Harry said. 'It's Idris.'

'Is he dead?'

There were few people in the world who Lahiri would, or could, be that frank with. The concern appeared genuine, at least.

'He came close. Somehow he ended up getting co-amox even though he's penicillin-allergic. VT arrest, shocked him out of it.'

'Ah, Jesus. How the hell does that happen?'

Harry didn't answer that question.

'That's not why I'm calling,' he said.

'Care to elaborate? I'm running thirty minutes late.'

'When do you think you'll be done today, then?'

'Last patient's at five-twenty. Paperwork, letters, seven or so, I would guess,' he said. 'What the hell's this about, Harry?'

'Are you free this evening?' Harry said. 'I think we should talk.'

Harry pictured Lahiri in his office, with cold eyes and clenched teeth. 'Do you, now?'

'About Solomon Idris,' Harry clarified. 'You knew him. You mentored him.'

'We should leave that to the police,' Lahiri said.

'Sure. But they're not investigating it, and there's a lot that's suspicious. Like the gun going off outside the shop, and his allergy mysteriously disappearing. I think there's something going on.'

Another student, much portlier than the first, came up from the basement in pursuit.

'I don't see how I could help you out,' Lahiri said.

'Did he ever tell you about Keisha Best?' Harry asked. One final gambit.

'He mentioned a girl called Keisha,' Lahiri said. 'A while back, though. Maybe October or something.'

'She's dead,' Harry said. 'Suicide, last November. In the chicken shop, Solomon told me he was doing it all for her.'

There was static on the line and background noise, and Harry could almost hear the conflict in his friend's head. Lahiri was weighing up the decision about whether his patient, the kid he felt he'd been somehow responsible for, who was fighting for his life in the ICU, was worth letting Harry back into his life for.

'You know where I'm living now?' Lahiri said.

'The boat?'

'Yeah,' Lahiri said. 'South Dock Marina, over in Surrey Quays. You can get the Overground to Canada Water. Ask the guy at the gate to give me a call.'

The line went dead, and Harry stood for a moment in the stair-well, watching as two more students in sports gear continued their run. All of them were drenched in sweat – maybe they did the East Wing last of all. He and Lahiri had met in medical school, and after both had been accepted for army cadetships, had lived together for three years in a dingy student bedsit off East Street. Now Harry had his sixth-floor flat with his rooftop terrace and the double bed only he occupied. From the terrace, he'd often pick out the flame-scarred New Cross tower block he'd shared with his mother. Lahiri had grown up in an East Sussex fishing village surrounded on three sides by the sea, before his stockbro-ker father had sent him to boarding school. After separating from his wife, he had traded their stylish house in Dulwich Village for a forty-three-foot motor yacht he used as an upmarket houseboat. He had a mooring on the Thames and another on the south coast. He'd chosen life at sea, or as close as he could get to it.

He must know something's wrong, Harry thought as he walked down the stairs towards the hospital's basement exit. He knows I wouldn't want to spend an evening with him unless I thought something was at stake. The first medical student he'd seen over-took him, now on his way back down, heading on into the car park. The captain was waiting, stopwatch in one hand, bottle of gin in the other.

Harry thought, that used to be us.

Sunday's snow had returned and it melted in Harry's hair as he stepped off the 345, joining the human throng moving through Peckham High Street. Plenty of those on the bus, pressed up against their fellow commuters, had been hospital staff going home after a long day. He looked up and down the road, pulling his coat tight to his body, and though there were no blue lights it was obvious from the two police vans parked near the junction with Peckham Hill where the crime scene was.

The road was open and the traffic flowing, but the bookmakers was closed, the door sealed off with a cross of blue-and-white police tape. The closest Harry could get was a cordon set up between two lamp-posts, blocking the pavement immediately in front of the betting shop. A young, long-haired man in plain clothes ducked underneath the tape and nodded to the two uniformed officers, and Harry got his attention.

'Excuse me,' he said. 'Is DI Noble through there?'

'Who are you?'

Harry dug in his wallet for his police ID. The detective laughed.

'Don't think we need a doctor, mate, but I'll ask.'

As Harry turned, he noticed a sidearm on the officer's belt and raised his eyebrows. A bus drove past, its wheels digging into a puddle of melted snow and splashing the back of his coat. He patted himself down, and Noble emerged from the betting shop, exchanging words with the long-haired detective. She approached the cordon and Harry held it up for her.

'Evening,' she said. 'I hope you don't mind coming down here.'

'Not at all,' Harry lied. 'What's going on?'

'Gang job,' Noble said. 'Two hours ago, seven teenagers burst into the place, all of them waving knives about. One of them, the oldest, goes up to the counter and puts a gun up against the glass, says he'll start shooting unless they hand over everything they have. While the poor bastards are emptying the till, the rest of them rob everyone else in there. They're in and out in three minutes, get away on foot, disappear into the local estates.'

'They get away with much?' said Harry. The cold was starting to numb his fingers, and he found himself tapping out random rhythms on his thigh to keep them warm.

'Eight grand from behind the till,' Noble said, 'not to mention eight or nine phones and wallets from the punters.'

'They got away with eight thousand and you've got time to chat to me?'

'It's an armed robbery. Flying Squad take the lead. I'm just here to supervise the usual shit – evidence collection, CCTV, cataloguing the witnesses. Shall we get in my car? I don't fancy freezing to death.'

Harry nodded.

'I'm in the car, if DS Alcock needs me,' Noble shouted, and they set off. She was parked around the corner, near the library, and they practically ran through the thickening sleet to get there.

'Get the bloody heater on,' Harry said as they slid into the seats. 'Shouldn't you be at the station? Doesn't look like you've got much to do round here.'

'They'll give the case back to us in a couple of weeks, once it becomes obvious that it's a local lot who's done it,' said Noble. 'It sounds like the TPB. They've done this sort of thing before.'

'TPB?'

'Tiny Peckham Boys. They're the dominant street gang in Southwark. Most of the local outfits we see round here are offshoots. They're relatively new, compared to their competition in Brixton and Lewisham, but they know how to rob a bookies.'

'It doesn't sound to me like a professional job,' said Harry. 'Speaking as an amateur, of course. Sounds like bloody chaos.'

'Nah, they know the system,' said Noble. 'They go in, seven black guys, all dressed identically, all similar ages, masks and gloves. Not one ID under those circumstances will stand up in court. They bring the gun, even though they're not gonna use it, because they know that if there's a firearm involved, we won't turn up until we've got armed back-up. That buys them an extra five minutes, even in Peckham. They hassle the punters so they're not gonna be paying attention to the guy doing the real work, and none of them will try any heroics. Then they get out, disappear into the estates, and they're laughing.'

A wave of hot air passed over Harry's knees and he shuffled in his seat. Both of them still had their coats on.

'So what about Idris?' Harry said.

'The poor bastard who shot him's been suspended on full pay,' Noble said. 'But that's standard procedure. Word from the top is that this one can get brushed under the carpet. No one needs to be made an example of. There's been hardly any media coverage, which is fortunate. For us, that is.'

Harry nodded as if he cared. His opinion was firmly that Solomon Idris had posed no threat to anyone, and that it had been quite obvious at the time. He could see how someone could have got a different impression – hearing a gunshot, seeing Harry on the floor – but armed police officers didn't act on impressions, or on things that civilians like Harry did or didn't shout at them. Just as he had, they took their jobs knowing that they would have to make brutal choices, and that they'd have to accept the consequences if they made the wrong ones.

'Come on then,' Noble went on. 'What happened today? Cause if you came up here to come on to me, I'll deck you.'

Harry ignored the joke and leant forward, directing more of the warm air around his legs.

'Basically, Idris had an allergic reaction to one of his antibiotics, and it almost killed him. We knew he was allergic beforehand, and it was on our electronic patient record system, both from his previous visits and after he came in to A&E last night. But when we checked this afternoon, it wasn't there. Vanished mysteriously. Someone deleted it.'

Noble shifted in her seat and turned towards him.

'Do you know where I live?'

'No.'

'Kew,' said Noble. 'That's another thing the Met does when you piss them off; they stick you on the other side of the city, so you've got to spend an hour and a half on the tube to get to work every day. And the same again to get home. So that means every bloody day I get to read the *Metro* and the *Standard*, cover to cover. So even I know that the NHS makes a mistake every now and then.'

'People don't delete allergies,' said Harry. 'That just doesn't happen.'

'What are you suggesting happened?' she said. 'I mean, you've obviously got suspicions or you wouldn't be here. Spit it out.'

Harry shook his head.

'The hospital are investigating it internally,' he said. 'Not necessarily because they're suspicious, but because it was a serious incident and a patient almost died. I'll keep you updated with what they find. But it still doesn't sit easy with me.'

'Bollocks,' said Noble.

'I'm sorry?'

'Stop with the cover-your-arse bullshit,' Noble said. 'You think someone deleted that allergy off the computer system so that Solomon Idris would be given a drug he was allergic to, because they wanted to kill him.'

Harry didn't know whether to be relieved at the fact that she'd verbalised the scenario in his head, or concerned that she had read him so easily.

'I think it's a possibility,' said Harry. 'I can't explain what happened any other way, what with the wristband, too.'

'The wristband?' said Noble.

'Patients with allergies have red wristbands,' said Harry. 'It's meant to prompt nurses to double-check before they give the drugs. But Idris's wristband was gone. Someone got rid of it.'

'Maybe someone just forgot to give him a wristband at all?'

'That's one of the things the internal investigation is looking at,' Harry said.

'Who's conducting that?' Noble said.

'Helen Liu, our Director of Patient Safety,' said Harry. 'She's thorough. If there's something going on, she'll find it.'

'No she won't,' said Noble. 'You don't believe that any more than I do.'

Harry took a deep breath.

'It just makes me uneasy,' he said. 'That gunshot outside the Chicken Hut last night. So it's not actively a threat to Solomon, but it causes Trojan to almost kill him. And then an allergy disappears from his notes, and once again he's at death's door. Now, that's either two episodes of incredibly bad luck, or someone's out to get him.'

Noble leant forward over the handbrake, her face unreadable. Harry had no idea whether she was taking him seriously or merely indulging him. 'So let's run with it,' she said. 'If someone wanted to do that, how would they? Make an allergy disappear?'

'Easily, if they were on the system at the Ruskin,' said Harry. 'It's a computer system like any other. Probably about ten thousand staff have log-ins.'

'Who?'

'Doctors, nurses, ward clerks, pharmacists, physios. Even medical students. Practically anyone who comes into contact with patients.'

'Surely an allergy would be in the paper notes as well?' said Noble.

'It would, yeah,' said Harry. 'But in the ICU everything's digitalised. The patient's paper notes aren't by their beds, and the nurses just check on the computer. In theory, you can only access the patient records from a hospital trust computer, but I guess there's probably a way to get into the system from off-site.'

'There will be,' said Noble. 'No computer system's totally safe.'

She said nothing else, but reached into her pocket to look at her phone.

'You think I'm crazy, don't you?' Harry said.

Noble laughed. 'Hey, I'd rather be listening to your crazy theories than having some jumped-up DS from the Sweeney ordering me around like I'm his PA.'

Harry watched her stare out of the windscreen, flicking the wipers on to remove the snow, imagining the cogs ticking in her brain. He'd seen the night before that the detective had a low tolerance for bullshit, and the fact that she'd agreed to meet him at the very least implied that she gave his opinion some weight. He reckoned he might as well play all his cards at once.

'There's more. I had a coffee with the pathologist who did the post-mortem on Keisha Best, too.'

'Oh, right?' said Noble. 'Go on.'

Tapping at the windscreen and Harry jumped in his seat, turning to see an older man in plain clothes. Noble flicked a switch and Harry's window came down, the cold air rushing in. He leant backwards as Noble leant forward to address the visitor.

'Everything alright, Derek?' she said.

'DS Alcock wants to know if any of the witnesses we interviewed reported hearing gunfire. Forensics recovered this.'

The detective held up a clear plastic evidence bag with a bullet inside. Harry couldn't stop himself thinking about the one they'd taken out of Idris. What was it Gunther had said? *Two inches higher, it would have been his heart. Three inches to the right, his aorta.*

'Tell Alcock he's a fucking idiot,' said Noble.

'I'm sorry, ma'am?'

'That's an unfired round. You can see the bullet's still in its casing. Go through the tape again, at some point our friend with the gun pulls back the slide to look cool.'

The detective turned and shuffled back towards the high street. Noble shook her head.

'Kids these days,' she muttered. 'They learn that on TV. Pull the slide back when it's loaded, all it does is eject a perfectly good round. You probably know that, though, don't you? Anyway, tell me about Keisha Best.'

'Well, she was HIV-positive. And recently infected, too.'

'What's recently?' said Noble.

'Less than a year, probably less than six months. She probably didn't even know about it. But that's not the interesting bit.'

'Tell me the interesting bit, then,' Noble said.

'She'd been pregnant, very recently,' Harry continued. 'Second trimester. Between one and two weeks prior to her death, she either miscarried or had an abortion. Dr Wynn-Jones thinks it was the second one, and I'm inclined to agree with her.'

'So what?' said Noble. 'It's Southwark. Eighteen-year-olds have abortions all the time.'

Harry felt his face burn red.

'So what?' he repeated. 'The thing is, she was at least twenty weeks gone. So if she miscarried, she would have needed medical help. And she doesn't show up on records for any hospital, clinic or GP's office south of the river, not even any of the confidential ones. So if she miscarried, she didn't go and see anyone about it. And if she did get an abortion, who performed it?'

Noble opened her mouth to speak, but he stopped her with an outstretched palm.

'I'm not finished. Your friend DC Kepler and his team searched her bedroom, and they found a blister pack with just two pills. That's exactly the packaging that the abortion pill would come in.'

'CID didn't investigate?' said Noble.

'Kepler said it could have been the morning-after pill, apparently. The pathologist gave the impression that CID were fairly snowed under, and they didn't see much point,' said Harry.

'Bloody hell,' Noble said.

'What if that abortion was against her will, illegally procured?' Harry said. 'She was forced into it, and that pushed her over the edge and she killed herself. That'd be reason enough for Solomon Idris to get angry, wouldn't it? If he cared about her. If he knew what happened to her, and that the police hadn't investigated it. Blamed himself for her suicide.'

'Do you think it was his kid?' said Noble.

'I've got no idea,' Harry said. 'The way he spoke about her, it was obvious that she meant something to him, at least. Enough to do what he did last night.'

'They were both HIV-positive,' said Noble. 'I don't buy that's coincidence. They must have been sexually involved.'

'We need to talk to someone who knows them,' Harry said. 'They must have friends, surely?'

'That's Mo's department,' Noble said, clarifying after seeing Harry's puzzled expression: 'DS Wilson. Moses, Mo. He should be round here in a bit. He's got lots of friends in very low places.'

'I'm working on that, too,' Harry said.

'And how are you doing that? Going undercover on the estate tonight, are you?'

'James Lahiri, Solomon Idris's GP, is an old friend of mine,' Harry said, trying not to choke on the word 'friend'. 'He mentored Idris as part of the Saviour Project.'

'What's that?'

'It's a public health initiative, treating victims of gang violence with therapy. To try and reduce recurrence rates. I'm seeing him once we're done here. Who knows, maybe he can shed some light on it.'

'Hopefully,' Noble said. Her face seemed unimpressed.

'Come on,' Harry said, pissed off. 'You guys are hardly pulling out all the stops, are you? You should have seen that kid last night; he was on the edge. Seemed like he didn't care whether he lived or died. And someone wants him dead. And what did you say? *We can sweep this one under the carpet.* Bullshit.'

'Harry, I don't think—'

But he was riled now, and cut her off. 'There are people like him all over this city, Frankie. Lost causes. People like Solomon Idris have no one to fight their corner. I don't mean to patronise you, but I know what that's like. And if someone hadn't fought for me, I don't know where I'd have ended up. It sure as hell wouldn't have been medical school. So if we don't advocate for him, no one will!'

They lapsed into silence again, the only sounds the wipers clearing sleet from the windscreen and the static on the radio. Outside, two ambulances raced down the high street in tandem, blue lights scattering over the dashboard, heading for the Ruskin, followed by a third in quick succession. Busy night for A&E, he thought.

'What about the wristband?' Noble said after a while.

'What?'

'Back to our little thought experiment earlier. You want to get that allergy off the computer system, so Idris gets his bad medicine and doesn't wake up. How do you get rid of the wristband?'

Harry started thinking. It was a bizarre experience, picturing himself wandering through the hospital, working out how to get a patient killed.

'Assuming that we didn't fuck up and forget to give him one,' said Harry, 'then you'd have to go right up to him, and take it off.'

'That changes everything.'

'I know,' he said. 'I know. But it could have happened any time from when he came into A&E, went to theatre, the CT scanner, or back to the ICU.'

'Oh, bloody hell,' Noble said, throwing herself back in her seat. Maybe it was what she was wearing, but Harry had a sudden episode of déjà vu. Noble was sitting exactly how the shrinks had done when they'd been assessing him after he'd got back from Afghanistan. Waiting to see how he'd react.

'Harry!' said Noble. He realised he'd been staring into the darkness. His heavy, quick breaths had left a disc of condensation on the windscreen.

'You won't say it, will you?' Noble continued. 'The obvious implication of everything you just told me. Even though you've already figured it out. You won't say it, because you don't like where it goes.'

Harry said nothing. After looking at him for ten seconds or so, Noble went on.

'Somebody with access to Solomon Idris in the hospital. And who could provide Keisha Best with the means for an abortion.'

'It's possible,' said Harry. 'It's one theory, I guess.'

'You think we're looking for a doctor,' said Noble. 'And it's obviously been weighing on your mind, with what you've raised about this allergic reaction. The only person who'd be able to orchestrate that would be someone in the NHS.'

'I've got no proof of anything,' said Harry.

'I know,' said Noble. 'Believe me, I know.'

Another tap on Harry's window. This time he was ready to see the old detective again, the one with the scarred face, but instead was met with the sight of the giant DS Wilson, wearing the same street attire as he had on the Camberwell Road: jeans riding low, a camouflage-pattern hoodie and a puffa jacket.

'They said you'd be here,' Wilson said. 'Can we get some food, guv? I'm starving.'

'You can go get dinner, Mo. Some of us are working.'

DS Wilson advanced his huge frame through Harry's window, waving a sheaf of papers.

'I got something you'll want to read,' Wilson said.

Noble moved to get out and Harry did the same, Wilson retreating from his side of the car.

'Go on, then,' Noble said. 'Dr Kent will join us, if that's OK.'

'PFC?' Wilson suggested as Noble locked her car. 'Or are we banned from chicken shops after last night?'

He laughed at his own joke and Noble joined him, and Harry followed them out into the snow in silence.

It wasn't a fried chicken shop, but the yellow light of the Burger King they found themselves in was far too reminiscent of the previous evening for Harry's liking. At least it wasn't cold in here.

He looked at his watch. Seven-fifteen. Twenty-four hours ago, he'd walked into the Chicken Hut and seen Solomon Idris for the first time. The teenager now felt like his charge, despite the fact he knew very little about him. He recognised the similarity with the girl with the pink hair, a different story perhaps, but the same themes. Somehow, Harry felt responsible. In both cases, no one else was there to speak for them, and so maybe he filled that void. Or maybe that was just his attempt to rationalise it. Because thinking about it like that was better than trying to track down her identity just so he had something to do, something that kept him from staring out of the window wishing he could sleep.

It was the eyes, Harry decided as Noble and Wilson returned from the counter, trays piled with food and coffee. He needed to know what had given Solomon Idris that look in his eyes.

'Ketchup,' said Wilson, and headed back to the counter.

'Does he always dress like that?' Harry said.

'He used to be Trident,' Noble explained. 'Just been seconded to CID 'cause so much of what we see is gang-related. Runs about thirty CIs in this borough, maybe five or six in Lambeth, too.'

'CIs?' Harry asked. Even though he'd been working with the police for a few months, the jargon went over his head now and then.

'Confidential Informants,' Noble said. 'Grasses, to you and me. Mo's basically spent the afternoon talking to his friends, and finding out if they know anything or heard anything about Solomon Idris. Anyway, this one's yours.'

Harry graciously took the burger from her and started unwrapping it as Wilson returned from the counter. Once he was done showering his fries with sauce, he reached into the inside pocket of his jacket and pulled out three A4 files, each in its own plastic wallet, with a photograph paperclipped to the first page. Though it was an old photo, Harry recognised the top one immediately as Solomon Idris.

'Here's our mate Sol,' Wilson said. Then he pulled off the top file to reveal a school picture of a mixed-race girl, hair braided either side of her face, tie loose, embarrassed smile on her face.

Harry knew who he was looking at before he saw the name typed on the file beneath it.

'Keisha was his girlfriend,' Wilson said.

'For sure?' said Harry.

'Well, for some time at least. I had a couple of sources on these two. The first one's a housing officer who's based on their estate, not sure if it's because she's a masochist or what. She said that Solomon spoke to her about trying to get a council house, because

Keisha was pregnant, but they were too young, and anyway they both had suitable housing with their parents.'

'When was this?' said Noble.

'First week of October.'

'So both of them knew that Keisha was pregnant at least six weeks before she killed herself,' said Harry. 'Did your source know whether it was planned?'

'Idris didn't discuss it much,' Wilson said. 'He got angry when she said they wouldn't qualify for council housing, and left.'

'At least we know they were together,' Harry said. 'That's something.'

'Don't speak too soon,' said Wilson. 'Princess had plenty to say about the both of them.'

'Princess?' said Noble.

'I can't tell you his real name,' Wilson said. 'But let's just say he makes me look like a ballerina. His information's the only reason he's not inside for GBH. Anyway, he works as an enforcer for a local piece of work called Martin Santos. He's a mid-level dealer for the TPB. That's the—'

'I've introduced Harry to the Boys,' Noble said. 'Go on.'

'Anyway, the Albany is Santos's ends, so it's his business to know the local faces,' Wilson continued. 'He said Idris and his best mate, Shaquille Dawson, used to be fairly high up in a small crew called the Wooly OC. Wooly's Walworth, and OC means they were affiliated with the Organised Criminals, a big Brixton outfit that got broken up around 2009.'

'Used to be high up?' Harry said. 'And then Idris got stabbed and went straight?'

'Well, kind of. You have to realise that these crews aren't big operations. Most street gangs in London are comprised of maybe six, seven key members who control a small area, and then you get allegiances formed between the local groups, which means lots of affiliated street crews but no central leadership. Two years ago, the Wooly decided to switch camps and ally themselves to the TPB, the OC's main rivals. Some boys in one of the Brixton crews took it on themselves to teach Idris and Dawson a lesson.'

DS Wilson paused to remove the lid from his coffee and blow on it. Noble was still chewing down on her burger, and Harry took a bite of his and tried to put that information together in his head.

'Idris got attacked in July 2011,' Harry said. 'He'd have been sixteen. So these days you can be high up in one of these gangs and still be in secondary school?'

Harry hadn't grown up too far from the Albany estate, in terms of both geography and deprivation, and a few of his contempories had been mixed up in the local gangs. But back then it had been the Yardies who'd run the streets, and teenagers were only the foot soldiers, peddling weed on street corners.

'It's a fucked-up world,' said Noble. 'We know he was involved when he was fourteen, 'cause of that A&E visit in 2009.'

Perhaps it should have been less surprising – the youngest kid Harry had ever treated for a gang-related attack had been a nine-year-old boy who'd been acting as a mule for a gang in Lewisham, too young to be stopped and searched by police. A rival crew had caved in his skull with a cricket bat and left him to die on the street in order to rob him of his stash. The kid was walking now, but not talking much.

'If there's only ten key members to a gang, then yeah,' Wilson said. 'The Wooly OC was formed out of kids from the Albany, who went to the same school. The leaders were a trio of nineteen-year-olds, three years ahead of Idris and Dawson. One of them was Dawson's cousin, Burke.'

'I remember them,' said Noble, slurping at her own coffee.

'What happened?' Harry said, though he regretted asking almost before the words left his mouth. He didn't imagine it involved a happy retirement to the countryside.

'Two weeks after the Brixton crew shanked Idris and Shaquille Dawson in 2011, they came for the big dogs,' Wilson said. 'About twenty of them found Burke and his two mates at a house party in Camberwell, dragged them out onto the street and beat them to death. The poor lads didn't have a chance.'

'Fucking hell,' said Harry. If almost dying wasn't reason enough to agree to some lifestyle counselling, then your mate's cousin being killed on the street had to be.

'Anyway,' Wilson said. 'After that, Princess said that Idris and Dawson packed it in. Kept their heads down around the estate, started going to school. Around the start of last year, Idris stopped picking up from Santos. Previously he'd been a regular, just for skunk, nothing serious. But apparently he just stopped coming.'

The time that the mentoring scheme would have kicked in, Harry reasoned.

'And in the summer, he started being seen with Keisha Best,' Wilson said. 'Together.'

'More evidence for the happy couple?' said Noble.

'Well, that's where it gets interesting,' said Wilson. 'Our friend used some colourful language to describe her. The first time Princess mentioned her it was *And then he started gettin with that sket Keisha.*'

Harry and Noble shared a look and shook their heads, and Wilson kept talking.

'Turns out Keisha had been one of the girls that Martin Santos had on the go, and he considered her his property. That fact that she was going out with Solomon Idris pissed him off big-time. Santos wanted Keisha tagged. Know what that means?'

'I don't think I want to, do I?' Harry said.

'I'm surprised you haven't seen it,' said Wilson. 'Basically, these monsters cut girl's faces to "mark" them as dirty, having slept around. So then the other members of a gang know not to go there.'

'Fucking hell,' Harry said, a memory returning of one of his first shifts at the Ruskin, when he'd been an SHO in A&E. A fourteen-year-old girl with a V-shaped cut in her cheek. 'I did know that, but I think I deliberately forgot.'

'Yeah, well, thank God, Princess wouldn't do it. Says he doesn't hurt kids and he doesn't hurt women, neither.'

'Small mercies,' said Noble.

'But he said that in September, Martin Santos slept with Keisha Best on at least one occasion. He was sure about that.'

'She cheated on Solomon?' said Harry.

'Probably not with malice,' Wilson said. 'It was probably closer to gang rape. Kids like Santos will organise house parties, where there's lots of drink, lots of drugs – GHB's a favourite – and then they and their mates take advantage of whoever they like.'

'Christ . . .' said Harry. It was another sad chapter in a sad story, most of which was missing, but which ended in front of a commuter train and in the mortuary at the Ruskin. Harry was about to ask whether Santos could've been the source of Keisha and Idris's HIV infection, but then remembered that the numbers suggested Idris had been infected a good few years ago, and Keisha more recently.

'That's all he had on them, though,' Wilson finished. 'Didn't even know that Keisha was dead. Hadn't seen either of them since at least last October.'

'Who's in the third file?' Noble said.

'Shaquille Dawson,' said Wilson, moving the file out from underneath the other two. The police mugshot had bloodshot eyes, lip curled downwards to reveal stained, yellow teeth. If it was taken at the same time as Idris's, then Dawson was fifteen in the photo. He looked at least five years older.

'He'll know what was going on between Keisha and Idris,' Harry said. 'What would have driven him to do what he did. I take it you guys are speaking to him?'

Noble and Wilson looked at one another, before Wilson broke into resigned laughter. Harry tightened the muscles in his face to try and stop his cheeks flushing red.

'In an ideal world, yes, we would,' Noble started. And then Harry realised why Wilson was laughing. Even if Dawson was no longer criminally active, a former gang member would sooner turn on a family member than speak to the police. The potential consequences were too great. He guessed that it was exactly the kind of problem that the Saviour Project had been set up to deal with.

'No chance,' said Wilson. 'Even if he's gone straight, no kid from that estate will ever speak to a copper.'

'What if it wasn't a copper who interviewed him?' Harry said.

Noble looked up at Harry. Finished chewing her mouthful.

'What do you mean?'

'I could do it.'

Noble shook her head and reached for her drink.

'No, no, no—'

'Hang on, hear me out,' said Harry, raising a hand. 'I spoke to the GP who runs this Saviour Project today. He said they do assemblies in schools. And the school that Idris and Dawson go to, it must have its fair share of problems with gangs, violence, stuff like that?'

'Albany Road Academy,' said Wilson. 'Thirty per cent of the upper school has a record.'

'So why don't I speak to him and see if we can organise an assembly at the school? Dawson's year. Short notice, maybe, but it could work. Get the docs in, and then take the kids one by one to chat in some rooms or something, and fix it so Dawson's in with me. It'll be a good cover, especially if all the kids have to do it.'

Even as the words came out of Harry's mouth, the idea was still forming in his brain. Dawson knew Keisha, knew Solomon, might know why one of them had climbed down onto the track and stared a commuter train in the face, and the other had walked into a chicken shop with a loaded gun and waited for the police to kill him after he'd told his story to the world. Again Harry thought about a story with blank pages. They knew the beginning and the end, they just had to figure out the middle.

'You think this GP would cooperate?' Wilson said.

'He told me he'd help in any way he could,' Harry said. 'He seemed to take what happened to Idris personally. He'll help.'

'I like it,' said Noble. 'We'll do it tomorrow. If it works out.'

Harry tried to stop a smile forcing its way onto his face. Couldn't work out whether he was happy that what had happened to Solomon Idris and Keisha Best was being investigated properly, or that it would be him who got to do it. There was something to be said for not relying on the promises of others.

'Get this doctor on board and get back to me,' Noble said, looking at Harry. 'If we go ahead, you'll be the one sitting down with Dawson, so I'll brief you beforehand. Mo, I take it you can't go in there as a body in the room?'

Wilson shook his head. 'Too many kids at that place know me. But we could use Hannah.'

'OK,' said Noble. 'You and me can be in a car outside with a couple of uniforms, near enough to get inside if there's any trouble.'

'You think there'll be trouble?' said Harry.

Wilson stood up and pulled his coat around his broad frame.

'You ever been inside one of these schools?'

'I went to Deptford Green,' said Harry.

'Then you know exactly what I mean,' said Wilson.

Harry conceded the point.

'Thanks for the food, guv,' Wilson said. 'I'll do the paperwork to get the bodies for tomorrow. Be in touch.'

'Just you and me,' Harry muttered once Wilson was gone. Noble had finished her meal, and was wiping her hands on a sheaf of napkins.

'Well, piss off and make phone calls, then,' Noble said. 'I'm gonna tie up this clusterfuck as best I can so I have the time free to work on this.' She tapped the personnel files, gathering them together, then stood up and fixed Harry with hard eyes.

Harry got up from his seat, energised. Headed for the automatic doors and the cold night outside, pulling his phone from his pocket. Examined Duncan Whitacre's business card in the light of a street lamp, and started to dial the number.

The Overground was busy with late-night commuters, and he had to wait for ten minutes on the platform at Peckham Rye. As he stood there, an express train passed, the livery blurred. He thought about only 468g of brain being present for examination, owing to distribution at the scene.

After he left Canada Water it took a while to get his bearings. He wasn't familiar with the territory, but he asked one of the people waving copies of the *Standard* outside the station. The marina was five minutes away on foot, through the old ship-yards named after countries that had long since ceased maritime trade with London, the glass leviathans of Canary Wharf leering from across the river at their undeveloped neighbours, One Canada Square lit up like a prehistoric obelisk calling to religious followers.

The wharf behind him, Harry passed over a canal and headed in a three-quarter circle around one of the quays. Small grey flakes were drifting down from above, landing on his shoulders and in his hair, and he dug his hands deep into his pockets to avoid the biting cold. The marina was spread out in front of him, the boats ranging from luxury motor yachts with jet-skis moored on the stern to barges which looked as if they had rooted into the water and would never leave.

As he approached the gates, his phone buzzed.

The text was from Whitacre, confirming that everything was in place for tomorrow. They'd spoken at length, and Whitacre had jumped at the chance to assist. Solomon Idris was his patient, he'd said, and he felt duty bound to help in any way he could. Whitacre would meet him tomorrow at twelve, along with another doctor and Charlie Ambrose, the youth worker who ran the scheme day to day.

Back to school, Harry thought. He wondered what question he'd ask Shaquille Dawson first. So far, everything he'd found out about Idris had just made the picture murkier.

They killed Keisha, and the feds didn't give a shit.

The marina was surrounded by wrought-iron black fencing, the single gap occupied by a gate and a guard hut.

'Can I help you?'

The watchman was dressed in a turtleneck fleece and a woollen hat, his booth heated only by a three-bar electric fire. There was a book lying face down on the bench entitled *How to Pass the UK Citizenship Test*.

Harry produced his hospital ID. 'Can you call through to James Lahiri, please? Tell him Harry's here to see him.'

'You're Harry? Mr Lahiri tells me you were coming,' the guard said, releasing the gate. 'Go on through. Berth twenty-nine. Turn left, second jetty on your right.'

Harry went through the gate and followed the guard's instructions. He caught sight of the Dome between the blocks of flats, a vague memory rising, a visit with his mother just after his eighteenth birthday, a few weeks after his interview at medical school.

Lahiri's boat was called the *Time and Tide*, a forty-three foot motor yacht whose sleek design reminded Harry of a sports car, two glass doors leading into the main cabin, with leather sofas and mood lighting. There were a couple of feet of clearance between the dock and the aft deck, and Harry made the jump with no difficulty. The boat had probably cost at least half a million, he thought, and Lahiri still had a hefty mooring rent to pay. Few other outgoings, though. No mortgage. No wife. Not any more, anyway.

'This a boarding party or something?'

The voice came from the side deck on the other side of the boat. Lahiri, wearing a diamond-patterned wax jacket, was just finishing a cigarette, flicking the ash over the side into the water.

'You started again?' Harry said, genuinely surprised.

'Yeah.'

'You're the only person I know who managed to give up in Afghanistan.'

'Thing is,' Lahiri said, looking out across the river, 'when I got back, I found out some bastard had been shagging my wife.'

Harry's heart hit the floor. Lahiri threw the butt over the side and headed down into the boat's lounge, which held two sofas, one looking out through the doors onto the aft deck, the other facing a plasma-screen television and a satellite phone on an asymmetrical carbon-fibre table.

'Take a seat,' Lahiri said. He went to a cupboard in the galley. Beyond it were two half-flights of stairs, which looked like they led down to a living area and up to the helm. Harry settled into the sofa and Lahiri picked up an open bottle of wine from the side and two glasses. 'You drinking tonight?' he asked.

Harry hadn't planned to – he tried not to drink if he was working the following day, but tonight could be an exception. 'Go on, then.'

Lahiri passed him a glass, and Harry took a sip. It was acid sharp. Probably the first glass of wine he'd had since the hospital's Christmas party.

'I saw that face,' Lahiri said. 'Looks like none of Alice's more cosmopolitan tastes rubbed off on you.'

Harry said nothing. Lahiri raised up the glass and spun it between his fingers.

'This is good stuff. Macon-Villages Sauvignon Blanc, the 2012 vintage. Feels bad to be wasting it on you, really . . .'

Lahiri laughed and Harry pretended to join him. Those kinds of jokes used to be second nature, more often than not going in the other direction. Jokes about Lahiri fucking ponies while Harry drank jellied eels by the pint glass.

'I'll happily take a Stella if you've got one,' Harry said.

'Afraid not,' said Lahiri. 'Anyway, what are Solomon Idris's chances? Fifty-fifty?'

Harry sipped more of the acid wine.

'If that,' he said.

The silence rolled over them with the spray of the wind, blowing droplets of sleet against the windows. Harry regarded his friend in the quiet, London's light blurry through the wet glass behind him.

'Be a damn shame to lose him 'cause of a bloody clerical error, after fighting so hard to get him through last night. Shouldn't happen in the twenty-first century, should it?'

Harry opened his mouth, ready to voice his suspicions. But then he decided against it.

'Systems work through people,' he said instead. 'People fuck up.'

'Yeah,' said Lahiri, finishing his wine. 'They do.'

Harry wished there was music or television in the background. Something to dull the oppressive edge of the silences.

'Such a relief that you turned up in that ambulance,' Lahiri said after a while. 'I mean, Kinirons is a safe pair of hands in Resus, but George bloody Traubert . . .'

Harry laughed. He was glad to know he wasn't the only one who thought of Traubert that way. 'Tell me about it,' he said. 'He's my boss.'

'Even I was getting nervous,' said Lahiri, 'and I'm a bloody GP.'

Harry laughed. It was the first self-deprecating joke of the night. A glimpse of the old James. Another silence.

'How did it feel?' said Harry. 'When you recognised Solomon, in A&E?'

Lahiri poured himself another glass of wine and scratched at the hair he had left above his right ear. He did that when he was thinking, or nervous. Harry remembered that during their surgical rotation, he'd had to keep his fingers interlocked so he didn't scratch his hair with his sterile gloves.

'Just the same as how it felt when I came into the sick bay and saw you and Tammas lying on the floor,' said Lahiri. 'Perhaps a little less acute, granted. But still the fear. I felt like every single experience in my life had been training me for those few minutes. In A&E, I had you, I had the rest of the team. Back then, I was on my own.'

'You saved my life,' Harry said. 'If Idris lives, you'll have helped saved his, too.'

'Yeah, well, you did the hard work,' said Lahiri. 'You and Mr Gunther.'

Harry shuffled on the seat, trying the wine a third time, and managing a decent enough gulp. If he didn't hurry up, Lahiri would drink the whole bottle. Maybe that would be a good thing.

'How well did you know Idris?' said Harry.

'I'd already set up the job at Burgess Park,' said Lahiri, resting back on the sofa, hands behind his head. 'Duncan even let me postpone it after I decided to go back to Afghan. When I got back, he introduced me to the Saviour Project. Idris started with us in 2009, but he only really engaged after he got attacked in 2011. Duncan did his initial sessions, then he got put on my list when I joined. I kept on seeing him, about once a month.'

'What do you see him for?'

'Check-up,' said Lahiri. 'That's how the project works. They come in for a clinic, they talk to me, Duncan or Lisa for ten minutes, then they go chat to a youth worker.'

'Tell me about him,' Harry said. He didn't care how the wine tasted any more, just wanted it down him.

'Why do you want to know?' said Lahiri.

'Because I have no idea why a seventeen-year-old kid would try and get himself killed like he did last night,' Harry said. 'And why someone would want to make sure of it.'

'I don't follow you.'

'The police recovered a spent shell casing from an alleyway off Wyndham Road, behind the Chicken Hut. Someone fired a gun hoping that the police would storm the restaurant and kill Idris, and they almost succeeded. And today his penicillin allergy disappeared from the hospital system. Somebody wants this kid dead.'

Lahiri said nothing. Just spun an empty wine glass between his fingers and looked at Harry. Another memory rose. The Maudsley, third-year psychiatry. A young student had walked into the consulting room, sat down and told them both that MI5 were beaming thoughts into his head. James had looked at that man in exactly the same way.

'Just tell me what you know,' Harry said. 'And then I'll leave you alone.'

Outside, a particularly vicious wind had started, and occasionally a handful of sleet would pound against one of the windows. Lahiri took a deep breath, refilled his glass, topped up Harry's, and began.

'As far as I know, Sol had a pretty crap start in life. His dad pissed off back to Nigeria when he was about seven, left his mum to bring him and his brother up. He started getting involved with gangs from when he was about ten, because sometimes his mum's benefits couldn't cover them. He wanted new clothes, and an Arsenal shirt, and football boots for school, and the older kids on the estate would pay him a fiver to deliver bags of weed to their customers. Police don't search the young ones.

'Before he knew it, he was involved in the Wooly OC. Four years ago, he had to initiate himself by attacking a member from a rival gang. Waited for him outside his school in Loughborough Junction, stuck a knife in him as he came out.'

'Solomon Idris stabbed someone?' Harry said, voice cracking.

'Yup,' said Lahiri. 'Initiation. They all had to. He didn't do that much damage, thank God. Said he didn't want to hurt the guy, aimed for his arm deliberately. Gave him a nasty scar but nothing else. A couple of the other guy's mates caught up with him and gave him a bit of a hiding, but he managed to get away with only a broken rib.'

The hospital visit in 2009, Harry thought. Solomon Idris had been treated in the Ruskin's A&E for superficial injuries. When he'd read that earlier, Harry had assumed Idris had been the victim, not a perpetrator.

'Idris told you all this?' Harry said. 'That he'd stabbed someone?'

Lahiri nodded. 'He had to. It was an initiation. That's how it works with these guys.'

'I know that,' he said. 'But he trusted you enough?'

'He told me everything. I'm his doctor. Everything we talk about is confidential. That's why the Saviour Project works. Because the kids trust us not go to the police. Anything we're unsure about, we go to Whitacre and he makes the call.'

'I didn't realise that.'

'It's the only way to make them trust us,' said Lahiri. 'Without that, kids like Idris wouldn't come anywhere near us. And if they can't tell us what they've done, and face up to their past, how the hell are we supposed to get them straight in the future? Do you know how many gang members under the age of nineteen have symptoms of PTSD? Forty per cent, Harry.'

'It sounds like a good idea,' said Harry. 'But if that's all confidential, then why did you tell me?'

'Because you're you,' said Lahiri. 'You get it.'

Harry nodded his understanding. Took another gulp of wine.

'Anyway,' Lahiri continued, 'two years ago Idris's friend's cousin got killed. Revenge attack after their gang switched allegiance. He ended up in the Ruskin for a week after he got stabbed. I think that scared him, 'cause that's when he really started to engage with Whitacre and then with me. By the time I started working with him last September, he seemed improved. Out of the gang lifestyle, he had a plan.'

'What kind of plan?'

'He wanted to move out, not just out of the estate, but out of London. I mean, he was studying catering at college, he had this girlfriend, he was looking for jobs. He'd found this flat in Nottingham that he was obsessed with moving into, planned this new life for himself and Keisha.'

The mention of the name sent the cold of winter rushing through the hole in Harry's chest.

'Keisha Best, was she your patient too?'

'No. Don't think she was at our surgery,' Lahiri said. 'Why, what do you know about her?'

'Idris's girlfriend, from the same block as him on the estate. She was HIV-positive, and it looks like she got it from him. She died last November. Climbed down onto the tracks at Peckham Rye and stared a train in the face.'

'Christ,' said Lahiri. 'Sol didn't tell me that. All I knew was that she died.'

'How'd he take it?'

'It devastated him. But he kept face, just said that shit happened, and that was what London did to people. I think it amplified his desire to leave. The first meeting we had after Keisha died, all he did was tell me about Nottingham. Tried to make conversation. But I could tell that it'd ripped him apart. He kept going on about how London was a bad place, how he just needed to get out. He seemed just as scared as he had been the weeks after he'd been attacked.'

'What about the next time you saw him?' Harry said.

'We didn't talk much. I only saw him once more after that, the first week of December. He said he was close to moving out, that he was saving up, he told me he'd found a job as a waiter in some restaurant around Westminster.'

'You didn't believe him?' said Harry.

Lahiri leant back, puzzled. Harry was feeling the warmth of the boat's central heating, or maybe it was the wine. He resisted an urge to tug at his collar.

'What makes you say that?' said Lahiri.

'You said *he told me he'd found a job*,' said Harry. 'Not that he had. You didn't believe him.'

Lahiri shuffled on his seat. Looked out at the sleet hitting the windscreen, stood up and stared across at the boats knocking against one another on black water, wine glass in hand.

'Week or so before Christmas, I was out for lunch. One of the places on the river between London Bridge and the Tate, you know 'em? Greek. Anyway, we were sitting by the door, and he comes in. Sol. I barely recognised him at first, he was in a shirt and trousers, a stack of CVs underneath his arm. But he saw me. I nodded to him, and he just turned around and ran out the door.'

Harry looked at his friend's face reflected in the boat's sliding doors. Blank, as if the memory was baseline, neither a pleasant nor an upsetting one.

'So if he had a job, and he was still at school, why was he putting his CV in at other places?' Harry said.

'Exactly,' Lahiri said. 'I didn't think much about it. But after that he didn't return my texts. I was worried about him.'

Lahiri turned around, finished his glass and put it down, reaching for the bottle to pour another. Harry thought about what it could mean, Idris lying about whether or not he was working. It raised the question of what he was really doing with his time, and if he was still getting money from somewhere, where it had been coming from. Harry looked across at Lahiri, thought he could see moisture in his friend's eyes, but he said nothing, waited for it to come out.

'He always looked so fucking scared, man. I'd worked with him for months, all my other kids had been making such progress. But he still looked terrified every time I saw him. He reminded me of those Afghan kids we used to see round the camp in Helmand.'

Lahiri took a long pull of wine, before resting the glass on the table and leaning forward.

'He had this look in his eyes, you know,' he said.

Harry closed his own eyes and was back in the Chicken Hut, Solomon Idris's hand resting on the gun on the table.

'I'm going out on deck,' Lahiri said.

Harry rose from the sofa and went out to join him, pulling his coat from the sofa's arm, sliding his arms through the sleeves. Trying to trap heat within. Lahiri leant over the boat's edge, lighting a cigarette.

'You should be working with us, Harry, doing this stuff,' Lahiri said. 'You'd be perfect, with your background. Much better than a Charterhouse boy like me.'

Harry inhaled a little of Lahiri's smoke and it mixed with his own breath as he blew it back out.

'I'd get bored if I was a GP,' he said.

'Do it part-time, then,' Lahiri said. 'Traubert would give you the time; he helped out when Duncan set up the project.'

'Well, I'm busy,' said Harry. 'I work with the police now as well. Since about last February.'

'I still can't get my head around that; you always hated the filth.'

Harry shrugged. 'Wanted to try something different.'

Lahiri smirked. 'Nothing to do with a young girl with pink hair, then?'

Harry spun around, resting on the ship's rim.

'How do you know about her?'

'Everyone knows about her,' Lahiri said. 'The whole hospital knows about Dr Kent's little obsession. It's admirable, really. You should hear how people talk about you.'

Harry was silent for a while, gripping the boat's aft railing with his numb hands.

'How do people talk about me?'

'They wonder what you do when you go home,' Lahiri said, wrapping his lips around the filter. 'They picture you sitting in that flat, making phone calls with a collage of newspaper articles on your wall like retired cops have in TV shows. And I don't think they're far off, you know.'

Harry tried to stop his face going red. There was nothing worse, he thought, than being on the wrong side of someone who knew you intimately, knew exactly where to twist the knife. He tried to think of a response, briefly considered pointing out one of the bones on his skeleton of a social life, then realised how pathetic that would sound. *I don't know what you're talking about, me and Rafeek went to a comedy night back in October.* So he went on the offensive.

'What about you? Why did you stay in London, after Alice left? I thought you'd piss off back to the coast. Let's face it, redeeming inner-city kids isn't really you, is it?'

Lahiri laughed.

'I'll give you that. It was all for the CV, I'm afraid. And maybe a little for the soul. Maybe I wanted to prove I'm a human being.'

That fucking smile again, Harry thought. Lahiri flicked his cigarette butt into the black water but made no movement back inside, instead turning and leaning against the railing. Harry was sure that he either knew or suspected far more about Idris than he was letting on. He knew the man well enough to know when he was holding back.

'Who were you out for lunch with?' said Harry.

'What, when I saw Solomon?' said Lahiri. 'Why does that matter?'

'It probably doesn't,' said Harry. 'But you stumbled when you talked about it. Who was it?'

Lahiri folded his arms, a flake of snow falling from the covering above them and landing in his hair.

'Georgia Henderson.'

The name was familiar, and he rolled it around in his brain for a while. Maybe a member of staff at the hospital, a mutual colleague. Then it clicked.

'Gavin Henderson's missus?'

Henderson had been a corporal with the Royal Anglians, the regiment with which Harry and Lahiri had been embedded on their first deployment. He'd been part of the firefight which had put Harry and Tammas in hospital, and he was one of the few men from the Anglians who'd volunteered to go back out after their tour had ended, just like Lahiri had. As it had turned out, going back had been the worst decision Henderson had ever made.

'She's a midwife,' Lahiri went on. 'Works over at Colchester General. I met her at the funeral.'

'You're seeing her?' said Harry.

Lahiri nodded, his teeth gritted. Harry wondered if he was glad because his friend had moved on, or because it partly assuaged his guilt.

'And don't you fucking dare judge me,' Lahiri said. 'When me and Gav got blown up, you know where you fucking were.'

Henderson had died fourteen hours after Lahiri had dragged him into a helicopter in a field outside their forward operating base, sixteen hours after stepping on the IED. Harry had been at Lahiri's house, in his bed, with his wife.

'Well, if you're happy,' Harry said weakly. 'That's the most important thing.'

Lahiri strode back through the open doors into the boat's living compartment and picked up the wine bottle, emptying what was left into his glass.

'I went back to try and do right. Because I wanted to be part of the team that got those bastards back for what they did to you and to the boss. And then I got home,' he paused, downing the glass in one, 'to find I'd lost my wife. And my house.' He looked up and held eye contact with Harry. 'And my best friend. And you know what? I deserved every single bit of it.'

'James, you can't—'

'Oh, fuck it, Harry! Me and Alice were nothing! I cheated on her so many times I can't remember.'

Harry almost threw up. He remembered when Lahiri had found out about him and Alice. She'd told her husband one evening in September, two days after Lahiri had flown back from Afghanistan. He had flown into a fit of rage, she'd sobbed to Harry over the phone. He'd smashed up their kitchen, thrown a chair through the window, kicked a door off its hinges. Her infidelity had apparently sparked in him a primeval anger Harry hadn't even seen on the battlefield. Harry'd asked if Alice wanted to come over. She'd said she needed space. Turned out she'd been in the taxi on the way to the airport, and it was the last time Harry had spoken to her.

And now Harry realised that all of Lahiri's hate, all of the anger, was directed inwards. Living on a boat, engulfing his sorrows with cigarettes and fine wine, James Lahiri hated himself more than anyone else. Harry thought about his conversation with Tammas the previous night, when he'd lost it. *James fucking brave fucking Lahiri.* Well, maybe he was only brave enough to hate himself rather than transfer it onto someone else.

'When?' Harry said.

Lahiri stared into his wine glass.

'Loads of times. Conferences, mostly. Nights out.'

He shrugged.

'That night we got back the first time, when we flew you and the boss back to Birmingham. I spent one night up there before I came back down to Alice, pulled some civil servant in a wine bar, and took her to my hotel room, and fucked her in the same shower I'd used to get the shite out of my hair and the blood off my face. You know how it feels, right? Same reason funerals make you want it. When you survive something like that, you just want to shag the living daylights out of anything you see, so you can prove you're still alive. You can understand that, can't you?'

'I guess,' said Harry. He wasn't sure that he could. The one time he'd survived something like that he'd woken up in the ICU in Birmingham, the other side of the world, a week and a half later. The drugs had made him see a purple sky above him and smell lavender from his bed.

'I'm sorry,' he said softly.

'It's alright,' Lahiri said, still staring into the glass. 'Me and Alice, we were a sham. She wanted the status of being a doctor's wife, and then the pity of being an army wife. Didn't want to support me, just wanted me around, someone to fall back on. And she knew I resented her for it. She knew that was why I went back to Afghan, just to get away from her. I suppose, in some warped way, I should thank you really. For finally giving me a reason to leave the bitch.'

Harry wanted to believe every word that his friend said. He stood up and circled the table, coming over to Lahiri's side. His emotions, as always, were muddied. He hadn't loved Alice, and when she'd disappeared from their lives, like a tornado dissipating into dust clouds, he hadn't missed her, either. But he had a deep desire to know what had happened to her, and that gnawed at him.

'Have you heard from her?' he said.

'Alice?' said Lahiri. 'No, but I found her on LinkedIn. Staff nurse at Christchurch Hospital. Couldn't find any trace of her otherwise. She won't call either of us. And I'm thankful. The other side of the world is a bloody good place for her to be, as far as I'm concerned.'

The place behind Harry's sternum expanded and ached as cold wind from outside passed through it. Lahiri kept talking, the wine glass's rotations increasing in speed.

'Let's hope that it's some poor Kiwi bastard who gets strung along now, eh?' Lahiri's head rolled down to his lap and he began to sob. 'Four years of fucking marriage. And she wasn't worth a fucking day. Lord, she really wasn't.'

Harry pulled Lahiri's head close into his shoulder and held him. They hadn't spoken once after it had all happened. Harry had been too much of a coward to call and had spent the week sitting in his old house with a bottle of Jameson's, waiting for the furious knock on the door.

'You're a bastard, Harry,' Lahiri said. 'I'm just glad she fucked you over as badly as she fucked me.'

And that's God's honest truth, Harry thought. Rain or snow or sleet hit the window and rolled down it behind them, and all he could feel was the cold.

The westbound tunnel between Bermondsey and London Bridge, the noise and vibration fighting to get into Harry's head. He stared at the *Standard*'s pages, and tried to forget the conversation he'd just had. He was far too exhausted to attempt processing it. The last words Lahiri had said to him, as he'd disembarked from the *Time and Tide*, circled in his head.

'Don't let this drop, Harry,' he'd said. 'Solomon Idris deserves someone like you.'

Harry felt the train slow as they approached the station, and bounced a little in his seat. One of the usual announcements cut through the noise.

'There is no southbound Northern line service from this station. This is due to a person under a train at Moorgate. Customers are advised to continue to Waterloo and change for the alternative branch of the Northern line for stations to Morden.'

A person under a train, Harry thought. Like so much in life, the tragic had become routine. He looked around him as he rose from his seat and headed for the doors, the tutting, the head-shaking. 'For fuck's sake,' grumbled his neighbour. Perhaps an extra fifteen minutes to their journeys, that was all. Harry had treated people pulled from under trains when they survived, which was more often than one would think. He'd seldom wondered what had motivated them to take that jump, much less so when he was delayed because of such a desperate act.

Jumping was one thing. Climbing onto the track and waiting for the train to hit you was another. The pathologist's voice in his head again. *She would have had a chance to save herself.*

Harry thought about Keisha Best as he rode the escalator out of the station. Normally he would have taken the tube down to Borough, but there was little point taking a bus half a mile, so he'd walk. This part of London at this time of night, at this time of year, wasn't bad. It had an edge, Harry thought, watching a train thunder over the bridge against the backdrop of the cathedral, still far enough north to be free from the dirty reality that crept in south of the river.

Harry wasn't even sure how he'd managed to find the phone in his pocket, let alone dial Tammas's number with numb fingers. He was almost home.

'Marigold House.'

'Hi. Room one-oh-nine, please.'

There was the usual sequence of clicks and whirls as the call was connected. Harry crossed over, passing a couple having an argument outside Borough station.

'Hello?'

Tammas had a telephone on his bedside table, which responded to voice-activated commands, with a microphone perpetually taped to the side of his mouth. He often joked that the sci-fi stuff was only available to quadriplegics.

'Sorry to call late, boss.'

'What is it? Harry. Half eleven? That's not. Late for. You?'

Harry said nothing, just looked over his shoulder before he turned onto Borough Road.

'What have. You been. Up to?'

'On Lahiri's boat. We were catching up.'

Tammas's ventilator cycled a few times.

'And how. Was that. For you?'

'Alright, I guess,' said Harry. 'He didn't kill me. We were talking about the kid, you know, the one I saw last night. Lahiri was his GP. But we ended up talking about Alice. He thanked me, can you believe that? He thanked me for giving him a good enough reason to leave her.'

'Oh what. A tangled. Web we. Weave when. First. We practise. To deceive.'

Tammas lacked the cadences, but the quote still resonated in Harry's mind.

'Shakespeare?' he guessed.

'No, you. Bastard. It's Scottish. Don't know who. But it's. Scottish.'

Harry laughed.

'How involved. Are you. With this kid?'

'The police are dragging their heels,' Harry said. 'Today I found out that he's likely infected his girlfriend with HIV, and she threw herself under a train in November. There's more than one reason this guy could have snapped. He's seventeen, boss. I remember how shit I felt when I was seventeen. I just—'

A deliveryman on a blue-and-silver motorcycle passed Harry and turned off ahead of him, into the same alley that led to his block of flats. Tammas interrupted him.

'You're doing. It again,' Tammas said. 'Distracting yourself. Deal with. You and James. That matters. That really. Matters. Let the police. Handle the rest.'

Harry headed up to the door, ready to punch in the code. The deliveryman was dismounting from his bike, walking up to the same door as Harry.

'What do you mean, doing it agai—'

The first punch came straight into the side of his face, sending him staggering towards the front door of his apartment block. The next blow, a kick to the soft of his abdomen, put him down. Hands on his hand, going for the phone. Harry let it go. The deliveryman grasped the phone with his leather glove, and stepped over him. He relaxed his muscles, waiting for another blow, but it didn't come. He arched his back, scrabbled backwards across the ice-covered tarmac.

Doesn't feel right, Harry thought as he rolled onto his back. This isn't worth it. Bringing the bike, turning in ahead of him to mug him for a phone. The man behind the motorcycle helmet wanted Harry, wanted him specifically. His phone. There was nothing on his phone worth having, not to anyone.

'HELP!' Harry roared, his voice cracking. Not out of fear, but because he wanted to take control back. Nobody would come, not at this time of night. The deliveryman was out of range, by his bike. If he came closer for another kick, then Harry could go for him. Being on the floor didn't put him out. If he tried to get on his bike, then Harry could jump him, but that was riskier. The motor was still running, and all he'd have to do was gun the engine and run him down.

Harry pulled himself to his feet, and the deliveryman responded. Reached for a pouch on his belt and pulled out a kitchen knife, serrations in the blade. Held it at arm's length. Harry's eyes darted from the knife to the deliveryman's other hand, where the phone was open, emanating blue light. The deliveryman's fingers were tapping something out, and after a few seconds the arm came back. Harry braced himself for a fight. If the deliveryman rushed him now with the knife, with his back against the wall, Harry's chances weren't good. He'd have to hurt him, and the motorcycle helmet and leathers were good defences against that.

But the rush didn't come. The phone came spiralling through the air, and Harry caught it with both hands, before immediately dropping it onto the pavement. He needed his hands to be free.

The distraction of the phone had given the deliveryman time, enough time to mount the bike, rev the engine, and sail past Harry before he could reach him. Harry turned to watch the bike veer right, towards St George's Circus, the number plate covered with mud, unreadable.

His jaw stinging, Harry knelt on his doorstep to pick up his phone and punched in the code to the front door. In the communal hallway, he sat up against the wall and let out hard, quick breaths. In the moment, there had just been adrenaline. Now there was fear, and the pain that started behind his sternum, and spread through his chest, and eventually seeped out of the scars.

Not a mugging. Not even close.

Harry turned his phone and saw the screen was cracked. But he could still read what was on it: a text, no recipient, all in capitals.

IF YOU WANT TO FUCKING LIVE, FORGET SOLOMON.

Harry flicked the phone back onto his recent calls, found Noble, and dialled.

The pain was fading as he held the bag of frozen chips to his face, the towel they were wrapped in starting to get damp. The chair he'd chosen to recover in was in the middle of his living room, pointing towards the window, facing north. The door was locked and bolted. He would hear anyone who came in that way. He'd have time to get a knife from the kitchen drawer before they made it out of the hallway.

His phone began to vibrate, drilling against the glass table.

'Frankie,' he said.

'I'm outside your building,' said Noble.

'Nine four six eight,' said Harry. 'Come up to the sixth floor.'

He stood up, took a sip of whiskey from the tumbler on the table. Went to the door and stared at it until he heard the chime of the arriving lift, when he released the chain and bolt and opened it.

Noble was on the landing, her hair damp, wet patches on her leather jacket. Harry glanced around to make sure there was no one else waiting, before letting out the breath he hadn't even realised he'd been holding.

'Jesus, are you alright?'

'I think so,' he said. 'Come in.'

'You've been cut,' Noble said.

'Have I?'

'Yeah.'

He'd rung her and given her a brief description of what had happened. He'd said he'd been attacked outside his home, and that he was OK. That whoever had done it had got away on a blue and silver motorcycle with a dirty number plate, heading towards Waterloo. She'd asked for his address and told him she'd be twenty minutes.

'It's my jaw that hurts,' Harry said as they walked into his living room. Noble stopped in the doorway, before heading to the window and staring out.

'You've got one hell of a view,' she said.

'Not bad, eh?' said Harry. He put the frozen chips back against his jaw.

'Are you sure you're not hurt?' said Noble. 'You don't want it checked in A&E?'

'It's just a bruise.'

Noble picked up the bottle of Jameson's.

'Decent,' she said. 'Have to say I prefer scotch, though. I'd deprive you of some, but I'm driving.'

She pointed down at the tumbler.

'Is that one your first?'

Harry nodded.

'I had a few glasses of wine earlier this evening.'

'Didn't have you down as much of a wine drinker.'

'I'm not,' said Harry. 'James Lahiri is, though.'

Noble turned and leant against the glass window, looking down at Harry in the chair.

'You get anything out of him?'

'Yeah,' Harry said. He kept quiet about the money and the flat in Nottingham, though. If Idris had told Lahiri, his doctor, about those things in confidence, he wasn't sure he should disclose them to the police.

'You think what happened has something to do with this?' Noble said.

Harry looked over at her, slowly, took a sip of the whiskey, felt it burn into a cut on the inside of his bottom lip, and pulled his phone from his pocket. Unlocked it through the cracked screen and held it up for Noble to see.

'He took the phone off me, typed that, and then threw it back.'

'Jesus,' said Noble. 'What happened, again?'

Harry told the story, starting with when he first noticed the motorbike pull in towards his apartment block, and ending with him on his knees, crawling towards the front door. By the time he was done the tumbler was empty, and the adrenaline was beginning to give way to a haze.

'You can't remember anything about this guy?'

'He was in leathers,' said Harry. 'I remember the bike.'

'Height?'

Harry closed his eyes, and the feeling behind his sternum came back. He could feel the tension in his body. What he was going through was normal – psychiatrists called it an acute stress reaction, and the usual course was reasonable. Looking over your shoulder for a few days, anxiety when you left the house. This time next week, he'd be fine. But the feelings, and what they reminded him of, were unwelcome.

'I'm five eleven,' said Harry. 'And he maybe had a couple of inches on me. So six one, six two?'

'Right,' said Noble. 'Skin colour?'

'No idea.'

'And you couldn't see the plate on the bike?'

'It was covered in shit, Frankie. So there was no way I could ID it, but if he got stopped then he could just say it needed a clean.'

'If you saw that bike again, would you recognise it?'

Harry shrugged.

'Maybe.'

Noble looked between Harry and the table.

'You got another glass?' she said.

Harry got up, went to the kitchen and put the bag of frozen chips back in the freezer now that his jaw was sufficiently numb. He returned to the living room with an empty tumbler.

'Fill it yourself,' he said. 'If you're driving, that is.'

Noble poured liquid into the tumbler and took a reticent sip. Harry was fairly sure that traffic cops who pulled over detective inspectors didn't reach for the breathalyser once they saw the warrant card, but he kept silent.

'Knife,' Noble said. 'That's interesting.'

'Why's it interesting?' said Harry.

'Well, we know that we've scared the shit out of them,' said Noble. 'But this – it's a careless move. Before today we only had bullshit hunches to say that there was anything going on with Solomon Idris. Now they're spooked. The logical conclusion is that this is the same person who let off a shot in the alleyway behind Wyndham Road.'

Harry cut in before Noble could finish.

'But the guy who jumped me used a knife,' he said. 'And if he had a gun, and he wanted to scare me, then why not use it?'

Noble nodded.

'Two different people?' said Harry.

'Fuck knows.' She downed the whiskey and put the glass down on the table. 'I'm gonna put my brain on this overnight. Are you still alright to go into the school tomorrow?'

Harry nodded.

'More than alright. I'm there.'

'Great,' said Noble. 'I really need to get off. Will you be OK?'

'I'll be fine,' said Harry.

'You got a girlfriend? Friend who might be able to come over? Family?'

He felt wounded by the question, and that surprised him. He'd been without a family for over a decade now, so he'd adapted to that. Of course he had friends, people he drank with after tough shifts, who he shared lunch with in the mess, but when it came down to moments like this, there were two names that he considered: Tammas and Lahiri. One bedridden, the other with all bridges burned.

'It's late,' said Harry. 'I'll be fine.'

'Suit yourself,' said Noble. 'Good luck tomorrow.'

Harry heard the front door shut as he settled back in the sofa, rocking his glass in his hand, rolling the liquid around. He was still feeling the effects of the adrenaline in his system. He'd not popped a pill since the morning, but now he knew he'd have to chase sleep around the caverns of his head, that it wouldn't just come to him. His phone buzzed – three missed calls from Tammas. Through the smashed screen, Harry managed to type a text saying all was OK, and send it. He wasn't in the mood to talk, to be told again how poor his life choices had been.

He looked across at the bottle. About half of it left. Would have done the trick but he was working the following day. Harry had never worked drunk and he never would. He'd quit either working or drinking if it ever got to that. He got up from the chair, moving slowly, picked up his laptop, a Billy Joel album, just one more glass, help him sleep, back into the chair. Went through his emails, agreed to a half-arsed request to examine medical students in the spring. Lingered over an invitation to a new online dating website exclusively for doctors, nurses and emergency service workers. He couldn't think of anything worse. But he signed up anyway, a month's free trial.

After an hour the tiredness began to descend, Billy finished singing, and he tried to track his thoughts away from Idris, covered in wires and tubes, or the image of a teenager staring at a train. Settled on a girl with fading pink hair, and moved to James Lahiri, khaki shirt, pistol on his belt. Tried to remember what Georgia Henderson looked like, but couldn't. Mountains full of lavender, the smell of lavender, a purple sky. Alice in the green dress she liked to wear.

He fell asleep in the chair just after midnight. The light would wake him up.

Tuesday, 22 January

He'd slept more than he'd expected to, but Harry was still tired as he changed in the locker room. Stress, withdrawal, it didn't matter what he called it. He felt the warmth of freshly laundered scrubs against his skin, and the grit in his mouth from the large, strong coffee he'd washed down his morning aspirin with. He made it to the doctors' office on the surgical ICU by 8.25, five minutes before the handover from the night team was scheduled to begin. He entered the room, recognising Aoife Kelly, Saltis, as well as Tammy Shelton, another of the senior registrars.

'Oh, hi, Tammy,' Harry said. 'You on today as well?'

'I am now,' said Shelton. 'Rashid called me late last night, said that you were away and would I mind covering. Please don't tell me that I've come in for nothing.'

Harry was about to answer when Rashid came in, his chest hair bursting out of the V in his scrubs, which were far too tight.

'I know, I know,' Rashid said. 'We've got twenty bloody operating theatres but no extra-large scrubs, I keep telling them.'

'What's with the registrar rota today?' Shelton said.

'Ah,' said Rashid, sitting down and turning to Harry. 'Harry emailed me last night, about this assembly thing. I mean, we're busy, so I asked Tam if she wouldn't mind coming in for the day. I'm sure you can cover one of her shifts next month. Work it out between yourselves.'

'Sure,' said Harry, a bit pissed that he'd come in when he wasn't needed, but then again it gave him a free morning, and the unit was busy. An extra pair of hands was always useful, especially if there was another slip-up with Idris's allergies.

'That said,' Rashid continued. 'Solomon Idris's mother is coming in again at about a quarter to nine. You could speak to her, if you're around. You've already built a rapport.'

'Sure,' said Harry.

It would be a chance to find out more about Idris, Harry thought, before chastising himself.

'I'll go see how he is, then.'

Rashid nodded, and Harry left. He walked into the unit, the

familiar smell of disinfectant hitting his nose. There was a different police officer keeping vigil in Idris's side room, a young face,
weapon on his belt. Harry nodded to him as he entered, putting
on an apron and gloves, muttering a greeting.

'S'cuse me, sir, could I take your name?' said the PC.

'Harry Kent. I'm one of the ICU doctors.'

'Can I see your trust ID please?' the copper continued. 'I'm
sorry, I've been instructed to security-check and keep a record of
everyone who visits this patient.'

'Good,' Harry said, pulling his lanyard from inside his scrubs
and showing the copper his ID. 'Who do you report to?'

'Detective Inspector Noble, sir,' the PC said. 'She's with
Southwark CID.'

Harry nodded. It was nice to know that at least someone was
doing their job properly. If the deletion of the allergy from Idris's
record had been done internally, and not by an outside hacker,
then he was at risk every moment he was in hospital.

He was about to ask where Idris's nurse was, but then Gladys
Lane walked into the sink room, carrying a new catheter bag.

'Mornin', Dr Kent.'

'Hi, Gladys. How's he doing?'

'Better. His urine output's good, he's stable, and he's been off
the vasopressors. Still needs his oxygen, but I think his chest's
sounding better.'

Harry grabbed a stethoscope from the wall and took a listen for
himself. It still sounded crap. PCP infection was a treatable disease,
but it took time to clear, especially when the patient's body was as
weak as Idris's. Everything else was promising, though: he was
producing urine, which meant that the kidneys were recovering,
there were no signs of heart failure, and while there was little
chance of him breathing unassisted any time soon, he was having
no issues with the ventilator. Luckily it appeared the allergic reaction he'd suffered hadn't caused any lasting damage.

'Know anything about the plan for later?' Harry said.

'They'll be over in the ward round soon,' said Lane. 'But the
night nurse said something about an angiogram. And the HIV
team are up to see him.'

Harry nodded. It all sounded about right. As with so many of his patients, once the acute phase was over, and they were stable, it was about waiting for things to clear up, and managing the issues which would emerge as a result of being in a medically induced coma for so long. In cases like this, the recovery could be weeks, even months.

Harry wandered over to the central nurses' station and waited around for Idris's family. One of Tammas's favourite phrases went something like: Think about what you know, and think about what you need to know.

I know he's an ex-gang member with a few grudges still going. I know he loved a girl who killed herself in November. I know he told Lahiri that he was working but he probably wasn't, so he was getting money from somewhere else. I know he had something he wanted to tell the world, or at least he thought he did. At the start, Harry had thought that might have been paranoia, mental illness, too much skunk, but now he was convinced. Because his girlfriend was twenty weeks pregnant, and lost it maybe days before she killed herself. That child, Harry thought. He needed to know about that. It was the child, and the loss of it, which had precipitated Keisha's death, and which in turn had caused Idris to do what he had done.

Harry's thoughts were broken by the arrival of two figures he had grown to recognise. Joy Idris, wearing her charity-shop coat and slightly dragging one foot. Junior Idris, gaunt and quiet, in the same school uniform that Solomon had been wearing in the photograph clipped to his police file.

'Hello, Doctor,' said Joy.

'Hi, Mrs Idris. I'm Harry Kent, one of the doctors. We spoke to one another late on Sunday night, but you may not remember.'

'I remember,' said Joy. Harry's stomach twisted.

'Shall we go somewhere private?'

Joy Idris nodded slowly and they shuffled towards the relatives' room, freshly stocked with a new day's supply of tissues. The way she moved was funereal, Harry thought, like she had already resigned herself to the fact of losing a child. It was the opposite of the pious optimism Harry had seen on Sunday, and he instantly regretted coming in on his own, but the rest of the doctors and the senior nurses were in handover, and the other nurses were all making sure that their patients didn't die.

'How are you doing?'

'I am praying every hour of every day,' Joy Idris said after a while. 'The devil is trying to take my son. I am praying for God to give me my son back, but he does not answer me. And I can have no more days off. I must go to work today.'

Harry nodded solemnly. He wondered what Joy did for a living, but didn't feel like asking.

'Even today, I will be docked two hours as I will come late. And Junior will be late to school, but they don't care.'

I bet they don't, Harry thought. From last night's conversation with DS Wilson, Harry was fairly sure that the Albany Road Academy had bigger problems than Year 9 students skipping their first lessons. He let the silence pass.

'What do you know about Solomon's condition?'

'He had an operation yesterday. They took part of his spleen away. The surgeon explained it to me.'

Harry nodded as she spoke. He was trying not to be obvious about the fact that he was studying Junior Idris, whose face was sinking into the off-white shirt collar, the tattered black school jumper. Junior was gazing at a point on the wall over Harry's shoulder, and there was something about him that was unsettling. Maybe it was the resemblance to his older brother.

'Yes, the operation went well,' he said. 'But I'm afraid there were some problems afterwards.'

Joy bowed slowly, and Harry wondered for a moment whether she was praying, before her head started to shake. Junior broke his gaze from the wall, reached down for a tissue and passed it to his mother, then returned to his default stare. Harry waited until Joy was looking up before he continued.

'What kind of problems?' Joy said, wiping tears from the side of her face. She didn't look distraught, just exhausted.

'Well,' said Harry, 'Solomon had an allergic reaction to one of the antibiotics he was given. I'm really sorry, it's a mistake that shouldn't have happened, and we're trying to find out how it did. His condition became quite serious, and at one point his heart stopped briefly. We were able to restart it.'

'My son's heart stopped?'

Joy Idris's mouth hung open, her face expressionless.

'For a short period of time, yes,' he said.

'His heart has never stopped before.'

'I know this must be so distressing for you, Mrs Idris,' Harry said. 'But the important thing is that we started the heart again very quickly. Now, sometimes when patients go through something like that, it can have very serious consequences. But there's absolutely nothing to suggest that Solomon is suffering any major after-effects.'

'So he's going to live?' said Joy.

The million-dollar question.

'I don't know,' said Harry. 'I'm really sorry, but I can't tell you the answer to that. He's stable, but he's still critical. He's very sick, and we need to work really hard to get him better again, and it might not be possible. The one thing I can promise you, Mrs Idris, is that we will do absolutely everything we can. I can promise you that.'

'God will decide,' said Joy. 'You can do everything you can, but at the end God will decide.'

The cynical part of Harry's brain said that Joy's words were as good an appraisal of the situation as any he could have come up with. She repositioned herself on the table, a dry tissue folded, waiting in her right hand.

He briefly considered asking about HIV, about whether Joy had known anything about it, but they had already checked with the Burgess Park Practice and the local GUM clinics, and there was no record of Idris ever attending for testing or diagnosis. At seventeen, Solomon Idris was effectively an adult. And Harry was loath to break the news of an adult patient's status to a family member without their permission, especially one in Joy Idris's emotional state.

'Our team are looking after him twenty-four hours a day,' Harry said. 'As I said before, Mrs Idris, we will do everything we can.'

Joy rose slowly, and for a second Harry was sure she was about to topple forward and collapse. She was shaking with every movement, her lips trembling, the tissue gripped in a tight fist. Harry rushed forward to catch her, but Junior got there first and batted his arm away.

'Don't you touch my mum, you fuckin' faggot.'

Harry backed off, only to watch Joy Idris push her son away. 'Junior!'

She turned to Harry, tears still wetting her eyes.

'I must go to work. Thank you, Doctor.'

She headed for the door. Harry rose to show her out, but her free hand had already opened it, and he stood awkwardly beside the table as Joy left. Junior followed his mother out, his head cocked back, facing Harry. The teenager's eyes, bloodshot and wrought with adolescent fury, never left Harry's, and he thought long and hard about the look he had seen in Solomon's eyes on Sunday night. He thought about the message that the man who'd attacked him had left on his phone. Wondered if that was all he should do. Forget Solomon Idris, hope he got better and walk away.

Harry followed what remained of the Idris family out of the door and closed it behind him.

Once the family had left, Harry went to Idris's bed and checked the plan from the ward round. He was to be reviewed that day by both the surgical and the HIV teams, continued on the anti-fungals, have one litre less of fluid than yesterday, and be trialled on a lower oxygen concentration. The CT scan was booked for lunchtime, and Dr Shelton had agreed to escort him.

'I hate CT,' Shelton had said. Most doctors did. Sick patients had a habit of deteriorating on the way either to or from the scanner, and some even arrested when they were in the machine itself. Of course, the scanners were invaluable, but the 'doughnut of death' still made doctors twitchy, and Harry was among them. That said, Shelton was a safe pair of hands if anything went wrong. Harry had asked if there was anything he could do to help out, but the team had everything under control.

He was in the stairwell on his way to the doctors' mess when his phone rang.

'Hi, Frankie.'

'Where are you?'

Noble sounded worried, but her voice was almost a whisper. Harry pictured her in a corridor, or maybe smoking in the car park, trying to disguise the conversation from prying ears.

'The hospital,' said Harry. 'Is everything alright?'

'No, it's fucking not,' said Noble. 'I've got to be quick, but basically your IT people have been talking to our IT people. They've traced the source of the entry which deleted the allergy on your system.'

Harry stopped on the stair, leaning sideways against the wall. Felt his scrubs stick to his body with sweat.

'Who was it?'

'It wasn't an external hack,' Noble said. 'The deletion was made in the early hours of Monday morning, from a trust computer. They don't know which one yet, but they know it was on the East Wing servers.'

'Fuck!' said Harry. Two physiotherapists passing him on the stairs turned their heads, then kept going. The East Wing was home to A&E, the ICUs and the emergency theatres, and hundreds of acute ward beds. Hundreds of computers. And someone inside one of those departments had deleted the allergy as Solomon Idris had been fighting for his life.

'Do they know whose log-in was used?' Harry said, his heart pounding. He doubted it – if so, they would have a culprit, and Noble would either have said so, or the police would be making an arrest.

'No, but they will soon,' she said. 'Either way, Fairweather's gone mental. He's launched a joint investigation with Homicide & Serious, and they've brought in a DCI from the local Murder Investigation Team. They're already at the hospital, setting up. Technical Services are gonna search through the accounts.'

'Shit.'

'They're looking at you, Harry,' Noble whispered. 'I told them what happened to you last night and it completely backfired. I'm sorry. They think that you're involved with Idris somehow.'

'Fuck. Thanks for the heads-up.'

Harry's head was spinning. The thought that he would be a suspect in an investigation he'd effectively started was a fairly ironic one.

'Are we still going ahead with the plan for this afternoon?' he said. 'The school?'

'Well, we've already made the arrangements,' said Noble. 'And

Wilson's ready. So let's go for it. It'll take that long for Fairweather to get things sorted, fingers crossed. Anyway, I've got to go.'

'You're coming to the hospital now?'

'Yeah,' Noble said. 'I'll see you later. I'll drop you a text.'

Noble hung up. Harry sat down on the stairs, put his hands against his temples, and forced himself to think. It wasn't anything to be worried about. He was innocent, he'd never even met Solomon Idris before forty-eight hours ago. That wasn't what terrified him. What scared him was the now-confirmed fact that there was a person who wanted Idris dead, who had tried to get him killed at Camberwell Road, and had probably procured an illegal termination for Keisha Best. And that person either worked inside the hospital or had access to someone who did.

There was someone who was a threat who might well be in the building right now, and Harry had no idea who it was. Whether it was the same person who'd brandished a knife at him last night.

'You alright there, my friend?'

Harry turned to the voice behind him. It was Rashid.

'Yeah,' said Harry. 'Just tired, that's all.'

'Well, forgive me,' said Rashid. 'I just had Dr Traubert on the phone. He wanted to see you.'

Harry rolled his eyes as he spun on his feet and headed upstairs. He had a terrible feeling that his day was about to get a lot worse. Told himself that as long as Solomon Idris made it back from the CT scanner alive, everything was going to be fine.

Despite his mood, Harry found the padded chair in Traubert's office relatively comfortable. The room was substantial, and Harry ran his eyes across the shelves of the large case of textbooks behind Traubert's desk, ranging from the classics of medicine, *Gray's Anatomy* and *Kumar & Clark*, to journal editions on anaesthetics and critical care. There were numerous texts in French and German, too, and the centrepiece, at the bottom: a carbon-fibre mini-fridge made by Porsche, which Traubert was reaching over to open.

'Can I offer you some Fiji water?' Traubert said. 'I'm afraid I don't have any coffee.'

'Sure.'

Harry had forgotten that Traubert was a health nut. On the opposite side to the bookcase was another shelving unit, which featured various awards and framed photographs, many of Traubert engaged in diverse forms of exercise – cycling, swimming, marathons. The alpine backgrounds suggested that a lot of them were from his native Switzerland, and Harry noticed that there were no pictures of anyone else other than members of a cycling team.

Traubert retrieved two bottles of water from the fridge, passing one to Harry. He unscrewed the top and considered the tropical scene on the label.

'What is this stuff?' he said, taking a sip. It just tasted like ordinary water, but cold.

'It's the purest water on the planet,' said Traubert. 'Fiji has unique geology, and the aquifers there are like nothing else in the world. As you may know, I'm teetotal, and I don't drink anything caffeinated. But pure, chilled water, there's nothing like it. It helps focus my mind.'

Harry couldn't help thinking of the amphetamine he'd washed down that morning with a glass from the Thames Water supply at his flat. He reckoned that did a much better job of focusing the mind. Traubert perched on the desk and delivered his soliloquy. Harry gathered that the board of directors were terrified that the press would discover the police were treating the deletion of Idris's allergy as a potential criminal matter, and typically they were far more scared of the damage to the hospital's reputation than the possible existence of a staff member who had tried to get a patient killed. As with any other super-massive organisation, when something like this happened in the NHS, the sharks smelled blood, and some of that could be Harry's.

The problem was, he wasn't really listening. He was thinking about the text message the man who had attacked him last night had tapped into his phone, and the photos on the files of Solomon Idris and Keisha Best.

'Does that make sense?' Traubert asked.

Harry was staring at the bookshelf again. There was a hardback French volume there, which didn't seem particularly medically related. It sounded romantic when he said the words in his head, even though he didn't have a clue what they meant.

'Harry!'

'Sorry, Dr Traubert. I didn't get much sleep last night.'

It wasn't really true. Harry glanced at the black-and-gold clock on the wall. Almost eleven. He sank back into the chair, trying to keep track of what Traubert was saying. He mentioned something about the chief executive getting involved, wanting to be kept appraised of the situation. People were worried about the presence of a police investigative team inside the hospital, particularly when they were looking at staff.

'I have to say, you're bad luck, Harry,' Traubert continued. 'Basically, what I'm trying to say is that I'm on your side.'

'Who isn't?' Harry said.

'Well, if you must know, a number of members of the board were pretty angry with you,' Traubert said. 'They didn't feel it was appropriate for you to tell the police that the allergy had vanished. Not until Patient Safety had completed their own investigation.'

'I was just speeding the process up,' Harry said. 'If they've got nothing to hide, why are they bothered?'

'Because they don't care about anything other than this trust's reputation,' Traubert said. 'Anyway, certain people want me to keep an eye on you.'

Harry rolled his tongue around the inside of his mouth, closed his eyes. When he opened them, he was briefly disappointed that he was still in his boss's office, and that Traubert was still there, still smiling.

'Well, you're keeping an eye, aren't you?' Harry said.

Traubert stood up, looking over Harry's shoulder as if he was expecting someone else to come in through the door.

'I have four departments to run in this hospital,' Traubert said. 'So I don't want this to take up any more of my time than is absolutely necessary, alright? I sat through a bullshit meeting this morning where someone even went so far as to suggest we suspend you.'

Harry said nothing. Traubert went on.

'I told them that if they did I'd resign in protest, and that if they wanted to scapegoat someone, they should wait until the police find the person who is behind all of this. That they shouldn't hang one of my best registrars out to dry.'

Traubert drained his bottle and tossed it into the recycling bin.
'You want another bottle of water?'

Harry shook his head.

'Suit yourself,' said Traubert. 'How involved are you with this?'

Harry shrugged his shoulders.

'I'm helping the police with their enquiries.'

'Come on, Harry. I can tell that you care deeply about this teenager.'

'Mmm,' was all Harry could manage. He was wondering where the hell his consultant was going with this, whether it was ground-work for an insult.

'You're helping the police in your role with them, this forensic thing?'

Harry nodded. 'In a way,' he said. 'I'm visiting Solomon's school this afternoon. It's part of the outreach scheme. The Saviour Project.'

'Ah,' said Traubert. 'That's Duncan Whitacre's project, isn't it?'

He pronounced the name *White-acre*, so Harry was briefly confused before he agreed.

'What a fantastic piece of work,' Traubert continued. 'Duncan should get a medal for setting it up; it's probably saved more lives than we ever do here. Stuff like that's the way forward, you know. Have you been involved before?'

'No,' said Harry. 'Just, um, helping out this once.'

'It's brilliant,' Traubert said. 'You know, I was a locum A&E consultant here back when Whitacre was setting it up. I helped find them an office. There was a similar thing at the Toronto General when I worked there.'

Harry's mind drifted back to Lahiri on his boat, and to meeting Whitacre on the ICU. How both of them had viewed what had happened to Solomon Idris as a failure on their part.

'Anyway, what I was trying to tell you is that you should watch your back. And I'll do my best to keep the bastards upstairs from directing their rage at you.'

'Thanks,' said Harry, suddenly uneasy.

'Don't worry,' said Traubert. 'I'm not asking for anything in return. You covered my back in A&E on Sunday night. I owe you for that. And you obviously think you're onto something here.'

Harry didn't say anything. Thought about how many times

Solomon Idris could have died already. Bleeding to death on the dirty floor of a takeaway. Traubert fucking up in A&E. Crashing on the table during the operation, the allergic reaction. And he was still only barely alive, he thought. He remembered what Joy Idris had said that morning. *The devil is trying to take my son.* At least if they'd suspended him, he could have spent more time helping out with the investigation.

'I think so,' he said.

'Well, let me know if there's anything I can do to help.'

Harry's phone buzzed in his pocket, the noise audible, and he resisted the urge to check it instantly.

'Take it!' Traubert said. 'Go on, don't let me bother you.'

The text was from Noble, styled with an efficiency Harry now knew to be trademark.

15 minutes. Boardroom, Jubilee Wing.

'I'll let you get on,' Traubert said. 'And I'm serious. If there's anything you need, if it all starts to get a bit much, you know where I am.'

'Thanks,' Harry said again.

He got up from the chair and had the door three-quarters open when Traubert spoke.

'Oh, there's just one more thing.'

Harry turned around.

'The police asked if they could have your computer records. They want to look at everyone who treated Idris since he came in, to rule out if anyone deleted the allergy by mistake.'

'Sure,' said Harry.

Traubert smiled and Harry shut the door. Felt the stress leave his body, just like the feeling of a cold beer on a Friday evening. He looked down at the text again, the screen still cracked from last night. He'd have to get that fixed, maybe the next weekend he had off. As he left the unit, he nodded to the young police officer on duty next to Idris's bed. Keeping watch.

Harry made it to the Jubilee Wing in ten minutes, and had even managed to change out of his scrubs into normal clothing, maybe a little less smart than normal for the school assembly. The board-room faced out onto a busy corridor near a coffee shop and the Friends' Bookshop, and he stood with his back to the wall, a little way down the corridor, coffee in hand, waiting for Noble to emerge. As he waited, Harry scoured the news applications on his phone for any mention of the shooting, eventually finding some-thing on the BBC News website, the local page for London. A seventeen-year-old male was 'stable' in an unnamed hospital after being shot by police on Sunday evening, and had been arrested on suspicion of firearms offences.

Standard fare for South London. Though the shootings usually made the news, the numerous stabbings and beatings didn't even make the *Standard*, let alone the nationals.

The door opened after a short while and two uniformed officers came out, followed by three or four young-looking detectives in plain clothes, including DC Kepler, the Professional Standards detective who'd interviewed Harry on Monday morning. The same detective who'd decided that Keisha Best throwing herself in front of a train not long after she'd been twenty weeks pregnant wasn't a crime. Noble came out next, scanned the corridor, spot-ted Harry and headed over.

'Morning,' she said. 'How you feeling?'

'Alright,' said Harry. 'Just the five of you?'

Noble turned and together they watched as the diminutive frame of Marcus Fairweather filled the doorway, nodding at both of them before moving away to reveal a woman, probably the wrong side of forty but holding on to her fresh face with an arse-nal of make-up. Dark hair, cream suit, a folder under one arm, designer handbag, shoes with an inch heel. Not much in common with Noble's leather jacket and Doc Martens.

'Who's that?' Harry said.

'Louisa Marsden,' said Noble. 'DCI with Homicide & Serious. She's a bitch.'

'Ha,' said Harry. 'Do you want a coffee?'

'Nah. I need a fag, though.'

They turned and headed for the hospital's main entrance.

'I take it there's no progress on who it was?' Harry said.

Noble shook her head.

'We've been busy,' she said. They emerged into the morning fog and made their way towards a smokers' cage, sandwiched between one of the medical school buildings and a bicycle park.

'Oh really?' said Harry.

'Yeah. I thought it would be a good idea to run down alibis, cross-check any of our persons of interest, see if they own blue-and-silver motorbikes. Wilson's been interviewing known associates of the gang who attacked Idris back in 2011, too.'

'You think this could all be revenge?'

'It's possible,' said Noble. 'But it wouldn't explain what happened yesterday, with the allergy.'

'Back to square one, then?' said Harry.

Noble shrugged her shoulders and smoked.

'Exactly. That's where Technical Services come in. We know that the change was made from a server on the East Wing, at seven-twenty, Monday morning, but the only way to find out who it was is to go through every log-in in turn and view their recent activity. So that's what we're doing, starting with everyone on duty Sunday night.'

Harry nodded, but he wasn't hopeful – the one thing that was missing from all of this was motive. He went down a mental list of the people who'd treated Idris in hospital, and couldn't think of a single reason any of them would want to cause him harm.

'You should look into his bank accounts,' said Harry. 'I think Idris might have been getting money from somewhere.'

'How do you know that?' Noble said.

'I can't tell you,' said Harry. 'Confidentiality.'

Noble looked at him, unimpressed. 'Well, he didn't tell you, unless he's woken up, which he bloody well hasn't. Which means you got this from your friend Lahiri, who's his doctor or his shrink or whatever the hell this Saviour Project meant.'

Harry tried not to betray anything with his face.

'Come on,' she said, pulling out her iPad. 'I'll show you mine if you show me yours.'

'You know that I can't,' said Harry.

'For fuck's sake,' said Noble. 'Confidentiality means I can't use anything Idris told his doctor against him. But I can use it to help us find whoever's trying to kill him, I reckon.'

'You got a law degree?' said Harry.

'Hell, no,' said Noble. 'A BA in philosophy, with a master's in bullshit. But fuck it. Tell me what you know. If it helps, we already know about the money.'

'What about it?'

Noble brought up some images from a folder on the tablet, scanned documents which looked like bank statements. Harry recognised the branch address. Walworth Road, near the Albany estate.

'These are Solomon Idris's finances,' she explained. 'As much as we appreciate your sage advice, one of the first things Mo did was pull his bank details. He had a junior saver's account. With an awful lot of money going in for a seventeen-year-old kid from the Albany estate, allegedly in full-time education. Something in the region of two hundred pounds a week.'

'Who was paying him that?'

'A numbered account,' said Noble. 'We're going to get a warrant to trace the payments, but the guy I spoke to in Organised & Economic said it could take months. But look at this.'

Noble's finger tapped a single record made on 22 December 2012. Ten thousand pounds had been deposited into Idris's account.

'Jesus!' said Harry. His thoughts immediately went back to the *Time and Tide*, Lahiri dropping the hint about Idris saving money, but without a job. Harry was sure Lahiri had been holding something back, and maybe this was it.

'Cash deposit,' Noble said. 'No way to trace it, either.'

'You think he was involved again?' said Harry. 'Drug money?'

'I don't know,' said Noble. 'I'd like to know. I'd like you to tell me what you know.'

Harry winced again, and the door of the smokers' cage clattered as a pair of shattered-looking catering staff entered, their roll-ups tucked in the pockets of their smocks.

'Can we get out of here before I get lung cancer, please?'

Noble scowled at him and they left, ducking into an alcove that separated the main hospital building from an old Victorian façade that now housed the neuroscience institute. Harry almost regretted the move. At least in the cage, it had been slightly warm. He moved to speak, but Noble got there first.

'Harry.'

'Yeah?'

'Do you trust me?'

Harry shuffled a little, dug his hands into his pockets.

'I guess.'

Noble smiled, and then leant against the wall and stared at him, a focused intensity.

'I know that means a lot, because I know you don't trust a lot of us. So I suggest we make a little pact. I believe that somebody tried to kill your patient, and I want to find them and bring them to justice. That's all. I couldn't give a fuck about the Met or your hospital or any of that shit. And I think you feel the same.'

Harry guessed she was waiting for a reply, so he just nodded.

'Good. So why don't we share everything we've got. And it stays between you and me, and we get this sorted. Deal?'

Harry nodded slowly at first, then quickly.

'Deal,' he said.

'I've shown you mine,' Noble said. They were briefly interrupted by a loud blast from an ambulance's airhorn as it came out onto Denmark Hill from the hospital entrance.

'I don't know much,' said Harry. 'James, my friend, is Idris's GP. He told me that Idris was saving money, but he reckoned that he'd lied about having a job. Said he bumped into him handing his CV in at a restaurant. Idris had plans to move out, move to Nottingham.'

'With Keisha Best?'

'It looks like it.'

'That ten grand came in just before Christmas,' said Noble. 'Keisha died in November.'

'Maybe Idris knows something,' said Harry. 'That's money to keep him quiet.'

'We'd thought about that,' said Noble. 'It'd give someone a motive.'

Harry's phone buzzed. A text from Charlie Ambrose, the youth worker with the Saviour Project, offering him a lift down from the Ruskin to the Albany Road Academy. Harry showed it to Noble.

'Let's hope we can find out, then,' he said.

'Too right. Keep in touch,' said Noble.

They headed back towards the main hospital building. Noble had almost turned away when Harry called after her.

'Frankie.'

She turned.

'Say this allergy thing is just negligence, a coincidence, whatever. And Fairweather wants to bury this all. You know you could get in a lot of trouble for swimming against the tide, right?'

'I've had nine years in the Met, Harry,' she said, coming back up to him. 'You don't need to tell me.'

'So why are you willing to risk it?' said Harry. 'I mean, I'm glad someone is.'

'Same reason you're not doing what that message told you to last night,' Noble said, and left.

Harry picked up a sandwich on his way into A&E and searched around for the Saviour Project office. It was tucked into a corner, upstairs, and he walked through the main shop floor as he looked for it, nodding to Rashid and Shelton as he passed them. They were leaning over a patient covered in defibrillator pads and monitor wires, with the ashen-grey face of someone who'd been brought back from the brink of death. He could tell by the look on their faces that the situation was grave. Harry made it to the office before he let himself exhale.

It was an underwhelming room, a door which could easily have led to a storage cupboard, an A4 piece of paper declaring its occupant as 'Saviour Project JRUH'. The door was open, revealing a narrow room with a desk overflowing with files, an old computer and two chairs when there was only really room for one. In the middle of this stood a young man with an armful of posters and leaflets, whom he presumed to be Charlie Ambrose. Harry remembered Traubert's spacious office a floor above them, enough room for his mini-fridge, and groaned inwardly.

'Come in!'

Harry stepped into the room.

'Hi, I'm Harry.'

'Good to meet you,' said Ambrose. 'I've just ordered a cab, there's no way we can carry this lot on the bus.'

Ambrose passed Harry a bundle of the materials, and they

shuffled awkwardly out onto Denmark Hill where the taxi was waiting.

'Their third period goes on until two,' Ambrose said as they arranged the boxes on the cab's floor. 'We're on after that.'

'OK,' said Harry. 'I guess I'll just be standing around. I want to keep my head down until I'm in a room with Shaquille Dawson.'

'Sure,' said Ambrose. 'Duncan does most of the talking, anyway. You'll enjoy it. He's quite theatrical. Inspiring, even.'

Harry nodded. In a weird way, he was looking forward to it. As if being in the environment that Solomon Idris and Keisha Best had shared would help him in some way appreciate the misery their lives had encompassed.

The taxi edged slowly through the lunchtime traffic around Camberwell Green, the cabbie cursing about the stupid pissing bus drivers, four or five buses in various stages of making stops and blocking their progress. Ambrose leaned forward and turned the intercom off.

'Where are you from, Harry?'

'Bermondsey, originally. My dad worked the docks.' It was half true. He'd worked the docks after he'd got back from the Falklands, and then six years later he'd walked out on Harry's mother and disappeared. 'What about you?' he asked.

'South Norwood,' said Ambrose. 'Well, Grenada on my mum's side, Trinidad on my dad's.'

'How'd you get involved with the project?'

'Roundabout way,' said Ambrose. 'I was a paramedic for ten years. Worked out of Oval, but I packed it in after I had my daughter. It's not a good job; you spend most of your day shipping drunks to A&E, or getting shouted at by managers. And you see so many of these poor children. I just . . . I don't know, I wanted to make a real difference. Improve some of their lives. I retrained as a youth worker, spent a few months with my church. But kids don't listen to religion anymore. There's no respect for it. Then Duncan got in touch about the Saviour Project, and I thought, hey, I've found my calling. This is it. And I've never looked back.'

Harry smiled and hoped it didn't look fake. The one thing that had struck him about everyone he'd met from the Saviour Project was the relentless optimism; in a way, it reminded him of the way

Joy Idris had been on the night her son had been shot. Confident that, against all the statistics, things would come out right. It jarred a little, almost felt naive. Maybe Whitacre and Ambrose just ignored the ones who fell by the wayside, and concentrated on the success stories.

'How's Solomon doing?' Ambrose said.

'He's stable,' said Harry. 'Not out of the woods yet, though.'

'Good,' said Ambrose. 'I got the call pretty late on Sunday; I was busy. I tried to go and see him yesterday morning, but I couldn't get in. Too many of you doctors. I said a little prayer, though. Felt like it was the least I could do.'

'You know him?' Harry said.

'Vaguely,' said Ambrose. 'That's the shame about this job. You get to see some of these kids grow up. Every time they're back in A&E, they're a bit taller. First time he came in, he wasn't really interested. He came to a couple of appointments and then just stopped, happens to about half the kids we take on. Then he was back, two years later, this time stabbed. I went to see him on the ward a few times. I told him it wouldn't end well.'

Ambrose shook his head, and Harry could see his distress. The awful state of affairs, when advice became prophecy.

'He was still in hospital when his friends were killed. All three of them, down at that house in Camberwell. After that, he let us in. Accepted our help.'

Ambrose sat back in the taxi, and Harry watched him roll his eyes towards the sky. Probably praying, if the youth worker's previous statements were anything to go by. A cyclist shot past the side of the taxi, prompting a horn blast and a tirade of muted swearing.

'I felt the same when I used to work for the ambulance service,' said Ambrose. 'You don't remember the ones you saved, just the ones you couldn't.'

Harry was fairly sure that depended on your outlook. He remembered a few he'd lost, but a few of the ones he'd helped, too. He wondered which category Solomon Idris would end up falling into.

'We're not sure if what happened on Sunday with Idris was gang-related or not.'

'We?' said Ambrose.

'The police,' said Harry. The pact. Him and Noble. That was the *we*.

'And I guess that's why you're here, and we're doing this,' said Ambrose. 'Duncan didn't really explain it. He says, we do. That's the kind of team we are.'

'Sounds like a good team,' said Harry. 'Sounds like you're doing some good work.'

'Yeah,' said Ambrose. 'Any kid we get out of that life is worth it, you ask me. Don't care how much money we spend. Some of the things they've gone through, so young. Let me ask you, Harry – how many gang members under the age of nineteen d'you think have symptoms of PTSD?'

'Forty per cent?' he said, smiling.

Ambrose laughed.

'Lucky guess,' Harry said.

'You been talking to Duncan?'

'No, James Lahiri. He's an old friend of mine.'

After last night, the word was becoming easier to say.

'Ah, James. He's a good man,' said Ambrose. 'Needs a few more months outside Middle England. No offence to him. That's one of the reasons Duncan has me at all the assemblies. Helps to have someone local up there. Gives us more credibility.'

Harry shrugged. From his experience, people like Solomon Idris didn't trust anybody.

'I guess some of them won't be helped,' said Harry. 'You never win them all.'

'They've got to want to help themselves,' Ambrose said. 'Galatians 6:7. A man reaps what he sows.'

Harry thought about that. He didn't like it much, the idea that because Solomon Idris had chosen a life of violence at one point, maybe he deserved what had happened to him. Harry had had few friends at his secondary school, and wasn't in touch with any of them any more, but during his time in sixth form one or two had ended up in prison, and he didn't feel that they'd been inherently bad kids. No worse than him, or the other two kids in his class of forty who'd made it to university. Idris had made mistakes, of course, he'd stabbed a kid, but that didn't mean he'd brought on what had happened to him. But then Harry thought, if that kid had died, and if it had been his son, or his brother, he might feel like Idris had got what he'd earned.

'We're here,' Ambrose said.

They got out and paid for the cab, Harry hefting both of the boxes as they started towards the school. The Albany Road Academy was an imposing structure: two huge slate-grey mono-liths linked by a series of covered walkways, all standing behind high wire fences. No barbs on the top, but still it looked more like a Scandinavian prison than a school.

'Let me take that off you,' said a voice from behind him. Harry turned and handed one of the boxes to an athletic-looking, red-headed woman in a short skirt and cardigan.

'Cheers,' said Harry. 'You one of the teachers here?'

'No,' the woman said, laughing. 'DC Gardner. I'm with Trident. But today, I'm a youth worker, aren't I?'

She didn't look like a copper, with frizzy red hair that came halfway down her back, which was probably why DS Wilson had sent her. They headed towards the school, where one of the teach-ers was holding the door open. Standing in the door frame was the familiar, patriarchal figure of Duncan Whitacre.

'Hi, Harry.' Whitacre smiled. He'd trimmed the beard from yesterday, but it still covered most of his face.

'Hey. Thank you so much for putting this together at such short notice. Honestly, we really appreciate it.'

He realised he'd said 'we' again without meaning to.

'Not at all,' said Whitacre. 'As I said, anything I can do to help.'

'Well, thanks,' said Harry. They kept talking as they entered the school, the box of materials in Harry's arms an awkward barrier.

'That said,' Whitacre continued, 'I appreciate that you have this agenda, which I totally support, but this is just a normal assembly for us. Many of the kids that we'll speak to today really do need our help, OK? I'd appreciate it if we try to disrupt that as little as possible.'

'Of course.'

'Great,' said Whitacre. 'The assembly hall's through this way. We're on in ten, so let's get ourselves set up.'

The security guards allowed them through the airport-style

metal detectors, the usual wall displays of various projects and subject areas bringing some colour to the building's interior, which Harry hadn't expected from its grey façade. He tried to picture Solomon Idris walking along this corridor. He was assuming that Idris had attended school the previous Friday, two days before he'd walked into the Chicken Hut. The thought sent the cold through his bones.

'You alright there?'

Charlie Ambrose had bumped into the back of him. Everyone was moving at a near-run, frantically setting up.

'Fine,' said Harry. 'Where does this stuff need to go?'

The assembly took about half an hour. Harry watched it leaning against the side of the hall next to Gardner, the undercover cop. Whitacre had the crowd in the palm of his hand, and Harry ventured it was probably the longest that this group of young men and women had ever paid attention to anything at school. He'd started with a video, a clip from a documentary that had been filmed in the Ruskin's A&E department the previous year and shown on Channel 4. It showed the team trying to revive a sixteen-year-old kid who'd been stabbed during a gang fight outside his school. The clip ended with a close-up of the kid's mother falling to her knees and being comforted by two nurses.

After that came the ministry. Whitacre had delivered his sermon with fraught passion, telling the assembled sixth form of the Albany Road Academy that however desperate a situation might seem, there was always a way out. He told them that he understood why they hated the police, because in London, the police were prejudiced against them. When he said that, Harry glanced at DC Gardner, who was nodding and smiling as if she agreed. Maybe she did. He explained how doctors were forbidden from telling the police things in all but exceptional circumstances, and how they could help.

'Violence *is* an illness. *Fear* is an illness. If you live with violence, or you live in fear, speak to us. If you had a chest infection, you'd come and speak to us, because you don't want it to get worse. You don't want to end up in hospital. You don't want to end up like the kid in that video.'

Whitacre seemed to be wrapping up. Harry scanned the faces, each one still attentive. So he was a little surprised when the slide show flicked forward onto a slide entitled 'First Aid on the Streets'.

'If it all goes wrong,' Whitacre said, 'you can save your friends' lives. Or anyone's life.'

He briefly talked about CPR, demonstrating it on a table in front of him. Then he talked about stab wounds and gunshots. How they should roll victims of chest wounds onto their injured sides so the blood would drain away from the good lung. Pressure and elevation to control serious bleeding.

'If you can't stop the bleeding by pushing on it, you need to use a tourniquet,' Whitacre said. 'Dr Kent, would you like to demonstrate?'

Harry tried not to look surprised when he came onto the stage.

'Sure,' he said. He scanned the table for the bright orange fabric of a tourniquet, before he realised that the item he was meant to use was a black canvas belt.

'You can use anything,' Harry said, trying to look at the kids and not appear nervous. 'A belt, a rolled-up shirt.'

Whitacre had stepped aside and extended his right arm towards Harry. Harry smiled at him.

'The important thing is to put the pressure on high up, and pull it tight. As tight as you can.' As he spoke, Harry looped the belt around Whitacre's bicep, pushed it up against his armpit, and fed it through the buckle. Whitacre gave a taciturn nod, still smirking, and Harry pulled the belt tight. Whitacre swore under his breath, the kids all laughed, and Harry noticed the head of sixth form at the back of the hall, shaking his head, while the other teachers smiled.

'Any questions?' said Whitacre, shaking the belt off his arm.

A hand at the back of the room, a sunken, heavyset figure. Two seats away from the boy Harry recognised as Shaquille Dawson.

'So where's the safest place to stab someone?'

A few laughs from the kids, the head of sixth form shaking his head again. Harry grinned, first thinking the teenager who'd asked had been joking, before he realised that he hadn't been. Whitacre's face was stony serious.

'There is none. If you stab or shoot someone, they're probably dead. Full stop. Arm, leg, chest, head. Makes no difference.' Whitacre raised his voice a little. 'If you make that choice, then it's their life over, and your life over, too. Murder. That's how the police see it and that's how we see it too.'

The words brought a reverent silence over the hall, which the head of sixth form broke by coming to the front and dividing the kids into groups for the one-to-one sessions. There were about fifty pupils, twelve each with Whitacre, Ambrose and two other youth workers who'd joined them for the assembly. Shaquille Dawson would be the last student in Gardner's group, and she would step outside and allow Harry to speak to him.

Harry sat in with Whitacre for the first few. Almost all of the kids had some experience of gang life, either as victims or perpetrators, or had some friends who'd been involved. A few spoke about their fear of getting caught up in it. A Year 10 student had been killed the previous September, beaten to death in Burgess Park, just opposite the school, and a lot talked about that. How the boy had just been a normal kid in the wrong place at the wrong time, not someone they'd expect to be involved. More railed against the police for shooting Solomon Idris.

Towards the end of the session, Harry sat in with Gardner, After she finished talking to the penultimate student, she got up and passed him a small black phone handset with a red button on it. He recognised it immediately. A panic button. Harry nodded, smiled, and took a seat. There were piles of leaflets from the Saviour Project spread out all over the table. *Finding Work in London. Opportunities in Sport. Choose a Different Ending. Breaking the Circle of Violence.*

Shaquille Dawson came in, his school jumper completely ripped away beneath both armpits, his tie hanging around the level of his breastbone. He had two square zirconia earrings in his right ear, and a long scar that started at the angle of his jaw and ran down his neck, disappearing beneath his collar. It must have been a superficial wound, Harry thought, or he'd have bled to death.

'Hi, there,' said Harry.

'S'up.'

Dawson sat down, the restless look of a bored teenager.

'Who're you?'

'I'm Harry Kent. I'm one of the Saviour Project doctors.'

Dawson shook his head.

'Allow this, i's a waste of time. I'm already with Saviour Project. I see Dr Lisa.'

'Oh?' said Harry, pretending he was surprised. 'How long you been with us, Shaquille?'

'Shaq,' Dawson said. He was politer than a lot of the teenagers Harry had seen so far. Looked him in the eye, at least. 'Two years. Since I got shanked.'

Dawson pointed to the scar on his neck.

'I was in hospital for two weeks, yeah? The docs told my mum it was fifty-fifty.'

'You were in a gang?'

'Not any more,' said Dawson. 'Look, allow this. Like I say, yeah, I already see Dr Lisa for this shit. I'm stayin' outta trouble. Aks Dr Duncan if you don't believe me.'

'I believe you,' said Harry. Then he took a deep breath, searching for the words to open up the line of conversation he needed. The worst he could do was freak the kid out, scare him off. And maybe lose the only chance we have to talk to someone who actually knew Idris, Harry told himself.

'I wanna talk to you about something,' Harry said. 'One of my patients is Solomon Idris. You know him, right?'

Dawson's expression hardened, and he gripped the arms of the chair hard enough to make his knuckles go white.

'Yeah, he's fam.'

'You know what happened to him, yeah?'

'Feds gone done him. Motherfuckers.'

'Do you know why Sol did that?' Harry said. 'Why he took that gun out?'

'Fuck knows,' said Dawson, the front giving way, moving towards upset. Tears. 'Man's off himself last few months, barely even talked to me. Like he was depressed or some shit. Maybe his doctor should'a keeped a better eye on him.'

Dawson fixed Harry with an accusatory glare. Look at James Lahiri like that, not me, Harry wanted to say.

'Depressed about what?' said Harry. 'Keisha?'

'Course about Keisha, da fuck you think?' said Dawson.

Harry wanted to ask about the HIV, but he couldn't let slip that Idris was positive if Dawson didn't know.

'Do you know if he has any medical problems?'

'Nah,' said Dawson. 'E's not been right, though. He's wasted, I don't think he's been eatin'.'

That fitted, the weight loss. Harry took another mental time-out. He had Dawson talking, and there was no reason to suggest that he didn't believe that Harry had been Idris's GP. That might change, of course, as his questions drifted.

'How was he with Keisha, before she died? Were they OK?'

Dawson shrugged his shoulders.

'They was fucked up. He kept saying they was gonna get away, move some place outta London.'

'Get away from what?' Harry said. 'What happened with her and Martin Santos?'

'Nah, he was over that. That was one time, one'a those fucks spiked her drink, innit. Or that's what she said, anyways.'

'But he still wanted to move away,' Harry said. 'And that's why he needed money?'

Dawson looked confused now.

'You po-lice?'

'No,' said Harry. 'The police don't give a shit. But I want to know who's trying to kill him. I want to protect him. Can you help me?'

Dawson said nothing.

'You know that someone tried to kill Sol, don't you? Somebody fired a gun behind the Chicken Hut. To get the police to shoot him.'

Dawson shook his head and pulled his bag over his shoulder, moving to stand up.

'Fuck this shit.'

'I know someone was giving him money,' Harry went on. 'Do you know where he was getting it from?'

Dawson's face changed, and Harry knew that he knew about the money. More, that he was surprised that Harry knew. Perhaps he'd figured out that only the police could have got that information. Dawson slid back into the chair, his left hand scratching at the long scar on his neck.

'What you tell me won't go to the police,' said Harry. 'I just need to know.'

Maybe it wasn't that much of a lie. The Medical Defence Union could fight that if it went to the GMC. He could break confidentiality if someone was at risk of immediate harm, and he could claim that with regard to Solomon Idris.

'Please, Shaq,' said Harry. 'You've got to help me. I don't care where that money came from, if he was back involved with the crew or whatever, I just—'

'He wasn't,' Dawson said, quietly.

'Sorry?'

'He wasn't back hanging with Wooly,' said Dawson. 'None of us are. Not after what happened to Burke.'

Dawson's cousin, Harry remembered. Beaten to death with the others at the house party in Camberwell. The reason both of them had gone straight. He opened his mouth to speak again, before Dawson cut him off.

'Sol was gettin cash off of someone,' he said. 'All he told me was it was peak, he knew some loaded doctor who was sortin' him out with grass. That's what Sol said.'

Harry's stomach began to clench. This was it. This was what they needed. Blackmail was one hell of a motive. A doctor who was supplying him with cannabis. Enough to get that doctor struck off.

'That still doesn't explain why he walked into that place with a gun,' said Harry.

Dawson stood up, and Harry's muscles tensed, as if expecting an attack. But then Dawson calmed, turned around, reached into his Nike sports bag, and pulled out a USB flash drive, branded with the Albany Road Academy's name and logo. He threw it onto the table.

'Sol gave me that,' Dawson said. 'Said if he got done, give it to the feds.'

'Why didn't you?' said Harry.

'Cos it was the feds what done him, innit?'

Harry nodded. Stared down at the USB stick. Maybe this was everything.

'What's on it?' he said.

Dawson shrugged.

'Dunno,' he said. 'Password.'

'Thanks for this,' said Harry. 'And you've got no idea who was giving him the money?'

'I got ideas,' said Dawson.

'Do you want to share those with me?'

Dawson shook his head.

'I said enough,' the teenager said, heading for the door. 'I ain't no snitch.'

'Shaq!'

Dawson turned around, one hand curled around the door handle, and Harry got up, realising how desperate he must look.

'Keisha's baby,' Harry said, whispering. 'Was it Solomon's?'

'Don't know nuffin bout no baby,' Dawson said, before his eyes widened as he appreciated what Harry had told him. 'Fuck.'

The teenager walked out, his bag over his shoulder, and Harry watched him go, thinking about the scar on his neck. He looked down at the USB stick on the desk in front of him, filled with a nervous excitement. Briefly wondered whether he should have recorded the conversation, but that would have been totally wrong without Dawson's consent, which he'd never have got without losing what little trust he had. Once Harry was sure Dawson would be gone, he got up and started looking for Gardner.

He found Whitacre first.

'How'd it go?'

'Good,' said Harry. 'I think we're onto something. Did you see Hannah?'

'She went out to see her colleague,' said Whitacre. 'He's parked out on Mina Road, the other side of the school.'

'Do you mind if I pop out to see them?' Harry said.

'Go ahead,' Whitacre said, grinning. 'You want to follow this corridor to its end, go across the playground, then get one of the teachers to let you out the back gate. It'll be shut now. They only keep it open for ten minutes at the end of the day.'

'Cheers,' said Harry. 'And thanks again for all your help. I owe you a beer some time.'

Whitacre's humourless face again.

'No, you don't.' But then the stare broke into a smile: 'Though I won't say no.'

Harry turned and headed for the exit, locating it after about a minute, and found himself in the playground in the middle of an after-school sports club – about sixty kids, maybe thirteen or fourteen years old, throwing basketballs towards each other. The playground had four hoops, and there were about ten kids around each one, trying to shoot. More often than not two of the balls collided in mid-flight. Harry could make out just two teachers, in high-visibility tabards, trying to keep order. Again, he was reminded of his own schooldays, fifty kids on a square of asphalt half the size of a tennis court, chasing a single football, more often fighting than playing.

He decided to do a lap of the playground, spotting that one of the teachers was by the gate anyway. As he reached a corner, he saw Junior Idris in an Arsenal shirt, dribbling away from two of his schoolmates, both of whom were body-checking him, trying to dispossess him in any way they could. One of them succeeded, and the ball bounced along the ground, coming to a rest at Harry's feet. Harry stopped it and looked up. Junior was standing right in front of him, If he recognised Harry, then he didn't show it.

'Ball.'

Said with no emotion. Harry was struck again by the family resemblance, and kept his foot on the ball, waiting for Junior to approach.

Once he did, Harry said, 'How are you, Junior? You remember me?'

'Don't talk to feds,' Junior said, the same venom in his voice. 'I don't talk to po-lice.'

'I'm not police,' Harry said. 'We talked at the hospital. I'm one of the doctors treating your brother.'

Junior looked behind him and feinted forward. The kids he'd been playing with had formed a line underneath one of the hoops, arms folded, shoulder to shoulder, all eyes fixed on their friend and the unknown man with his foot on the basketball.

'Don't talk to doctors, neither,' Junior Idris said. 'They's just as bad. Sol said they's worse.'

Those words made Harry's chest burn, and he rolled the basketball back to him. Junior picked it up, but kept looking at Harry, until one of his mates broke the line, ran forward and grabbed it from his hands.

'Excuse me!'

Harry turned to find a burly PE teacher in an off-white tracksuit, one hand on his phone, evidently suspicious of the stranger who'd wandered into his class. Harry showed his ID, explained he was one of the Saviour Project doctors, and the teacher walked him to the gate. He was starting to realise that lying got easy once you believed it yourself.

Wilson and Gardner were parked up on the road, far enough out of sight that they wouldn't seem suspicious. It was one of the Met's unmarked fleet that was deliberately poorly maintained in order to fit in around places like the Old Kent Road, an old BMW 1-series with peeling paint and a smashed brake light. Harry knocked on the windscreen, disturbing Gardner from the emails on her phone and Wilson from the psychology textbook he was reading. Wilson reached back and opened the back door, and once Harry was inside, he pulled out and started heading south.

'How'd it go?' Wilson said.

'Good,' Harry said. 'Idris was blackmailing someone for the money. Dawson doesn't know who. All he knows was that Idris said there was a rich doctor who was giving him grass. Those exact words.'

'Well, shit me,' said Wilson. 'That it?'

'No,' said Harry, trying not to sound proud. 'Idris gave this to him. Just in case anything happened.'

Gardner turned around, and Harry dropped the USB into her waiting hand.

'Jesus,' she said.

'Let's get that up to the station right now,' said Wilson. 'If we can't open it there we'll courier it down to Technical. Christ, that's mental. That's great work, Doc.'

Harry didn't know what to say. He was thinking about the look in Junior Idris's eyes and the scar running down Shaq Dawson's neck.

'You want us to drop you home?'

'Sure,' said Harry. He was drumming his fingers on his thigh. This was progress. This was good.

They got onto the Walworth Road and Harry felt the car rattle as Wilson put his foot down.

'Good job, Dr Kent,' Gardner said. 'Bloody good job.'

Wilson dropped him off outside his apartment block and walked him to his door in silence. Harry guessed that Noble had told him about the events of yesterday evening. They'd gone via Walworth station, where Gardner had gotten out of the car with the USB. Wilson had said that the Technical Services Unit for the South London region was all the way down in Sutton, so they'd have to organise a courier. Noble had to sign off on the funding. Best-case scenario, they'd know what was on it by the following morning.

Harry thought about that as he rode up in the lift. How the information wasn't the important thing. It was all about how the individual pieces of fact interacted. Solomon Idris was getting money off a doctor, possibly something to do with the supply of cannabis and whoever was willing to pay to keep that information quiet. Harry wondered how many doctors Idris knew. He wandered through his kitchen, putting on the kettle, running a hand through his hair. Thinking about James, and the way they'd spoken together the night before. Not mended yet by any means, but going in the right direction. Two lonely men who'd been through so much together.

Harry scolded himself after thinking that. It would be easy, wouldn't it, if it turned out that Lahiri had been paying Idris off. He'd often tried to do this, search for flaws in his friend, as if it justified what he'd done. But even then, a bit of weed seemed too little to kill someone over.

The kettle clicked but Harry ignored it. Looked at the bottle of Jameson's on the coffee table and then the clock on the wall. Sat looking out of the window for about ten minutes before he pulled a tumbler from the kitchen cupboard and picked up the bottle, then the phone. Got the Marigold House switchboard and dialled the extension for Tammas's room.

'Afternoon.'

Tammas sounded well, like he sometimes did after a good physio session, which were necessary to stop his muscles wasting.

'Boss,' said Harry. 'How's it going?'

'As ever. So you're. Alive, then?'

'I'm alive,' said Harry.

'Only. Last night. One minute. We're. Talking and then. The next the. Line just. Goes.'

Harry had completely forgotten. He'd been talking to Tammas, when the deliveryman had attacked him.

'Sorry about that,' said Harry.

'What happened? The. Battery just die?'

Harry said nothing, and drank whiskey as Tammas's ventilator cycled. Tammas liked the stuff, so now and then Harry brought a bottle of a nice single malt down, and one of the nurses would let him drink it through a straw. Tammas's brother was a naval lieutenant and his parents still lived in his native Dumfries, and the mother was getting old. Osteoarthritis, and now a stroke as well, so the family visits were few and far between.

'A man attacked me,' said Harry.

Tammas made a noise that was somewhere close to the word 'no', and Harry thought he could hear the tube rubbing against Tammas's neck, the kind of noise that would be made if he was shaking his head. That was one of the few movements still intact.

'Harry. I warned. You.'

'Boss, he tried to warn me off this kid. They wouldn't do that unless there was something going on. Something serious. Whoever's behind this has tried to kill him. Twice. And they'll do it again.'

'Well the. Police. Will protect. Him. That's their. Job.'

'I know, but I need to—'

'Harry!'

It was the loudest that Harry had heard Tammas's voice in a long while, and from the tone he knew that Tammas had come close to calling him 'Lieutenant'. He said nothing and waited for the rebuke to come.

'You're. Getting obsessed. With something. That doesn't. Concern you,' Tammas said. 'It's just. Like the girl. With the pink. Hair. All over again.'

Harry sat back in his chair and wanted to spit and shout, but resisted. Maybe it was a little bit like Zara, but that was because she and Solomon Idris had one thing in common – they were two human beings who had slipped through the cracks in society, two people who the rest of the world had decided didn't matter. And Harry had to fight for them, because if he didn't, then nobody would.

'And I'll. Tell you why.' Tammas continued, 'You. Speak to James. You're. Close to. Admitting. What you did. And. Worse than that. He's close. To. Forgiving you. And you. Can't deal. With that. You stubborn. Bastard. So you're. Going to run. Like you. Always do. Go and. Care about. A stranger who. Has nobody. Because you can't face. Caring for. Someone you love.'

Harry let those words echo around his mind and wondered how true they were. Ten cycles passed before he spoke.

'Speak,' said Tammas.

Harry took a deep breath and finished off the whiskey.

'We know that Solomon was blackmailing a doctor. Something involving drugs, apparently. Lahiri was his GP.'

'It would. Be quite. Like him. To try and. Solve. A problem by throwing. Money at it.'

Harry said nothing. There was a lot of distance, though, between paying someone money and trying to get them killed. He felt a buzzing in his chest, a pain in that place. Lahiri had been in A&E; he couldn't have fired a gun behind Wyndham Road. It couldn't have been him there. But he'd been in A&E, so he could have been the one who changed the medical record. It had been done at 7.20, and the shifts changed at eight. Christ, he thought. Jesus Christ. Lahiri had been cagey the previous night, like there'd been something he'd been holding back.

'You're. Thinking, Harry. Aren't you?' Tammas said after a minute or so of silence. 'It's always. Dangerous. When you're thinking.'

Harry couldn't help it.

'Not the time, Boss.'

'Just. Pretend you're. In medical school. Again. And think of. Horses. Not of. Zebras. Make the right. Calls. I always. Trusted. You to. Do that.'

Tammas hung up. The old, clichéd aphorism, imploring doctors to consider common diagnoses ahead of rare, unusual ones. But the horse in this case didn't feel right. He just needed to wait, to find something to occupy his time while the police did their work. Soon, they'd know what secret Idris had almost died for. And Noble's people running through the IT system at the Ruskin would find out who'd deleted the allergy. And then they'd unleash hell on them. They'd get a result on this, they wouldn't give up, not like they had with the girl.

Tammas's warning had been right, he realised. Lahiri had taunted him about it, too, on the boat. *The whole hospital talks about Dr Kent's little obsession.* He'd just brushed that off, but somehow hearing it from Tammas made him think a little more. At the start, when the police started losing interest, he'd been making phone calls every day to various departments and detectives, with little yield. Then he'd got in touch with missing-persons charities, newspapers, websites. The *Standard* had run a little feature about it, but the rest of the nationals, and the TV networks, were only interested if they had police cooperation. And the police wouldn't fund a media campaign over a case that had such a minuscule chance of being solved.

Now, he took a less concerted approach. Taking the job with the police had been a good decision – every now and then there was the odd promised favour, or a midnight coffee shared with some detective he would try and interest. But so far he'd had the same chorus of shrugged shoulders. *It's London, mate. People vanish all the time.* Hopefully, when all this was over, and the person who had tried to get Idris killed was behind bars, he could buy Frankie Noble a drink and persuade her to take up Zara's case.

She was someone's daughter, and presumably she'd disappeared from their life. Maybe she'd been gone already, so they didn't notice. These thoughts, and many others, had gone through his head a million times already.

Tammas had once asked him why he didn't just leave everything, move on. He hoped it was a stubborn, self-righteous refusal to be another person who just gave up. He didn't like to consider the fact that it was because he had nothing else to move on to. Apart from a career that was going nowhere, and a membership form for a dating website waiting in his inbox.

Harry didn't think about Tammas's words again. He needed to think about something else. The winter sun was coming in low through the living-room window, his view of the city obliterated by its light. He tried turning on the TV. Reading one of the research journals he tried to keep up with. None of that worked, so he went to the kitchen and decided he'd try cooking something, even though he wasn't hungry. Put some tomatoes in a saucepan and reboiled the kettle. There was pasta in a cupboard, and some sausages in the fridge.

Maybe Tammas was right. He'd got too involved, forgotten that he was meant to be a doctor, and that his duty of care was to his patients, not to the police, not to anyone else. He thought about Solomon Idris again. The fragile, emaciated figure, sitting in the yellow light of a chicken shop. The hard look in his bloodshot eyes still struck Harry to the core. He walked back into the living room, picked up the tumbler and the whiskey bottle on the way. When he got there, his phone was vibrating against the glass table.

Lahiri.

'Hello?' Harry said. For some reason he was already nervous.

'Harry, where are you?'

He stood rooted to the spot, aware his heart was racing. There was an alien timbre to Lahiri's voice, one Harry couldn't quite figure out.

'My flat.'

'You wouldn't mind coming over, would you?' said Lahiri. 'I think we'd better talk.'

'What about?'

'Solomon. I wasn't completely honest with you last night.'

Harry ran out of the living room with the phone still pressed to his ear, searching for his keys. He'd worked out what was bothering him about Lahiri's voice, the emotion he'd never heard in his friend before. Lahiri was scared.

'I'm on my way,' he said.

He got his coat on and headed out at a run, the door slamming behind him.

He pushed the car fast through the rain and the rush-hour traffic, using back roads to avoid the big roundabouts. If he got pulled over, he could always try the doctor-on-call line. He was trying not to think about the tone of Lahiri's voice – it was the kind of voice junior doctors used when they were calling him up about patients they thought were about to crash. The voice of men on the edge.

He checked his watch as he moved down Greenland Road. He was a minute away, not far at all. He tried not to think about Tammas's words, about his thoughts. Tried just to concentrate on the road. A light ahead turned amber and Harry sped up to catch it, only for a cyclist to change lanes and brake, forcing him to stop. The deceleration threw him forward in his seat, and he was about to swear when he felt his phone vibrating against his thigh.

To his surprise, it wasn't Lahiri.

'Frankie, I can't talk now, I'm driving.'

'Yes, you can,' said Noble. 'Pull over.'

He swerved left and pulled up against the side of the road. Kept the engine running. His heart was racing. Noble sounded agitated, too. Shouting in the background, like she was outside.

'What is it?'

'I need James Lahiri's address.'

'Why?'

'We audited all the accounts of people working in the East Wing on Monday morning. It was Lahiri's log-in which made the change. He deleted the penicillin allergy, Harry.'

Harry balled his right hand into a fist and slammed it down on the dashboard, feeling the whole seat shake.

'Are you sure?'

'Look, I don't want to get into—'

'Are you sure, Frankie?'

'It's all there in black and white. I'm sorry. Technical Services got the data and we've got a warrant for his arrest. We're at the address the Ruskin had on file for him, the one in Dulwich Village, and there's some Russian family living here now. They say they moved in last October.'

Harry scrunched his eyes closed. Maybe the world would vanish. All he saw was Solomon Idris. The thin, hopeless figure, sitting in the yellow light of a restaurant. And then his body jerking in the ICU as Harry shocked his heart.

'The fucking bastard!'

'The address, Harry.'

Tightness spreading through his chest, his head sore like he'd just taken three amphetamines instead of his normal two.

'He lives on a boat. South Dock Marina, Surrey Quays. It's called the *Time and Tide*. Berth twenty-nine.'

'OK,' said Noble. Harry heard her shout to whoever else was there. 'Surrey Quays! Let's move!'

He waited for her to move the phone back to her ear. Heard the clicks of car doors closing and the background noise disappear.

'Frankie?'

'What?'

'I'm on my way there. To Lahiri's.'

'What? Why?'

'He called me,' Harry said. 'Fifteen minutes ago. Said we needed to talk.'

'Shit,' Noble said. 'You don't need me to tell you, Harry, that if you warn Lahiri we're coming for him, I'll throw your arse in prison for obstructing an investigation. Is that absolutely clear?'

'Yes.'

'Keep him on the boat,' said Noble. 'Preferably inside. I'll see you in a bit.'

Harry hung up and threw the phone to one side. It bounced off the passenger seat and landed in the footwell, and he swerved out into the traffic and earned himself a horn blast and a torrent of verbal abuse from the Honda he'd cut up.

The road ahead was fairly clear for evening rush hour. Lahiri's old house in Dulwich was a fair way south, probably half an hour's drive. Maybe less if they used lights and sirens.

He wondered why he was angry, why he was even surprised. On reflection, he should have known the moment Shaq Dawson had said the word 'doctor'. Lahiri was the man with the secret. Solomon Idris had found out. And when the money wasn't enough to keep him quiet, he had to die. Harry just prayed Lahiri was naive, out of his depth, that he hadn't realised what he was getting into. That could be forgiven, if not excused.

The light ahead turned amber again. Harry put his foot to the floor.

Outside, the air felt heavy with rain, the twilight full of clouds as Harry parked his car by the marina's entrance. It was almost dark.

Behind the security fence, the boats had their lights on, projecting silhouettes of masts and beams onto the old dock walls at one side of the quay. The same harbour watchman was there, the same book open. *Chapter Five: British History.* He smiled in recognition. Opened the gate, waving.

Harry ran on. Turn left, second jetty on the right. Berth twenty-nine. It was high tide, and a sixty-foot Fairline with a Norwegian flag was manoeuvring out towards the river, the sound enough to disguise his footsteps as he approached the boat.

The *Time and Tide* pitched and rolled in front of him, the lights in the cabin dim. Harry grabbed hold of one of the mooring lines and swung himself forward, trying to land on the mooring rig and not the deck so as not to rock the boat and give away his presence. As he landed, the yacht blasted its foghorn. The fear inside Harry broke through its containment, and he swore under his breath. Inside, Lahiri had a TV programme on, loud; Harry could hear some muttered debate, the odd burst of canned laughter. He advanced along the port side of the boat, heading for the aft deck, where he'd stood and watched his friend smoke just the other night.

What had Lahiri done after he'd gone? Ordered his friend, his colleague, to attack Harry? Texted him his address, and opened another bottle of sauvignon blanc?

He reached the deck and tried to arch his head to look through the French doors. Lahiri was on the sofa, a steak dinner on his lap, a glass of wine on the table next to him. Red this time.

Harry vaulted around the corner and kicked the glass.

Not hard enough to break it, but the vibration reverberated through the entire boat, and Lahiri jumped up, the plate smashing to the floor, his mouth open in shock. Harry grabbed the door and pulled it open, the glass shaking as he slid it away. As he stepped into the light Lahiri charged forward, fists up and ready. He stopped about two feet shy, the look on his face a mixture of bewilderment and recognition.

'Harry, what the hell?'

Harry threw his punch, which was a good one. His first two knuckles hit the angle of Lahiri's jaw just as he was coming forward, so he was off balance, his weight forward, and the momentum sent him down. Onto the floor, his hands coming up to his face. Then he was back on his feet and charging at Harry, but Harry was expecting it and went with the tackle, running backwards and gripping Lahiri's shirt with tight fists, rolling him out of the door and onto the deck. He brought a leg up to lever Lahiri's weight to one side, swinging him around until his back hit the rail at the boat's stern.

He had him. He pushed him back over the rail until his feet started coming off the ground, and his head was arched over. Cold bullets of rain pounded down on his head and shoulders.

'Why the fuck did you do it, James?'

Harry punched him again.

'Tell me what's going on, or I swear to God, I'll kill you.'

'Harry, listen, please, just—'

Harry twisted his leg and flipped Lahiri so that he was face down, the rail digging into his friend's abdomen, both their faces staring down into the black water. The rain was coming quicker now, individual plops landing in the water in front of them. Harry had one hand on Lahiri's shoulder, pushing him down, the other digging into the back of his neck.

'First-year anatomy,' Harry said. 'You remember the atlas, this thin piece of bone around your brainstem? All I have to do is squeeze, mate, and if you're lucky, you die. If you're not, you end up as a vegetable and your only glory in this world is as a case study for ethics lectures. Now I want the truth, alright?'

Harry pulled Lahiri up by the collar and threw him against the half-open French doors, fracturing the glass into a kaleido-scope of cracks. Lahiri sat up against the window, wiping blood from the corner of his mouth. He was down. Harry stood on the deck, leaning back against the rail, let the rain come down on him, and waited.

'We gave him the money,' Lahiri sobbed. 'That's all.'

'How much?'

'Ten thousand. At Christmas.'

'That all?'

'Yes!'

'Two hundred and fifty a week, as well?' said Harry.

Lahiri shook his head.

'What was the money for?' Harry spat. 'To keep him quiet about the drugs?'

Lahiri looked up at Harry, the only committed movement he'd made so far. The rain was pounding onto the deck now, so they had to raise their voices, but Harry didn't feel the cold. He could feel the sweat under his arms, on his face. Lahiri's face was sallow, defeated, with the expression of horror you get when you realise someone else knows something they were never meant to. An expression of abject failure.

'Shit,' Lahiri whispered.

'The police are on their way,' Harry said. 'They're coming for you, and believe me they are gonna rip you apart when they get here. I mean, you'll get a great lawyer, I'm sure, but they will nail you to the fucking wall. So talk.'

'Police?' Lahiri squealed. 'Why?'

'Because they audited your log-in at the Ruskin, that's why. They know what you did. They know you deleted that allergy.'

'What?'

Lahiri tried to stand up.

'Look, Harry, that's a mistake!' he pleaded. 'I never deleted any—'

Harry charged forward, swung Lahiri around so that he bounced back off the rail and fell onto the deck. Through the rain, he saw two joggers in high-visibility jackets stretching on the other side of the marina, unaware of the men fighting a few metres away from them.

'Bullshit,' he said. 'The police know. Your log-in made the change. How the fuck could you, mate? What was it, you too much of a pussy to go and actually kill him?'

Lahiri shrugged. 'Well, the police are wrong, then. I'm being set up.'

'I've got no idea if I believe you, James. You know that, right?'

'Come on, you stupid prick! I know you're nowhere close to the friend I thought you were, but do you really think I'd try to kill someone?'

'You've killed people before!' Harry spat. 'And I'm sure that pressing a few keys on a computer's a lot fucking easier than slotting some Taliban bastard.'

'Shut the fuck up, Harry!' Lahiri shouted, tears in his eyes again. 'I didn't try to kill Solomon, OK? Christ!'

Harry rested back against the railing of the boat. Lahiri slid down the cracked door, running a hand through his drenched hair.

A faint siren in the distance. Noble and the cavalry, the entire Metropolitan Police Service, so it seemed, descending on one boat. The studious watchman at the front gate had no idea what was about to hit him.

'You called me here,' Harry said. The rain rattled against the boat and Lahiri scrabbled to his feet. 'Now tell me why. I reckon you've got two minutes.'

Lahiri nodded, pulled a wet cigarette out from his shirt pocket and tried vainly to light it.

'There was a bit of a scandal at the Saviour Project,' he said. 'We prescribed small amounts of recreational drugs to patients who used regularly, while they were trying to cut down. Only weed. It was to stop them having to buy from dealers, who were usually people from their old gangs. Obviously we kept it quiet, but somebody threatened to tell the press.'

'Idris?'

Lahiri nodded. GPs prescribing cannabis to teenagers, Harry thought. The whole of the Saviour Project's model was alternative by its nature, but that was more left-field than anything he'd encountered before. The kind of thing an editor at the *Daily Mail* would have a wet dream over.

'Is that what you didn't tell me yesterday?' Harry said. 'That you paid Idris off to keep him quiet?'

'No,' Lahiri said. 'He needed the money so he could move to Nottingham and start a new life. That's what he told me. I said no, and then he pulled out his threat. Fucking clever for a seventeen-year-old kid, but there you go. I went straight to Whitacre, and he said he'd sort it. Next thing I know Idris had a job and an income, and I didn't ask any more questions.'

'Why didn't you tell me yesterday?'

Rain harder still. Cold and unrelenting. Lahiri finally managed to light his cigarette.

'You fucked my wife, Harry. You'll forgive me for not opening up. A detective rang up the practice this afternoon, asked if he could make an appointment. So it looks like it's all going to come out now, and I'd rather have you on my side.'

We'll see about that, Harry thought. That might have been possible initially, but after finding out about the log-in, all bets were off.

'Why didn't you tell the police before?'

'They haven't interviewed me,' Lahiri said.

Harry stared at his friend, smoking in his Barbour jacket, and wondered when everything had changed. At what moment he'd stopped implicitly believing everything that came out of Lahiri's mouth. Even before Noble had called, he'd been suspicious. The sirens grew louder, and Lahiri stood up and came up to him at the railing, pressing his face into Harry's.

'I didn't delete that allergy,' he said. 'You believe me, don't you?'

'I'm not sure if I do.'

Internally, Harry was taking every single one of Lahiri's sentences apart, searching it for contradictions, assessing whether the passion in his denial was legitimate.

'There's more,' Lahiri said. 'I think Idris was involved in something else. I'm not sure what.'

'Tell me.'

Lahiri's eyes were red and wet now. He opened his mouth to speak, but the noise came first. A sound like a door slamming. Harry felt the tunnel in the air, and followed it with his eyes, fixing on the hole in the yacht's superstructure, about two inches from Lahiri's head. Next came sharp pain across the side of his face. That instant could have lasted for an hour, paralysed in time, and he wouldn't have known any different. Harry watched water fall down the drenched hair on Lahiri's forehead as his pupils dilated.

The second shot sent them both down. Harry rolled onto his back, felt a spray of something wet hit his face. Warm, much warmer than January rain. When he rolled back, Lahiri wasn't there. He'd fallen forward, his figure bent against the railing.

'JAMES!'

Then Harry was scrabbling. The third shot landed somewhere above him as he crawled across the aft deck, keeping close to the windows with the cracked glass. The shooter had to be on the jetty. It was the only place he could be, because the shots were loud enough to make out despite the rain. Harry kept on, around the starboard ladder, and edged against the short deck on the starboard side. It was about twelve inches wide. He spread-eagled himself against the hull, as flat as he could.

How long did it take to drive from Dulwich to Surrey Quays? Harry listened out for the sirens, but they were gone.

Then the pain in his chest came, starting behind his sternum, expanding to fill his chest, exploding out of his side. He closed his eyes. Tammas lay beside him, blood pooling underneath his head. The sky had turned purple. Harry was breathing twice per second now, and the world was starting to fade. He tapped his face and his neck and his chest, furiously. He hadn't been hit. He scrabbled at his belt for his sidearm. Man down, man down.

He had to get to him. Engage the threat, return fire, and reach the man. Reach James.

Fuck, fuck, fuck.

The boat rocked. The shooter had come aboard. He could feel the movement with each step, and the shooter took about four, then stopped. Probably to step over Lahiri. Harry closed his eyes and prayed that he didn't hear the *coup de grâce*, the point-blank shot into Lahiri's skull that would send him into the eternal dark. It didn't come. Harry considered his options. He could keep shimmying along the starboard-side deck until he reached the bow, clamber over it. Jump onto the jetty and run for land, but that was ten metres, he'd make noise, and abandon Lahiri. That was out. He could go back towards the aft deck, where the shooter was, and fight him. He looked around, searching for anything he could use as a weapon. Nothing. He looked down.

There was a ladder, back and to his right, leading from the deck down into the black water. The steps resumed, louder and quicker, moving towards him. He had to get back to Lahiri, had to get pressure on the wound, get him treated.

Harry inhaled deeply, closed his eyes again. Made his decision, and moved.

Hang the fuck in there, James, I'm on my way.

He made it in two strides, the first to the head of the ladder, the other swinging his body backwards, his hands gripping cold steel, holding on by instinct. Slowly, he let himself slide down. First his feet, then his legs went down into the water, the pain coming in brutal waves, and he bit hard on his lip to stop himself crying out. He heard the footsteps come closer and descended, the water up to his chest now, his legs floating free. Hands slipping down to the bottom of the ladder. A figure coming to the starboard side, above him.

Harry took one last silent breath and sank under the freezing water, his eyes scrunched shut, every fibre of exposed skin screaming. He knew that he could stay underwater for eighty-four seconds, but that had been in a swimming pool at Sandhurst, nine years ago. This was at four degrees in the Thames. The urge to breathe burned in him, like an addiction, a voice in his head tempting him to come up to the light, break water, drink the winter air. He felt the ladder shake as the man came closer.

He exhaled underwater and watched the bubbles rise to the surface. A keen-eyed gunman would spot that, he realised too late. He closed his eyes and waited for the bullets to come, cutting through the water, filling his lungs with blood. He could drown twice for his trouble.

He'd talked and thought about this lots of times. What happened at the end, whether life would flash past in front of him, what he would see as the blackness came. Now he wondered if what he'd always known had been confirmed: that there was nothing. Nothing to think about, no one to treasure the sight of in his last moments. Just an image, burned into his retinas. Not of family, or a lover, but a friend, folded over on the deck of his boat, bleeding out into the varnished teak.

In the dark water, Harry made his choice. As soon as the gunman moved, he would go up the ladder and rush him, and get to Lahiri. Even if it meant a bullet in the chest. He saw the purple sky, and knew again that he had been saved by the man who lay wounded above him.

The ladder rattled and the whole boat shook. Fast steps. The gunman, running. Harry broke the surface with just his nose and mouth, his head still below the water, and took in one huge gasp, a painful rush of frigid air filling his lungs. He willed frozen hands and feet to bring him up the ladder. There was noise now, shouting. The boat jerking and moving. Harry made it to the top. Pulled himself over onto the side deck, slipped and almost fell again.

I'm here, James, I'm coming. It's alright.

He thought he could see a beam of light, refracting through the glass windows of the boat's cabin.

'Is everything alright?'

Harry recognised the voice, the Slavic inflections of the watchman.

'Hey!'

The swearword that followed was in a language Harry didn't recognise, and it was cut off by the gunshot that followed it. The beam of light swung away and disappeared, the torch smashing as it hit the ground. Sounds of feet running down the jetty. Harry kept crawling towards the deck, but it was hard, every reach a battle. There was no pain from the cold any more, just numbness. He made it to the corner of the deck and kept going. If the gunman was still there, then fuck it. James Lahiri hadn't worried about his own life when Harry had been down, bleeding into the dust with two collapsed lungs. He looked up once as he pulled himself to his feet. The gunman was gone, the watchman lying on the jetty, clutching his thigh, screaming.

Harry was up now, scrambling towards Lahiri, still motionless against the aft railing.

'It's alright, James,' he said through machine-gun breaths. Knelt at Lahiri's side, grabbed the collar of Lahiri's shirt, and unfolded him, slamming his torso down onto the decking, his numb hands searching the chest for the bullet wound. It wasn't there.

'James, it's me, talk to me!'

Harry's eyes trailed up, the pressure in his chest unbearable, until he saw the small, puckered crimson diamond underneath James Lahiri's left eye. The chunk of his skull that had come away when the bullet had exited it. The smear of shiny cerebral matter along the polished wood. The glaze in his eyes, like a slaughtered animal.

Harry rolled over onto his back and lay down next to his dead friend. Tried to cry but hadn't the energy. The sky looked darker than he remembered. Then he closed his eyes.

* * *

They were ten minutes away from Surrey Quays, Wilson driving, Noble in the passenger seat with the *A to Z*, when the call came over the radio.

'All units be advised, gunshots reported at South Dock Marina, Rotherhithe. Trojan 138 en route, confirm response.'

'Did he say South Dock?' Wilson asked.

'Hit the lights,' said Noble. Wilson did, the sirens came on, and he pulled into the bus lane. A marked patrol car was in convoy behind them with two uniformed officers and two detectives, ready to search Lahiri's boat, and it too went on blues, scattering the traffic ahead. Noble grabbed the handset from the radio console between them.

'Control, this is DI Noble with Southwark CID, any more details? Over.'

Static on the line, competing with the sirens and the rain bouncing off the car roof.

'Er ... Multiple 999 calls reporting gunshots, at least one casualty, ambulance and HEMS dispatched, Trojan en route.'

'Control, we are en route also,' she said. 'Four CID, two uniforms.' As she spoke, she unconsciously reached to check the semiautomatic holstered under her armpit, a Glock 26 she carried as a leftover from her time in the Central Task Force. She'd go in alone if she had to, if there was active shooting. The words started to process. *At least one casualty.* Lahiri, she thought. Harry.

'Fuck,' she whispered. Wilson had his foot to the floor, the car weaving through the traffic, rush hour on the Old Kent Road. If Harry wasn't dead, she'd fucking kill him herself. She wondered if it was a mistake, not bringing armed support. They knew a gun had been used behind the Chicken Hut, but it couldn't have been Lahiri, he'd been in A&E.

'Fuck,' she said again.

'You OK, guv?' said Wilson.

'Just fucking drive. Third exit here, A2208.'

'Hold on, then.'

Wilson broke away from the car behind them, swinging around the back of a retail park and heading onto the Rotherhithe New Road, where the traffic was lighter. Noble looked down at the *A to Z*. It couldn't be more than a few minutes now, not on blue lights.

They would have to wait at the rendezvous point for Trojan to arrive and clear the scene before anyone could go in. Noble looked at the map again, then jolted forward as Wilson slammed on the brakes, looking up, panicked. A teenage girl wearing cup-sized headphones had stepped out onto a zebra crossing and Wilson hit the horn with a clenched fist, accelerating away down an empty street as the girl darted out of the way. Noble pulled the radio back to her mouth, pressed the transmit button.

'Trojan 138, come in,' she said. 'Confirm your ETA, please.'

Better be fucking soon, she thought to herself, the gun itching under her arm again. It had been years since she'd fired it, on a revalidation day. She chose the number five in her head, arbitrary and meaningless. If Trojan were more than five minutes away, she and Wilson would go in. She knew Wilson would go with her, and he was built so big it would take more than a few bullets to take him down. There was a taser in the back of the car he could take.

'Control, this is Trojan 138,' a Scottish accent said. 'ETA four minutes, over. All units please hold until arrival.'

'We'll be there in two!' Wilson said.

'Roger that,' Noble shouted. Wilson took a corner hard and she bounced out of the seat again, aware of her heart thudding in her chest. She wondered if Lahiri had somehow been tipped off, if Harry had been responsible. She already had images of Marcus Fairweather, sitting her down across a table, making her account for every single decision she'd made. Fuck, if Harry was dead, if Lahiri had killed him. She tasted bile and the metal of adrenaline.

A new voice on the radio: 'Control, this is Echo Five-Five. We are at RVP and holding.'

The first unit on-scene, a local uniform. Noble held the radio tightly.

'What can you see?'

'There's a white boat, third from the right as we're looking at it, guv. Appears to be one guy on the jetty, one on the boat, can't really see cause of the rain.'

They swerved into a side road and the masts of sailing boats came into view, silhouetted against the dark sky, blue lights mixing with sodium orange.

'Control, DI Noble. Can we get India 99 in the air, use the thermal.'

If the shooter had stayed among the boats, there was no way the three-man Trojan team would be able to search the marina effectively. India 99, the police helicopter, had a thermal imaging camera that would pick the bastard out wherever he was.

'Already tasked, guv.'

'We're here!' Wilson announced. They shot up a ramp, towards a gate and a guard hut, ominously unoccupied. *Fuck, fuck, fuck.* Another patrol car was parked across the gate, its two occupants crouched up against a low wall, torches out and ready. Noble was out of the car and into the rain before it had even stopped, opening the boot, pulling a vest over her head, throwing another to Wilson. She got one hand on her gun and advanced towards the gate, shouting to the uniforms.

'Which boat is it?'

'That one,' said the first uniform, pointing out into the marina. Noble risked a look over the wall, could see the figure on the jetty, fuck-all on the boat. The guy who was lying down was moving, struggling, obviously injured.

'Shit,' she said.

Wilson by her side now. 'I'll go in with you if you want,' he said. 'Just say the word, guv.'

She thought about it. For now, they waited. Only the sounds of rain and sirens approaching, a helicopter somewhere in the mist. Her hair already cold and wet, her hand wiping her eyes. She thought of Harry again, his anger when she'd told him about what they'd found, Lahiri's log-in deleting the allergy. She hoped he was the one who was moving on the jetty.

'Guv?' said Wilson again. The true cop in him. Ahead of them, in the rain and the chaos, there were people in need, and they were there to help.

'OK,' said Noble, reaching to draw her gun, but they were stopped by the sound of the Trojan 4x4 squealing as it pulled up behind them, the two officers in the back jumping out as it slowed, hands on their MP5s.

'Berth twenty-nine!' she yelled. 'We've got casualties.'

The officers sprinted up to the wall, the driver coming to join them, drawing his weapon. Noble met them there, her fingers clammy around the grip of her own gun.

'DI Noble, CID,' she said. 'We'll follow you in.'

'OK,' said the first Trojan officer. 'Stay close.'

He pulled open the gate and through they went, the three black-clad Trojan guys and Noble and Wilson following behind, heads low. There was a thin walkway snaking down towards the jetties, Lahiri's boat about a hundred metres from them.

'Armed police!'

Noble ran closer, sprinting through the rain. Watched as two of the armed officers hurled themselves at the railing on the side of the boat and pulled themselves up like commandos on an assault course. The third stayed on the jetty with the injured man.

Noble reached them and realised she was holding her breath. The man was wearing a security uniform, an obvious wound in the meat of his thigh. It wasn't Harry.

'Harry!' she yelled, into the sky, up at the boat. The ladder dangling down from the side deck had become dislodged, half in the water, useless. One of the Trojan guys appeared on the railing, a panicked look on his face.

'Ma'am, up here!' he called. 'I'll help you up.'

He extended a hand and Noble leapt and took it, her feet scrabbling for a hold on the ladder. She came onto the deck, slipped again. Turned and saw the two bodies lying on the aft deck, almost holding hands, like an old couple laid out on a picnic blanket.

'Harry! Can you hear me?'

'Fucking hell, is he shot too?'

'No, no, I don't think so!'

'Control, this is Trojan 138, get onto LAS, we'll need another ambulance and HEMS, we have two casualties and one fatal. Over.'

'Should we roll him on his side? He's wet, he's been in the water. Mo, go get a blanket or something.'

'Get him on his side, quickly, quickly!'

'Come on, Harry, wake up!'

The voice sounded ethereal. Had it been male perhaps he would have imagined it to be the voice of God.

Harry let out a low moan as hands on his shoulders shook him back into consciousness. He needed to find James. James was hurt. Tammas was coming with the rest of the team, to get him fixed, and back to Bastion. He could hear the helicopter. They were almost here.

'I need a medikit over here!' the voice called. 'Christ, Harry!'

He was still on the boat, could feel its motion beneath him. People coming aboard. His eyes were blinking open now, his limbs starting to send feedback to his brain. There was rain coming down, hitting his right cheek. He was wet, and on his side. Couldn't feel his extremities, and there was a dull pain in the side of his face, where splinters of the *Time and Tide* had ripped into his skin. He knew the voice now. He felt her breath, warm on his skin as she knelt next to him.

'Harry, are you hurt?'

He managed to moan something approaching 'No'.

He felt himself coming round. The hull shuddered, as it had when the gunman came aboard, and he became aware of other footsteps, someone running to Noble's side. He could hear the voices now as two distinct people. 'Paramedics are at the cordon, guv.'

For Lahiri, only Lahiri was stone dead, so they wouldn't be coming for him. Then he remembered there was the watchman, too.

'Get them through,' Noble said. 'Send them to the other guy.'

'What about him, there?'

'He's dead.'

Dead. Who's dead? Harry thought. Everything was still fuzzy. He was on James's boat, and James was dead. The watchman wounded.

Hands shaking Harry awake. Noble's voice.

'Harry? Can you tell us who did this? Did you get a look at him?'

Harry tried to form words, but nothing came. His throat was full of cold water. He really needed to throw up.

James isn't dead. He can't be dead. Not here, not in London.

'Get me some blankets over here,' Noble's voice shouted, clearer now. 'He'll freeze to death.'

Harry felt hands on him again. Noble was pulling off his wet coat, trying to get to his shirt. He tried to speak again, tried to undo the buttons, but his cold fingertips had lost all coordination.

'I'll do it,' Noble said, pulling off his fleece and his shirt. 'Sit up for me, Harry, can you sit up?'

Things were less grey now. He pushed up against the railing behind him, shuffling along on his backside, and hands under his armpits helped him. Someone came over and wrapped Harry's bare back in a blanket, followed by a layer of insulating foil.

'James's been shot,' he muttered. 'I've got to help him.'

'It's alright,' said Noble, stroking his shoulder. 'There's people here.'

A throbbing pressure in his temples.

'FUCK!'

'Harry, did you get a look at him? Who did this?'

Harry shook his head and felt his chest burn again, his eyes painful, like he'd been crying. Who did this? he thought. Who did this? Noble sat at his side and hugged him close, and he felt some of the sensation returning to his hands, tucked into his armpits. Another officer held him from the other side. He tried closing his eyes, as if that would make it go away, but all he saw was Lahiri's face as he rolled him over, the missing part of the back of his skull.

'Harry, you're starting to shake, I'm gonna get the medics,' Noble said.

'No,' he said, coughing. 'The watchman needs them. If I'm shivering it means I'm warming up.'

Noble turned his head with her hand to look at him. He saw her face for the first time, silhouetted against the blue strobe lights.

'Trust me,' Harry said. 'I'm a doctor.'

Noble's face didn't even start to smile. 'Exactly,' she said. 'You're a bloody doctor, what the hell were you doing here?'

'I was already on the way before you called,' he said. 'He called me.'

Just answer the questions, Harry told himself. Answer the questions and it will make it less real.

'What happened?'

'We had a fight,' said Harry. 'He said they'd given Idris the money. He was blackmailing them. But he said it was just to help him get away.'

'From what?'

Harry was still shivering but he was warming up now, his sentences no longer fragmented, his thoughts more coherent. 'They were prescribing kids weed at the Saviour Project. Idris was going to tell the papers for money.'

Harry felt a sudden need to pass out and buckled forward, before the blood rushed to his head.

'What about the allergy?'

Harry shook his head, and the stench of the water he was covered in hit, or maybe he just became aware of it. He burst out of Noble's embrace and vomited onto the deck, most of it dirty brown dock water.

'Said he didn't do it,' said Harry. 'Acted like he didn't know what I was talking about.'

'Acted?'

Harry shook his head, coughed, and vomited again.

'Fuck knows.'

He wiped his mouth on the blanket and started to look around. Go and ask him, Harry thought. Go and ask his corpse. The pressure was rising in him like a wave, and he felt the tears start to build behind the dam in his head, soon to overflow. Beside him, an officer spoke to Noble.

'Guv, this is a crime scene now. We need to get him off.'

'OK. Let's get you to your feet, Harry.'

Hands under him again, pulling him upright. He could taste shit and vomit.

'No chance of any chewing gum?' he said as he pulled the blanket closer.

'Richmond menthol?' Noble offered.

'Jesus, my chest hurts,' he said. They began an awkward walk off the boat, from treadplate to treadplate, a token gesture for sure. The rain was still coming in hard, and any forensic evidence the shooter had left would be long gone already.

'Do you want me to get the paramedics?' Noble asked.

'No, I'm fine.' He ran cold fingers over the scar on his chest, and threw up again, collapsing on the wood of the jetty, where

Trojan officers stood cradling their guns, and paramedics worked on the watchman. One of the fast-response cars that HEMS, the air ambulance, used after dark pulled up next to the cordon, the orange-jumpsuited crew rushing out towards them.

'This way,' said an officer, and pulled him towards the collection of vehicles, towards the noise. He closed his eyes, heard gunshots echoing around the docks. Saw Tammas, then Idris, then Lahiri.

Christ, Harry thought, his parents. Tammas. He'd have to tell Tammas that James was dead, that he'd let him down, too. The unreality of it all began to take hold. He looked around and it was like watching himself on camera, it was him but not really him. And then he saw a paramedic filling out paperwork. Behind the paramedic, a body lay underneath a blanket, pale fingers poking out, pointing to the sky. Harry stared. It was all real, and the reality sucked into the place behind his sternum like stars into a black hole. Ten minutes ago, he'd come close to killing the man with his bare hands. Now Lahiri was dead, and all Harry wanted to do was sit in a dark room and punch the walls until his knuckles bled.

They sat him down on the back step of the ambulance, Noble continuing to shield him with her body. His shivers were still frequent, but decreasing in their vigour. One of the paramedics put an oximeter on his finger, but Harry shook it off.

'Won't work,' he said. 'Too cold.'

Then a temperature probe into his ear. Noble got the hint and stood up, wiping the moisture she'd gained from him off her shirt. She was drenched, too, he realised as he looked up. Wearing only a short-sleeved shirt and a tactical vest.

'Are you alright?' she said.

'We need to find who did this,' Harry said.

'No, Harry,' Noble said, squatting so she was at his eye level. '*We* need to find them. Us. The police. Not you.'

Harry nodded.

'Do I stink like shit?'

'Yeah.'

'James,' Harry said.

DS Wilson came over. 'Didn't think getting shot at once in a week was enough, then?' he said.

'How's the security guard?' Harry asked. People who dealt with death every day took the piss to keep them sane, and Harry did that most days. It was different today.

'The HEMS docs think he'll make it,' said Wilson. 'He's still conscious. Good job you did there, mate.'

Harry looked over at him. 'What do you mean, good job?'

'Putting that tourniquet on.'

'What?'

Wilson looked across at Noble, and then at the crowd of medics around the wounded watchman, and then back to Harry. He crouched down next to Noble.

'Our friend over there got shot in the leg,' said Wilson. 'Straight through the thigh. Someone tied a belt around his leg, stopped the bleeding. We assumed it was you.'

Harry tried to stand up, but the medics stopped him.

'I never left the boat,' he said. 'I went into the water when the guy came onto the deck, then I came back up. Last thing I remember is hearing the watchman shout, and trying to crawl back around, but then . . . Then I don't know.'

'Christ,' said Wilson.

Harry looked up at Noble. She met his eyes and then glanced down at the floor.

'It must have been the shooter,' Harry said. The words felt foreign on his lips. Background noise grew, the team of medics getting ready to transfer the watchman into the waiting ambulance. Wilson ran back over, fresh from a conversation with someone in a white jumpsuit.

'Forensics have found a casing,' he said, panting. 'Obviously, we'll have to wait for ballistics, but it looks like nine-mil. Mick reckons it's the same gun as Sunday.'

Harry nodded. Tried to process the information. The same person who had tried to get Idris killed had been successful with James Lahiri. Everything linked up, got sucked into the same black hole. One of the paramedics ran up to them, waving them off the ambulance's back seat.

'Gotta move, guys, we're loading the patient up.'

Noble and Wilson lifted Harry, keeping him wrapped in the blankets. Harry resisted, holding onto the paramedic.

'Where's he going?' Harry demanded.

'The Ruskin,' said the paramedic.

'No!' Harry said. 'Go to the Royal London. The Ruskin's not safe.'

'It'll be fine,' said Noble. 'He'll have a Trojan escort. Have we got another ambulance coming for him?'

She pointed at Harry. They moved out of the way and the HEMS crew loaded the guard up into the vehicle. He was breathing oxygen through a mask, not a tube, which was a good sign.

'I'm not going to hospital,' Harry said. 'I don't want to be anywhere near that place. I'll be fine.'

The paramedic crouched down.

'I really think—'

Harry burst from the blanket and grabbed the front of the paramedic's shirt. 'Look, with all due respect, my best friend has just been killed, and there's a man out there with a gun who should have killed me too, and he'll know that a fucking hospital is the first place I'd go. So while I appreciate your concern, please, just accept . . .'

He let go and collapsed backwards into Wilson, his voice cracking, each word punctuated like a slamming door. 'I – will – be – fine.'

He closed his eyes and was back in the blanket, Noble's arms pulling him close. Wilson and Noble had a quiet conversation, but the siren from the departing ambulance blocked it from Harry's ears. She took Harry by the arm, leading him across the wooden planks, opposing the tide of white-suited forensic officers heading for the boat.

'I'll take you somewhere safe,' she said, but from the wobble in her voice Harry knew she was lying.

A uniformed officer was holding the back of a patrol car open.

'The heating's on already,' she said.

'Where are we going?' Harry said.

'Lewisham station,' said Noble. 'I'm sorry.'

He wasn't under arrest.

That was the first thing that Marsden, the saccharin DCI from Homicide & Serious, said when they arrived at Lewisham police station, he on his way in, she on her way out after setting up the incident room. Two detective constables called Deakin and Bambrough interviewed him in a room that was still cold even with the heating turned on full. They brought him tea but he didn't touch it, and they told him he could leave at any time, and he didn't need a lawyer, but he could have one if he wanted.

Harry didn't want a lawyer. He wanted to go to sleep, and to wake up after his Saturday night shift and find that all of this had never happened. He wanted the pieces missing from the back of James Lahiri's head to be back where they belonged. He wanted a warm room and a shower, and to get the specks of his best friend's blood off his face. He wanted existence itself to stop.

He told the detectives all of this, and more. They went through everything he'd done that day, from getting up, speaking to Idris's family, getting bollocked by Traubert, coming to the school with Whitacre and Ambrose, his conversation with Shaquille Dawson. Sitting in his apartment, thinking everything over, getting the call from Lahiri. Setting in motion a chain of events that ended with Lahiri dead and another man fighting for his life, and Harry freezing cold, in a police station, with his friend's blood on his face.

If he'd just stayed at home, and watched TV, and ignored that call, would Lahiri still be dead?

Probably, Harry thought. There was no way that whoever had turned up to shoot Lahiri could have known Harry would be there, unless they'd been following him. The main question was, was it his fault? However much he allowed himself to wallow in self-pity, there was nothing Harry could have done the moment that bullet had entered Lahiri's skull. But if he'd heeded the warning given to him the previous evening, in brutally violent fashion, would Lahiri still be alive?

At the start, the older detective, Deakin, had asked him to describe his relationship with James Lahiri. Harry had said simply, 'He's my friend.'

Yes, he was your friend. But he didn't trust you enough to tell you all he'd wanted to on that previous night, when you sat and drank acid wine together.

If Harry hadn't done what he'd done, maybe Lahiri would still be alive.

Harry knew he wouldn't sleep tonight, and he knew he'd lie awake for many more trying to answer that question. If the woman in front of him, with her tweed jacket, her perfect teeth and her nasal inflections, did her job and caught the person who'd killed Lahiri, then maybe it would be easier. Maybe there'd be answers.

Hours ago now, Tammas had said, *Make the right calls. I always trusted you to do that.* That sounded an awful lot like bullshit now.

They finished off by interrogating him about everything that happened on the boat. Harry left nothing out. There was no reason to lie. He recounted every accusation he'd levelled, every punch, kick and slap he'd rained down. Throughout, the two homicide detectives looked at him with poker faces, breaking eye contact only when their sergeant, an overweight East Asian man with a heavy Scouse accent, called them out to discuss something. Their pretence had been that they just wanted the facts, but he knew why he was really there. Firstly, he was their only witness to the murder, and secondly, they needed to rule him in or out.

So he gave them everything.

'You're sure Mr Lahiri said that it was just cannabis?' DC Bambrough said.

'Dr Lahiri,' Harry said, for the third or fourth time so far. 'As far as I can remember, yes.'

'And he denied that the money was to stop Mr Idris from speaking out.'

'No. He didn't deny it. He said Whitacre handled it.'

'Duncan Whitacre?'

'I assume so,' said Harry.

And then he told the rest of the story. How the first shot had missed them both, and then the second had hit Lahiri, and the third had clipped the boat as Harry ducked for cover. There wasn't much of use there, as Harry couldn't recall a lot after that. He remembered going in the water, coming out wet, dirty and cold, turning over Lahiri's body and hearing another shot before he passed out. He might have seen the watchman go down, or the shooter running away, but he wasn't sure.

'Can I go now?'

Bambrough, the younger detective, looked at Deakin, the older one, who shrugged and left, presumably to consult the boss. After a while, Harry sipped his cold tea, and Bambrough said, 'I'm sorry about your friend.'

It was only when Deakin came back in to tell him he was free to go that Harry realised he was crying.

Noble was in the incident room, briefing the Homicide & Serious team on everything they had so far on the investigation, but she stopped mid-sentence when she saw Harry in the door, a blanket still over his shoulders.

'Let's go,' she said.

'Don't you need to stay here?'

'Mo's on his way over. He'll bring the team up to speed.'

Harry nodded, and they headed silently into the car park. Still it rained. He was shivering again by the time he got into the car.

'There's another blanket in the back.'

Harry wrapped it around him. He was wet and cold, a film of dirt covering his face and hands. She had the heater on full and the radio tuned to a classical music station, the volume low. Quiet, brooding violins. As they headed north, through Deptford, Harry began to feel warmer. His fingers hurt, and his chest too. Maybe he'd cracked a rib somewhere in the chaos.

'Where are we going?' he said after about ten minutes of silence. There was an advert on the radio about bladder weakness.

'I'm afraid the Met doesn't really do those nice safe houses you see on TV.'

'I wasn't expecting one.'

'We've got a room at a place near Aldgate. Low-budget, but it'll do.'

Harry shrugged his shoulders. It was logical to assume that if their shooter wanted him dead, all the expected places weren't safe. That included the Ruskin and his home, maybe even his friends' houses, not that he had any who sprung to mind – he could hardly kip on the floor of Marigold House next to Tammas's bed. No killer, no matter how determined, could search through every hotel in London.

As they drove, Harry realised he had lost all track of time. It had been about four or so when he'd set off for Lahiri's. Now it could be anywhere from six to midnight, he didn't know.

'His parents live in Sussex,' said Harry. 'Peacehaven.'

'We know,' said Noble. 'There's a family liaison officer with them now.'

Harry pictured James Lahiri's stoic, dignified father, his mother, obsessive and perennially bored, disturbed during their evening to hear the news. The thought brought vomit rising into his throat. Parents didn't expect to bury their son. Maybe the Lahiris had, when James decided to go to Afghanistan, twice, but the moment that plane had landed, they'd have breathed sighs of relief. Having dinner on his boat, a workday evening. And then dead. All because of what?

Because someone was scared the media would find out they were giving weed to kids?

It still hadn't sunk in. James's death. The one who always landed on his feet, who always managed to climb out of whatever hole he found himself in, was on his way to Greenwich Mortuary with a tag on his toe and a bit of his skull missing.

Alice. He wondered who'd tell her. Lahiri's parents certainly didn't have any affection for the woman. She hadn't left any way of being contacted, anyway, if Lahiri had been forced to resort to stalking her via LinkedIn.

He thought about Georgia Henderson, too. It wasn't his place to tell her, but someone had to. The man she was seeing was dead. These were the people Lahiri's life had touched, and as their faces circled through his eyes he focused on watching the traffic on Tower Bridge so he didn't cry. Closed his eyes and maybe slept for a while, or passed out, he wasn't sure. When he opened them they were on the edges of the City, near Old Street. He reached into his pocket to get his phone, only to realise that it was in the footwell of his car, parked by the front gate of the marina. It would be impounded as evidence.

'Frankie,' Harry said through a trembling jaw. The car had ground to a halt, the hotel's sign bearing over them. 'I need to call someone.'

'Who?'

'His name's Peter Tammas. He was mine and James's commanding officer in the army. Mentored both of us. He needs to know.'

'It's made the news already,' said Noble. 'Word is, one of those boats belonged to an executive at Sky. He was live-tweeting from his cabin.'

Harry looked up at her as they exited the car into the rain. The street was deserted. Noble was scanning it in a certain manner, one which Harry recognised. She was his bodyguard now.

'He needs to hear it from me,' Harry repeated. 'Not the bloody news.'

'Is this guy a doctor?'

'He's not involved,' said Harry.

'On Monday, you said that about Lahiri.'

'Well, here's a fucking alibi for you, then,' Harry said. 'He's been bedridden for near on two years. There's a bullet in his spine. How's that?'

Noble looked back at him, pain on her face, then threw him her mobile.

'I'm sorry,' she said. 'Don't go out of my sight.'

'Thanks,' he mumbled.

They stepped through the automatic doors into the warm hotel lobby, the sight of a man in wet trousers and covered in blankets instantly drawing puzzled looks from the staff. Noble headed up to the desk. Harry leant against the wall and a cleaner passed him, catching the smell of the Thames and throwing him a dirty look. He got the operator at Marigold House and from the voice thought it was the receptionist with the dreadlocks he'd seen on Sunday night. He was put through quickly.

'Harry?'

He said nothing. The rattle indicated that Tammas was trying to speak.

'What's. Wrong?'

He closed his eyes and tried to force himself to say the words, to say what he said to people all the time. It was routine, if awful, when it was someone else's mother, who'd fought her failing body for decades, and was finally succumbing in A&E. Here, the false reality collided with the other one, like the paradox about the cat in the box who was both dead and alive until you opened the box and found out. If Harry said the words, they would become true.

'James is dead.'

Harry had never heard someone cry through a tracheostomy

tube before. It sounded like a wet iron gate being scraped along tarmac.

'No!'

Spoken like a father. Harry waited for the ventilator to cycle, for Tammas to speak.

'How?'

'Someone shot him,' said Harry. 'On his boat.'

'Have they caught . . . No. God. No. No. No. No.'

Harry's head fell forward to touch the cold metal of a leaflet rack. Tammas's sobs echoed out of Noble's mobile, each one a hammer striking the anvil inside his chest. Each one a fresh explosion of pain out of his side, a piercing wind through him.

'Was he. Involved?'

'I don't know. It was something to do with the kid.'

'Fucking. James. Fucking. Stupid. Fucking. Fucking. Bastard.'

Tammas's anger burst through, his voice collapsing into a hoarse fit of spluttering. Harry overheard a brief conversation as a carer burst into the room, asking him if he was OK.

'Fuck off. Leave me. Alone. You nosy. Little shit.'

'Boss, listen—'

'No!' Tammas roared.

Harry was silent. He pushed his forehead into the metal until it hurt. He could picture Tammas, filled with incandescent rage, but with no working muscles below the neck with which to express it.

'Who did it?' Tammas spluttered.

'I don't know. Someone he was working with, someone who wanted to keep it quiet. I'm going to find out.'

Tammas's breathing was laboured, every word spat as though it could be his last.

'Find. Him. I don't. Care. What. James. Did. You find. Who. Killed him.'

'OK, boss.'

'You find him. And you. Make. The Bastard. Pay.'

Harry felt water running down his face and looked up to see if it was rain or snow, then realised that he was standing indoors. He wiped his tears on the corner of a blanket. 'I will, boss,' he said.

Another wail, this one louder and more piercing than the last. 'Oh, Jesus. Harry. You can't. Hear me. Like this.'

'Boss, I—'

Tammas had hung up.

The hotel room had twin beds either side of a small table, walk-in cupboards and a badly designed bathroom where the shower door opened into the toilet. Harry sat on the bed nearest the window, the blanket still around his shoulders. Noble had turned the heating up fully and he wasn't as cold any more; two cups of tea rolled around inside his stomach. She was sitting on the edge of the other bed, fingers dancing over the keys of the iPad on her lap.

'What size are you?' she asked.

'I'm sorry?'

'I'm getting Mo to drop you off some clothes.'

'Medium,' Harry said. 'Thirty-four waist.'

'I'll get him to bring some food too, you must be starving.'

Harry said nothing, just nodded. He wasn't hungry. In fact, he couldn't picture himself ever eating again.

'Shoe size?'

'Ten.'

Facts were good. He could answer questions about facts, as he had done with the detectives at Lewisham. Noble tapped some more on her iPad.

'Remind me again why we have to share a room?'

Noble lifted the lapel of her jacket to reveal the holster and the gun underneath. 'Look at yourself. You shouldn't be alone tonight,' she said. 'But more than that, you could be in danger. And I'm sure you'd rather have me watching your back than some gorilla from Protection Command.'

Harry threw off the blankets and headed into the bathroom, where he studied his reflection in the mirror above the basin. His face was smeared with dried blood, not all of it his. The laceration on his right cheek was superficial. It had stopped bleeding but there was a sizeable sliver of laminated wood embedded in the wound, and his stubble was matted with dried blood and shit from the river. He started running the hot tap. He had some antibiotics in his bag at home.

'How come you're carrying?' he called through the open bathroom door.

'I told you, I used to work Central Task Force, the undercover unit,' Noble said. 'We all got authorised when we joined. Our last op went wrong, we lost track of some paperwork, and we ended up raiding a drugs shop in Finsbury with an expired warrant. And some very nasty people who were meant to go to prison didn't, and now they know my face. It's a standard precaution. In case they come after me.'

Harry winced as he eased the splinter out, and a line of fresh blood scored the white basin.

'That really happens?'

'They came after one of my team, the guy who'd been my inside man. Shot him up as he was coming out of the pub in Chiswick,' Noble said. 'He spent four weeks in St Mary's. So yeah, it does.'

Harry craned his head awkwardly to get his cheek under the tap. The hot water stung. He knew the tone of voice Noble was trying to put on, the one that implied she knew how he was feeling. The trouble was, he wasn't feeling. The system had reset. He was numb. He heard his own voice echoing in his head, telling Tammas. *James is dead*. Still it didn't sound real.

'I'm gonna take a shower,' Harry said, wiping his bloodied face with a towel. He retched again when he saw the mess he'd made – watery blood, and the greasy brown-black shit that coated his face and neck. 'That OK?'

Noble nodded and Harry locked the bathroom door, pulling off his damp trousers and underwear and starting the water. The hot steam rose up and filled the cubicle, the smell of shit that clung to his skin slowly giving way to whatever aloe vera rubbish they'd put in the shower gel. The water turned brown and grey and translucent as it ran down his body and pooled in the shower basin, swirls of dirty colour that mixed like the thoughts in Harry's head. He expected to feel more than this. Maybe it was shock, perhaps. Or maybe this was what grief was. A void.

The shower gel burned the wound on Harry's cheek, but he didn't particularly care. He folded slowly until he was cross-legged in the shower, staring down at the flecks of rusty red-brown in the water, Lahiri's blood spiralling into the drain. He stared for a few minutes, then closed his eyes, trying to shut down, to free up some bandwidth in his mind, but it didn't work. First the vomit came, then the tears, and then Harry rested his head against the perspex and both his body and soul shook.

It was a few minutes before he realised he was speaking, the same phrase being forced through trembling lips.

'I'm sorry.'

It took a while, but then he was done, and he stood up slowly, shut off the water and ran his hands through his hair, working in shampoo and bringing out twists of moss and slime. At least now the police couldn't drag their feet. A rich doctor was dead on his luxury houseboat. The Met would have to bring all of their resources to bear.

Harry stepped out of the shower and looked in the mirror. The cut on his face had stopped bleeding, but his eyes were red and raw. He recognised the look. The pain had been replaced by a deep hunger, and all he really wanted to do was sleep. He suspected that he would be unable to do that, and he longed for any chemical that would assist. Alcohol, a benzodiazepine, anything.

He could hear voices: Noble's and someone else's. He edged the bathroom door open and saw her standing with DS Wilson, who was holding a bag from Marks & Spencer and a small rucksack. Coca-Cola and pizza boxes.

Wilson passed him the M&S bag and Harry inspected the shrink-wrapped underwear, dark chinos, T-shirt and navy crewneck jumper. The rucksack had a change of clothes for Noble.

'Call it an operational expense,' Noble said. 'No one wants to end up wearing Primark after the day you've had, do they?'

She tapped the pizza boxes and slid them towards Harry.

'Tuck in,' she said. 'Two-for-Tuesdays; we might as well.'

He was suddenly starving, the smell of hot food trumping his nausea, making him feel like he'd not eaten for a week. When he'd finished getting changed, Wilson had left. He caught his reflection in the mirror and resisted a desire to go and wash his face again, as if there were microscopic traces of Lahiri's blood that he could remove. He opened a pizza box and wolfed a slice down in one bite.

'Thanks,' he grunted. Noble had the news on; recorded footage of the inauguration of the US president for his second term. Underneath the video, the headline ticker ran. Harry read, *Police confirm that a 35-year-old man has died following a shooting at a marina in Rotherhithe, South London.*

'Turn that shit off before the headlines come on,' Harry said. 'Please.'

Noble reached for the remote. The book said to use the silences, and they did, staring at a blank TV and eating pizza.

'You guys got anything?' Harry said after a while.

'Trying to trace a black Fiesta seen in the area going at high speed. Forensics are tough, obviously, with the weather.'

'What about the USB?' Harry said.

Noble shook her head.

'What does that mean?'

'It means they're still working on it,' she said. 'Christ knows what's on there.'

Harry closed his eyes and saw Lahiri again, holding that cigarette. Just before the hole had appeared in the back of his head. Harry felt the tears well up and inhaled deeply to try to hold them in. Noble broke the silence.

'Is there anyone I can call for you, any friends you'd like to speak to?'

Harry shook his head.

'Parents?'

'My mum's dead, and I haven't spoken to my dad in twenty years.'

Noble turned back to the window.

'Do you want a drink?' she said.

Harry looked down slowly. There was a half-litre bottle of vodka at her side, which had appeared from nowhere. It was supermarket brand, Marks & Spencer. Wilson evidently knew her too well. Noble had fetched two glasses from the hotel room's coffee table and filled them both half full. She had read his mind.

'I shouldn't,' he said. 'My old shrink told me I shouldn't drink when I'm feeling fragile. Something about making dark places darker.'

'You think it can get much darker than this?' Noble said.

Harry picked up the tumbler and emptied half of it into his mouth. The vodka burned down his throat, and the sensation reminded him of the way the vomit had burned up after he'd come out of the water. He shivered and smelt shit again, scrunched his eyes shut. Noble rose and reached into the plastic bag at her side, pulling out a packet of condoms. Durex Extra Safe. Harry shuffled in his seat, and she caught his eye and winked.

Once she was finished wrapping the condoms over the room's two smoke detectors, she sat back down opposite Harry, and lit up. The smoke swirled over towards him and he inhaled a little of it, hoping for a little passive nicotine. Looked back down at the drink.

'To James,' he said, raising it.

Noble touched his glass with hers, and each of them drained their tumbler in one long pull; two experienced imbibers getting to know one another. She reached to refill the glass, and Harry looked at her and wondered if alcohol was something more, filling a gap in her life that bereavement had created. She looked far too young to be a widow.

'I couldn't help but notice,' she said. 'Your back, when you came out of the shower . . .'

She was talking about the criss-cross of scars across Harry's right flank, all tributaries joining to the main track that ran across the right side of his chest and round to his back.

'Those are from the day James Lahiri saved my life,' he said.

'Oh, Christ, I'm sorry,' Noble said, covering her face with one hand. 'I'm a stupid—'

'No, you should know,' said Harry. 'I feel like I should tell you. He and I were MOs at a forward operating base in the valley above the Musa Qala river. Four hours by road from the next nearest base. We were the only doctors, with a company from the Anglians and a few dozen locals. We only had a skeleton kit – if anyone got seriously hurt we'd fly them back to Bastion, but it kept us busy enough. Weeks before, we'd had a bad job – five of the boys injured in a rocket attack a mile from our front door. Four of them made it. After that, Tammas, our boss, came up to visit, see how we were doing. We were sitting out in the main courtyard, having a brew. Lahiri went for a piss.

'First thing we heard was an explosion in the officers' mess, which was right behind us. Sounded like a grenade. We got up, and one of the local Afghan police ran out of the mess, rifle in his hand. He shot Tammas, then he shot me. Next thing I knew I was on the ground, groping in my pocket for a field dressing. I could feel my own blood coming through my fingers. That's one of the last things I remember. That's when the real fighting started. They'd been up in the hills above the base, waiting for this bastard to go before they attacked.'

Noble's glass was empty. Her eyes, widened by the alcohol, were fixed on him. He was waiting for the lump to rise in his throat, but it never did any more. He'd left out the part he always did, turning to see the policeman running out of the mess, one hand already unbuckling his holster. Shaking so much that he dropped his pistol, scrabbling to pick it up as Tammas fell beside him, and taking one in the chest before he could reach it. It would have been a clean shot, centre mass, if he hadn't fucked it up.

'He shot two more guys before they took him down. Four of our boys emptied their rifles into him. Lahiri was on us fairly quickly. Apparently he heard the shooting but he couldn't come out 'cause he couldn't stop pissing. He was just standing there holding his dick while the fucking Taliban were running around our FOB.'

Noble's face was strained, like she wasn't sure whether to laugh or not. Harry looked down and realised he was holding the tumbler hard enough to make his knuckles go white.

'Anyway, I had two collapsed lungs and my liver ended up split in two. The crappy Russian bullets they use fall apart the moment they hit you. Tammas took one through his spine, he was paralysed from the neck down. Still is. They flew in a Chinook to evacuate both of us, and two of the other injured guys. Saved my life for sure. James put two chest tubes in me, six units of blood, carried me up the valley to where they touched it down. There was lavender growing in the fields around the base. I remember that.'

'Christ,' she said after a long silence. The vodka was gone.

'Yeah. Three Afghan National officers dead in the mess, along with two of our lads. Tammas gone from the neck down. Everyone else made it. A shitty fucking awful day. Five for one, six if you count Tammas.'

'Thanks.' Noble said. 'You didn't need to tell me all that.'

'I know,' Harry said. 'But I wanted you to know what kind of man James Lahiri is. We were out in the open like sitting ducks, our perimeter was compromised, there were snipers and rockets in the hills. And he just knelt down, and got his kit out, and got to work. Like he was in A&E on a quiet Sunday afternoon, and it was just another job. That's the kind of man he is.'

Noble looked at him with a patronising smile, and Harry realised the tense he'd just used, and then stood up. He froze for a moment.

'Sorry,' he said. 'I thought I needed to be sick.'

Noble nodded, and went into the bathroom. Harry sat back down again, slowly. The alcohol was beginning to get into his system, blunting the edge of his pain. He felt a sudden lust for sleep he knew wouldn't come. Looked out of the window and wondered how many other people were lonely and getting drunk in a hotel room in this city, and wished he could just be one of them. At least he wasn't getting drunk on his own, he thought as Noble came back into the room, took her blazer off, and put her gun in the top drawer of the bedside table. The holster straps cut into her shirt, framing the defined, muscular shoulders.

'I might put on some music,' she said. Harry nodded and looked across at the bottle. Between them they'd emptied it in half an hour. James would have been proud of that. He went back to staring. Outside the window, streams of motorway light merged like rainwater along a cobbled street, and the sparse opening chords of a Beethoven sonata pierced the room.

'Oh, what's the fucking point!' Harry said.

He swivelled out of the seat and stood up but she was right there. His tumbler hit her shirt and the liquid spilled out onto the floor, his arm lurching to catch it. When he righted himself they were close.

'I'm sorry,' she said.

He looked down at her, nodded slowly, and she arched her neck backwards, pushing her face close into his, one hand pressed flat against his shirt. When it came, the kiss was desperate, it and the alcohol mixing in Harry's brain, summoning an army of chemicals to replace the fear and the grief. The pair of them stumbled backwards towards the bed, Noble pulling him down with her.

He rose and switched off the music, silencing the piano before the introduction was even over. She was waiting for him on the bed, the leather straps where the gun usually sat still cutting into a shirt one size too small. He pulled the holster off her, then the shirt, and then she took off his, and wrapped her legs around him, pushing his erection into her body. Harry glanced up at the door.

'It's locked,' said Noble. 'Anyway, I'm waiting.'

She tapped the bedside table on which the holster and the gun rested. 'Fuck it, Harry,' she said. 'If someone's coming, we may as well die like this.'

The sex was how sex should be, Harry thought. Unexpected, ambushing, intense. But the thoughts it left him with, alone in the bed as she showered, were bitter and unwelcome. He'd never felt this sick after sex before. He'd never cried afterwards either.

The last woman he'd had in bed had been Alice Lahiri, and at the moment Detective Inspector Frances Noble had wrapped her legs around his and brought him to climax he had thought of her. Once they were done, he heard Lahiri's voice, not condescending, but speaking in pained sympathy. *You know how it feels, right? Same reason funerals make you want it. When you survive something like that, you just want to shag the living daylights out of anything you see, so you can prove you're still alive.*

Sex with Alice had always been routine, cold, without anything that could be called passion, as if it were a necessary part of what they were doing, of their joint betrayal of the man they'd both supposedly loved. Harry was lying on the bed, listening to the hum of the shower as it pumped water over Noble's body. The sex had been primal, a path of least resistance to expunge the wrath that all the gods Harry didn't believe in had hurled down on them that day.

Four hours ago, he had seen his best friend die. And now he lay naked on a bed in a hotel room, with a drunken, grieving widow in the shower, thinking about his dead friend's wife.

Fuck that. Fuck it all.

He walked naked to the coffee table and tried to pour vodka from the bottle, but it was empty. His eyes scanned the room, running over the door, the line of light glowing beneath it, coming to rest on the bedside table. He thought about the gun on top of it, and the round in its chamber. Then he collapsed onto the bed and sat back up again, exhaling forcefully. He'd not had thoughts like that in a while. In fact, this was the first one this year and, though fleeting, it scared him to the core. They came at times like this, when he was staring into the unimaginable, face to face with his own weaknesses and the consequences of the decisions he'd made.

All the arguments against flooded into his head at once. Chief among them was one voice.

You can't let James down. You let him down before, and now he's dead, you can't do that. You owe him that much. Maybe you couldn't save him, like he saved you, but you can make sure that the bastard who did it rots in the closest thing they can find to hell.

He went over to the carrier bag that Noble's colleague had brought in with the pizza, and rooted for anything he could sleep in. He didn't want to be naked when she came in from the shower, even if they weren't sharing a bed. She emerged wrapped up in a towel, moving gingerly, the polar opposite of her professional bravado.

'You OK?' he asked.

She nodded. 'Yeah, I'm good.'

The water from the shower had covered it up, but from the red in Noble's eyes Harry was sure she'd been crying, too. She put her underwear on underneath her towel and pulled a sleeveless vest from her rucksack, letting the towel fall to the floor.

'I'm sorry,' Harry said as she climbed into her bed.

'Don't be,' Noble said, pulling the covers over her.

He looked across at her and wondered if she'd thought of Jack. She reached up and turned off the light, a thin sliver of orange still filtering in through the window from the city outside. The sheets were damp with their sweat.

After a few minutes, she sat up. 'I need to smoke,' she said. 'Want one?'

Harry said he didn't. The lights went back on. She took the empty vodka bottle to use as an ashtray and lit up, her face bathed in an orange glow. She was sitting on the end of her bed, facing the desk. He wondered if she'd planned it. While he'd been washing Lahiri's blood off his face, perhaps.

Harry lay in his bed, smelling her smoke, thinking of how stupid it all was. A rising anger that he'd let himself be seduced so easily. He knew why, too.

'You remember me, don't you?' he said.

'I remembered you the moment I saw you,' Noble replied. 'When you came through the cordon on Camberwell Road.'

The Ruskin, last April. Forty-one-year-old Detective Chief Inspector Jack Noble lay brain-dead in the ICU, his body an empty shell. Long since sunk into a coma for his own good, he was not in any pain, but there was no hope left. His wife, serene, professional, not a tear in sight, held his hand as the nurses switched off first the monitors, then the machines. The rest of the team, Harry included, stood silent at the back of the room, a guard of honour in pink scrubs. No drugs, no electric shocks, no one breaking ribs in an attempt to restart his heart. Just a man ceasing to be, forty years too soon.

'Did you remember me?' Noble said, lighting another. 'You persuaded me to donate his organs. I always felt guilty about that. Jack would have hated me for it.'

'Yes, I did.' Harry now sat up in his bed. 'And don't say that. I hope that it helped you. Knowing that some good came of it.'

'Someone got his kidneys, his liver. And his lungs and his heart. You wanted his eyes too, but I wouldn't let you have them. I couldn't stand the thought of walking along the street one day, and seeing someone with Jack's eyes. Even if that sounds ridiculous, I'd just think it was them.'

Harry remembered the full conversation now. He'd used all the usual lies. *Instantly. Painless. He wouldn't have suffered.* In fact, Jack Noble had likely been alive for a few minutes after his pushbike had disappeared beneath the Sainsbury's delivery truck at Vauxhall Cross. It had taken time for an extradural blood clot to squeeze his brain out of the hole between his skull and his spine. Harry hadn't told the grieving widow those details back then, and he had no intention of rectifying that omission now.

'There's been no one since him, has there?' he said.

Noble shook her head.

'Is that why you wanted me? Because I was there, at the end? Because I was connected to him?'

She threw the half-smoked fag into the vodka bottle and turned to him. She was sullen, upset, probably the closest Frankie Noble ever came to crying. 'Fuck you,' she said.

'I didn't mean—'

'Why do you even give a shit?'

'I—'

'Why can't you just accept what happened and forget about it and move on? Why can't you be a typical fucking man, and do that?'

Harry took a long deep breath. 'I can do that,' he said. 'I can not give a shit if you don't want me to.'

Noble looked across at him, her eyes hurt.

'I think it'd be for the best,' she said.

'OK.'

'You know, there aren't enough people in this world who do give a shit,' Noble said, tucking herself under the covers. Harry heard her words blend into one another and realised she was probably still a little under the influence.

'You give a shit, don't you?' she continued. 'I know that you give a shit about your girl from the riots. Zara, or whatever you call her. I did some research on you. I pulled the file. Since August 2011 you've made fourteen separate enquiries to the Met in relation to her. All different units. Missing Persons, Homicide & Serious, Sapphire, Special Projects, Major Case Review, Vice & Organised, Narcotics. Even Fairweather's gig, Professional Standards. That's giving a shit, isn't it?'

'You could call it that,' Harry said. He could close his eyes and picture Zara's fragile body, the hair, the T-shirt, the paralysed look of fear in her unresponsive eyes right at the start. The same dead look he'd seen on his friend's face in the rain, that very evening.

'Will she ever wake up?'

'Professor Niebaum's a world expert, and even he doesn't know,' Harry answered. 'There have been people where she is now who've woken up after weeks, months, even years. If she does, the chances are she'll have brain damage.'

'What's the difference between her and what happened to Jack?'

Harry felt his skin go cold. 'Jack was brain-dead,' he forced himself to tell her. 'He couldn't breathe for himself, or control his blood pressure, or anything like that. Zara can do all those things. Her body functions just fine, her brain is functioning, too. It's just her mind that we have to rescue.'

His words rang around the room, echoing off the glasses and the vodka bottle with the dead cigarette butts and ash.

'I hope she wakes up,' Noble said. 'One day.'

'Me too.'

Silence.

'James gave a shit,' Harry said after a while. 'At least he did at the start. He told me he thought there was something more going on with Idris, something else he didn't tell me on Monday.'

'Maybe he wasn't sure if he could trust you,' Noble said. 'There are lots of questions, Harry. Ask them tomorrow.'

'OK.'

They said nothing for a while. Harry sat upright in bed, looked over, and saw that she was asleep. She slept in a foetal position, to one side of the single bed, as if she expected someone to interlock behind her, someone larger. He turned away and looked at the door in front of him again. The darkness mellowed into a twilight, the blue of his adapted vision, and the orange filtering in from London outside. No matter how hard you tried, you could never block out that light.

This would be a long night, he thought. The longest in a while.

Wednesday, 23 January

The dream on Tuesday night was a chaotic rage of blood and fire and anguish. Harry was at the helm of the *Time and Tide*, pushing her through black waters. He was on a river that didn't exist, one as wide as the sea but with the smell of London. He found himself on the starboard deck, by the aft ladder. He backed away as James Lahiri came up out of the water towards him, climbing onto his own boat, his face ashen, a dark red hole in the back of his head. Then he saw faces in the water – Solomon Idris, Keisha Best, and Shaquille Dawson. Idris's brother Junior in an Arsenal shirt. Faceless young men and women. Afghan boys and girls. All clawing to get onto the boat. Shouting out to him with wordless screams.

A sound like a slamming door woke him up.

They ate breakfast in the hotel restaurant. Harry filled his plate with bacon, greasy sausages and hash browns, poured coffee, and barely touched any of it. The promised snow had fallen overnight, a couple of inches that was quickly turning to slush on the roads and wreaking inconvenience rather than havoc across the city.

Harry watched as Noble received a call, before offering the phone to him.

'It's for you,' she said. 'It's your friend.'

Harry took her phone and she went to refill her coffee, probably to give him privacy. So he went outside to stand in the snow, the cold an unwelcome return.

'Morning. Harry,' said Tammas. 'Did you. Sleep?'

'No,' Harry said. 'You?'

'A little. I got woken. Up at. About. Six. Forty-five.'

'What happened?'

'I got a. Visit. From some. Detectives. Up your end.'

Harry felt the cold go through him faster than it should have. Three lanes of angry rush-hour traffic on the Old Street roundabout were competing with the congestion and the snow. He moved around to another wall to shield himself from the noise. 'Who were they?' he asked.

'Homicide. They said. From Southwark. One of them. Oriental.

Stank of. Cheap fags. Like the ones. You used. To get from. The mess. The one. In charge was. Female. Blonde. Not bad. Would have. Given me. A hard-on. If I had. A spinal cord.'

Shit, Harry thought. The sergeant from Homicide & Serious, the one who'd supervised his interview at Lewisham, had been East Asian, probably Chinese, and the woman sounded suspiciously like DCI Marsden, especially if she'd been in charge. They'd driven all the way down to Kingston to speak to Tammas first thing, rather than wait for the morning. And the senior investigating officer had done it herself, not delegated it.

'Bastards!' Harry said. 'Why the hell did reception let them in?'

'I let them. In, Harry,' said Tammas. 'You know. How much. I appreciate. Visitors.'

Harry took a long, hard breath.

'What did they say?'

'They wanted. To know. About. James.'

Harry rested his head against the wall, and spoke in a voice an imitation of Tammas's own, every word punctuated.

'What did you tell them, boss?'

'I told them. He was. One of the. Best. Doctors. I ever took. Under my wing. I told. Them. That if it wasn't. For him. Lots of. People. Would be dead. You. And me included. And that. He went back. For seconds. Even though. It probably wrecked. His life.'

The eulogy was appreciated, but it didn't really matter. There was only one thing which did.

'Boss, did you tell them about what happened with Alice?'

'I didn't. Have a choice.'

Harry punched the wall.

'Fuck!' he spat. 'Fuck! Fuck! Fuck!'

The police were obeying the universal law of entropy, moving from order to chaos. The answer to why James Lahiri was dead started and finished with Solomon Idris, sitting feverish in a Chicken Hut. The patient he'd been trying to help, or that he'd let down, depending on which way you looked at it. If they were trying to look more widely, to treat his murder as a coincidence, then they would have a field day and get nowhere.

'I wasn't. Going to lie. To them. Harry.'

'I know, boss.'

'I told them. You didn't. Do it.'

'What?'

There was a vent in the wall blowing out warm air, and Harry edged along to stand beside it.

'I said. That however. Much you might. Have wanted. To do. It. You wouldn't. Have the balls.'

Harry didn't know whether Tammas was being tongue-in-cheek or condescending. He let the warm air run through his hair and listened.

'They were. Saying. Things,' Tammas continued. 'About. Lending money. Giving. Drugs to teenage boys. Changing things. On some. Computer system.'

'That's bullshit,' Harry said. He wasn't sure if he believed it or not. James had deleted that allergy, or at least someone with access to his computer log-in had.

'I told them. It doesn't. Matter what. James did. That he's. Still dead. And someone should. Still pay.'

'Harry!'

He turned to his left and briefly raised his arms as the phone was snatched from his hand, only to lower them when he realised it was Noble, one hand inside her jacket.

'Jesus Christ, what part of *don't go out of my sight* is difficult for someone with a medical degree to understand?'

Harry opened his mouth to speak, but Noble cut him off, grabbing his hand.

'What happened to your hands?'

Harry looked down. The cold had outmanoeuvred the pain, and he hadn't even realised he was bleeding. There was a pair of cuts on the knuckles of his right middle and index fingers that looked deep, and were still oozing black-red blood.

'Oh,' Harry said. 'I, erm, had a moment.'

Noble regarded him with suspicious eyes. It almost looked like pity. He could still feel the tightness behind his sternum. He wanted to scream, for everything inside him to just explode out of any hole it could find. It felt compressed, as if the scars on his chest were sealing it all in. He longed for Lahiri's scalpel to open it again, to release the pressure just as he'd done on Harry's collapsed lungs halfway up a foreign mountain.

'Do you want to finish your phone call?' she said, passing it back to him.

Harry put the phone up to his ear, but Tammas had hung up.

'Fuck's sake,' he said.

'Don't worry about it,' Noble said. 'Wilson wants me over at Lewisham. He says he's found something I should see.'

'I'm coming with you.'

'Harry, I'm not sure—'

'Frankie, we made that deal yesterday, remember. That hasn't changed. I was part of this from the start, and I plan to see it through to the end.'

Noble shook her head.

'This is fucked up.'

A chunk of snow fell down from the roof, and landed between them. The cold went through Harry again, and he leant against the wall to catch his breath. She lit a cigarette and turned towards her car.

'Come on, then.'

All the other times Harry had been to Lewisham station it had been to the custody suite or the interrogation rooms. He'd never made it into the inner sanctum, a seemingly infinite maze of offices, meeting rooms and training classrooms. Noble explained that they often transferred major investigations to Lewisham when they needed the extra facilities. He trudged to the station through the slush in the car park, still unused to the new shoes they'd got him. The jumper he'd been bought was reasonably thick, but the temperature was still hovering around zero outside and there was no one about without a coat. Hence the tattered black fleece from the boot of Noble's car that Harry sported. The Metropolitan Police insignia was present on the chest, but if he folded the collar over it was just about covered. At least it helped him blend in.

In the meeting room, all fifteen stone of DS Moses Wilson sat perched on a worktop. It was an old-fashioned classroom, with yellow-stained walls, a projector at one end, and wooden desks arranged in rows. It still stank of the cigarette smoke that had once hung from the ceiling, though it had long since been banished.

Wilson was in a suit, which was bizarre, and almost made Harry feel underdressed for the occasion.

The computer in front of him was locked, a Met Police logo above the log-in boxes. Plugged into the console was the USB drive Shaquille Dawson had handed over the previous day. Harry thought about that, how it felt like a different time. A lot could happen in eighteen hours.

'Technical Services cracked it this morning,' Wilson said. The detective looked rough, like he'd been up all night. There was a coffee stain on his tie. 'You'll never guess what the password was.'

Harry said nothing. Thought about what a seventeen-year-old would use as a password. A footballer's name, maybe, or a rapper.

'141112KAB,' Wilson said.

Noble shook her head. 'I don't get it.'

Harry got it, but Wilson explained first.

'14 November 2012,' he said. 'The day Keisha Best died, followed by her initials.'

Harry became aware of his heartbeat again, and silence descended. They could hear muffled conversations from the adjacent conference rooms.

'What's the delay?' Noble said.

'I thought we'd wait for DCI Marsden's team,' said Wilson. 'They're having a briefing upstairs.'

'Sod that,' said Noble. 'Show us now. You've seen what's on it, right?'

Harry watched Wilson shuffle, and knew that he had, and whatever he'd seen had scarred him. He had the same look he'd recognised in Solomon Idris at the Chicken Hut, and it all fell into place. Just like that, he knew.

A seventeen-year-old boy with eyes that had seen too much.

An eighteen-year-old girl, recently pregnant, with the fortitude to stare down a commuter train.

Both of them HIV-positive.

'Oh, Christ,' he said. 'It's sexual, isn't it?'

Wilson nodded.

'Abuse?' Harry said.

Wilson nodded again.

'Some of the worst shit I've ever seen. I told Marsden, I had to, guv. I've sat through it once, and I'm not gonna watch it a second time. Respectfully, the less times this video gets seen by human eyes the better.'

'You're right,' Noble said. 'Fuck.'

Harry felt numb. They stood in silence for a minute or so until the door opened without a knock. Harry recognised DCI Marsden from when he'd seen her at the Ruskin, now dressed in a dark red power suit, her entourage surrounding her like acolytes around a cardinal. The same people had been at Marigold House that morning, questioning a grieving man about who might want to kill his departed friend. He recognised other faces: the Chinese sergeant, sweat patches under his arms, the two detectives who'd interviewed him after the shooting. Last into the room were two people Harry did not want to see at all: DCI Fairweather, complete with damp trenchcoat and an even smaller suit this time. Kepler, his lapdog, trailed behind, a new sheaf of A4 paper tucked under his arm.

'Detective Inspector,' Marsden said, nodding towards Noble.

'Morning, ma'am.'

The detectives from Homicide & Serious, at least eight of them, filed into the room and formed two rows behind the chairs that Harry and Noble were sitting on. One of them spoke up.

'This is from the stick Shaquille Dawson handed over, right?'

'To Dr Kent, yes,' Marsden said. 'Let's play it.'

Harry felt eyes burn into the back of his neck and wondered why she had felt the need to point that out. At the computer, Wilson nodded solemnly and brought up a media player. He clicked play and bowed his head forward. To Harry, it looked like he was praying.

The video buffered for a while, and then the scene appeared. Keisha Best was face down on a double bed with lime-green sheets, naked, her hands tied to the headboard with thin plastic cord, something stuffed inside her mouth. The image was jerky, as if the camera was hand-held, but the quality was good: not quite high definition, but not far off. Good enough to make out a trickle of dark blood running from Keisha's left buttock down the inside of her leg. She was moaning, a terrible sound Harry recognised as the low vowels of intoxication. He'd heard them enough times in A&E. What was it that the post-mortem had found? Benzodiazepines, ketamine and GHB?

Solomon Idris entered the picture, also naked, facing away from the camera. His eyes were red from crying, and from the way he moved it was obvious that he was drugged, too. He moved closer to the camera, knocking into the bed as he did so, and then the image revealed the shackle around his right ankle, a length of chain running off into the distance. Like a dog tied up outside an off-licence. Slowly, Idris turned to face the camera.

'Please,' he said.

Seventeen years old, Harry thought. Perhaps when he'd seen him in the Chicken Hut, in a coat too big for him, fingers wrapped around a gun, Solomon Idris had looked like a man. Here, he was undoubtedly a boy.

Whoever was behind the camera did something, silently, and Idris flinched. Then he turned to face the bed and mounted the girl strapped to it, his body visibly trembling as he wept. Both the bodies shook and cried. Harry had to look at the floor, but somehow that just made it worse. Wilson had been right. This was the worst sound he had ever heard, the worst thing he had ever seen. This darkness had no place in the world. Behind him, one of the homicide detectives rushed to a bin and vomited.

A new sound came from the speakers, and it made Harry look up. It was a voice, from behind the camera, but it sounded electronic and garbled, low and menacing.

'You know that's not good enough.'

Harry looked across. Noble was still watching, unblinking, her knuckles white around the armrests of her chair.

Idris, begging again: 'Please. Make it stop.'

'Do it!' the mechanical voice commanded.

'No!'

The camera moved, up and closer to the bed, and then Harry realised that whoever was holding it had stood up. A pair of hands came briefly into view. They were wearing pale blue non-latex gloves, exactly the type used in hospitals. Idris flinched as the man behind the camera approached.

'Hit her!' the voice said.

Idris sobbed again, raised his hand, and brought it down on the side of Keisha Best's face, and both of them cried out.

'Do it again!' the voice shouted, and Harry felt the anger rise in him, and turned around, and wanted to find another wall to punch. By now, the chorus of silence among the gathered police officers had started to break, people swearing, heads in their hands. At the back, Fairweather and Kepler were arguing in whispers.

DCI Marsden broke through, standing up.

'I think we've seen enough,' she said. Wilson reached over and paused the video. The still frame caught Idris with a distraught expression on his face, while Keisha thrashed beneath him. Wilson, flustered, tried to minimise the window but missed a couple of times before the image finally disappeared.

'You've seen it before, Detective Sergeant?' Marsden continued. Wilson nodded.

'What happens?'

Harry watched Wilson swallow hard, still staring at the floor, before meeting Marsden's eyes. 'That continues for about four or five minutes. He hits her repeatedly. The man behind the camera taunts Idris about his inability to reach orgasm. He then approaches the bed and rapes Miss Best himself, while forcing Idris to watch. Then the video cuts out and back in again, and we see Idris performing fellatio on the offender. The whole thing lasts about thirteen minutes, ma'am.'

'Thank you,' said Marsden. Harry looked around the room. The DCI was probably the only person who wasn't visibly distressed by what they had just seen. Instead she looked cold.

'He rapes both individuals?'

'It appears so, yes,' said Wilson, his voice cracking.

Harry felt stupid for not working it out earlier. It hadn't been about embarrassing the Saviour Project by leaking stories about giving kids cannabis to the press. That was no reason to kill another human being. Making sure a video like that one wasn't watched by anyone but the sick, depraved fucks who would pay for that sort of thing was. The silence lasted about thirty seconds, until Marsden spoke again.

'Right,' she said. 'This is one investigation now. Under my

control. We work together, and we work our arses into the ground until we've found the people responsible for this, and put them in prison. Enhanced Protection Wings – they'll get what's coming to them. Understood?'

The chorus replied: 'Yes, ma'am.'

Harry looked behind him. Fairweather had his arms crossed and was typing an email out on his phone, evidently pissed at having been sidelined. Marsden continued.

'Let's summarise what we know so far. We know that a computer account at the Ruskin belonging to Dr Lahiri deleted the penicillin allergy on Solomon Idris's medical record. It's reasonable to assume that this was intended to kill Solomon. We also know that a firearm was discharged in the vicinity of Wyndham Road while Idris had hostages there, again with the likely intention of causing his death. And we know that Dr Lahiri was murdered yesterday evening. That's about all we know for sure. So, let's talk.'

Noble stood up.

'Mo, what else did Technical Services have on the video?' she said.

Wilson looked down at his notepad.

'They reckon it was filmed on a GoPro, guv. It's a compact camera that you can fix to something mobile. They're designed for skiing, sports, stuff like that. They think he attached it to his body with a strap, or a headband, or something. They've seen it before in child porn, hardcore stuff.'

'Traceable?'

'Afraid not, guv.'

'What about the rapist? Nothing on his identity?'

'The only parts of his body that come into view are his hands and forearms, and he's wearing a long T-shirt tucked into those gloves,' Wilson said. 'They can estimate his height as between five-nine and six foot, but that's it. The voice was electronically modified with audio editing software after the video was filmed. They might be able to get something on that, but it's going to CEOP for specialist analysis. Could take weeks.'

'Shit,' said Noble.

'What else do we know?' Marsden said. She had moved to the

front of the room now. If it wasn't for all the suits Harry could have been back at medical school, in some tutorial where he didn't know any of the answers.

'There's something,' Harry said. All the faces turned to look at him, and Noble nodded at him to continue.

'It's possible the offender is HIV-positive.'

'Really?' said Marsden. 'On what basis?'

'Keisha Best was, and Solomon Idris is,' said Harry. 'I take it that none of them use protection in that video?'

Wilson shook his head. 'We don't see any other part of his anatomy in the video. He's clever like that. But there's no evidence of condom use, no. And serial sex offenders tend not to.'

'Don't want to ruin the experience,' Kepler said. 'Motherfuckers.'

'If he is positive then how would we spot it?' said Marsden.

'Well, once you've got a suspect in custody we can take a blood sample,' Harry said. 'With their consent. Whoever it is would have to take regular medications, several every day. But if it's well controlled, then you'd have no idea.'

'Right,' Marsden continued. 'Anything else? This is open forum.'

'Access to a blue-and-silver motorbike,' said one of the other detectives. 'And access to the gun.'

DI Noble stepped forward, next to Marsden, who regarded her with a suspicious sideways glance. Another alpha female was pissing on her territory, Harry thought.

'Statistically, we're looking for a male aged between thirty and sixty,' Noble said. 'Point one: we know those kids were drugged. The post-mortem on Keisha Best found a long history of benzos, GHB and ket. I know stuff like that isn't hard to get hold of these days, but he knew exactly how much to give them so they were compliant, but not passed out.'

Harry shuffled on his seat, fully aware where Noble was going. When he'd said the same things, freezing his arse off in the front seat of her car on Peckham High Street, it had just been conjecture. In retrospect, it looked terrifyingly prophetic.

'Point two. The evidence suggests that Best had a termination shortly before she died, but there are no records of her going through any legal channels. So someone arranged it on the sly. I

238

think we're looking at a healthcare professional, probably a doctor, with access to the Ruskin's computer system.'

'Good work,' said Marsden. 'This project, what's it called, Saviour?'

Noble and Wilson nodded.

'It's an obvious place to start,' Noble said. 'It's the only significant contact Solomon Idris had with the healthcare system in four years, aside from two visits to A&E. If he was supplied with cannabis, that could have been used as a way in, a grooming strategy. And it seems likely that the offender accessed Keisha Best through Solomon.'

Harry listened to the words, still processing what they meant. Someone in the project, someone he potentially knew, was responsible for *that*, the horrors he'd just seen.

'Who runs this gaff?' asked Deakin, the detective who'd interviewed Harry.

'It's the GPs out of the Burgess Park Practice,' Noble said. 'And some A&E staff at the Ruskin.'

Deakin held up a computer printout.

'The tech report says that our mate Lahiri made his change to the allergy at 07.20 on Monday morning. Are we thinking he still did it, or was it someone else using his account?'

Harry almost stood up to speak, but Noble got there first.

'Keep an open mind,' Noble said. 'It's possible Lahiri did it, for whatever reason. It's possible he was involved. But it's also possible that someone else who knew his log-in details could have done it.'

Harry's skin burned hot, and he felt sick again. *It's possible he was involved.* Not with that, Harry thought, not with that abomination I've just seen.

'Really?' another detective said. 'Wouldn't a stranger stick out in the hospital?'

No one said anything and Harry realised all eyes were on him. He tried to suppress his anger at Noble's previous comment and answer the question plainly.

'Not necessarily. There are a good few hundred doctors at work at the Ruskin every day, and most of the time there's some locums in, especially in A&E, so an unfamiliar face wouldn't raise too many alarm bells. You put a stethoscope around your neck, you can get just about anywhere in a hospital.'

'Mmm,' Marsden said, obviously fighting for control of the room. 'We'll cross-check all Saviour Project staff with those who may have been at the Ruskin around that time. And let's not forget, it's possible that there's more than one person involved here. We could be looking at a group of offenders. A ring, so to speak.'

That thought resonated around the room for a short while, before Wilson piped up.

'There's something else,' he said. 'Whoever shot James Lahiri last night wounded the harbour watchman as well, but he took the time to put a tourniquet on. And he knew how. That's another indicator we're looking at a medic here.'

'So he's a nonce who works in a hospital,' a young detective said. 'Surely they couldn't get a job, with that kind of record.'

'We know how clever some of these fuckers can be, Helen,' another copper replied. 'They can stay clean for years.'

'He's not a paedophile,' someone else cut in. 'Those are teenagers, not kids. It's a different type of perv we're looking at, and that's important.'

'Good point, Mike. Also, sexual activity with both a male and female, that's unusual.'

A few more voices shouted out, until one cut through them, the booming, didactic tone that belonged to DCI Fairweather.

'Gentlemen, ladies, please,' Fairweather said, standing up. 'I'm sorry to tread on your toes, Louisa, but it does strike me that we're making a very dubious assumption. We're all talking like we're sure that the murder of Dr Lahiri yesterday evening is linked to all of this.'

'With respect, Marcus—' Marsden began.

'I'd like to hear a better idea if you've got one,' Noble interrupted. 'Sir. Lahiri was Idris's GP. They're linked. Like I said, there are two possibilities. Either Lahiri was involved in the abuse, and he's been taken out by his co-conspirator to stop him coming to the police. Or he's not involved, but he knew something that would tip us off. He told Harry about the scheme to prescribe some of the Saviour Project patients cannabis.'

Harry had never felt an urge to hit a woman before, but he was getting close. Lahiri was dead, and Christ, he hadn't been a perfect man by any means. But the suggestion that his friend was a sexual sadist set Harry's blood rising, and he was finding the words to attack Noble's statement when Marsden started talking.

'We know they're connected,' she said, turning to DCI Fairweather. 'It's the same gun.'

'What?' Noble said. 'Ballistics confirmed that, did they?'

'They did indeed,' said Marsden. 'Worked overnight for us. DS Cheung got the report through this morning. Terry?'

Cheung stood up and addressed the crowd. Harry was struggling to concentrate on what he was saying, still furious at Noble's earlier suggestion. She was the one he trusted, the one who'd made a pact that they would find out what had happened to Solomon Idris, and now she was just wrong.

'We recovered two shell casings from the marina,' Cheung continued. His accent was almost comical, the Scouse obvious, but with a breathless, sweaty voice that reminded Harry of a man who'd often frequented the pub he'd worked in during medical school. 'Nine-millimetre rounds. Firing pin markings on the casings were forensically matched to those recovered from the Wyndham Road crime scene on Sunday evening.'

Cheung was playing with a laptop, opening up an email attachment.

'They ran it through NABIS and got nothing. The gun's not been used in any previous crimes. But we do have a lead on the ammunition.'

The detective zoomed in on the round, brass surface of the base of a cartridge casing. Harry squinted to look at it, the markings stamped into the metal vaguely familiar.

'That's army-issue,' Harry said. Underneath the NATO motif was a military L number, a designation system which was only used by the UK.

'Yeah, it is. Radway Green, manufactured in 2004. Apparently, we've seen this ammunition in London before.'

Next to Harry, DS Wilson spoke up.

'Fitz,' he said.

'Sorry?' said DCI Marsden. 'Who's Fitz?'

'He's a gun dealer,' Wilson said. 'CID are investigating him in a joint operation with Trident. He popped up on our radar just before Christmas. We don't know his full name, but everyone calls him Fitz; we think it's an abbreviation of his surname. He's local to the Elephant & Castle area, been seen drinking in the Wetherspoons there. He exploits a loophole in the law with respect to antique firearms – goes over to Europe with a few mates posing as collectors and buys old World War One pistols at antiques markets, which you can legally import into the UK.'

'Well, it's legal until he puts live ammunition into them and sells them to teenagers,' Noble added.

'And he uses military ammunition?' Marsden said.

'According to our sources,' Wilson said. 'He's a double ampu-tee. We heard he used to be in one of the engineering regiments – might have been bomb disposal. But Trident haven't got anywhere with an ID.'

'More than that, though,' Cheung said. 'That ammo's from the same batch recovered in seized weapons known to have come from him.'

'Christ,' Harry said. Ordnance disposal was done by ammuni-tion technicians, whose other duties included acting as armourers during deployment. It wasn't exactly a transferable skill, unless you were willing to break bad.

'Right,' said Marsden. 'Any other forensics?'

'Potentially,' said Cheung. 'Scene of Crime recovered a DNA sample from the belt our shooter tied around the security guard's thigh. They're running it against all known parties. Might have something back by this afternoon.'

'Great work on the gun,' Marsden said. 'That's one hell of a lead if we can bring this guy in and sweat him. DS Wilson, that's your action. Get it done. Terry, I want you to coordinate with my team and run the backgrounds of everyone who worked with the Saviour Project team. Prioritise anyone with a previous convic-tion, even if it's not sexual, and anyone who would have had access to the computer system at the Ruskin. Frankie and Marcus, my office, and we'll draw up the Major Investigation Plan, make sure we're not missing anything.'

Marsden turned around, preaching now. Harry shuffled on his chair as people stood up, sure that his omission in her list of orders hadn't been merely accidental. He was thinking of the video and the look in Solomon Idris's eyes.

'It's the easy stuff which will win us this one, guys,' Marsden continued. 'Let's do it right.'

Some of the other detectives spat out platitudes in response. Harry stood and locked eyes with Noble, who cocked her head towards the door.

When they got out into the corridor, Noble opened a fire exit and stepped out into fresh, powdery snow. Harry looked at the ground while she lit up. He was rehearsing his words in his head, trying to work out how to put his argument. The snow wasn't sticking.

'I can't—' Noble said.

Harry leant forward and picked the cigarette from between her lips.

'Fuck you,' he said.

'Sorry, I was just trying to—'

'Not for that,' Harry said. 'I mean fuck you for what you said back in there.'

'What are you talking about?'

'Two theories,' Harry quoted. 'You think Lahiri was responsible for what we just watched? You think he did that? You think he got his kicks from raping teenagers?'

Noble stared Harry down, retrieved her cigarette from his fingers, and smoked it.

'What I think is that there has to be a reason for someone to kill him,' she said. 'So either he was involved, or he knew enough about it to be a reasonable witness against someone who was.'

'He wasn't a rapist,' Harry said. 'I knew him for fifteen years, and he was my best fucking friend.'

'Harry, I've heard wives say that about their husbands. We all have.'

'Well, not this one,' Harry said. 'He's dead now, OK? And it is fucking me up, and I promised the boss I'd find who did it, and ignorant coppers who didn't know him talking shit about him is not fucking helping!'

He finished, his cheeks hot despite the cold. Two community support officers jogged around the building, come to investigate the commotion. Noble dismissed them with a gesture, and Harry felt like crying again. Wished he could find the pressure valve and let everything out.

'Sorry,' he said.

'It's OK,' said Noble. She reached out to touch his arm, but Harry drew it away. She laughed. 'I'm being friendly, alright? I'm not gonna try and fuck you in the car park.'

Harry shook his head.

'I'm serious,' he said. 'Lahiri wasn't that man. If you go down that road, then you'll waste a lot of time, OK? You've got to believe me.'

Noble nodded.

'I believe you,' she said. 'But in this line of work we never assume a thing. You can understand that, can't you?'

'He called me over,' Harry said. 'He told me about the cannabis prescriptions, about all of that. Why'd he do that if he was guilty?'

'Misdirection,' Noble said. 'Trying to get us to focus elsewhere.'

'Then surely he'd direct us away from the Saviour Project, wouldn't he?'

'Maybe. But there's no point agonising over stuff like this. I hate to say it, but Marsden's right on this one. Whoever's behind this will have a record and a history. We'll get there with old-fashioned hard work. Knocking on doors.'

Harry nodded. Snow fell down and cooled his face, and he thought about the sound of Tammas crying through his tube. Behind them, someone came out of the fire escape. They both turned to look. It was Wilson.

'There you are, guv,' Wilson said. 'DS Cheung's looking for you.'

'Well, aren't I the lucky one,' Noble said, crushing out the cigarette. 'Mo can sort you out – speak to uniform and organise you a minder – and then you'll want to go home, I guess?'

'I'm not having a minder,' Harry said. 'And I'm gonna head to the hospital first. Check on Idris.'

Noble shook her head.

'Harry, this is our case now. Don't cause us grief.'

And with that, she strode away. Harry watched her jog along the corridor, the dark jeans tight around her legs, remembered his

drunken fumblings of the night before. Adrenaline, alcohol, corti-
sol, the right combination of brain chemistry for two sensible,
professional people to do something wild and stupid. He hadn't
even been attracted to her when they'd first met. Wilson beckoned
Harry into the corridor.

'I'm not having a shadow,' Harry said. 'I'll take my chances.'

Wilson breathed in.

'The guv said—'

'I know what she said,' Harry said. 'Tell her I ran off if needs be.
But I'm getting out of here.'

'Take your chances, then. But stay the hell out of trouble.'

Wilson smiled. Harry could tell he knew that he wasn't going to
honour those words and smiled back. They got out into the car
park and stood under an alcove, watching uniformed coppers
scrape snow and ice off patrol car windscreens.

'Do you need a lift to the hospital?' Wilson said.

'I'll get a cab. You don't have a spare phone I could borrow,
do you?'

His own was still in the evidence locker. Wilson reached into his
pocket and handed him an old Samsung.

'Take mine for now. I'm sure I'll see you later. I've got my work
one anyway. That's got Frankie's number if you need it.'

Harry nodded. He was thinking about what Marsden had said,
about their best lead bearing on Wilson finding the man who'd
likely sold the gun which had killed Lahiri. A man with no legs
who spent most of his time in a chain pub in the middle of
Walworth couldn't be too hard to find.

'Tell me what you know about Fitz,' Harry said.

'The gun dealer?'

'Yeah. You think it's short for his surname?'

'I reckon so,' Wilson said. 'Fitzgerald, Fitzwilliam, you know,
something like that. I'm not on the team investigating him, but one
of my CIs has heard of him. My guy runs an off-licence on the
Elephant & Castle roundabout, reckons that this bloke comes in
pretty much every day for two six-packs of Special Brew.
Sometimes has people asking after him.'

'So he's a heavy drinker?' Harry said. 'And he's in a wheelchair?'

'Yeah, so I've heard,' Wilson said, sounding confused. Harry had an embryo of an idea, something that would probably get him struck off if he went through with it, so he stayed quiet. Wilson looked at him suspiciously, but let it go.

'My work number's in there,' he said, nodding at the phone. 'Gimme a text if there's news about Idris.'

Harry nodded and headed off, the thin fleece little protection against the cold. He took the high street up towards the railway station, where there'd be a taxi rank for sure. On the way, he passed a pair of freezing-looking students in Goldsmith University hoodies, carrying football kit, one white, one Asian. Mirrors of himself and James Lahiri, taking the train from Guy's down to the medical school sports ground in Brockley every Wednesday afternoon, then the bus up to Tommy's Bar for the obligatory post-match beers.

He'd never drink with him again. Even though they'd not really spoken for months, Harry was coming to realise that he'd viewed it all as temporary, a phase they were going through, that they'd eventually reconcile. But there'd be none of that now. Lahiri had died angry and scared, seeing in Harry a broken, paranoid, unfaithful man, ready to accuse him of murder.

He found a cab at the station and got in. He had cash. Forty quid in dried-out tenners he'd rescued from his wallet the previous evening.

'Where you going, mate?'

'John Ruskin University Hospital.'

'Right you are.'

Most days, the noise of the hospital excited him, even made him feel at home, but today the feeling was different. The buzz of activity that made the place feel alive was ominous in light of the knowledge that a man capable of the acts he'd just witnessed could be walking the same corridors.

The news would already have spread among the staff, he knew. Nobody would talk about much else for weeks. But then one of the consultants would be spotted in a local restaurant with a new house officer, or something like that, and Lahiri's death would be old news. A&E would find another locum, Burgess Park would find another GP, and the world would turn again. Unless the police's investigation became public knowledge, or the rumours of paedophilia and sexual abuse began to spread. Then he'd make the headlines again.

Harry reached the ICU but walked past the corridor to the ward, heading into the changing room instead. Unlocked his locker and found the aspirin bottle, deciding whether to take three or four. Two was the usual – he'd never taken four at the same time before. And this would be his third day in a row, which was breaking another rule. But he hadn't slept in twenty-four hours, and it would a long day yet before he got the chance.

He washed four pills down with water and popped his trust ID badge into a lanyard, aware that in his police-issue fleece and chinos he didn't much look the part. The ward round was done, and he found the duty consultant sitting at the nurses' station, making notes at the computer. Rashid's three days on call had finished, and it was a new consultant waiting, Dr Amos. She looked up and it took her a while to recognise him.

'Harry,' she said. 'What happened to your face?'

'Cycling accident,' Harry said, air rushing through his chest again.

'Oh,' said Amos. 'You're on the rota today?'

'No,' Harry said. 'I was hoping to check in on Solomon Idris.'

'Sure, let's go,' she said, standing up and heading for Idris's side room. 'Marek told me about what you did on Sunday night, he sounded very impressed.'

Harry ignored her. Amos had only been at the hospital since Christmas, so maybe she didn't know about Lahiri and his connection to Harry, or maybe she hadn't yet heard. He arched his head to look into the side room at Idris's monitor as they washed their hands and donned gloves and aprons. The vital signs were stable, particularly his blood pressure, which from the look of the infusion pumps running into him no longer needed stabilising with drugs. Only forty-five per cent oxygen going in through the ventilator. They stepped inside and Harry nodded at the police officer on protection duty, who was reading the *Mail*.

'What's the plan?'

'The surgical team are happy,' Dr Amos said. 'Touch wood, he shouldn't need to go back to theatre. It's just a case of clearing his lungs up now. Continue with the physio, get him off the ventilator.'

Harry felt a tight band around his chest as he looked down at Idris. There were only slightly fewer tubes and lines than there had been yesterday, but the wasting in the muscles between his ribs was becoming more pronounced. The worst thing wasn't the teenager's frail appearance, though, it was the reminder of the last time he'd seen him. Begging the man with the mechanical voice not to make him rape his own girlfriend, the sedatives taking all of the fight out of him. The tears in his eyes as he'd hit Keisha, all to satisfy some other bastard's sadistic tastes.

'Harry? You OK?'

Harry looked up at Amos.

'Yeah,' he said. 'How're the haemodynamics?'

'Not bad, in light of his arrest,' Amos said. 'We'll do another echo later, but the numbers look good.'

'OK,' Harry said. Looked at Idris and silently promised him again that he'd have justice, that Harry knew about Keisha now and he'd punish the people who'd made him do what he'd done. Then he balled up his apron and his gloves and threw them into one of the clinical waste bins. He thanked Dr Amos and headed out of the ICU, aiming for the staircase that led down to A&E. He almost made it before he heard his name called.

'Harry?'

He turned. Traubert was standing in his office doorway, leaning against the wall, a pained smile on his face. Harry stood his ground.

'Come here.'

He swore under his breath as he walked over to Traubert's office. The consultant retreated into the room and sat on his desk, his hands folded into one another, as if he'd read a book about body language and was trying to imitate the picture beneath the heading 'compassionate'. Harry didn't shut the door. He had no intention of staying.

'I'm so sorry, I only just found out,' Traubert said, his voice lowered. 'How are you doing?'

Harry garbled fragments of stock phrases, *Been better, Pretty crap, As expected.*

'What the hell happened? Have they caught who did it?'

Harry opened and closed his mouth for a while before he found the words.

'My friend's dead,' he said. 'I feel terrible, Dr Traubert. And I need to go.'

'Well, I'm shocked you're even here, Harry. That's why I wanted to talk to you. I wanted to let you know that I've already sorted the rota, and you can take as much time off as you want. A whole month, if you need it. Just do let me know when you think you'll be ready.'

Harry looked at Traubert, the consultant smiling with every word, and waited for him to trail off.

'Thank you,' he said. 'I really need to go, I'm sorry.'

'I was wondering if we could sort out some kind of tribute to James,' Traubert went on. 'Perhaps something—'

The impulse was so strong, it happened before Harry could stop it. He looked down at the shaking base of the door he'd just kicked, and then back up at the horrified expression on Traubert's face.

'I'm sorry,' he mumbled. 'I'm not thinking straight.'

'Go home,' Traubert said. 'Look at yourself. Go home, Harry.'

Harry tried to focus on the consultant's mouth, but the room was spinning. He got up and left, his head pounding with pain and terror. Started down the staircases towards A&E, slipped on the bottom step of the first flight and fell, his hands crumpling against the wall. As he pulled himself up he felt a shooting pain go up his jaw, and then came the palpitations. He stood upright against the wall, and caught his breath. Four pills had been a mistake.

A&E was busy as he walked through. Two nurses were trying to restrain a screaming young girl with disturbed, psychotic eyes. In another bay, Bernadette Kinirons was writing up a prescription chart for a woman with an obviously broken nose and a black eye, while a uniformed police officer texted on his phone in the background. Kinirons made eye contact and touched her scrubs where her heart was, and Harry nodded back.

He came out of Resus and found the triage desk, the large room where the senior A&E nurses decided how urgently patients needed to be seen. It was the front line, quite possibly the most difficult job in the hospital, and the nurses who did it were all formidable in their own right. The first one Harry saw wasn't the one he was looking for.

'Hey,' he said. 'Is Josh working today?'

'Aye, he's just in the charge nurse's office. And I'm so sorry to hear about Dr Lahiri. I know youse two were close.'

The use of the past tense made him wince, but not in the way he'd expected. It wasn't the statement that Lahiri was gone which cut him, it was the implication that they had been close, once, and the knowledge that the reason they no longer were was his doing.

Harry arrived at the office, and was met by the sight of a man in a grey tabard hunched over a computer screen. People often underestimated Josh Geddes. He looked young, though he was well into his thirties, his hair styled with great effort like a nineties pop star, edges of tattoos poking out of his sleeves. Truth was, Geddes was perhaps the best nurse Harry had ever worked with. He lectured at the nursing school, had written two books, and he would still take an hour out of his day to hold the hand of a homeless man who was dying alone, or calm a frightened, senile patient.

'Oh, Christ,' Geddes said, spinning on his chair. 'Shut the bloody door, won't you. I'm so fucking sorry.'

'So am I,' said Harry.

'You look like shit,' said Geddes. 'When did you find out?'

'Last night,' he said. 'I was there. I watched him die.'

Geddes clasped a hand across his mouth. 'There's nothing I can say, Harry. Sit down.'

'I don't want to talk about it,' Harry said, closing the door behind him. 'Not now.'

Geddes was a good friend – when Harry had worked in A&E they'd often been on night shifts together, and had spent many a morning at the pub just uphill from the hospital, indulging in a morning Guinness and fry-up before heading home to sleep. He needed someone he could trust for this.

'I need you to find a patient for me,' Harry said.

'Sure,' Geddes said, turning back to the computer. 'What's the name?'

'I've only got a partial surname. But don't search now, they're not in at the moment.'

'How do you know that they'll be on the system, then?'

'I don't,' Harry said. 'But the patient's local and he drinks twelve Special Brews a day.'

Geddes looked up at him, his face changing as he followed Harry's thought processes. Few hardcore alcoholics managed to go a year without at least a short stay in hospital, and for every admission there were usually numerous A&E visits. Falls, fights, gastric ulcers, detox, seizures. Assuming Fitz's habit was as entrenched as Wilson had thought, then he'd be on record, and the Ruskin would have his address.

The problem was, it was against the rules to access someone's personal medical record unless you were involved in their care, and Harry wasn't at all. If he passed that information to the police, then he could well be struck off. And from the expression on Geddes's face, that wasn't lost on him.

'Harry, they're auditing all of our computer use after what happened to that ICU patient. You know that, right?'

'I know,' said Harry. 'If they come asking, say that you stayed logged in but I did all the searching. I'll take the rap.'

Geddes threw himself back in his chair.

'If I help you find this man's address, what are you going to do? Give it to the police?'

'No,' said Harry. 'It looks like this man sold the gun that killed James to whoever did it. I'll pay him a visit, and maybe he'll tell me who he sold it to. I'm sure he won't report me to the GMC.'

Geddes got serious again, and bowed his head. Looked from side to side like he was checking if there was anyone else in the room to hear what he was going to do.

'No police.'

'No police,' said Harry. 'They'd never be able to use it in court, anyway.'

'Give me the name.'

'We've got a partial surname. Begins with "Fitz".'

Geddes winced.

'Christ, Harry, there'll be hundreds.'

'You'll narrow it down,' Harry said. 'Our man is white, he's aged between twenty and fifty, and he's a double amputee, both his legs. His address will be near Elephant & Castle, either SE17 or SE1, and he's a drinker. Look for alcohol-related admissions.'

Geddes nodded.

'OK,' he said. 'I'll be in touch. I never enjoy my lunch breaks, anyway.'

Harry took a deep breath, and felt the air in his chest twist, and made the mistake of closing his eyes. Saw James's face turn and then disappear, the red spray on the fuselage of the boat. He made to leave, then turned back.

'Oh, Josh, one other thing.'

'This illegal, too?'

'No,' Harry said. 'Did you have a trauma call come in yesterday? Just after six? An Eastern European guy, gunshot leg.'

Geddes nodded.

'Yeah,' he said. 'Emile Giurescu. He's up on Kipling Ward now, in traction, but he should do alright. When he came in, he still had some geezer's belt around his thigh. HEMS doctors said it saved his life.'

Harry took Geddes' number, put it into Wilson's phone, and then drop-called him so he had a number to call when he found Fitz's address.

'Thanks for this, Josh,' Harry said. 'I owe you one.'

'I'm not doing it for you,' Geddes said. 'I'm doing it for James.'

Harry nodded and headed for the door.

'Where are you going, anyway?' said Geddes. 'You're not working, are you?'

'Nah. I'm off to see the doctor.'

Noble didn't want people to speak to her while she smoked, so she got into her car and lit up. She sat back, inhaling deeply, thinking about Harry. He'd been wrong, what he'd said last night. There had been many men since Jack had died, probably too many, though none as intense, none as desperate as Harry had been. Understandable given the circumstances. In a different light she would have seen that as passion, but Christ alone knew what it had been in him. She finished the cigarette, and, after ensuring she was unobserved, ducked into the glove compartment where she kept the hip flask engraved with the Metropolitan Police's logo and a blue number fifteen, the number of years that Jack Noble had served as a police officer when he'd received it. She unscrewed the top and let that day's second taste run down her mouth, the heat in her throat a glorious contrast to the cold outside.

And then it came, the feeling that every drinker seeks. Every hair on her body stood on end, all the stress and hatred left through her skin, and her hands and face glowed with life. For that single second, the hollow inside her was full of bright warm joy.

A tap on her window made her jump. 'Didn't mean to startle you,' DCI Fairweather lied.

Noble got out of the car and Fairweather backed off. She made a point of standing downwind, scrabbling in her pockets for chewing gum. 'Can I help you, guv?'

'You can indeed, Frankie, you can indeed. Come with me.'

They walked alone through the car park. Only a year or so older than her, Fairweather was already a chief inspector, almost certain to be in command of a unit within a few years, maybe even the Met's first ever black commissioner, some said. He was already ticking one of the boxes with an anti-corruption job. She could shoot him in the back of the head right now and few would be the detectives who turned up to arrest her rather than take her to the local and buy her a drink.

She followed him into the station, to the room where they'd had the briefing, now littered with coffee cups and empty water bottles. DCI Marsden sat at a table, laptop open in front of her. When they came in she smiled and shut it. Fairweather locked the door and pulled down the blinds. Noble looked across at Marsden, trying to read her, to work out what she was there for. The presence of Fairweather, the only other senior-grade detective on the investigation, was ominous.

'Sit down, Frankie,' said Marsden.

Noble did so, thought for a moment, and then decided she had to take the high ground. 'With all due respect, guv, will this take long? I'm halfway through organising the interviews—'

'This can take as long as you want it to,' Marsden said. Fairweather stayed standing, leaning against the wall to her left. A classic pincer movement. If they wanted her to feel like a suspect, they were going to have to try harder than that. Noble looked between them, trying to work out who was in charge. They'd spoken about this, planned it. It was Fairweather who spoke first.

'How much do you know about Harry Kent?'

'How long is a piece of string?'

Fairweather rolled his eyes and refolded his arms. 'Come on, Detective Inspector. Let's not make this harder than it has to be.'

'Harder than it has to be?' Noble said. 'Why does it have to be hard? What's going on here?'

Fairweather looked over at Marsden, then back at Noble.

'What I'm asking,' he said, walking over towards her, 'is how much you know about Kent's past.'

'He grew up near here,' Noble said. 'Ex-forces. Studied at Guy's, where he met Lahiri. Served together with him in Afghanistan for a year and a half. Got wounded in action, Lahiri saved his life. Came back in 2011, been working at the Ruskin ever since.'

Fairweather nodded. Leant back a little.

'Is he married?'

Noble shot through every piece of information she'd gleaned. He lived alone, no ring, never mentioned any woman. He didn't act like a married man, or a divorced man. Men with families who stood for the things which Harry Kent stood for had something to lose, and acted accordingly.

'No,' she said. 'What are you getting at here?'

'Any recent relationships?'

'Sir, I've got a growing feeling that you know the answers to these questions much better than I do, so why don't you enlighten me?'

The silence hung in the room and Noble briefly tasted a little vodka again, or maybe it was just acid on the back of her throat. She was afraid now. Afraid that she'd fucked up. Fairweather looked over at Marsden again, who nodded. He leant forward, folded his arms.

'We've been running the background on James Lahiri. Well, Louisa's team has. It turns out that after Kent got wounded, Lahiri decided to go back to Afghanistan for a second tour, during which time his wife, Alice, had an affair. Would you like to take a wild guess at who that affair was with?'

Noble threw herself back in her chair with such force it almost toppled, and used all of her restraint to avoid swearing. In retrospect, there had been signs. The way Harry had talked about Lahiri had been distant, his grief conflicted – because he'd fucked up their friendship long before Solomon Idris had walked into the picture.

Fairweather was still talking.

'I take it from the expression on your face that this is a surprise to you, Frankie? He'd kept it from you, hadn't he?'

'If I'd shagged my best mate's wife, then I wouldn't broadcast it either, sir.'

'Especially not to someone I was hoping to get into bed,' Marsden said.

Noble rolled her eyes slowly over to Marsden, wondering whether she knew what had happened in the hotel room or was just winging it. That was the trouble with working with detectives. Very little remained private, however hard you tried.

'I beg your pardon?'

'You know what I meant, Frankie,' Marsden said. 'You spent the night in his bedroom.'

'I was armed,' Noble objected. 'I was protecting him.'

'Really?' said Marsden. 'And did you fuck him, as well?'

Noble looked at her, wondering whether an open-handed slap or a rabbit punch would be the best approach. She wanted to leave a sting, but not a mark. Noble knew what the dynamic was now. Marsden was calling the shots, Fairweather a mere attack dog.

'Yes,' she said through gritted teeth. Fairweather shook his head in disgust.

'Do I need to tell you how grave a breach of trust it is to have sexual relations with a witness in a murder investigation?' he said.

'He's not a witness,' said Noble. 'He's a colleague.'

'Come off it, Frankie,' said Marsden. 'He's a witness to a murder now. The only witness, I might add, given that our Bulgarian friend can't remember a single thing. So I think we need to go back to square one here.'

'What do you mean, go back to square one?'

'I think we need to bring Dr Kent in for questioning and

examine his story. We need to look at the physical evidence surrounding the South Dock crime scene and see if it matches up with his version of events.'

'We already did,' said Fairweather, turning to Marsden. 'Louisa, your team asked him about the nature of his friendship with Lahiri. He didn't mention the affair once. In my book, that's attempting to pervert the course.'

'That's ridiculous,' Noble said.

'He had a motive. He was at the crime scene, and he's done his best to remain involved in the investigation and potentially direct it away from himself. That makes him a suspect. In fact, it makes him the most likely suspect.'

There were two types of detectives. Some, like Fairweather, like Louisa Marsden, were calculators: they worked on facts alone, critically analysing everything they saw, going on balances of probabilities. Noble was the other kind, like Jack had been, like he'd taught her to be. She judged people, she went on her instinct. Harry Kent was a good man. The light still shone in his eyes, however mortally wounded his life was. She tried to switch off the emotion, to talk in facts. Turned to Marsden, knowing it would piss off Fairweather.

'Ma'am, we know the gun is the same as the one from the take-away. And he sure as hell didn't fire it then.'

'So he's working with someone,' said Marsden. 'Christ, maybe he's the one behind the camera in that video. Maybe he's been pulling the strings all along.'

'We only have that video because of him!' Noble protested. 'You haven't thought this through at all, have you?'

'Then it's a cover,' Fairweather said. 'He's wanted to kill Lahiri for ages. He found out about Idris and the abuse, and thought it was the perfect opportunity. Or, he found out about the abuse and decided to dole out the punishment himself.'

Noble shook her head vigorously. Opened her mouth to protest but Marsden cut her off.

'Last night I went to see the guy they'd both trained under – he's in some hospice thing down in Kingston. According to him, the sun shone out of Lahiri's arse. Kent was good, but he was only good. Never brilliant. Kent managed to get himself wounded, his boss ended up paralysed on the battlefield, but James Lahiri comes home with a medal. Kent's lived in this guy's shadow for most of his life, so he gets his own back, takes his wife away. But then she pisses off to New Zealand. And finally he's snapped.'

Noble listened to the theory and saw about seven holes, but decided to plump with the largest.

'Oh, come off it, that's ridiculous. There's no way in hell he could have predicted we'd call him to the takeaway with Idris.'

'But what if he did?' said Fairweather. 'Because he knew it'd be the perfect alibi. He got his accomplice to fire the gun on Sunday night, then he took it off him and went to do in Lahiri. The gun's probably in the river, we'd never be able to dredge that marina. Don't you think it's convenient that he just happened to be on his way there when Lahiri died?'

'It's not convenient at all,' Noble said. 'The shooter might have been following Harry for all we know. They attacked him Monday night.'

'So he says,' said Marsden.

'There's CCTV, for fuck's sake!' Noble said, turning to Fairweather. 'Let's imagine, for one crazy fucking second, that you're right, and Harry did have an accomplice who fired that shot at Wyndham Court. Why risk going to the boat at all? Why not get his accomplice to do it?'

'You've worked the murder squad, Frankie,' Marsden said. 'You're not stupid. You must've seen murders motivated by simple jealousy. He had to do it himself. Every day of his pitiful life since he met Lahiri, the bastard did everything he did, but better. He needed to look him in the eyes and pull the trigger.'

Noble refused to believe it. She remembered the fire in Harry's eyes, the passion, as he'd spoken about Solomon Idris, about Keisha Best, about their stories. That hadn't been an act.

'But he didn't do it,' she said. 'He didn't fucking do it, and you know it!'

'You're probably right,' said Marsden. 'But I'm not satisfied we can eliminate Harry Kent without knowing exactly what went on between him and Lahiri. So I want him in for questioning. I've sent two officers to pick him up.'

'Under caution?' said Noble. They sure as hell didn't have

enough to pick him up on suspicion of murder, whatever bullshit case they thought they could build.

'Ideally, yes,' Marsden said. 'But if he refuses, I'll have uniform arrest him on a common-law perverting the course charge. I'll direct the interview myself, but I want you in the window, right next to me. If even one thing he says differs from what he's told you, he's had it.'

The rage inside her was building like smoke up a chimney, and she longed for her skin and face to glow again. How long had it been without a drink? Ten minutes, maybe?

'With respect, ma'am, this is a gross waste of time during a vital phase of the investigation. Have you forgotten what we all sat through this morning? Somebody is out there drugging teenagers and raping them. That's what this case is about. Solomon Idris, Keisha Best, and what was happening to them. And how James Lahiri connects to it all. Bringing Harry in would be a fishing trip, that's all.'

'Maybe you're right,' said Marsden. 'But I'm going to eliminate the only person we can place at our crime scene. I'm in the process of applying for a search warrant for his home. And if you don't cooperate, then you're obstructing, and that's grounds for a disciplinary complaint.'

She smiled, venomously. Noble decided on the rabbit punch, and slipped her hands underneath her thighs. Fairweather turned the knife.

'I suspect that any such complaint would receive significant sympathy.'

Noble stood up.

'He should be with us in an hour,' Marsden called after her. 'We'll do him in Room Three; they've had the heating off all morning.'

'This man has just lost his best friend!' Noble yelled. Marsden merely smiled and shook her head, and Noble headed for the door. She had to get back to her car. A chain-smoke and a few more fingers, and a phone call to Wilson to form a plan. They might go for Harry, but he would fight them off easily enough. If Marsden was going to fuck up this investigation, though, then Noble owed it to Solomon, Keisha and Lahiri to make sure that someone went after the real monsters.

She was almost out of the door when Fairweather blocked it.

'It's such a shame,' he said quietly. 'You had such potential. Having sex with him was an oversight, but letting it cloud your judgement, that's unforgivable.'

Noble said nothing, moved forward, but Fairweather stayed put, his breath humid by her ear.

'You should have walked after what happened in Finsbury,' he grunted. 'You shouldn't even be a police officer, let alone a DI. And now you've fucked a witness. I'll have you, Noble, you mark my words.'

'Get out of my way,' Noble said. 'Sir.'

Fairweather remained still and made a tutting noise. 'Dear me,' he said. 'If Jack could see you now . . .'

Noble slapped him. Hard. He went down, swearing, and for a brief second she imagined drawing her gun and driving it into his temple, just to watch his face as he wondered whether she'd do it or not. But instead she levered past him with her knee, and shouted back to Marsden.

'I'll be in my car,' she said. 'Ma'am. Call me when I'm needed.'

From A&E, Harry walked down the hill into Camberwell, retracing the route he'd taken on Sunday night, sirens echoing off the buildings. There were always sirens, he thought, if you tuned your ears to the sounds of this part of the city. They made him think of the boat last night, and he tried to count cars, or look in the shop windows, to get the memory out of his head. Every so often, he could still taste the dock water. Even the cold reminded him. On the way, he rang the hospital switchboard and asked to be put through to Dr Wynn-Jones at the mortuary.

'Hello?'

'It's Dr Kent. We spoke on Monday.'

'Yes?'

Her office was quiet.

'I can't talk much now,' Harry said. 'But I thought you should know. You were right about Keisha Best. She was being sexually abused. The police have it on video. They're launching a full investigation.'

There was a heavy breath on the other end of the line, and

Harry wondered how she felt. Vindicated, because she was right, and upset, because she wished she was wrong.

'Thanks for letting me know,' she said. 'If there's anything else I can do, be in touch.'

Harry hung up and made the rest of the journey to Burgess Park Practice at a jog. The surgery was a good few streets away from the park it was named for, sitting between two pre-war terraces, a building site and an old church with a stripped roof and plywood in place of stained glass. It was a modern, angular building, not unlike the Albany Road Academy, automatic doors set into sand-coloured concrete pillars. When he entered, the clinical smell of alcohol gel filled his nose, signs directing him to a touch-screen console to book himself in. He proceeded to the desk.

'Is Dr Whitacre with a patient?' he said.

The receptionist looked up slowly.

'Dr Whitacre's all booked,' she said. 'He's teaching medical students.'

'Great,' said Harry. 'I'll surprise him.'

He walked down the corridor towards the doctors' rooms. A set of stairs headed up to the first floor, a column of nameplates above it. Dr James Lahiri, third from the top. Dr Duncan Whitacre, two beneath. Harry headed up the stairs, leaving damp footprints on the carpet. At the top, a man with a drooping face held the door open for him, a letter in his hand. Bell's palsy, Harry thought. On his way to A&E for some steroids.

Harry walked past Lahiri's office, and spotted the plastic tuft of blue-and-white police tape still caught in the door. Someone from Homicide & Serious must have been around earlier to search it. He wondered what they would have seen: Lahiri was fastidiously tidy, had been since boarding school, so it wouldn't have taken long. He stood and stared at the door for a while. On the boat, Lahiri had said, *I went straight to Whitacre, and he said he'd sort it.* Had that been part of the deception? Whitacre had told Lahiri it was just about cannabis, when actually the things he had been paying Idris to keep quiet about might have been far worse. And he remembered the first time they'd met, how Whitacre had been so keen to cooperate with the investigation, his personal interest almost unusual, overcompensating.

'Shit,' Harry whispered.

Whitacre had been on the ICU after the Monday morning ward round. He could have been there from half past seven, made the change on the system. He might well know Lahiri's log-in and password, if he used the same password on the practice network.

A text from Noble.

Where are you?

Harry told her. Then he moved down the corridor to Whitacre's consulting room, and kicked in the door.

Whitacre was slouched forward, his demeanour far removed from the demagogical passion Harry remembered from the assembly. He was at his desk, his shirt open at the collar, his cuffs halfway up his forearms, his red eyes familiar to Harry from the mirrors he'd looked in that day. The two medical students, both in the uniform of chinos, striped shirt, stethoscope and crumpled logbook, turned to face him, their faces terrified.

'Harry,' Whitacre said, standing slowly. 'Did you want to talk? We could step outside if you—'

'Let's talk here,' Harry said. 'And now.' He turned to the medical students. 'What are you guys? Third-year?'

They nodded fervently. Behind his desk, Whitacre ground his teeth together, sipping water from a glass, running a hand through his beard. Harry could tell he was getting to him, that Whitacre had no idea what he was going to do next.

'You'll do the SJT soon, so here's a scenario,' he said. 'Professional ethics. You're a GP. A patient threatens to talk to the press about a controversial treatment. What would the consequences be if that GP paid them money to stop them from telling—'

'That's enough!' Whitacre bellowed, turning to the students. 'Why don't you two make yourselves scarce. Er, we'll catch up next week.'

The students shuffled around Harry and headed for the door. The silence grew and swallowed the room. Harry looked across Whitacre's desk. Photographs of his sons, the resemblance striking; one in a fireman's uniform, another in a conservatory on a sunny day, holding an infant. A snow globe with a diorama of the leaning tower of Pisa. One snap of a younger Whitacre, holding hands with a long-haired woman, palm trees behind them. Harry thought about the crime-scene tape outside Lahiri's consulting room, and wondered what knick-knacks would have been on his desk. Photographs of the wife who'd left him, or the friends who'd betrayed him.

It struck Harry then how alone James had been, how those now grieving in the wake of his death were those who'd abandoned him in life. He felt the pain rise up in his chest again and sink into his stomach. He'd never get to make that up to him. But those thoughts, and others, could be dealt with later. His business now was in this room, with the man in front of him.

'Well?' Whitacre said.

Even with his shocked, haunted face, he still looked like a cartoon of a family doctor – had the right body language, the good habits that were so ingrained. Leg crossed on the opposite knee, fingers clasped together, body leant forwards.

'You were prescribing cannabis to Solomon Idris,' Harry said. 'Among others.'

Whitacre's face hardened and he rose from the chair.

'Are you here on police business?' he said.

'No,' said Harry.

'So why the hell do you care about that?' Whitacre spat. 'That, that . . . stuff. It pales into insignificance. A friend is dead. Killed for no good reason.'

'You're wrong there,' Harry said.

'I beg your pardon?' said Whitacre, red eyed.

'He wasn't killed for no good reason,' Harry said. 'He was killed because he knew something that somebody wanted to keep quiet. Something about Solomon Idris. That's why he died, and that's why I'm here.'

It took Whitacre a good few seconds of soundlessly opening and closing his mouth to process the words. 'Are you accusing me of something, Dr Kent?'

'Not yet,' said Harry. 'Now tell me about the weed.'

Whitacre sank back into his chair.

'It's a harm reduction strategy. Most of these kids are going to smoke cannabis, whatever we do or tell them. Gang rehabilitation is all about reducing the number of contacts between the patient and their old life, and if they're going to their old gang to buy drugs, then that increases their exposure to the people likely to draw them back into their old lifestyle. If we prescribe it to them, they don't have to be exposed to those environments. Simple. If it was heroin, we'd give them methadone, which is Christ knows how much more harmful.'

'Right,' said Harry. 'If you're so proud of it, why keep it a secret?'

'It's not a secret!' Whitacre protested. 'We ran the whole thing past the Home Office – we had to, so we could get access to the drugs. Anyone who files a Freedom of Information request can find out all about it.'

'But you still paid off Solomon Idris when he threatened to tell the papers about it?'

Whitacre's face dropped in surprise, the same way Lahiri's had when Harry had told him he knew about the cannabis, and he slapped the desk with the palm of his hand. Harry watched the particles settle back down to the bottom of the snow globe and waited for Whitacre to speak.

'A lot of people have worked very hard for the Saviour Project,' he said. 'Not least James Lahiri.'

And look how he ended up being repaid, Harry thought but didn't say. Wilson's phone started vibrating in his pocket, but he ignored it. He had Whitacre alone now, and the way he'd reacted when Harry had brought up the money told him he was onto something.

'Solomon was difficult,' Whitacre said. 'He'd told us that the only way he was ever going to be able to start anew was if he got out of London. Maybe he was right. But the council wouldn't rehouse him on account of his age. So he asked James for money, and James came to me, and we said no. Because if we did it for him, we'd have to consider others, and we just don't have the budget.'

'So Solomon came back, and he said that if you didn't give him the money, he'd tell the press that you were prescribing kids weed?' Harry said.

Whitacre nodded. Pulled an e-cigarette from his desk drawer and sucked from it, the tip glowing purple.

'I don't need to tell you, Harry, that the NHS is under attack from all sides,' he said. 'That kind of leak would be certain death for the project. One story in the papers and the commissioning board would shut us down. Ten thousand was worth it.'

'You made that decision, then?'

'I did,' Whitacre said. 'And I'd do it again. I took it out of my own bloody savings so it wouldn't show up on the accounts. I kept James out of it, though I'm sure he worked it out.'

Harry looked at him, seeing the pride. Shook his head, and tried to look as disapproving as possible.

'You covered it up.'

'Yes, I covered it up,' Whitacre said. 'I won't pretend I didn't. Refer me to the GMC. Call your friends down here and arrest me. Sometimes you've got to do something bad so that something worse doesn't happen. I would have thought you would have known that.'

'Something worse?' Harry said.

'These kids,' Whitacre said, an arm outstretched to the window, the sleet and concrete towers outside. 'For some of them, the Saviour Project is the only hope they've got. Everybody else has given up. They don't have families, the education system sees them as failures, the police see them as criminals. If we go under, then eight years of hard work gets wasted, and what do you think would happen to the patients? Society has given up on these people. We're all they have.'

The preacher was back. Whitacre's face was as red as his eyes, and Harry saw the righteousness he'd first seen in the assembly hall of Solomon Idris's school. It reminded him of the fanaticism of some of the locals they'd met in Helmand Province, human beings so committed to a cause that it had utterly consumed them, to the point where their goals trumped anything else. That worried Harry, because it made him wonder if there was a limit to what this man would cover up to protect his project. As much as it had riled Whitacre, Harry knew this wasn't about a few joints of cannabis. It centred on a much more unspeakable horror than that.

'Well?' Whitacre said.

'Idris was keen to get out of London, wasn't he?'

'Yes, he was.'

'Any idea why?' Harry said. He had no idea whether his feigned ignorance was convincing or not.

Whitacre shrugged. 'I wish I'd known more about him, Harry. You think I don't regret that? We failed Solomon, both me and James. And it appears he's paid a price for that.'

'There was no one else in his life, other than Keisha Best?' Harry said. 'Nothing romantic? Nothing sexual?'

He watched Whitacre intently, waiting for the giveaway, that initial micro-expression of shock that would come with the last question, but it didn't. Whitacre stared at him hard and said, 'I don't know. If anyone would have known, it would've been James.'

Six frantic knocks on the door.

'Come in,' said Whitacre.

Another man with a haunted face entered the room. This one belonged to Charlie Ambrose, and he was out of breath and sweating hard. The youth worker had on a heavy coat, scarf and hat, which were wet from the sleet outside. His eyes looked wet, too, and had the look of a child seeking reassurance.

'I take it you've heard, Charlie,' Whitacre said.

'They told me when I turned up for work at the Ruskin,' Ambrose said. 'I went straight to my church, I couldn't . . .'

'Sit down,' Whitacre said. 'We'll talk. Dr Kent was just leaving.'

'That's not it,' Ambrose continued, and now Harry got worried. The look on his face wasn't just shock, it was panic. 'There's a police car outside. Two of them in reception, asking for your office. They told me not to come upstairs and warn you, but I—'

Whitacre bolted to his feet. For a brief moment Harry braced himself, expecting a punch, but it never came. Just a meaty finger, aimed right at his chest.

'You bastard!' Whitacre shouted. 'You self-righteous arsehole.'

What have they found? Harry thought as he stared at Whitacre. Tried to picture him as the man in the video, imagine his voice as the mechanical one of the man who'd raped one teenager and forced another to do the same. The thought made him instantly furious. He felt Ambrose step closer to him at one side, turning for the door. There was noise in the corridor outside, and before

Harry could speak two uniformed coppers entered, one male, one female, hands on their belts.

'Arsehole!' Whitacre repeated, jabbing his finger at Harry again, before turning to the officers. 'You're arresting an innocent man! This is bullshit!'

Ambrose going to Whitacre's side. 'Don't give them an excuse, Duncan!'

'I will tear you guys apart!' Whitacre continued as the police officers approached. Harry backed away from him, looking straight at the coppers. The female one, older by a few years, stepped forward.

'Sir, calm down!' she bawled. 'We're not here for you.'

Whitacre stopped, his rant terminated mid-sentence, his mouth hanging open in confusion. Harry was confused, too, but when the male copper turned around, everything fell into place. He closed his eyes and waited for the copper to speak.

'Harry Kent, I have received a request for you to attend Lewisham police station for questioning in relation to the murder of James Lahiri. You are not under arrest—'

'Good,' said Harry, bursting for the door. But the male officer got there first, holding his waist with a thick arm.

'What the fuck?' Harry said. 'Let go of me!'

The copper gripped harder, and Harry had to restrain himself. The officer didn't have a good hold, and with a well-placed head-butt Harry would have been free, but he stopped himself. When he looked forward, the female officer was in front of him.

'Harry Kent, I am arresting you on suspicion of attempting to pervert the course of justice. You do not have to say anything but it may harm your defence if you do not mention when questioned something which you later rely on in court. Anything you do say may be given in evidence.'

Despite the arrest, he wasn't put in a cell or processed, just taken straight to an interview room at Lewisham. In the car, he'd said nothing other than repeatedly demand to be put in touch with Noble, but the uniforms had just used the usual bullshit about being the people who executed the warrant, not the people who wrote it. On the journey, the man had asked him if he was the doctor who'd been at the Camberwell Road shooting, and then the woman had told her partner to keep his mouth shut. They'd put him in a cold and small room and told him that people were coming down to speak to him. He knew how this worked. They'd be going through his house, and his locker at work. Silently, he congratulated himself on switching the labels on the aspirin and amphetamine bottles. A drugs charge would be a gift for the police, letting them remand him in custody and giving them even more time to trump up charges, when they should be out finding the bastard who'd killed his friend and raped two teenagers.

On the drive, he'd come to a few conclusions. Tammas had told them about the affair with Alice Lahiri, which he'd neglected to mention when the two detectives had questioned him yesterday evening. They had to. Maybe, if the police had nothing, it would make sense to interview him, to push him a bit, but not when everybody knew the reason Lahiri had been killed. He remembered walking into the interview room that morning, looking around at the people whose job it was to find justice for his friend, and going through the hell of watching that video. Twenty-odd people who were scarred together, like soldiers who'd fought side by side. No one who hadn't been in that room could really understand what it had been like.

And it made him fucking furious that the man responsible was walking around London while they came after him. His pain, his anguish at the death of his friend, could wait – had to wait. The hell that Keisha and Solomon must have gone through eclipsed it completely.

The door opened, and the same two detectives who'd interviewed Harry after Lahiri's death came in, the older one, Deakin, in a stained white shirt with a mustard-coloured jumper and a paisley tie, and Bambrough, the younger one, in a royal blue suit, open-collared shirt. Harry looked past them and saw the woman standing in the doorway in the same blood-red dress she'd worn to the meeting that morning. DCI Marsden darted away once she met Harry's eyes, but he didn't buy it. She'd wanted him to know that she was the one directing this interview, that she would be just the other side of the one-way mirror set into one wall of the room.

DC Bambrough inserted a fresh CD and flicked on the

recorder. Deakin was chewing gum, working it all around his mouth. He leant back in his chair, staring straight at Harry. He had a pink-coloured folder on the desk in front of him, which he opened and started to file through. Bambrough started talking, identifying himself and Deakin and stating the time and location, and as he spoke Deakin picked up a rollerball from his shirt pocket and scrawled something on a piece of paper, which he held up to show Harry.

Harry felt his face burn. When he spoke, it was more like a hiss.

'For the tape, Detective Constable Deakin has just held up a piece of paper on which he has written: *Frankie said you were a crap shag.*'

Bambrough looked across at his colleague, laughed and shook his head.

'Worth a try,' he said.

Noble sat at the back of the antechamber adjacent to Interview Room Three, watching the two DCs from Homicide & Serious go through the motions with Harry. DCI Marsden was in front of her, watching with her face up close to the window, condensation forming on the glass. As if she didn't have better things to do, a fucking murder investigation to command. No, she was turning the knife, relishing watching them break a man who was already broken. Noble was still furious that they'd arrested him at all, as there was no way in hell the CPS would even consider pressing charges. An omission in an interview was a long way from a lie to a direct question by a police officer, and any half-competent solicitor could get the charge thrown out. So she sat, cross-legged, and thought about what she'd done since her meeting with Marsden.

She'd spoken to the officers who'd searched Lahiri's office at Burgess Park. He'd written his passwords on a Post-it attached to his computer monitor. That gave pretty much anyone in the Saviour Project access to his log-in, so she'd tasked Wilson and a couple of other DCs with some basic police work. Interviewing all male Saviour Project staff systematically, checking their alibis for Sunday night, Monday morning and Tuesday night, and running full background checks. The tasks which should have been directed by the woman in front of her.

Harry started speaking, the intercom distorting his voice, and Noble looked up from the floor to listen.

'For the tape, Detective Constable Deakin has just held up a piece of paper on which he has written: *Frankie said you were a crap shag.*'

Noble was up, the stool she was sitting on crashing to the ground, as she stormed to the front of the room, got into Marsden's face.

'You self-righteous cunt!'

Marsden, spinning around, for a split second genuinely afraid, until her face returned to stone.

'Face the consequences of your actions, Detective Inspector.'

'You fucking bitch!'

'I didn't tell them, Frankie,' Marsden said. 'You know what coppers are like. Gossip spreads, doesn't it?'

Noble threw the door open and slammed it behind her, running for her car, trying to stop the tears building up.

Harry was wearing a woollen jumper and his Met Police fleece, and the interview room was still cold. The detectives seemed to be suffering too, Deakin with his hands tucked into his armpits, leaning back, Bambrough rubbing his hands together as he kept on talking.

'As you know, Dr Kent, you have been arrested on suspicion of attempting to pervert the course of justice. I'm sure this is just a misunderstanding, but information has come to light indicating that you gave a false answer to a question my colleague asked you on Tuesday, 22 January. Is there anything you'd like to say to that?'

Harry said nothing. Deakin had started writing on a notepad in the folder, taking notes, and Harry wondered what the need was given that the entire thing was being recorded. Then he passed Bambrough a sheet of paper, which he read from.

'Last night, my colleague asked you the question, *What was the nature of your relationship with James Lahiri?* And you replied, *We met in medical school, we served in the army together. We were friends.* I then asked you, *Were you close friends?* And you replied, *Yes. We were.*'

Harry thought about that. He could hardly remember being

interviewed after James had been killed. He knew that it had happened, but his memories of the previous night were a series of vignettes, jumbled, disordered. Noble putting a blanket around him on the boat. Driving through the City. Calling Tammas, and hearing him cry through his tube on the end of the phone. But worse was the fact that, even if he'd said that, he'd been telling the truth. *Were you close friends?* They *were.* They had been, before Harry had fucked things up.

And the horror, the shadow between the idea and the reality, was that if it hadn't been for the affair, then Lahiri would have told him what he'd hidden on Monday night, if not before, and he wouldn't be dead. The weight built in the hollow space in his chest, and the more DC Bambrough talked, the less Harry listened.

'We have received information that you and James Lahiri had not spoken to one another in almost a year before this week. The reason being that you had embarked on a sexual affair with his wife, Alice Lahiri. Is this true?'

'No comment,' Harry said quietly. Fuck you. He'd been held once by the police, fifteen years old, on suspicion of criminal damage. Some kids had trashed a cop car when the officers had been inside the Co-op, getting lunch. Harry'd been in the wrong place at the wrong time, wearing the wrong clothes. He'd been young, but wise enough to answer no comment to everything then, just as he would now.

Deakin spoke for the first time: 'It would be pretty bizarre for you to forget that you'd shagged your best mate's wife, wouldn't it?'

'No comment.'

'Or that he had broken off all contact with you? You wouldn't forget that, would you?'

'No comment.'

'So the obvious conclusion is you deliberately misled us last night, didn't you?'

'No comment.'

Deakin shook his head and passed the pink folder over to Bambrough, who pulled out a plastic wallet and started thumbing through the papers. Deakin kept talking.

'It's clear to me you hid the fact you shagged your mate's wife.

Who wouldn't, eh? But then that got us wondering what else you might've left out, and Jamie did a bit of digging, didn't you, Jamie?'

Harry ducked his head lower, digging his knuckles into his temples, imagining himself sixteen again, in his tracksuit, blocking out the sound. But he couldn't do it, not when Bambrough pulled out the top sheet of paper and slid it across the table to him. Harry tried not to look at it, but he did when he saw the army crest on the top of the document. He couldn't read it from where he was, but he saw that it had come from the Defence Medical Services.

'How do you pronounce that, Dr Kent?' Bambrough said. '*Heed-ley* Court? *Head-ley?*'

He looked around the room, driving his fingernails harder into the palms of his hands. Settled his eyes on the recorder, as if reminding himself that he was being recorded would in some way make it less likely that he would blow up.

'Nice place, was it?' Bambrough said, looking up at him. 'As good a place as any to do your rehabilitation, I suppose. And all those injuries, I had no idea you'd been through so much! I mean, I don't have a clue what a pulmonary contusion or a haemothorax is but it sounds pretty nasty to me. Mind you, I do know a bit about post-traumatic stress disorder.'

Look at the floor, Harry told himself, just look at the floor. Don't give them the satisfaction.

'One of my best mates from Hendon was the first officer into the tunnel at Edgware Road,' Bambrough went on. 'He was never the same afterwards. But you get a very different take on it, y'know, when it's a shrink's words.' The detective picked up another sheet and read. '*The patient harbours an intense feeling of survivor guilt over the serious injuries sustained by his colleagues, but has managed to adapt well to civilian life. Observed sleep and patient self-reporting indicates paranoia, hypervigilance and delusions consistent with moderate PTSD.*'

Harry slammed a fist on the desk. 'Those are private and confidential medical records!' he shouted. 'How the fuck did you get those?'

Bambrough smiled and cocked his head to one side the way a teenager who'd just won an argument might.

'You gave them to us,' Deakin said. 'When you applied for a job as a Force Medical Examiner.'

'Did you read them all?' Harry asked. 'If you did, you'd see that I've been discharged as of January 2012. I had problems. I had therapy. I got fixed.'

'Who are you trying to convince, Dr Kent?' said Bambrough. 'Us or yourself?'

'Fuck you.'

'I did some reading on PTSD,' Bambrough continued. 'Very interesting. There was one phrase which really stuck with me. *A propensity to react disproportionately to stressful stimuli.*'

'You've got no idea what you're talking about,' Harry said. 'I want a lawyer. No comment.'

The room descended into silence. Deakin sat back in his chair, arms folded, taking his chewing gum out and sticking it under the table. Bambrough pulled his notes close to his chest, reading over them. Harry saw the game they were trying to pull, letting the silence envelop him, in the hope that their quiet judgement would become an itch, something that he would eventually give in to. He fought it, and then Wilson's phone buzzed twice, the way it would if he had got a text. Geddes, maybe, with the address of the man who'd sold the gun to Lahiri's killer.

The gun, Harry thought. That was his way out.

'I was in the meeting this morning,' he said. 'DS Cheung said that the gun which killed Lahiri was the same one which was fired behind Wyndham Road.'

The detectives nodded. Harry knew that they were both DCs, that the person really running the show, DCI Marsden, would be behind the one-way mirror, so he turned his body and shouted directly at it.

'I couldn't have fired that gun. It's someone else. I made mistakes with Alice, I'm gonna have to find a way to live with that. But I was not involved in James's death, and you all fucking know it. Go find the man in that video. Stop wasting your time.'

'There's a turning point in every interview I do,' Deakin said. 'Where the bad guy switches from *I didn't do it* to *You can't prove I did it.*'

Harry shook his head. The phone in his pocket buzzed again, the text still unread. He had an urge to read it, but he didn't want to draw attention to the fact that he still had the phone, that he hadn't yet been searched.

'Well, I think I can say whatever the hell I like,' Harry said. 'Given that I haven't yet received the lawyer I've repeatedly asked for, and therefore everything I say now would be very shaky in front of a judge.'

Bambrough looked across at Deakin, the poker face wavering slightly.

'You've requested a solicitor and we are obliged to honour that request,' Deakin said. 'Anything you say from now on may be given in evidence and will be taken as an indication that you have waived that right.'

'Fuck you both,' Harry said. 'Take that down and give it in evidence.'

Bambrough shuffled on his chair, looked at him.

'What was James's reaction when he found out about you and Alice? How did he find out?'

'No comment.'

A knock on the door.

'Come in!'

All eyes turned. Harry had never thought he'd be glad to see the bald, angled face of DCI Fairweather, who spun into the room, one hand holding his glasses onto his nose, the other resting on the door.

'Detectives, I think it's time we put an end to this tiresome charade.'

They scowled and got to their feet, Bambrough turning off the recorder with a closed fist.

'Interview suspended, twelve forty-one.'

As soon as they were gone, Harry checked his phone. The message was from Geddes, short and to the point.

Niall Connor Fitzpatrick, d.o.b 3/7/1979, 105 Rodney Place, SE17 1PP. Adm with #fourth metacarpal, March 2011, also UGI bleed, Oct 2012.

The hashtag was a medical abbreviation, and it meant that Fitzpatrick had fractured the bone under the ring finger of one hand. It was a common injury in those who'd thrown a punch, so common that it was called a boxer's fracture. The upper gastrointestinal bleed wasn't surprising either. Over time, heavy drinkers eroded the lining of their stomachs, and the repeated vomiting weakened the wall of the oesophagus. As the liver failed, the arteries in the gullet wall could swell up and burst, and that was catastrophic. It was how Harry's own mother had died.

Rodney Place was a name Harry recognised. The road was on the border of the Heygate estate, a failed housing project on the eastern side of the Elephant & Castle roundabout. Now the council had decided to pull it down but were still working on evicting the few stragglers who clung on within, so it existed mostly fenced off, abandoned. He could get there by taxi in fifteen minutes if the traffic was good.

But first, of course, he'd have to get out of this room.

There was noise from the corridor, men and women arguing. It appeared to be Fairweather who was running the show now. Harry strained, listening for Noble's voice, but he couldn't make it out.

Then the door opened, and Fairweather walked in alone, sweat on his bald forehead in tight, organised beads. He shut the door slowly and quietly, then paced towards the CD recorder.

'I'm not saying anything else until I get a lawyer,' Harry said.

'Shut up,' said Fairweather. Harry had expected him to turn the recorder on, but he didn't. He was checking that it was off. Then he retrieved the CD, slid it into a plastic jacket, and put it in his coat pocket. Remained standing, hands forward, leaning on the table. Harry shuffled backwards on his chair.

'I'll start by apologising,' Fairweather said. 'What happened was unnecessary, in my opinion. You're no longer under arrest. You're free to leave.'

Harry shook his head, disgusted. He knew it'd been a mistake, six months ago, to start working with the police. Done, of course, with the best of intentions, of somehow building bridges, finding some hotshot detective and convincing them to take up Zara's case, to do his bit putting a name to the face lying there.

'What are you going to do with that CD?' Harry said.

Fairweather smiled.

'It's going to disappear. No record has been made of your arrest, and none will be. That's my offer. On one condition.'

Harry felt his skin begin to itch under his clothes, looked up at Fairweather. When he said nothing, Fairweather kept speaking.

'Your assistance in this inquiry is no longer required. Until further notice, your only contact with any serving Metropolitan Police officer will be if you are requested to attend a formal interview at a police station. You are not to contact any witness or person of interest in this investigation or any other, and if you are found to have done so I will not hesitate to arrest you on charges of obstructing an investigation. Is all of that clear?'

Harry thought about the text, thought about handing it over to Fairweather or Marsden, letting the police process the information. But he was fairly sure that Niall Fitzpatrick wouldn't talk to anyone with a warrant card, and he remembered the promise he'd made to James Lahiri, alone in the shower, washing his blood off his face, and said, 'Crystal.'

'You've done more to hinder this investigation than to aid it, Dr Kent,' Fairweather said, finally sitting down. 'Feel free to resign as a Forensic Medical Examiner, if you wish.'

Harry stood up and headed for the door. Turned around, decided to have one last shot.

'Go fuck yourself.'

Fairweather smiled again, pulled the CD from his jacket pocket, tapped it, and put it back.

'Goodbye, Dr Kent,' he said.

Noble was outside and on her third cigarette when she saw the Mercedes pull into the station's car park, and recognised the two figures in the front. Professional Standards. Some of the older coppers called them the rubberheelers, because you'd never hear them coming until you turned around and there they were. Christ knows where they'd been – probably over to Tulse Hill to meet with the area commander, given how long they'd been gone. She said nothing as Fairweather strode past her into the station's back entrance, the apologetic, bleary face of Tony Kepler following behind. She knew how he felt, a good copper having to do a bullshit job. She remembered now why she hated Louisa Marsden, why they'd never got on. Every detective enjoyed turning the screw on a suspect, and there was no more satisfying feeling than when some fucker who'd offed his wife collapsed and confessed all. But Marsden had to be a sadist, drawing some weird pleasure out of breaking down a man who'd already lost his best friend, and done more to help their investigation than most of her team.

She finished her smoke and went back inside, trying to form a plan for what she'd do with her afternoon now Harry was gone. Wilson was working through the Saviour Project staff. When they'd picked him up, Harry had been at the Burgess Park Practice, talking to Dr Whitacre, the project's founder. Lahiri had mentioned him on the boat. It seemed as good a place as any to start.

She headed to the interview room corridor, and heard two voices in shrill combat, Fairweather and Marsden, standing in the corridor so they didn't disturb the interviews. Two DCIs on one investigation was always a recipe for disaster. As Noble got closer, she saw Fairweather bang on the door to the interview room, heading in, then Bambrough and Deakin, the detectives from Homicide & Serious, leave, shaking their heads, swearing.

'Boys, come with me,' said Marsden, heading past Noble towards the incident room. The detectives were still cursing, and Noble wasn't sure if they were angry at their time being wasted, or the fact they hadn't got to finish taking Harry over the rack.

They left Noble alone in the corridor with DC Kepler, a pained look on his face.

'Bet you fucking regret transferring now,' she said.

Kepler came closer, his voice quiet. Noble recognised the look on his face now. It was the same one Harry had had when he'd sat her down in the ICU and told her that Jack wasn't going to wake up.

'I need to have a word, ma'am,' he said quietly.

That's when she knew. In the five or six years Noble had known Tony Kepler, he had never once called her ma'am, despite her superior rank. He called her guv, like Wilson did, like all her colleagues who were also friends.

'Jesus, Tony,' she said.

'I'm sorry, ma'am,' Kepler said.

'Don't fucking ma'am me,' said Noble, 'Just get it over and done with.'

Kepler pulled a piece of lightweight yellow paper from his

pocket and handed it to her. She'd seen a Reg Nine notice once before, after the job in Finsbury.

'Detective Inspector Frances Noble, I am informing you under Regulation Nine of the Police Conduct Act that you are subject to an investigation by the Professional Standards Directorate following a report of an incident of misconduct, which is detailed in this notice. You are advised—'

She didn't read it, just took it, cut him off, stuffed it into her jeans pocket.

'Get out of there while you can, Tony,' she said, patting him on the arm. 'You're too good for those pricks.'

Kepler nodded sullenly. 'Thanks, guv.'

Noble turned and left, needing to be away, ran through the car park, pulling her phone from her pocket, calling Wilson, but he didn't pick up. Fucking load of bollocks it all was. She looked around the unfamiliar surroundings of Lewisham High Street, but it didn't take her long to spot the nearest pub, the Joiners' Arms. Directly across from the police station, so probably a coppers' bar, but fuck it. She went inside, headed straight to the bar, ordered a double vodka-lemonade and a straight double vodka on the side and crawled off into a corner booth, where she pulled her phone out and saw one unread text, one unread email.

The text was from the phone Wilson had lent to Harry, and it read, *Can I still trust you?*

She replied, one word. *Yes.* Then she checked the email, which was from the detective superintendent in charge of the Flying Squad, regarding the betting shop robbery on Peckham High Street. It outlined his opinion that the matter would best be handled by local CID, and requested that DI Noble take over the investigation, effective the following morning. Marsden and Fairweather had both been copied into the email. The bastards had moved quickly.

Noble took a single gulp of her drink, trying to clear her thoughts. The Reg Nine notice, Harry naked on top of her, the taste of vodka in his mouth. Misconduct was certainly the right word for it, but the fire that had taken hold in her when Fairweather had mentioned Jack's name had burnt out and now sat as embers of guilt, smouldering away. And all this, distracting her from what she needed to do. She thought about the video, the fear in Keisha and Solomon's faces as a man had hit and raped them. She thought of James Lahiri, still and cold on the deck of his boat. She'd promised Harry that she would help him bring the person responsible to justice, and she couldn't do that sat in a bar, drowning her sorrows.

Her phone buzzed again. Harry had replied.

Have Fitz's address in Elephant and Castle. Going there now. Where are you?

Noble replied, *Clearing my head.*

Then she looked down at her glass of lemonade, an inch or so gone from the top. Checked that she was unobserved, poured the two shots in and filled it back up to the top, mixing it with her finger. Took a long gulp, and pulled the Reg Nine form from her pocket, scanning the words. The artificial, formal language left her in no doubt that Fairweather was the author. In some places, the phrasing was comical. *During this time, it is alleged that you had sexual intercourse and/or sexual relations with the witness.* Made her sound like Bill bloody Clinton. But nowhere in the form did it say anything about suspension, or restriction of duties.

So she finished her drink in one straight pull, the burn and the sting making her eyes hurt and her skin glow, took her coat and headed out, crossed the road towards the police station, making for the incident room. She might only have a day left on this case, but there was plenty that could be done in a day of proper graft. The way Marsden had stitched her up, she'd have every right just to go home and leave her to it, but the job was about more than that. Jack would be proud of that, whatever Marcus fucking Fairweather thought.

The Heygate estate was a wasteland, a concrete sarcophagus bordered by thick plastic walls, health-and-safety signs, random orbs of off-white light illuminating broken windows and crumbling brickwork. People had left the Heygate in herds – even five years ago, the estate's residents had numbered only fifty of their original three thousand, and they were the diehards who saw the shithole as home because it was the only one they'd ever known.

Now all but a handful had left, and the bricks and mortar would be dust before the next year was out.

Rodney Place was the road leading in from the south, and Harry told the cabbie to stop as soon as he saw the sign, paying him and leaving the taxi at a run. Once the cab had left, turning back onto the New Kent Road, Harry squeezed through a gap in the fence, heading for a staircase that led into the main residential block. He'd texted Noble on the way and had been unnerved by her answer. He hoped she was still on his side, because right now she and DS Wilson were the only people he trusted. As he climbed the stairs, he briefly considered what he would do if Fitzpatrick wasn't around, or unable to provide any information. Perhaps he could make his way to Kingston and find some comfort in Tammas. When he thought of that, he heard Tammas's voice again. *You find him. And you make. The bastard pay.*

Harry followed the signs for the hundreds, darting up onto a walkway where broken glass and used syringes crunched beneath his shoes, some of them caked in dirt and mould. The sun was low in the afternoon sky and flecks of snow hung in the orange street lights of London's rising night. The dusk accentuated those few homes within the estate which had lights on, the last few stoic hangers-on. He spent a while on the concrete walkway, passing boarded-up doors, until he realised that it was just the even numbers on this level. The odd numbers were a half-floor down, facing the other way at ground level, opening onto the estate's central oblong. On the staircase, a rat darted against him and he jumped, fists balled, ready to strike. Held his fleece tight and shivered as the wind hit, then moved forward.

A few steps later Harry was in the central square, looking over the rest of the estate towards Lambeth and Vauxhall, skyscrapers whose lights never died. In a hall of residence, he thought, the central area would have been called a quad, with students sitting out in the sun pretending to revise or throwing snowballs in winter. Here, those people who hadn't fled bolted their doors after dark. He looked down the abandoned corridor of boarded-up maisonettes, and saw a light. The flat closest to him was number 97. He counted. The light was over number 105.

Harry pulled off the fleece with the police logo on it, and threw it onto the floor, moving side-on to the door under the light. There were no boards, just a thin line of dust where perhaps they had once been attached.

He knocked hard. Got no answer, so he knocked again.

The sound of wheels scraping along the floor emerged slowly from the apartment, before giving way to the click of bolts being drawn across and the creak of the door. Harry stood with half of his body open to the door, the other half protected, so he could throw himself against the wall if rushed. There was no sign of a dog, which was good. The man he took to be Niall Fitzpatrick opened the door in a metal wheelchair that looked like a prop from a wartime medical drama. Between the stumps of his legs, which were covered by thick tracksuit shorts, a trembling hand held a sawn-off shotgun, its twin barrels oriented upwards towards Harry.

'Who the fuck are you?' Fitzpatrick said.

There were about four feet between Harry and the gun, not too far to reach if the need arose. The problem, however, was the wheelchair. With a standing opponent, you could take them off their balance, and gain the advantage. But he couldn't do that with Fitzpatrick.

'I hear you sell guns,' Harry said.

Fitzpatrick looked up at him with yellow, bloodshot eyes. He stank of alcohol and vomit, and had pieces of old food and dead skin matted into his red beard. He wore a large camouflage coat over several layers of jumpers, stained with dirty brown marks. Harry tried to picture the man as a fresh-faced ordnance technician in a combat uniform, walking out towards a ditch. Harry felt lucky for what he had, which seemed ironic.

'Who the fuck are you?' Fitzpatrick repeated.

'A client,' he said. 'A potential one, anyway.'

'You alone?' Fitzpatrick said.

Harry nodded. Fitzpatrick said nothing and turned his chair around, wheeling into the apartment with the shotgun between his thighs. The flat was silent but for the scraping of the wheels on the hard floor and the wind howling through the damned walls. Inside, there was a workbench with a vice, some files, and several hand drills Harry assumed were for altering the firearms Fitzpatrick made his income trading. Removing serial numbers, converting between calibres. Underneath the bench was a pile of cans, Skol Super.

Fitzpatrick turned to face him.

'Sit down,' he offered, waving to a mouldy sofa opposite a desk with a plasma television set, plugged into a DVD player. Whoever said crime didn't pay had obviously never been south of the river. There were box sets of *Band of Brothers* and *The Pacific* spread beneath the TV. What a life, Harry thought. Drinking, selling guns, and watching war series.

He remained standing. 'What you got for me, then?'

'Nine-mil automatics, mostly. A sawn-off if you'd like, but you'll have to pay for that. Extra, I mean. If you're happy to wait, I could get you something special.'

Fitzpatrick coughed and spat some dark bile onto the floor. Harry thought about Solomon Idris, coughing in the Chicken Hut, with that look in his eyes. Wondered if it would be better if he'd never known what had given it to him, and reminded himself why he was here, freezing his arse off in a place where if the man in front of him decided to shoot him dead, he'd likely not be found for months. Not until the asbestos removal men came to rip down the walls.

'What kind of nines?' Harry said.

'The fuck do you care?' Fitzpatrick grunted. 'You don't look like no collector to me. In fact, you don't look like my normal clientele, either. I bet yer wife's off with some geezer, and you're gonna do them both, aren't you? Or her and the kids, and then yourself.'

'I just want something reliable, that's all.'

'All my gear's reliable,' Fitzpatrick said. 'Take my word for it, or piss off.'

'How much for a nine, then?'

'Twelve hundred. You bring it back unfired, and I'll give you five hundred back.'

'Ammo?' said Harry. Twelve hundred was pretty cheap. That much for the life of James Lahiri, and maybe Solomon Idris, too.

'A full clip,' said Fitzpatrick, reaching onto the workbench with one hand and pulling a can of Skol Super to his mouth. 'You want any more, you can pay for it. Only two clips, mind you. I'm not selling my shit to some weirdo who's gonna run into a school and get on the news.'

'What's your ammo?' said Harry.

'Fucking good shite, alright!' Fitzpatrick said. 'Now buy summat or fuck off.'

Harry tried not to appear flustered, even though his heart felt like it was close to bursting out of his chest. He needed to stay calm, to keep his peripheral vision on the gun between Fitzpatrick's stumps, but not let on that he was looking. He scanned the chair, looking for the wheelchair brake. Spotted the serrated metal lever by Fitzpatrick's right foot.

'I'm buying,' said Harry. 'Maybe. Let me take a look first.'

Fitzpatrick grinned, revealing brown, broken teeth, and put his left hand to the left wheel of his chair, spinning like a basketball player. Reached to open a drawer beneath his workbench, and then used both hands to lift up a weathered Browning. That was his second mistake, though he hadn't yet realised it. The first one had been underestimating the exhausted, broken-looking man who'd knocked on his front door.

Harry's first move was to rush up behind the wheelchair and stamp his foot on the brake, before wrapping his left arm around Fitzpatrick's neck and grabbing the sawn-off with his right, holding it by the breech and pulling it up into the air, sliding his hand downwards as he did so that the trigger guard ended up in his right hand, the twin barrels directed at Fitzpatrick's head.

'You fucking piece of—' Fitzpatrick spluttered, his hands scrabbling for the gun on the worktop after they'd tried, and failed, to spin the chair's wheels.

'Shut up,' Harry shouted. 'And let me see your hands. You ever seen what a shotgun does to a skull at close range, Niall?'

He released the pressure on Fitzpatrick's neck and backed away, putting both hands on the shotgun. Now he was shitting himself. Fitzpatrick still had a gun on the table in front of him. Maybe it wasn't loaded, but he had to assume that it was. If he went for it, Harry couldn't pull the trigger. Couldn't shoot a man in the back of the head. The pain behind his sternum came back and the cold wind rushed through his chest.

'How the fuck do you know my name?' Fitzpatrick said.

'I know a lot of things about you,' Harry said. 'First things first, that gun there on the table. Pick it up by the barrel, with your left hand.'

Fitzpatrick did so.

'Fuck you,' he said. 'I know people who'll make you pay for this. You won't even see 'em coming. They'll stick a knife in your skull and you'll be dead before you hit the floor.'

'Throw the gun away,' Harry ordered.

The gun hit the wall at the side and cracked the plaster, leaving a long rip. Harry kept his eyes on Fitzpatrick, whose hands hung in the air, shaking. Whether the tremor was from fear or the liver failure Harry wasn't sure.

'You're filth, aren't you?' Fitzpatrick said.

'No,' said Harry. 'I'm not. No rules for me.'

'You're gonna regret this, you cunt. Who the fuck are you?'

'I'm army, like you,' Harry said. '256 Field Hospital. You deployed, didn't you?'

'Me and a thousand others,' Fitzpatrick said. 'Don't try that brothers-in-arms crap on me.'

Harry couldn't see his face, so it was hard to tell whether the attempt to build rapport had been in any way successful, though he suspected it hadn't. He decided to cut straight to the chase.

'Look, mate,' he said. 'I feel sorry for you. You shouldn't be in a shithole like this. Maybe I can help you out.'

'What the fuck d'you want?' Fitzpatrick said. Harry was writing the sentences in his head before he said them, and a lump was forming in his throat. Before he knew it, the words were coming out strained.

'I had a friend,' he said. 'He was a medical officer, too. Saved my life and God knows how many others out in Helmand. Last night someone went onto his boat and shot him dead with Radway Green nine-mil, 2004 batch. Sound familiar?'

Fitzpatrick swore loudly.

'I just sell the gear,' he said. 'I dunno what people are gonna do with it. 'S not my problem.'

'I know,' said Harry. 'That's why I'm not here for you. I want the guy you sold it to.'

'No way,' said Fitzpatrick.

'You don't look like you're in a position to negotiate,' Harry said. Fitzpatrick's foot was repeatedly striking the wheelchair brake. Eventually it gave way, and he started to turn around.

'Stay fucking still!' Harry yelled.

The sound echoed around the room, and in the silence that followed Harry realised that his hands were so sweaty they were slipping around the shotgun. His fingers were nowhere near the triggers, but Fitzpatrick didn't know that.

After a while, Fitzpatrick said, 'How am I supposed to know who it was who killed your friend? I don't ask no questions. An' I've sold three or four nines these last few months.'

'Anyone seem out of place?' Harry said. 'Like me? Older guys, seemed like they might be professionals?'

'You think hitmen buy their guns from me?'

'Not professional killers,' Harry said. 'Professionals. Like lawyers, or doctors.'

Fitzpatrick shrugged his shoulders.

'I dunno. There was an older guy.'

'White guy, with a beard?' Harry asked. 'In his fifties?'

'Not that I remember,' Fitzpatrick said.

Harry switched the sawn-off to his left hand and reached for Wilson's phone with his right, brought up the internet browser. It took him a while to type using only one hand, so he stalled.

'Think! Anyone out of place?'

He could hear Fitzpatrick's breathing, fast and laboured, and see it too, quick pulses of white air into the room. Soon enough, Harry had managed to type *Saviour Project* into the search engine. The first hit was a press release from the project's own website, and it came with a picture, which was what he needed. The photo had been taken at an awards ceremony at City Hall, the mayor standing with assorted figures: Lahiri, some of the youth workers, Kinirons, Traubert, Josh Geddes and some of the other staff from A&E. Duncan Whitacre front and centre, beaming ear to ear.

'Turn around,' Harry said. 'Keep your right hand in sight.'

Fitzpatrick did so and Harry crept closer, keeping the shotgun back. He held the screen forward, zoomed in on the picture. Fitzpatrick leant in and squinted, trying to make out the faces.

'You recognise anyone there?'

'Yeah,' Fitzpatrick said. 'I sold a gun to Boris.'

'Don't fuck with me,' said Harry. 'Look at all of the faces.'

Maybe Whitacre had disguised himself somehow when he'd come to buy the gun. Shaved, and worn a wig or a cap.

'Oh, shite,' Fitzpatrick said. His eyes widened, and he coughed again, more bile spluttering over his camouflage jacket. Harry turned awkwardly, rotating his body so he too could see the screen, follow Fitzpatrick's line of sight.

'Someone there?' Harry said. He felt as if every blood vessel in his body were about to burst, every molecule of his concentration focused on the alcoholic amputee in front of him. A Trojan team could have burst into the room behind him and he wouldn't even have noticed.

'Three weeks ago,' Fitzpatrick said. 'I sold him an old Luger.'

'Who?' Harry said, leaning in. Tapped the screen with his thumb, just above Whitacre's face.

'No, not him,' Fitzpatrick said. '*Him.*'

Harry's eyes followed Fitzpatrick's finger straight to the smiling face of Charlie Ambrose, in a purple shirt and dark suit, and he felt a stone sink into the space inside his chest. It made sense. Ambrose, the man who'd first converted Idris to the hope of a better life, who sat in his office in A&E, unseen by the rest of the staff. Went into the school, engaged with the kids on their level. The eyes and ears of the Saviour Project.

Shit, Harry thought. Backed away slowly, sliding the phone into his pocket, until he was in the doorway. Eyes fixed on Fitzpatrick, he opened up the shotgun's breech and let the cartridges fall out, threw it on the floor, backed out of the door and started running.

He ran until he found the covered walkway he'd entered the estate from. Kept going up onto a ramp that would take him over the New Kent Road and into the housing block on the other side, except it was boarded off, a large white plastic barricade stopping him. He almost ran straight into it, slipped on ice as he tried to turn, and ended up with his back there, sliding down it. He was breathing too fast now, sweat gluing his clothes to his skin like some terrible sclerotic disease. He scrunched his eyes closed and punched the barrier until his knuckles were numb and blood ran in smeared trails down the white plastic. He fell forward and the tears came, and when he opened his eyes Lahiri was there, carrying him from the battlefield as he bled out from his wounds.

I'll get the bastard, don't you worry. I'll get him.

Harry fumbled in his pocket for Wilson's phone. Wiped his bleeding knuckles on his trousers, then unlocked the phone. It went straight to the broswer page, Ambrose's face smiling back at him, and he retched before he went to the contacts and called Noble.

She replied immediately.

'Harry?'

'I know who did it.'

'Where are you?'

He took a deep breath. He didn't care what they did to him any more, as long as somebody picked up Charlie Ambrose and put him a cell.

'The Heygate,' Harry said.

'What the hell are you doing there?'

'Niall Fitzpatrick lives here. I've just paid him a visit.'

'Who?'

On the other end of the line, Harry heard anxious static. He wondered if he'd been put on speakerphone.

'The gun dealer. Fitz. He sold a gun to Charlie Ambrose,' Harry continued. 'About three weeks ago. He's sure, Frankie. ID'd him from one of the pictures on the Saviour Project's website.'

'Oh, bollocks,' Noble said. Now it sounded like she was moving, and quickly.

'What is it?' Harry said.

'Get on the New Kent Road,' Noble said. 'By the traffic lights. I'll pick you up. Don't do anything stupid.'

She hung up, and Harry got to his feet. He didn't even think about running, just walked towards the road. It was snowing again, and he looked up, let the grey flakes cool his face. He briefly thought about Fairweather's warning, but if the cavalry came for him and threw him away, then so be it. He'd had enough.

Noble made it to the New Kent Road ten minutes after he called, not bad going from Lewisham, her unmarked Volvo skidding to a halt, the blue lights in the front grille reflecting off the bus stop where Harry was waiting.

'Get in!' Noble said. She was wearing a dark police polo shirt with a black tactical vest, a parka over the top to keep out the cold.

Harry pulled open the passenger door and slid into the car. He clicked himself in as Noble raced forward, turning the siren on and heading to Elephant & Castle.

'You need your head examining,' Noble shouted over the noise. Harry's vision went briefly grey, and he leant forward, expecting to pass out or vomit, but he didn't.

'Are you OK?'

Harry looked up to meet her eyes. Everything hurt. Noble came up against traffic at the roundabout, slammed on the airhorn, and waited for the buses to move out of her way.

'I'm alive,' Harry told her. 'What the hell's going on?'

'We're up shit creek,' Noble said. 'But thanks to you, we might have a paddle.'

Noble swerved left and leant over the dashboard as they approached a red light, checking they were clear before she jumped it. They had to shout to hear each other over the siren and the noise of the traffic. Noble took the south-west exit from the roundabout, towards Kennington and Clapham. Made Harry wonder where the hell they were heading on blue lights.

'What's the rush?' he yelled.

'I called Marsden after you called me. This afternoon, we had the team work up everyone in the Saviour Project, ready to split into pairs and question all of them tomorrow. Half an hour ago, one of her DCs rang Charlie Ambrose to ask him to come in tomorrow morning.'

'Shit,' Harry said, realising what it meant. 'So he knows we're on to him.'

'Maybe. With luck, he doesn't know we're coming now,' Noble said. 'But he knows his days are numbered. We've got to get to him before he runs.'

'Where does he live?'

'Pulross Road,' Noble said. 'Brixton. Jesus Christ, Harry, you'd better be right about this.'

'Fitzpatrick picked him out from a photo,' Harry said. 'I was trying to find a picture of Whitacre, for God's sake.'

The radio squawked from the car's central console as they flew past the Imperial War Museum, an inspector with a Trojan call sign asking for Noble. Harry picked up the conversation: Ambrose was known to be armed, so they would hold at the house before getting an armed response team to go into the house and arrest him. They were coming in two vans from Whitechapel, and would arrive in twenty minutes.

'They know about us,' Harry shouted once Noble signed off on the radio.

'I know,' Noble shot back, 'Fairweather wants me done for misconduct.'

'Shit,' said Harry. 'I'm sorry.'

Noble swerved onto the wrong side of the road and then cut into the traffic as it merged into a junction. They had to be covering ground faster than Harry ever had in London before.

'You should've told me about the affair, Harry,' Noble said. 'You made me look like a right fucking idiot.'

'I'm sorry,' Harry said. 'I didn't think it was important.'

'What, that you had an obvious motive for doing in Lahiri? Christ, if you hadn't just broken my case, I'd be letting you sweat in a cell, you bastard.'

He sat back in his seat and watched a group of tube passengers scatter as they ran the traffic lights opposite Oval station. They were closing now – Harry didn't know where Pulross Road was, but they were approaching Brixton. He wondered if Ambrose would come quietly or try and make a run for it. Or worse, fight his way out. Wondered what was about to unfold. They passed another branch of Chicken Hut on the left, and Harry thought back to Sunday evening, when everything had started. Perhaps everything ended here.

'Shit, that's Mo calling,' Noble said. 'Answer it, will you.'

Harry reached forward and took the call on Noble's phone, which was plugged into the car's hands-free system. Wilson's voice filled the car, too quiet to hear.

'Speak up, Mo!' Noble yelled. 'Hang on.'

She reached down and killed the siren. They were approaching

Stockwell station now, and Harry realised that they were close enough that Noble didn't want Ambrose to be forewarned by the sirens.

'I've got background on Ambrose, guv,' Wilson's voice said. 'He sounds like our guy. I checked his record with LAS. He was never a paramedic, just an ambulance technician. Left the service back in 2007 with a clean record. But I just got off the phone with his old line manager. She said a teenage boy he was driving to hospital claimed Ambrose groped him while his crewmate was out of the vehicle. Ambrose resigned rather than face the investigation.'

Noble's palm slammed against the car's steering wheel as she swung the car off the main road, heading through a residential area now, the new Brixton – old Victorian terraces home to professionals who cycled to their City jobs and ate at the start-up restaurants in the covered market. Harry tried to picture Charlie Ambrose as one of them, to remember every detail of their conversations.

'Any family?' Noble said.

'Yeah,' said Wilson. 'Seven years old. She's at school. His wife's a secretary; she's at work.'

'We're coming up,' Noble said. 'I'll see you in a bit, Mo. Good work.'

She hung up and slowed the car right down, the blue lights off now. Harry looked up at the satnav near the hands-free phone and spotted Pulross Road, running at right angles to them. They were coming up to the junction, and Noble crawled along and parked right at the bend.

'Number twenty,' she said, pointing. 'That's him.'

They were lucky, as the junction allowed them to watch Ambrose's house from the next road while blending in among the other parked cars. The house was in a terrace in the shadow of an elevated railway arch across which commuter trains rumbled. The kerb outside the house was empty, so if Ambrose had a car, maybe he was out. The living-room lights were on, though.

Noble picked up the radio.

'This is DI Noble,' she said. 'Am at target location. Trojan please update.'

'We've hit traffic,' the reply came. 'Accident on London Bridge. Should be there in one-five.'

'Shit,' Noble said. An upstairs light came on, and she looked over at Harry, who looked back at the house. He was still processing what they'd found. Ambrose was good for everything. He'd been abusing Idris and Keisha Best, and he'd grown tired of the blackmail. The weekly payments, not the lump sum that Whitacre had paid at Christmas. So he had followed Idris, looking for the right moment, and when he broke down and went into the Chicken Hut, he'd decided to make sure Idris stopped talking to the police. But even that hadn't worked, so he'd gone onto the computer system in A&E using James Lahiri's log-in and deleted the penicillin allergy. It didn't explain why he'd killed Lahiri, but there would be plenty of time for that.

'Eyes up,' Noble whispered.

Harry looked up. Charlie Ambrose had opened his front door, and stood staring at the winter's evening in a grey tracksuit. His hands were empty apart from a set of keys. To Harry's right, Noble drew her gun, finger wrapped around the trigger. There was nowhere on the tracksuit Ambrose could conceal a weapon, so they were probably safe. For the minute, at least.

'If you can get down slowly, do.'

Harry slid back in his seat and watched Ambrose walk to the sheet-metal garage door set into the house, unlock it, and pull it up. It was dark inside the garage and Ambrose didn't turn on a light, but Harry could still make out the vehicle inside. A blue-and-silver motorbike, sparkling clean, recently washed.

'Bastard,' he whispered.

'We've got him,' Noble said. 'We've got this pervert, don't you worry.'

Ambrose left the garage, not bothering to close the shutter. He was carrying something large and heavy, and Noble got one hand on the car door, ready to go out and challenge him. It was only when Ambrose turned his back to them to open his front door that they could see it was a red plastic jerrycan. Then Ambrose stepped inside his house and shut the door behind him.

'He's destroying evidence, isn't he?' Harry said.

'Why the hell else would he bring petrol inside?' Noble snapped. 'Fuck!'

She grabbed the radio from the central console with one hand, reaching into the back of the car with the other and retrieving a Kevlar vest identical to her own, throwing it to Harry.

'All units, all units,' she said. 'Male suspect Charlie Ambrose wanted in connection with murder and sex offences, in process of destroying evidence at 20 Pulross Road, Brixton. I repeat, all units please assist at 20 Pulross Road, SW9. Suspect is believed armed and dangerous.'

Harry fed his arms into the vest, not bothering to clip it tight. Blinked and saw the open door of the Chicken Hut on the Camberwell Road, Solomon Idris with his pleading, haunted eyes – first in the takeaway as he fell to the ground, and then again looking at the camera attached to the man who'd made him rape his girlfriend. Lahiri, mouth open in surprise, the back of his head missing. He opened his eyes and unlocked the car door.

'You're staying here!' Noble yelled, opening her side.

Harry ignored her and got out of the car.

'I'm doubling the odds,' he said.

There was a siren loud in the air, from the direction they'd come in. Harry hoped it was Trojan, or at least a nearby patrol unit who'd heard the request for assistance. He followed Noble towards the house. She led with her Glock out and held low, aiming for the front door. It was a crisp, clear evening, the kind which in the countryside might be accompanied by smells of firewood and pine needles. But it was the stench of petrol which filled Harry's nostrils as he assumed a position beside the door.

Noble knocked three times, and the whole frame shook.

'Charlie Ambrose!' she shouted. 'Armed police! Open up, now!'

Nothing. Harry leant down and moved to lift the letterbox with his fingers, but Noble batted him away.

'Look through that and he'll blow your head off,' she whispered. 'There's a crowbar in the boot. Go on!'

Harry sprinted back towards the Volvo, his unfastened vest bouncing against his shirt. The sirens were getting much louder, but still it felt as if they were alone. Two against one. He pulled the boot open, grabbed the crowbar, ran back towards the house. Just a little further, James, he said to himself, just a little further.

At the door, he looked up at Noble, who nodded. He dug the crowbar into the gap between the door and the frame and levered it forward, pushing down with his weight. Noble stepped behind him, readjusting her stance, her gun still trained on the door. When the first gunshot came, it split the air. The hole which appeared in the door drew Harry's eye, the blue paint cracking around the wound in the wood, just as the fuselage on Lahiri's boat had.

He knew what came next. Threw himself backwards as the next shot sounded, his eyes closed. The world moved in slow motion. He knew this place. The brain's evolved survival mechanism, the ability to decelerate time in those milliseconds between life and death, when the senses become hyperattentive, every muscle group working in tandem to fight or flee. Harry knew he was fall- ing, despite the fact all he saw was darkness. In that moment, he felt Tammas fall to his right, and was sure that somewhere, within the stench of petrol, was the smell of lavender.

The punch came to the top of Harry's left shoulder, complet- ing his fall backwards, and as he rolled to the ground, bouncing down the concrete steps that led up to Ambrose's house, he assessed the pain. Rounded, cascading through his torso as the shock wave dissipated. He knew what a gunshot wound felt like. Sharp, incisional, like a tunnel of fire. It wasn't like that. The vest had done its job.

Harry opened his eyes. He was on the floor, the door gaping open above. His backwards motion as he'd fallen had levered the crowbar and broken the lock. Noble came into view, her body hunched, shaking twice as she returned fire, three shots directed into the hallway.

Her hand on the scruff of his neck, dragging him back behind the safety of the low wall in front of Ambrose's drive. Screaming into her radio with one hand, the other holding the gun up.

'Shots fired, shots fired! Shit, Harry, are you hit?'

'I'm good,' Harry said, scrabbling to his feet. Hugging the wall for cover, peeking up at the house. The open door, a dark corridor behind it. No sign of Ambrose.

'Did you get him?' Harry said.

'No idea,' said Noble. A patrol car pulled up at the T-junction next to Noble's Volvo, and she yelled at the officers to get down. They got out, rolling for cover behind their car, one of them losing his hat. Harry risked another look at the house. The hallway was no longer dark. A bright glow of orange burned from deep inside the building, the heat carried by the wind, registering on Harry's skin. There was no pain, just adrenaline and fear.

'Shit,' he whispered. Beside him, Noble was yelling on her radio again, demanding an ETA on the Trojan units. One of the uniformed officers joined them by the wall.

'Fire and Rescue on their way, guv,' he said. Noble was about to reply when Harry saw movement in the periphery of his vision, coming out of the house. He looked up, and in that moment, he knew what he saw would stay with him for the rest of his life. Like so many things he'd seen that week, it would haunt him forever.

Charlie Ambrose exploded from the front door, fire burning from his chest and face, arms cruciform. He spun onto the pavement, his screams drowned by the roar of sirens and the burning blaze behind. Harry jumped up, turning his face from the heat, and sprinted to Noble's car. Went to the boot, still open, and grabbed the fire extinguisher that had been next to the crowbar. Ambrose was on the floor, writhing, while a copper beat him with a rolled-up high-vis jacket. Harry pulled the pin on the extinguisher as he ran. Squeezed the levers together, covering Ambrose with powder, screaming until the canister ran dry. Another copper arrived beside him with his own extinguisher, letting off blasts of water.

Noble, on her knees, her voice breaking as she held down the radio's transmit button. 'Ambulance request at 20 Pulross Road. Category A. I need LAS here now!'

Around him, more police cars screeched to a halt, officers spilling out to seal off the roads. Ambrose's arms and legs were flexed, the way burns victims' often were when the muscle tendons contracted, but his lips were moving. Harry leant in, trying to hear what he was saying.

'. . . who art in heaven, hallowed be thy name . . .'

'Charlie!' he shouted. 'Can you hear me?'

Half of Ambrose's face was white, where the powder from the fire extinguisher had hit him, and the other was his natural dark colour, but blistered and red, with areas of yellow fat where the skin had burned away.

'. . . be done, on earth as it is in heaven . . .'

'Charlie, listen to me!' Harry yelled. 'Is there anyone else in the house?'

'. . . our daily bread, and forgive us our . . .'

'Charlie!'

Harry grabbed the front of Ambrose's jaw and tried to put his face in front of his mouth, but his right eye had burned closed and his left darted across the sky. He was expecting Ambrose to recoil with the pain, but he didn't, because the fire had burned through all of the nerve endings in his face. He looked up and around, hoping that paramedics would have materialised from somewhere, but there were just more police officers, rolling tape between trees and holding back terrified residents. Noble appeared beside him.

'Is he alive?'

'For now,' Harry said. 'Where's that ambulance?'

'On its way. Are you alright?'

'I'm fine,' he said. 'Fuck.'

Both of them spoke through heavy, laboured breathing. Harry paused to wipe sweat off his face. Somehow, he still felt cold. He looked back down at Ambrose, his lips still moving. The man couldn't just die here. Even if it was like this, it was too easy. He deserved to sit in front of Frankie Noble and answer her questions, face the choices he'd made. In the house, something exploded, and everyone ducked down. The blaze had spread, the front room and hallway now well alight, the glass in the windows popping.

Harry looked down at Ambrose. You've treated bastards and murderers before, he told himself. You can do it again. But without kit, there was little he could do. Ambrose needed fluid resuscitation, pain relief, and an endotracheal tube to stop the swelling in his tissues crushing his windpipe. Ambrose came to the end of the Lord's Prayer and Harry took his moment and leant down.

'Charlie, you listen to me,' Harry whispered. 'If you want your God to forgive you, then how about you tell me something. Help us out. Tell us why you killed James, Charlie. What did he know?'

Ambrose's good eye flickered towards Harry, and then back to the sky.

'Our father, who art in heaven . . .'

Harry swore. Heard the sound of a large vehicle pulling up behind him, and turned, hoping to see an ambulance. Instead, a bulky fire engine roared into the cordon, blasting its horn to scatter the crowd of police out of its way. Firefighters leapt out, rushing to unravel hoses. One ran over to him.

'Just the one casualty?' he shouted.

'Yeah,' Harry replied. 'I'm a doctor. You got a medical kit on that thing?'

The firefighter nodded and returned from the engine holding a first-aid bag, but it was only very basic, no drugs or fluids. Harry switched on the oxygen cylinder and fitted a mask over Ambrose's face. Most of his tracksuit top had melted into his flesh, but on the legs, where the petrol had only splashed rather than soaked, it hung off in strips, which Harry cut off with shears. As he cut, he tried to assess the damage. Practically all of Ambrose's face, neck, chest and back were burned, the shoulders and upper arms, too. He swore under his breath. He needed to put a line in, start some fluids, if only to feel like he was doing something, futile as it might be.

Harry put on a pair of gloves – better late than never – and looked up. Two of the firefighters were standing in front of the house's front room, a hose team directing water inside, while another pair fought through the hallway. When he turned back, Noble was at his shoulder again.

'Frankie, where the hell's that ambulance?' he demanded.

'It'll get here when it gets here,' Noble said. At the cordon, an unmarked car pulled up, Fairweather and Marsden getting out and running towards them. Harry grabbed Ambrose by the hand and tried one last time.

'Come on, Charlie, speak to me!'

Ambrose was silent, the movement in his lips desperate, and when Harry listened to his chest it was obvious he was struggling to breathe. He grabbed a bag-valve mask from the first-aid kit and pulled it open, sealing it over Ambrose's face, feeling the waxy skin beneath his fingers. He looked at Noble and nodded down at the bag.

'Connect the oxygen up to that,' he said. 'Squeeze it every six seconds.'

Noble did so, connecting up the tubing and pumping the bag between her hands, panicked.

'Slower than that,' Harry told her. 'Nice and easy.'

He felt movement behind him and looked up to see Fairweather kneeling beside them both, his face contorted with fury. He was staring up at the house, watching the firefighters advance into the hallway. Then he turned to Noble and hissed in her ear. 'What the hell were you thinking, going in without back-up?'

As the detectives argued, a paramedic car arrived behind the fire engine, followed quickly by an ambulance. The first medic to him took over holding the mask on Ambrose's face, and Harry turned to the second and demanded a half-litre of saline and the biggest cannula they had.

'He was destroying evidence, sir,' Noble protested. Another medic relieved her of the task of squeezing the rescue bag. Harry found a vein in Ambrose's wrist, that part of the body having been relatively spared by the flames, and placed the line.

'Did you fire your gun?' Fairweather barked. 'Give it to me, now!'

Harry administered a shot of morphine and connected a fluid infusion, standing. Tapped Fairweather on the shoulder, who spun, mid-rant, his coat flapping in the wind.

'What?' he demanded.

'Hold this up as high as you can,' Harry ordered, handing him the bag of fluid. Fairweather almost dropped it, but as he caught the bag his gaze settled on Ambrose's half-burned, half-whitened face, and the blood slowly drained from his own. Above them, a helicopter circled. Harry looked up, wondering if the air ambulance had been scrambled, but it was the police chopper. Another paramedic fixed a second line in Ambrose's neck and started another bag of fluids, while a fourth retrieved the trolley from the ambulance.

'Do you want to intubate him here?' one of the paramedics asked. Harry did indeed, before the fluid leaking into the burned tissues swelled and obstructed his airway, but he didn't have the necessary drugs.

'Sats?' Harry asked.

'Ninety-six per cent on O_2.'

Holding. Harry looked around, trying to localise himself among the mass of emergency vehicles, chaos and destruction. They were just behind Brixton Road, no more than five minutes from the hospital.

'Just get him to the Ruskin, fast.'

The paramedic nodded, and together they loaded Ambrose up, still squeezing oxygen into his lungs, fluid into his veins. Harry watched as they wheeled him towards the ambulance, one of them taking the fluid bag from Fairweather. He thought about Solomon Idris, crying as the man with the mechanical voice told him to hit his girlfriend, again and again, until the teenager's protestations dissolved into sobs, and the man moved to finish it himself. He kept thinking about that until the ambulance was out of sight, and Noble grabbed him by the arm, and pulled him away.

The Professional Standards team at the crime scene wouldn't let Noble take her own car, so they chased the ambulance in a patrol car driven by one of the uniforms, Noble and Harry in the back. The journey to the Ruskin was a blur of scenery in the windows, lit up by blue lights. The hexagonal tower blocks of Shakespeare Road, the railway bridges at Loughborough Junction, the terraced houses on Coldharbour Lane. For most of it, Harry was in a daze, his body recovering from the metabolic effort of the last few hours. He looked down at his hands, his knuckles scabbed over from punching walls.

He glanced at his vest, and saw the wisps of fibre where the bullet had caught it. Fingered it, feeling for the metal. Its brother, the one three places higher in the magazine, had passed through James Lahiri's skull and out the other side. That was a sobering thought. He had another still to add to his collection of images that would never leave him, the macabre dance of a burning man as he burst from a burning house.

'What are his chances?' Noble asked as they turned up Denmark Hill. This was the end of the same journey Harry had made with Solomon Idris, trying to stem blood flow, place lines, save a life. All rivers flowed to the sea, he thought.

'Sorry?' he said. Noble repeated her question. Harry just shook his head. Tried to picture Ambrose's prostrate, writhing figure, and calculate the surface area which had been burned. It had to be at least three-quarters, maybe even eighty per cent. Harry had heard of survivors with that degree of injury, but they were notable exceptions. He thought about his phone call to Tammas, crying in the rain outside the hotel the previous night. About the promise he had made, to find the man who'd killed Lahiri and make the bastard pay.

Well, Charlie Ambrose was paying now and he'd pay for the rest of his life, however short it was. Whether that was justice or not, Harry didn't know.

They arrived at the hospital barely seconds after the ambulance, jumping out of the car as the trolley carrying Ambrose disappeared into A&E. Harry followed them through at a run, sprinting into Resus. The team were arranged as normal, except that they had two consultant anaesthetists present, one rushing to the face mask, the other checking the vital signs. A burns victim was an anaesthetist's worst nightmare, especially if the patient had inhaled hot gases. Ambrose's burns meant his tissues would fill with fluid and swell, and if that happened in his throat it would obstruct his windpipe. In some cases, it was impossible to secure an airway at all. Harry glimpsed Josh Geddes, checking the lines in Ambrose's wrist and neck, and getting another one in the other side. The trauma team leader, an A&E consultant, stood with gloved hands resting on the lectern at the end of the bed, shouting out orders. Wallace the porter stood beside him, ready to run.

The team, together, working as something more than just a group of individuals. Just as the department had done for Solomon Idris three nights ago. It didn't matter who the person on the trolley was, old or young, rich or poor, abused or abuser.

They set up more infusions and the anaesthetists agreed on a tracheotomy, which they started to set up for. They gave Ambrose more morphine and sedation, too. Harry stood outside the bay and watched. Normally, with a burns victim or anything similarly graphic, they would close the curtains to spare the other patients having to see, but there were so many people working on Ambrose that there simply wasn't room to do it.

Harry kept watching, his eyes darting between the doctors, the vital signs monitor and the patient. Time had stopped. He had no idea if seconds had passed, or minutes, or hours. He didn't notice the hand on his shoulder for a while. He turned, his head heavy, his vision greying. It wasn't Noble – it was Dr Kinirons, the A&E consultant who'd treated Idris.

'Harry,' Kinirons said. 'It's Charlie Ambrose, isn't it?'

He tried to form the words to reply in the affirmative, but he lacked the strength. There was something wrong.

'Harry?'

He focused his vision on Kinirons's face, her hands coming around to his side, fumbling at the buckle on the police vest he was still wearing. She looked concerned, and he could imagine why. Something wasn't right. He looked down at the floor, and saw the three drops of blood, dark red against the yellow-white linoleum.

'Oh, Christ!'

That was Noble's voice, Harry thought, but he couldn't see her. Kinirons unclipped his vest and the blood which had gathered between it and his sodden shirt poured out, slapping onto the floor.

'I need some help over here!' Kinirons roared as Harry slumped, feeling Noble's hands around his back.

'Come on, stay with me!'

Everything else was dark. He thought about how the hearing was the last sense to go, and the first to come back, and let the darkness take him.

Saturday, 26 January

The winter evening sun looked good over London. It always did.

Harry sat in his living room looking out of the window, his arm in a sling, a half-eaten plate of steak and salad on the table beside him. That was one of the things the junior doctor who'd discharged him yesterday lunchtime had told him, that he was mildly anaemic owing to the blood he'd lost. Only two units, so they'd not needed to transfuse him, but he ought to be careful. Not much exertion, and plenty of bed rest and red meat.

The bleeding had stopped by itself, but they'd needed to go in to remove the bullet. One of Abe Gunther's registrars had performed the operation and Gunther had explained it all to him on the ward on Thursday evening. He'd been so out of it that he hadn't taken anything in, so he'd found his notes in a quiet moment on the ward and read them. The vest Noble had hurriedly thrown him had saved his life, by directing the bullet upwards, away from his vital organs, sending it into his shoulder, over his collarbone and out of the meat of his trapezius muscle. Most of the damage was to his musculature, thankfully, so he'd not been on the table for long, just enough to clip the single vein that had been caught, and make an attempt at restoring some aesthetics to the exit wound. His shoulder and back would likely be stiff for some months, but there was little chance of any lasting damage.

They had been kind enough on the ward to take the remaining splinters from the *Time and Tide* out of his face, and he'd been discharged on the Friday with antibiotics to prevent infection and tramadol for the pain, which had the advantage of making him tired. The first thing he had done on returning home was to fall into his mattress and sleep for fifteen hours; a deep slumber inter-rupted only by vague dreams of burning men.

On Saturday the snow arrived for good, though the predicted blizzard that would close the airports, shut down London and cause a mini-apocalypse never materialised. With the snow came the detectives: faces Harry didn't recognise from a case review team at Scotland Yard entrusted with going over the entire inves-tigation, starting with the shooting at the Chicken Hut and ending with the fiery destruction of a house in Brixton. The detectives had taken statement after statement, asking few direct questions but writing endless notes, enough scribbles and scrawls to fill a thick book. The interviews had been conducted in his flat and had taken most of the day, as well as using up all the coffee he had in the kitchen. Harry told them everything, even what had happened at Fitzpatrick's apartment on the Heygate estate, and how he'd got the address. If the GMC wanted to come for him, they could. He'd take his punishment.

He opened his eyes and got up, his shoulder stinging, music playing. He thought about all of the lives irrevocably altered by what happened that week, not least his own. Outside, the city was constant, pulsing, unchanging. The Eye was close enough for him to make out its rotations, still turning, as it had been even when the whole city was on fire. Anarchy reigning on the streets, but there'd still been tourists to be fleeced. One of the nurses at the hospital had been caught stealing a pair of headphones from a branch of PC World during the disorder. Someone had made the usual comments about never really knowing anyone.

But it hadn't just been anyone who said it, it had been James Lahiri, in the pub as he mulled over whether to go back to Afghanistan. That was the irony Harry mused over as he poured a glass of Jameson's, looking over the only city he had ever known. Tom Waits was finishing 'Burma-Shave' when the doorbell rang.

Harry answered it in a T-shirt and tracksuit bottoms, his hair and face a mess.

'You're looking better,' said Frankie Noble.

It was she who was looking better, Harry thought but didn't say. She had a smart office dress on underneath a fur-lined coat, and he suspected that she too had spent the day being interviewed by senior people. He stepped aside and led her into the kitchen. In the sink was a pan of tomatoes he'd been cooking when Lahiri had called on Tuesday evening. He'd not been back since.

'Drink?' he said.

Noble nodded. 'Just the one,' she said. 'I'm the duty inspector nine-to-five tomorrow.'

Harry brought the bottle and two tumblers into the living room, remembering five days ago when he'd done the same after

Ambrose had attacked him. Noble sat down and made a face at the music.

'Sorry it's not Beethoven,' Harry said.

'He sounds like he's just woken up from a coma,' Noble said.

Harry thought of the girl with the pink hair, lying in a bed on Tennyson Ward. He hadn't been to see her in over a week now. Probably the longest such interval in a good while.

'Any news on Ambrose?' he said.

'He's still alive,' said Noble. 'And he's conscious. But you know what doctors are like. They won't tell us anything. No idea if or when we'll get to talk to him.'

'And the investigation?'

'We recovered a nine-millimetre Luger from Ambrose's house,' she said. 'It's a match for both the Wyndham Road shooting and Lahiri's murder, and he doesn't have an alibi for either of them. We've got the motorbike in his garage, we've got the fact that he burned his computer hard drive to pieces – that's where he started the fire. Basically, if he ever gets out of hospital then he'll go straight to prison for the rest of his life.'

Harry didn't expect Ambrose to survive, and if he did, it would feel like one hell of an injustice. He'd seen boys and men burned that badly out in Afghanistan who'd succumbed, usually not in the hours after their injuries, but in the days and weeks after. It gave them time to suffer, time to appreciate their imminent mortality, to say goodbye. He didn't know how he felt about that.

'It looks like there are more,' Noble went on. She'd drunk her whiskey, so she poured herself another glass.

'More?' said Harry, finishing his own drink and offering his tumbler up for a refill.

'More kids,' said Noble. 'We've passed the case over to the Child Abuse Investigation Team, and they're looking for any other kids who went through the Saviour Project and worked closely with Charlie Ambrose, who might have been abused. They've found one already, I think they're planning an interview next week. It's turning into a big operation.'

'Jesus Christ,' said Harry. 'How old?'

'Seventeen,' said Noble. 'A kid called Jerome Vincent; he's in a Young Offenders Institution. Ex-gang member, but he got arrested last year after he indecently assaulted an eleven-year-old boy at a swimming pool. The child psychologist said it was the behaviour he'd expect from a teenager who'd been sexually abused himself. Textbook, apparently. Ambrose worked with Vincent for two years, 2009 to 2011.'

'Shit,' said Harry.

'Olujide Okiniye,' Noble went on, reading from notes. 'Sixteen years old, spent a year with the Saviour Project in 2010. He made a complaint about being sexually abused to a schoolteacher, who thought he was just trying to get out of going to parole meetings. His parents took him back to—'

'Stop it,' Harry said. 'I don't need to know. I don't want to know.'

Noble nodded, looking down at the floor.

'I'm sorry,' he said, moving closer. 'I didn't mean to sound like I don't care. I do, you know I do. It's just . . .'

He trailed off, drank more whiskey, felt it burn.

'I've heard enough shit like that this week,' he said. 'We both have.'

He moved closer to her, to put his hand on her shoulder, but she pulled her head away and he retreated to his chair. The music kept playing, and they looked out of the window as the snow started again, the lights of invisible landmarks blurred and pixellated. Both of them drank slowly, looking across at each other, then back out at the sky. Eventually, Noble broke the deadlock.

'Tell me about Alice Lahiri.'

Harry looked up at her slowly, the screws in his heart tightening, 'Why?'

'Because I need to know what happened.'

He watched her face, tried to work out whether her need was professional or personal, then he looked into the glass, and started talking.

'James met her at a mess party when he was an SHO down in Portsmouth. It was a bit of a whirlwind, they'd moved in together after six months, married after a year. I didn't really get to know her until what happened with me and Tammas. James got flown back on the plane after ours, and he'd come up to visit us at the Queen Elizabeth, and then at Headley Court, and she'd come with him. After he went back to Afghan, she kept popping in to see me. Bringing me cakes and shit like that, keeping an eye on me. One night she brought a bottle of wine.'

Harry left the story unfinished, aware he was now probing a place in his memories he rarely visited, mostly because of the guttural sensation it produced in his stomach. He couldn't even really remember how or exactly when it had started, but he knew that this was how it ended. Lahiri's corpse about to be cremated, and Harry on the verge of tears, hand shaking around a glass of whiskey.

'I've got to tell you something,' Noble said.

Harry looked at her, and nodded. Her face had fallen, an expression he recognised from doctors whose patients had a fatal diagnosis. A mixture of dread and pity.

'We recovered Ambrose's phone intact,' she said. Harry's mind raced as he tried to anticipate the hit, to work out what truth would shatter over his head. She paused, as if she too was hoping that Harry would realise what was about to come. But he didn't.

'Go on,' he said.

'There were about twenty calls between Charlie Ambrose's phone and James Lahiri's made since November.'

Harry stared at her, paralysed. Even if he'd wanted to, he couldn't have moved.

'There were six calls made this week,' Noble went on. 'Including one which took place in the early hours of Monday morning, shortly after Solomon Idris was brought in to the Ruskin. And another on Monday evening, after you visited him on the—'

'Stop!' Harry shouted. 'You're wrong!'

Noble continued, unflinching. 'CAIT are investigating Lahiri to see if they can find anything else, but the current line of inquiry is that he was involved in the abuse of those kids. His log-in made the change on the hospital computer system. I'm sorry.'

'You're wrong,' Harry said, crying now. 'You're just fucking wrong. Anyone could have had access to that log-in, you said it yourself, the stupid arse wrote his password on his desk.'

'Harry, I know—'

'What've you got on him?' Harry demanded. 'Some phone calls? That doesn't prove a thing. You couldn't convict him if he was alive, so how the hell can you do it now he's dead?'

'Does it matter?' Noble asked. 'He's dead. Ambrose is going to be punished, one way or the other. Does it matter, at the end of it?'

'Of course it matters!' Harry said. 'They're cremating that man tomorrow, and I need to know what kind of man they're burning.'

His voice echoed around the room and back to him. Tom Waits had run out of songs, and the silence rolled in between them. He wondered how much evidence it would take for him to concede, to accept even the suggestion that Lahiri had been the man responsible for the video he'd forced himself to watch on Wednesday morning. Stuff on his hard drive? DNA? Remaining convinced by one's opinions in the face of overwhelming proof to the contrary was the definition of fanaticism, the very thing he and Lahiri had fought against, side by side. Tammas couldn't know, Harry thought. He'd see him at the funeral tomorrow, and he wouldn't tell him about the police's theories. It would destroy the man.

'What if you're wrong?' Harry said. 'What if you're missing something?'

'It's not my investigation any more,' said Noble. 'CAIT have the case now. They'll rip apart anyone who even came close to Solomon Idris and Keisha Best. Our best hope is that Idris wakes up and starts talking.'

Harry nodded. He'd requested regular updates on Idris from his hospital bed, and as of Friday afternoon, he was stable and making good progress. The plan was to take him off the ventilator on Monday morning, and if all went to plan he could potentially be awake by that afternoon.

Noble said she needed the toilet, and Harry thought about her while she was gone. Remembered the night they'd spent together, a night when it had felt like the world was crashing down around them, and every moment of pleasure that could be taken had to be, as if it was their last opportunity.

'I guess I should thank you,' Harry said when she came back.

'For what?'

'For trusting me when the rest of you bastards were trying to put me in the frame.'

She laughed and threw her hair back.

'I think Marsden just wanted to rule you out,' she said. 'And establish herself as the alpha in the investigation. Perhaps I'd have done the same in her shoes. But Fairweather's a nasty piece of work. All he cares about is the politics. Didn't matter if you were guilty or not, he just wanted another scalp on his way to the top.'

'And what about your scalp?' Harry said.

Noble smiled. 'I've not heard anything else. I have a feeling Marsden put in a good word, given that they'd have tipped off Ambrose if we hadn't got to him. I probably have you to thank for that. Fingers crossed it'll go away, and I'll get off with a written warning.'

'Here's hoping,' Harry said.

They clinked glasses.

'Whose investigation is it now? Fairweather's?'

'No way,' said Noble. 'Homicide & Serious are handing over the files on Idris and Lahiri to the CPS, and they'll prosecute Ambrose if he makes it. CAIT have the rest. All Professional Standards get to do is investigate whether we did anything wrong at the Chicken Hut. I suspect they won't do anything. Excessive force isn't the flavour of the month any more, not when we've got DCIs selling information to the *News of the World*.'

She finished her glass and Harry watched her again. Outside, an ambulance coursed along the street, heading for Waterloo. It was both a comforting and a sad thought, that whatever hell his life became, whatever happened to lost souls like Solomon Idris, or Keisha Best, or the girl with the pink hair, the city would keep going.

'I know that James was a good man,' he said. 'If he did what you think he did, then those were despicable acts. But that doesn't change what he did for me.'

'Maybe we're wrong,' Noble said. 'And in all likelihood, we'll never know. So maybe that's a good way to think about it.'

Harry finished his drink. He wasn't sure how firmly he held that conviction, though he'd said it with strength and sureness. He suspected, with time, he'd change his views. That was the temporal nature of relationships, after all. Lahiri was a man whom he'd alternately loved, hated, befriended and betrayed. When he'd been alive, Harry's last act had been to accuse him, and since he'd died, all he'd done was defend him.

'I should go,' Noble said, standing up. She offered up her empty glass, and Harry moved over to take it from her. When he did, he stood between her and the door.

'You shouldn't,' he said. 'Not if you don't want to.'

He stood up, and she kissed him, and he led her to his room, and outside, the city kept on going.

Sunday, 27 January

Harry woke up alone in his bed at about half-past ten and dragged himself to the shower. The side of the bed that was usually neat was a mess, and held the smell of a woman for the first time. She'd not woken him leaving. Neither of them had cried this time, but the sick feeling in his stomach wouldn't go away, despite the fact it was the second night in a row that he had slept properly. He wasn't sure what it was: the sex, the alcohol, or the events of the past week. He spent half an hour or so sitting on the shower floor, letting lukewarm water wash down over him, cleansing, baptismal. Then he toasted a couple of bagels and scrambled some eggs, washing the breakfast down with half a carton of stale orange juice and coffee. The harsh winter sun lit the apartment as if he was on stage, so bad that it hurt his eyes.

The service was at one, at Lahiri's old school, just south of Guildford. He took care to dress himself well, putting on his only black suit and a neatly pressed white shirt, ironed as only a soldier can, not a crease in sight. The man himself would have been proud of that one, Harry thought as he pulled the warm fabric over his body, doing up the buttons, selecting a sombre tie from the rack in his wardrobe. Their colleagues who still served would turn up in dress uniform, and it was likely Lahiri would get the full works, right down to the coffin draped in the Union flag. His school were sending pall-bearers from the Combined Cadet Force. The man was a war hero, after all.

He looked at the mirror, running a hand over the scar on his face. The scabbing had evened away, but the line where a splinter of Lahiri's boat had sliced into his flesh remained, a constant reminder of what had happened. His eyes looked less worn now, his hair something approaching even. In the dark suit he could almost pass for someone normal.

The location worked out conveniently, as Kingston-upon-Thames was on the way. The drive took an hour or so, some of the lunchtime traffic holding him up. He took a diversion, going through the park, slowing to look at the deer standing in the snow, a herd of them fleeing as a family walked dogs. One of the deer ran behind the group, stumbling on an injured leg. The runt of the litter, Harry thought. He'd been trying for most of the morning to pin down the feeling that was itching at him, the lingering suspicions. He wondered if it was entirely selfish, his agony over Lahiri's guilt or innocence. Because if it turned out that his friend was a child molester and a party to murder, it made what Harry had done to him somehow more acceptable?

Lahiri had made phone calls to a guilty man. And his computer log-in had made a change that had almost been a death sentence to a victim of horrendous abuse. As he'd said to Frankie, that wasn't enough to convict someone alive. But he couldn't shake the thought.

Tammas picked up Harry's turmoil but said nothing. They had a portable ventilator at Marigold House with a battery life of eight or so hours, enough time for the service, the wake and the return journey. But by a quarter past twelve, they still hadn't left.

'We'll be late,' Harry said.

'Then go. Without me,' Tammas spat in reply. He was already hooked up to the machine, sitting in a wheelchair with the ventilator at his side on a trolley, wearing full No. 1 dress complete with medal bars. Tammas had never officially been discharged, and as a lieutenant colonel he would possibly be the highest-ranking officer at the service. Their delay had been due to his objection to the mode of transport Marigold House had arranged.

'I'm not going. Anywhere. In the back. Of an ambulance. Unless you're. Taking me. To the bloody. Hospital.'

'Boss, please—'

'Put me in. The back of. A Transit. I'm not. Going in that. Thing.'

The private ambulance drivers had refused to leave until they'd been paid, and with the care home refusing to shell out Harry had paid them himself, before arranging for a taxi large enough to accommodate Tammas, a nurse, his wheelchair and the portable ventilator. When they finally left, Harry had followed behind in his own car.

They made it to the service by five to one. It didn't look like a school at all, more like a country estate; the grand memorial chapel constructed from huge sandstone pillars, bounded by snow-covered fields and skeletal, anorexic trees. Harry shivered as he wheeled Tammas into the chapel, the ventilator humming among the gathered crowd. He recognised plenty of faces, a handful of friends from medical school, and others in military dress, former army colleagues, both from the medical corps and the Royal Anglians. Georgia Henderson was somewhere in the mix, standing with a couple of her dead husband's comrades-in-arms. There were faces from A&E as well, and Harry nodded to Kinirons, her sharp features accentuated by her black dress. He recognised a few more, some of the other junior doctors. George Traubert, looking up at the masonry in a charcoal suit, not black. And the other doctors and youth workers from the Saviour Project, filling two pews on the other side, the forlorn figure of Duncan Whitacre among them, head bowed.

To his left, Tammas was trying to speak, so Harry leaned close.

'Go up. The front. Don't sit here. And babysit me.'

Tammas had lost the ability to whisper, and the rear two rows of the congregation turned to see what was making the bizarre rattling noise that sounded something like speech.

'I'm fine here, don't you worry,' Harry said. He'd rather be at the front – it would make the walk to the pulpit less conspicuous for his reading – but the figure he'd spotted in the second row made him wish he wasn't there. She still did her hair the same way, hanging over the right shoulder. Alice and James Lahiri had never divorced, even though they'd been about as separated as it was possible to be, so it was still her husband's funeral that she'd flown halfway around the world to attend.

Harry thought of the beds they'd shared and felt the space under his ribcage empty again. He looked across at Tammas as the vicar began the welcome, and remembered the conversation they'd had waiting for the taxi.

'You look like. Death. Harry.'

'I've had a rough few days.'

'You. Got the. Bastard. Who did it. Didn't. You?'

Harry explained about Ambrose, that he was now in limbo. He'd mentioned eighty per cent burns, and Tammas had looked up at the sky and smiled. Tammas had seen enough burns patients during his career to know what it meant.

'I hope. He pulls. Through. And spends. The rest. Of his. Miserable. Life just like. Me.'

Harry had spent the drive over trying to work out whether to tell Tammas about what the police thought about Lahiri. The man had little left to live for: a distant family, and two surrogate sons, one of whom had been brutally murdered, whether it had been deserved or not. Now, as they sat listening to the bidding prayer, he was unable to stop the tears.

Tammas asked him what was wrong.

'I treated him like shit, boss,' Harry said. 'He gave everything to me, he loved me so much, and I threw it all back in his face. Why? Why the fuck did I do that?'

Tammas moved his head with great difficulty to answer the question.

'You hated him. For treating. You. Instead of. Me. You hate. Him. For saving. Your life.'

The sentiment hung in the air like the smell of cordite after a battle. Harry felt a deep pain swell in his chest and burst upwards, into the place he thought his soul might be. He remembered saying those words himself, but still, the verbalisation of them by someone else, by the only man in the world he unshakeably respected, was a new condemnation. The vicar finished the prayer, and the organ struck up the first hymn. 'Nearer, My God, to Thee'. Harry tried to sing out the words, the tune's rhythm disrupted by the rotation of the ventilator to his left. The second verse came around, and through the noise Harry could make out Tammas, vainly hoping only Harry would hear his words.

'Wasn't this. What they played. As the *Titanic*. Went down?'

They formed a line heading out of the chapel, each visitor shaking hands with Lahiri's parents. He didn't have any other immediate family, and the others were all back in West Bengal, so it was just the two of them thanking the mourners, faces sombre. His mother wore a blank, lifeless smile that Harry suspected was the result of sedatives. His father had his back ramrod straight, and was looking everyone in the eye and shaking their hand, trying his best to be as British as possible. Everyone except one person, Harry observed. When Alice came to the front of the chapel, her black hair like a veil over her face, they turned aside and looked at the ground. Harry watched her slink away, hiding in the throng of mourners, and felt an urge to vomit.

It was the worst thing he had ever done, and he would never get the chance to get anywhere close to reconciliation. The line of people moved forward, and Harry pushed Tammas closer to the huge oakwood chapel doors. The Lahiris would be faced now with two men, one who had made their son the man he was, another whose actions had meant he'd lived the last year of his truncated life bitter and alone.

Harry was fighting back tears when he reached the front. He knew Lahiri's parents well, having spent a few summers during medical school at their house in Sussex. Football and tennis in the garden, excursions on the sailing boat, swimming in their heated pool. Harry's mother had died when he was nineteen, and in the years that followed Lahiri's parents had gone out of their way to look after him. As Lahiri's father stooped to shake Tammas's limp, lifeless hand, his mother threw her arms around Harry, weeping openly into his shoulder. Harry wept, too.

As he held his dead friend's mother, Harry realised that Lahiri must never have told them who Alice had embarked on her affair with. That guilt swelled in him, pushing against his lungs. He didn't know how long it had been when the vicar moved him on, pointing him down the stairs, and towards the long gravel drive that led back towards the school, filled with the 4x4s and Aston Martins of Lahiri's friends, waiting to drive them onwards.

Harry drove over to the wake, while Lahiri's parents escorted their son to the crematorium. They'd asked him if he wanted to come along, but he'd said he had to look after Tammas. A couple were turning their only son to ash, and that was something which Harry couldn't bear to witness.

They'd hired out a function room at a pub in a countryside village not far from the school, the kind of place where all the farmhouses were owned by CEOs and hedge fund managers who commuted into London and used the stables for their daughters' ponies, and the barns for their swimming pools. Harry got a Glenmorangie for Tammas and a Coke for himself, and asked for a straw, and the barman put the straw in the Coke, so he asked for another one and put it in the whisky.

There was a trio of officers from the RAMC standing with Tammas and his nurse, medics who'd gone through Sandhurst with Harry and Lahiri. They were making war talk and telling stories about Lahiri, so Harry joined them for a while, allowing his thoughts to wander. He'd come to a decision, while he'd been holding Lahiri's mother, that today was about grieving for Lahiri as the best man they all knew, and judgement, if it came at all, could come later. He cursed the fact that he would have to drive home, that he couldn't participate in what seemed to be a fairly heavy session among several sections of the crowd. Doctors drank a lot. People at wakes drank a lot. Two plus two made five.

Harry wandered between groups of old friends from medical school, asking them how their husbands and wives were, where they were working. Most were consultants or GPs, and all talked about how close he had been to Lahiri, and how hard it must be for him, which just made it worse. A few of Lahiri's friends from school who Harry had met at birthday parties and nights out tried to speak to him, but after a few sentences they got the message and left him alone. Stooped over the bar with his head in his hands, like a figure in an Edward Hopper painting.

Fuck it, he thought, and ordered a Jameson's. By the time it came there was someone beside him, a delicate hand on his shoulder.

'Hey, Harry,' said Alice. 'That was a nice reading you did.'

A touch of Kiwi in her voice now, even though she'd been there only a few months. That was her in a nutshell, though; the ultimate shapeshifter. All things to all men.

'Yeah,' Harry said. He'd read the poem *If*, words about fortitude, strength of character, an unbreakable spirit. Things which James Lahiri had had in spades, which he might well have used to become an even greater man. Transforming the lives of young men. As he'd read it, his stomach had swollen with horror. The fleeting thought, however improbable, that instead those traits had helped him become a monster.

Harry always remembered names. It was a skill he'd had forever and never appreciated. Now he repeated in his head the ones Noble had said the previous night. Solomon Idris. Keisha Best. Jerome Vincent. Olujide Okiniye. And they were the ones who the

318

police knew about. The phone calls to Charlie Ambrose. Harry couldn't explain those. Not with the information he had. He realised then that it was possible he would never know what James Lahiri had been. That he might question it for the rest of his life. Maybe Solomon Idris would wake up, and tell all. Point the finger. But maybe he wouldn't.

'That poem was in our downstairs toilet,' Alice said. 'In the old house, I mean.'

The old house where he'd held her and kissed her so many times, each one a betrayal. Oh, you self-righteous prick, Harry thought. Trying to denigrate your best friend's memory just so you can feel less guilty about screwing his wife. He opened his mouth, about to utter some platitude about how Lahiri had been a good man, better than both of them, but there was no point. She would hear, but not listen. She might cry, so that a man would comfort her, and people would talk about her, and then she would fly back to New Zealand and carry on with her hollow life.

'Go fuck yourself, Alice,' Harry said. Saw his whiskey off in one, turned and searched for the first face he recognised that wasn't Alice.

It was Bernadette Kinirons, standing with Traubert, the two consultants concealed in a corner of the pub, she nursing a glass of wine, he a bottle of sparkling water. Harry made eye contact with them and headed over. Kinirons gave his arm a squeeze, and smiled at him.

'You did well, Harry,' Kinirons said. 'We've all lost a good man, you know. The world has.'

Harry said nothing and nodded. Kinirons's eyes were misting, genuine, and Harry held them for a while. He remembered the fury in her voice as she'd led the effort to resuscitate Solomon Idris, and knew that she would have done the same for Charlie Ambrose, and that she was the kind of doctor everybody wished to become. The antithesis to that stood beside her, and he leant forward and put a condescending hand on Harry's shoulder.

'I happened to be having lunch yesterday with the medical school sub-dean,' Traubert said. 'We're going to set up a memorial award in Lahiri's name. A bursary for a disadvantaged student who upholds the values that James stood for. I'm sure you'd be a welcome addition to the awarding committee.'

Harry mumbled something in response.

'Maybe later, eh, George?' Kinirons said, sliding her arm around Harry's back. 'You're doing really well, Harry. I know you feel like you have to keep it all together at moments like this, but you're a young man. You shouldn't be burying your friends. It's alright to let it out sometimes.'

'Thanks,' Harry said, and meant it. Beside them, Traubert shuffled awkwardly to one side.

'Well, you're doing better than he is, at any rate,' Kinirons continued. Harry followed her gaze and found a group of GPs from the Burgess Park Practice sitting around a table, eating finger food. Whitacre had at least three empty pint glasses in front of him, and another three-quarters full of Guinness, some of which had been spilled down his shirt. A woman whom Harry presumed to be his wife was trying to get the stain out with a handkerchief, while Duncan shouted at her to leave him alone, and someone else begged them not to make a scene.

'He's taking it hard,' Traubert said. 'Poor man. I'll go over once things have calmed down.'

A phone rang loudly, and Traubert dug into his trouser pocket, making his apologies.

'Oh, bloody hell,' he said. 'I'm on call this weekend; I'd hoped they wouldn't bother me.'

Harry watched him leave. On his way out, he headed over to Whitacre's side and embraced him warmly, two good friends consoling each other. Harry watched him, trying his best to conceal his contempt. Kinirons read his look, though, and laughed.

'I know you hate him, Harry,' said Kinirons. 'I would, too, if I was his registrar. But he likes you. He was singing your praises on the drive down here. It'd do you good to make friends, alright? Think about the future, eh? You're not going to be a registrar forever . . .'

Harry thought about that for the first time in a long while. It was one of those small-talk questions that junior doctors asked each other in quiet moments on call, at parties and conferences. What their career plans were, whether they wanted to specialise or not, which training programmes at which deaneries they were applying to. Most people had a plan, did research to get the places that they wanted, but Harry had just been bumping between registrar jobs for years now. The future was a distant place, out of his reach. After this week, there were lots of people who didn't have much of a future.

'So, unless I can tempt you with a job in A&E,' Kinirons went on, 'I suggest you have a few more bottles of Fiji water in the near future.'

Harry laughed and Traubert came back over, shaking his head.

'I've got to head in,' he said, pulling his coat on. 'Neuro think there's a case of Guillain-Barré in A&E.'

'Was he OK?' said Harry. 'Whitacre?'

'He's saying that there might have been other people involved, people other than Charlie. Are you still in touch with the police? Is that true?'

Harry looked across at Whitacre, who was draining his current pint, and saw his eyes briefly harden as they met his own.

'It's not clear,' Harry said. 'They've passed it over to a specialist team who deal with child abuse and that sort of thing. But all being well, Solomon will be awake and talking next week. Hopefully they'll get a lot from him.'

'How's he doing?' Kinirons said.

Traubert made a forlorn frown. 'The plan's to give him a trial off the ventilator tomorrow. You know how it is, patients who've been on the unit that long, it might be difficult. But we've got to try. Anyway,' he went on, 'I've got to head in.'

'Well, looks like that's us, then,' said Kinirons. 'George here is my chauffeur.'

Harry shook both of their hands and walked with them to Traubert's car. When he came back inside the pub was loud with noise, its focus the table of Lahiri's colleagues from Burgess Park. Duncan Whitacre was at the centre of the circle. He was on his feet, obviously drunk, his wife trying to calm him down as he shouted at one of his colleagues.

'. . . fed up of this bullshit!'

'Come on, Duncan, please, let's just go home.'

'I'm not going anywhere!' Whitacre roared. 'All of this is a sham! Room full of sad losers, deluding themselves!'

The hairs on Harry's neck stood on end. He knew what was driving the rage inside Whitacre, and he knew that it was only a matter of time before it erupted out.

'Mate, why don't you get some fresh air?'

The suggestion came from one of Lahiri's school friends, said in the kind of condescending voice that could only inflame the situation. Whitacre swept the empty glasses off the low table, spitting as he did so.

'Look at you! All of you! Standing around, patting yourselves on the back, telling each other what a good man he was! Well, you're all full of shit! Do you want to know what kind of man James really was? Do you?'

Harry rushed forward, trying to be as non-threatening as possible, but the table was between him and Whitacre, and he knew he wouldn't be able to stop him delivering the punchline.

'He was a fucking nonce!' Whitacre bellowed. 'Him and that black bastard Charlie! Kiddie-fiddlers, both of them!'

Half of the crowd were caught speechless, in shock, while the others – the younger, drunk, male half – charged him. The first punch came from a doctor Harry and Lahiri had lived with at university, catching Whitacre awkwardly on the right ear, before two of Lahiri's school friends bundled him to the ground. Somewhere in the melee, Whitacre's wife erupted into tears. At the edge of the crowd, Lahiri's mother wailed loudly and collapsed into her husband's arms.

As people rushed into the scrum, four of Whitacre's work colleagues pulling him away, Harry backed off slowly, finding himself near the door with Tammas and his nurse. Harry looked down at him.

'You. Never really. Know. Anyone, do you?' Tammas said.

'We knew James,' Harry said. 'And he wasn't that.'

He looked over at the fight, which the bar staff were breaking up, and felt the tears come again.

'I'm getting out of here, boss,' he said.

'Good idea,' Tammas said.

He walked to his car, got in, and pulled away too fast, gravel spinning out of the wheels and the car stalling. He punched the dashboard and swore, checking his mirrors to see if it was safe to set off again. It was clear, apart from Duncan Whitacre, stooped over on a kerb, crying and vomiting.

Harry put the car in gear and clamped his foot down.

Noble called him when he was well into London, on the A3, after she'd finished work. She was in the pub, or rather outside it, smoking, and wanted to know if he had any plans that evening, suggesting she bring a curry over to his place. Just for the convenience, she said, because she had a meeting at eight on Monday morning at the station on Borough High Street, and Harry's flat was just up the road. Eventually, they got on to talking about the funeral and the wake, and how the ugly accusations had come out.

'I wish we'd have just been able to say goodbye. Give him a day of respect before all the accusations started.'

'We'll know eventually,' Noble said. 'It's just a matter of time. These investigations don't get results overnight, you know that.'

'I know,' said Harry. 'I just wish Whitacre had kept his fucking mouth shut. I mean, what are his parents supposed to think now?'

Harry had wanted to have a few private moments with Lahiri's parents, maybe to apologise by proxy, but the mood had been unendurable. He would call, or write, or something.

'No idea on when Idris will wake up?' Noble said. 'He'll know who's responsible. CAIT are preparing to interview the others, too. If Lahiri's innocent, we'll clear him.'

'They'll try and take him off the ventilator tomorrow,' Harry said. 'Well, that's the plan, anyway. There're no signs of brain damage, but it could be a week before he's ready to talk. Maybe longer.'

Harry was navigating the roadworks by the north end of Clapham Common, so it took him a while to realise she hadn't responded.

'What is it?' he said.

'It's nothing,' said Noble. 'I'm tired.'

'No,' said Harry. 'What is it?'

'I'll tell you later.'

'If it's about Idris, you should tell me now,' he said, 'and you will.'

A loud roar burst out of the static on the hands-free. Harry suspected Noble was in one of the pubs by Walworth station, waiting for him to get home, and a football team had just scored. Once the noise subsided, he heard her take a deep breath.

'I had a word with one of the DIs from CAIT today,' Noble said. 'They did HIV testing on Lahiri at the post-mortem, and on Charlie Ambrose, too.'

Harry was sure that she didn't know he was holding his breath.

'They're both seronegative,' said Noble. 'So unless Idris and Best got HIV from some other source, they figure there's someone else involved. They've gone back to square one now, looking at everyone in the Saviour Project again.'

Harry hit the dashboard with a flat palm.

'Why the hell wouldn't you want to tell me that?' he shouted, changing lanes. 'It's more evidence that he's innocent! You people have nothing on him!'

'I didn't want to get your hopes up,' said Noble. 'It might still turn out that he was involved. I don't want you to hurt any more than you have to if things go that way.'

Harry thought about that, and how he was just regressing to the worst kind of human behaviour, demanding to see the world in black and white because it was easier that way.

'How far away are you?' Noble said.

He ignored her.

'He's not a rapist,' he said. 'I don't need to prove that to you. He's not.'

Silence again. The traffic was sluggish, particularly for a Sunday afternoon, and Harry felt the frustration starting to build.

'What's going to happen to Idris?' Noble said after a while. 'After he's discharged?'

'If I have anything to do with it, he'll go straight into psychiatric care. The Maudsley has a specialist adolescent unit, we'll refer him there. After what that kid's been through, it's what he needs.'

'I meant with being HIV-positive. What's his life expectancy?'

Harry hit a red light and yawned. 'It's unusual for someone so young to present with such a serious lung infection, so that suggests he's particularly susceptible to the disease. He must have been infected three years ago, at least. But with modern therapy, HIV is a chronic disease rather than a life-shortening one. It's like having diabetes. More of an inconvenience than a disability, really.'

'Inconvenience?' said Noble. 'What do you mean?'

'Well, you've got to have monthly blood tests, take about ten pills a day,' he said. 'Some of the medications need to be kept refrigerated, little things like that.'

Noble said something, but Harry didn't hear it. His own voice was echoing back to him like a hallucination. *Some of the medications need to be kept refrigerated.* And then another man's voice, as patronising as ever. He felt the colour draining from his face. It was how realisations like this always happened, like a drop of cold rain striking his head as he stepped outside.

'Fiji water,' he said.

'What?'

'Frankie, I need you to meet me at the hospital,' he shouted into the phone. 'I'll be there in five minutes.'

The light went green and he indicated left, moved into a bus lane, cut up a taxi, accelerated along the tarmac, watching the road. Rummaged in his door pocket for his doctor-on-call card, slid it onto the windscreen for all the good it would do. He'd take the back road, Acre Lane to Brixton, and then on to Camberwell.

'Harry, what the fuck?' said Noble.

He could tell from the sound that she was getting into her car, starting it. A speed camera flashed as Harry went past it, doing fifty in a thirty zone.

'I'll explain in a second,' he said. 'Get driving and get some back-up. Then call me, and I'll explain. Do it, now!'

With that he hung up, and accelerated.

Harry parked on a double-yellow outside A&E, leaving the car unlocked, running to the entrance, where Noble waited for him. James Lahiri was an innocent man, he was sure, but that could wait. There was a guilty man who didn't know they were coming for him. He started talking as they headed into A&E. For what felt like the tenth time, Noble was trying to understand his logic.

'He's got a fridge in his office?' she said, struggling to keep up as he paced through the department. 'You want me to arrest someone because they've got a fridge in their office?'

'HIV medication needs to be refrigerated,' Harry said. 'That's what made me realise. But everything else fits. He used to be an A&E consultant, back when they set up the Saviour Project. He told me that's how he knew Whitacre. He'd have known Ambrose, too.'

'Harry, I can't arrest someone on that!' Noble shouted.

'Why not?' said Harry. 'It all makes sense. He must have used the computer that Lahiri was still logged on to to delete Idris's penicillin allergy. He couldn't have risked doing it from his own account, because he knew it'd be audited.'

She followed him through the main hospital and up the East Wing staircase at a run, heading towards the second floor.

'How do you even know he's here?' she asked.

'He's on call today,' Harry said. 'He was at the funeral. I told him we'd find out who was behind everything once Idris woke up.'

He rounded the corner, sliding to a halt in the corridor between the medical and surgical sections of the ICU. He was still in the black funeral suit, his shirt glued to his chest and back with sweat. The name on the plaque on the office door in front of him taunted him, as if reminding him of his failure, the fact he'd been blind for so long. Dr George Traubert, Clinical Services Director, Emergency Department & Perioperative Care.

On the drive up, Harry had realised that he'd been missing it all along. On the night it had all started, George Traubert had twice screwed up with Idris. First, he'd taken minutes trying to find a vein, even attempting a venous cutdown, a procedure decades out of date, while every second the teenager was bleeding to death. Then he'd spent so long trying to intubate him that Kinirons had had to step in. Harry had derided both as acts of a doctor out of his depth, but as the thoughts circled in his head he realised the truth was far more sinister.

Traubert hadn't lost control, he'd known exactly what he was doing. Because he never wanted Solomon Idris to wake up. Exactly the same when he'd kept asking Harry how everything was going, whether the police were any closer to finding out who was behind his shooting. Again, Harry had found it merely annoying, when in reality Traubert had been checking up on whether or not he was safe. You sick bastard, Harry thought.

'Harry! We need a warrant! Harry!'

He tried the door handle. It was locked.

'Harry, if he's guilty and we need to prosecute then I can't use any—'

Harry looked at Noble. He wasn't a copper. It wasn't his job to preserve the chain of evidence or turn a portfolio over to the CPS. He was running on a much baser instinct than that. He swung his body into the office door and the lock gave way with a crack.

'For fuck's sake, Harry!'

He leapt round Traubert's desk, finding his way in the dark, knocking over a sheaf of papers. Noble came in behind him, switched on the light. Harry found the mini-fridge, sat in chrome metal between the rows of medical textbooks, the Porsche logo embossed on the bottom-right corner. Yanked the door open, and the light from inside illuminated his face, refracted by the polygonal water bottles, which Harry grabbed, sweeping them out onto the carpet of the office until the fridge was empty.

Apart from the single leaf of kitchen roll on the bottom shelf. Harry closed his eyes and lifted it up.

'What is it?' Noble asked.

Harry opened his eyes and saw the pill boxes, processing the names. Entricitabine. Atazanavir. Drugs that were keeping George Traubert alive, preventing the virus inside him from consuming his immune system. The same virus he'd transmitted to Keisha Best and Solomon Idris during years of rape and sexual abuse. He lifted the boxes and read off the colour-coded labels on the ampoules. Diazepam, for injection. Ketamine. There was no good reason for a consultant to have sedative drugs like those in his office. And then the one at the bottom, a single dose of Mifepristone, the abortion pill. Just in case the first one didn't work. He should have got rid of it by now, Harry thought – Keisha Best and her child were long dead. It was a mistake, and one which would help put Traubert in prison. Where he belonged.

'Bastard!' Harry shouted. 'Bastard!'

Noble pulled him out of the way, her own eyes settling on the medication boxes at the bottom of the fridge.

'Is that enough to make an arrest?' Harry said, realising now that he was shouting. 'Ring the officer who's with Idris!'

Noble's face went white. 'There isn't one. We stood them down after we got Ambrose.'

'Fuck!'

She stepped forward, trying to calm him down. 'There's officers on the way, Harry, we'll get him, don't you worry.'

But he was already gone, out of the office, sprinting for the ICU, bursting through the doors into the nurses' station. The chief nurse, Valdez, stared at him, and Harry realised he was still in the black suit he'd worn to the funeral. He looked down the corridor towards Idris's side room, scanning the windows for the tall, stooping figure of Traubert. He wasn't there, but neither was the patient.

'Where's Idris?' he demanded.

Valdez looked at him, smiling.

'Oh, you've just missed him,' she said. 'He's gone to the CT scanner.'

He gripped her around the shoulders, his forehead burning with rage. Shouted a question that he already knew the answer to.

'Who's with him?'

Valdez laughed. 'Harry, calm down, he's fine. The registrar's busy in A&E, so Dr Traubert said he'd escort Idris himself.'

'Angie, listen to me! Fast-bleep security and get them up to CT now!'

He spun and ran, swearing and cursing as he did so. While there was a CT scanner directly below them in A&E, it was kept free for emergencies, so non-urgent scans would take place in the radiology department in the South Wing. To get there, Traubert would need to wheel Idris to the lift lobby Harry had just come out of, go down, take him along the main hospital corridor to the South Wing lifts, and then up to the first floor.

Harry took the steps in the East Wing stairwell four at a time, jumping from landing to landing. Harry had told Traubert at the funeral that they would know everything when Solomon Idris woke up, and Traubert couldn't let that happen. He'd tried to ensure that in A&E, and again when he'd deleted his allergy, but it hadn't worked. There were too many people in an ICU to walk in and kill someone without suspicion, even if you were a consultant. He had to get somewhere where he'd be alone with Idris, and he

could do it then. Not the CT scanner itself – there were radiographers and nurses who'd be suspicious and raise the alarm. But any
of the corridors along the way would be fine.

He got to the main hospital corridor, his legs beginning to ache,
his muscles tiring. Tried to think like Traubert. Everything the
bastard had done so far had been misdirection, calculated to point
as far away from him as possible. Setting up Lahiri, getting
Ambrose to do the dirty work. If he was going to murder Idris in
cold blood, he'd do it in a way which would look like natural
causes, or a complication of his condition. These were the actions
of a man who planned to kill, get away with it, and keep on fucking teenage girls and boys, not the desperate last stand of someone
who knew the game was up.

Harry turned a corner in the corridor, hearing Noble shout
behind him. The South Wing lift lobby was about a hundred
metres ahead, off to the left.

'Uniform are on their way!'

Out of hours, the hospital's emptiness was eerie, particularly
along the main corridor, which hosted the outpatient departments, the canteen, the lecture theatres and coffee shops that were
the focus of activity in daylight hours. Most of the time, Harry
found the stillness of weekend and night shifts comforting, relax-
ing, even serene. Now, the loneliness was forbidding. Somewhere
ahead of him, a doctor was waiting to murder his patient, unseen,
and the only noise Harry could hear was the machine gun fire of
his feet on the vinyl floor, and the panting of his breath.

A muted chime filled the empty walls, another part of the usual
hospital chorus. A lift, arriving.

The lift. That's where he'd do it. Alone, no witnesses. Solomon
Idris would be wheeled into the lift alive, Traubert would inject
him with something while they were inside, and he'd arrest in the
corridor, or in the CT scanner. Harry willed his muscles to find
any extra speed they could. The lactate in his legs burned, and his
chest filled with fury and rage, his head cloudy with adrenaline.

He turned the corner, and there they were, waiting for the lift.
Solomon Idris, the tubes and wires from his body attached to
portable ventilators and monitors strapped to the chassis of the
trolley, feet pointing towards the open lift. Beside him was George

Traubert in raspberry scrubs. He looked up as Harry charged towards him. Briefly Traubert's face changed, as he recognised Harry. The mask of the genial, bumbling consultant was gone, and for a split second Harry saw the man with the mechanical voice, the one who had ordered Solomon Idris to hit his drugged girlfriend harder.

'Harry?' Traubert said, trying to sound surprised. 'What the hell are you doing here?'

From the wobble in his voice, Harry could tell even he didn't think he would get away with that one.

'Get away from him, George,' Harry said. 'It's over.'

He'd meant to shout, but it came out hoarse, defeated.

He heard Noble arrive behind him but kept his eyes locked on Traubert.

'Police!' she called. 'Show me your hands, now!'

Traubert's hands came up from by his side, and Harry stepped forward, his eyes darting towards them, focusing on the white plastic in Traubert's left hand, the growing dark patch on his trousers. He charged forward, all of his weight behind the tackle, pinning Traubert against the trolley. Went for the arm, wrapped his hand around Traubert's wrist.

'He's got something!' Harry yelled.

His fingers scrabbled as he pulled Traubert's hand up, revealing the twenty-mil syringe he was holding, finger and thumb over the plunger, doing his best to empty it into the fabric of his scrubs so they didn't find it on him. Harry threw his other hand onto Traubert's wrist, levering all of his weight onto the consultant. Noble was there now too, her hands on the scruff of Traubert's neck, lifting him up, her face red, screaming.

'Hands behind your back! Drop it! Drop it now!'

Harry's grip loosened for a second, and Traubert lashed out with an elbow, catching him right on the bridge of the nose. He fell back, crashing onto the floor. The momentum was enough, though, and Harry brought the syringe with him, watching it bounce across the vinyl and disappear under Idris's trolley. Harry tasted blood but came up anyway as Noble got an arm around Traubert's neck. He managed to stay on his feet this time, delivered a kick between Traubert's scrabbling legs. Traubert squealed and doubled over, and Noble took the advantage, flipping him forward and pulling his hands behind his back.

'What's in the syringe, you fucker?' Harry screamed.

'Hold him,' Noble said, her knees digging into the small of Traubert's back. Harry did so, holding the consultant's hands in place as she slid on the cuffs, clicking them into place. He leant down, his face right by Traubert's, smelling sweat and his stupid fucking cologne.

'You're gonna rot, you know that, George?'

'George Traubert, I am arresting you on suspicion of conspiracy to commit murder. You do not have to say anything but it may . . .'

More footfalls behind them, Valdez arriving with one of the FY2s, faces aghast at the commotion. Harry continued to spit, getting to his feet.

'Everyone's gonna know what you are, George, you hear me? Everyone's gonna know what a pervert you are.'

His hand went to his shoulder, sore from the stitches, from Ambrose's bullet. He moved it up to his face and it came away with blood on it, just a split lip, nothing serious. Noble was coming to an end.

'. . . rely on in court. Anything you do say may be given in evidence.'

Harry was suppressing the instinct to kick Traubert again. Behind him, Valdez and the junior doctor were joined by Tammy Shelton, whom Harry assumed was the day registrar.

'What the hell's going on?' she demanded.

Harry ignored her, going to the head of the trolley to examine Idris from top to toe, checking over each and every port, line and tube. He checked the monitors and the ventilator settings, the portable oxygen supply, everything, making sure that in the few minutes Traubert had been alone with Idris he had done nothing else. Two more figures ran into the lobby, but not doctors, police; Noble's back-up. To be there so quickly, Harry guessed they'd already been in A&E, usually a safe bet at the Ruskin.

Harry looked over at Traubert, watched the coppers drag him to his feet, his body half vertical, hands cuffed behind his back, head bowed. As they did, his face came into view of the gathering crowd, who reacted with shock, disgust, disbelief. Valdez kept saying Traubert's name, over and over again. Shelton repeated her earlier question, and Harry snapped a reply.

'What does it look like?' he said. 'Go and ring Dr Fairbanks. Get her down here.'

Fairbanks was the most senior consultant on the unit, had held Traubert's job before him, and was now on the hospital's board. She would arrange for another consultant to cover the rest of the day, which would no doubt be the least of the board's worries after the news got out.

Noble stepped out from behind Traubert, shaking her hair free from her flushed face.

'Been a while since I've been in a scrap,' she said.

'You got an evidence bag?' Harry said.

'No.'

'I do,' said one of the uniforms. Noble took it from her and Harry nodded to beneath the trolley. Noble put gloves on, got down on her knees and reached underneath, retrieving the syringe and holding it up inside the polythene bag. Traubert hadn't managed to empty it all – there was at least three or four millilitres left, enough for forensic testing. Traubert, silent, couldn't resist looking up at it, and bowed his head again when he was done. Harry walked over to Traubert, grabbed his jaw with his hand, looked into his eyes.

'Look at that, George,' he said. 'That's a fucking slam dunk. You're finished.'

Traubert said nothing, and Noble swept Harry's arm away, folding up the evidence bag and calling in on her radio.

'Let's get him out of here,' she said, leaning into Harry and continuing under her breath: 'Before you do anything stupid.'

'I'm staying,' said Harry. 'They'll need all the help they can get.'

Valdez looked across at him, her face still paralysed with horror. Noble nodded, and they watched as she helped the police drag Traubert into the lift, hitting the button for the ground floor. Harry turned to Valdez and the FY2, taking his position at the head of Idris's bed. The teenager had remained unconscious and unaware throughout the entire ordeal. He would have no idea, until they told him, how close the man who had hurt him for years had come to taking his life.

'Let's get him back to the unit,' Harry said, wiping his lip with the fabric of his suit jacket. Valdez nodded, and they started to wheel the trolley back into the ICU.

As they did so, Harry looked down at Idris, lying supine on the trolley, eyes taped closed, tube in his throat, wires in his arteries, lines in his veins, heart beating. Chest rising and falling, weak muscles between his ribs, but stronger than they had been. The numbers on the screens merged into one another, but what they all meant was that the person they were attached to was alive, and that was all that really mattered. He thought about all the promises that had been made over the last two weeks, and in his head he heard the echo of the words he'd said to Traubert, two of them repeating.

It's over.

Friday, 1 February

The snow had come and gone and January was over, but London was still held in the crisp, melancholy half-light of winter. It was as dark as midnight as Harry got off the bus, though it had only just gone five. He'd just got a new haircut and a new phone, and the police had returned his car, which they'd gone to the trouble of cleaning, so in some ways he felt like a new man. He hoped that below the surface things were renewing as well. His shoulder hurt less, and he didn't need the tramadol. The scars on his cheek and his knuckles were beginning to pale, no longer turning heads when he went out.

The pub was just off Camberwell Green. It wasn't the closest to the hospital, but that was why he liked it, the fact that it wasn't swamped with healthcare staff. He went inside, ordered a coffee and sat at the bar. There was a folded-up copy of the *Evening Standard* there. Page five carried the story, a picture of the Ruskin's distinctive Victorian edifice and the headline DISGRACED CONSULT-ANT FACES RAPE CHARGES.

He folded the paper up and went to the back pages and read about football. Noble arrived after he'd been waiting for about ten minutes, dressed in the same black leather jacket she'd worn two Sundays ago. She sat next to him and ordered a large glass of house red, grinning at Harry. She'd just finished work, the final nine-to-five in a long week, with a weekend off to look forward to. Harry was about to start, working Friday through Monday, from 8.30 at night to the same time the following morning. Lots of the other registrars had covered for him while he'd been away, so he owed a few people favours.

Noble picked up her drink and they headed over to a booth at the back.

'What's this, then?' she said, sipping at her wine. 'Our first date?'

Harry laughed. 'Something like that,' he said. 'Though if you're hoping to stay at mine tonight, you'll have to make do with an on-call room.'

'That's very presumptuous,' said Noble. Harry finished his

coffee and took a look over the food menu, but it all sounded a bit too artisan. He needed something calorific enough to prepare him for a twelve-hour night stint.

'How was work?' he said.

'Good,' said Noble. 'I was up with CAIT for most of the afternoon. They're handing over Traubert's file to the CPS on Monday morning. They're covering the exploitation side, all the sexual stuff.'

They'd only spoken over the phone in the intervening week, not seen each other in person. Harry had spent most of it asleep, either at home or after long, cathartic sessions down at Marigold House. From what he'd gathered, Traubert had answered no comment to every single question asked of him.

'What about the conspiracy charge, then?'

Both of them had given statements to the Homicide & Serious team in Lewisham about what had happened at the hospital. Traubert had been seen drawing up a syringe in A&E, and the police believed he had done so with the intention of administering whatever drug it contained to Idris somewhere between the ICU and the CT scanner, but had then emptied it to try and destroy the evidence when he'd been confronted. According to Noble, if the syringe contained something deadly, they would have enough to charge Traubert with conspiracy to murder.

'Forensics got back to us on the syringe, said it contained potassium chloride.'

Harry nodded. On the wards, potassium was kept in separate cupboards from other preparations, and in pre-filled syringes with red stickers on them. Injected into a patient who didn't need it, the drug would stop the heart within seconds. It wouldn't show up on a post-mortem either because cells leaked potassium after death, so the rise wouldn't be noticed. The clever bastard, Harry thought.

'Then you've got him, surely?' he said.

'They'll have a hard time proving that syringe was intended to kill Idris,' Noble said. 'And that was the only question he bloody answered. Gave a prepared statement saying he'd found the syringe in A&E and was waiting to dispose of it properly.'

'Bullshit,' said Harry. 'There's no reason for anyone to draw up a twenty-mil syringe of potassium; that's a massive dose. They'll never believe him.'

Noble shrugged. 'It's circumstantial. People are still innocent until proved guilty in this country, Harry.'

'Even rapists? Even paedophiles?'

'He's not a paedophile,' said Noble. 'His victims were adolescents, not children, and he abused both females and males, which means it's not paedophilia in the classical sense. Most paedophiles are attracted to a certain gender, a certain age range, and they justify their actions as normal sexual behaviour, a form of love. But here the abuse was driven by violence. CAIT have a psychologist attached, and she told me she thought Traubert was more of a sadistic personality, that it was the act of controlling them which turned him on, and teenagers were just who he happened to have access to.'

Harry shook his head. All along, people had suspected James Lahiri of heinous acts, and made the comments about never really knowing somebody. Under their noses had been a monster, and they'd all missed it. How long had Harry worked with George Traubert; how many times had he sat in his office wishing he was somewhere else? Those questions, and more, occupied his thoughts, the way a schizophrenic's hallucinations refused to give him peace. Where had Lahiri crossed paths with those men, their activities and their plans, and why did he have to die?

Noble reached out and touched his knee, but he pulled back, almost on instinct. She looked up at him and tried an understanding smile.

'Harry, don't beat yourself up about it,' she said.

'That's easy for you to say,' he retorted.

'Do you know what the CAIT psychologist told me?' Noble said, lowering her voice. 'She said that the type of personalities who commit crimes like that, sexual sadism, are usually the types who go on to commit serious sexual violence. Eventually, the violence and the rapes aren't enough to satisfy their urges, so they go on to worse. Serial murder. Much as I hate to admit it, without you we probably wouldn't have caught Traubert. Christ knows what he might have gone on to do.'

'You're saying he might walk, though,' Harry said.

'On the conspiracy charge, maybe,' said Noble. 'But on the other stuff, we've got him nailed to the wall. We've got the drugs

339

in his office, and even if they're shaky in court we've got everything CAIT found at his house. Sophisticated video recording and editing equipment, a spare room with lime-green sheets, the exact same ones we saw in the video. They couldn't get any DNA off them, but Technical analysed the lighting pattern in the room and they can stand up in court and say that video was filmed in his house. His bank account had withdrawals of two hundred and fifty pounds a week which coincide with the payments to Idris. And his hard drive's got stuff on it that would make your blood run cold. They've sent it across to CEOP for analysis. They've got about two thousand images and videos, most of it Category Four and Category Five.'

'What does that mean?'

'Penetrative sex, imagery of a sadistic or violent nature. Most relating to adolescents, some children. They're charging him with rape, indecent assault, possession of a controlled substance, making and possession of indecent images. You name it. He's history, Harry.'

'He'll be out in ten years,' said Harry, stirring the black clumps left in his coffee cup.

'Bollocks,' said Noble. 'There's no judge in the country that will go easy on him. And however long he gets, he's a middle-class sex offender whose face will be all over the papers. He won't last a month inside Belmarsh.'

Harry thought about that. In his elective at medical school, he'd spent four weeks with the medical unit at Wandsworth prison, and he'd seen the things that the inmates did to sexual offenders, particularly paedophiles. He'd seen one patient who'd had bleach poured onto his genitals while three other inmates held him down. He thought about things like that happening to George Traubert, and then about Charlie Ambrose dying slowly in a hospital bed, his burned skin slowly crushing him to death. He wondered what kind of thing was called justice.

'The images of Solomon went back as far as 2009,' Noble went on. 'It looks like that's when he started abusing him, right at the beginning of the project.'

'Four years, and it took his girlfriend to kill herself before he decided to try and escape?' said Harry. Solomon Idris would have been thirteen years old. It explained how he'd managed to get advanced HIV disease by the age of seventeen, and it explained what had haunted Harry the most, the look in his eyes, that thousand-yard stare.

'Who knows what his mindset was that night,' Noble said. 'You know as well as I do the psychological damage that kind of abuse does to people, especially teenagers. For all we know, you could have been right. It could have been a suicide attempt.'

Harry stirred his coffee some more.

'Well, he came bloody close. And I hardly helped him, did I?'

He thought about Fairweather's words, inviting him to pack in the police work. After what he'd seen of the organisation over the past weeks, writing a resignation letter was climbing up his to-do list.

'I'm glad you were there,' Noble said. 'You stood up for what you thought was right, even though the easy thing to do was walk away. Most people take the easy route, but you didn't.'

She got up to go to the toilet, and her words sat in Harry's stomach like a lump of undigested food. He was listening to Tammas's thoughts about life, remembering the words he'd said. How everybody had a hollow inside of them, which they strove their whole existence to find something to fill. Maybe Noble had filled it with her husband, and now he was gone, she filled it with her work. And when it came to people like George Traubert, maybe it was filled with something unspeakable, or maybe it was empty, closed off by some psychological valve to the rest of the human world. Whatever it was, Harry didn't understand what could drive a man to do that, and he hoped he never would.

Noble came back on the phone, and sat down again. She was talking in French, and went on for about a minute before she hung up.

The choice of language suggested to Harry that she'd been making enquiries in George Traubert's country of origin.

'Switzerland?' he said.

'Yeah, the federal police,' she explained. 'Like I said, the statistics say that Traubert's offended before, but he doesn't have a record in the UK. We've been in touch with both the Swiss and the Canadian police, to see if there's anything they can use in court.'

'Christ,' said Harry. He remembered Traubert telling him how he'd given Whitacre the benefit of his experience in Toronto, doing something similar to the Saviour Project. Outreach work with disadvantaged teenagers. How many did they suspect from London? Noble had mentioned four, but maybe since then the Child Abuse Investigation Team had uncovered yet more lives which the man had ruined. The teenagers they'd already identified were undergoing testing for HIV, though thankfully none of them was yet showing symptoms. Further interviews with the Saviour Project administrators had revealed the first point of contact: in 2009, Solomon Idris had had five initial consultations, three with Duncan Whitacre. Two with George Traubert. Assuming the abuse had started not long afterwards, Idris had been a victim of the most horrifying crimes for nearly four years.

'We ran his credit cards,' Noble went on. 'He took holidays to Thailand, twice a year. Alone. God only knows what he got up to over there.'

'Well, you just make sure you put him away,' said Harry. 'You owe them that.'

Noble looked up at him. 'We will.'

'And make sure that you tell everyone that James Lahiri's an innocent man.'

'We will.'

'Good. What about Idris, the charges?'

'The guy I spoke to at the CPS peddled some bullshit about him having to cooperate with the police. You know what they're like with guns, mandatory five-year sentences and all that.'

'Fuck's sake,' said Harry. The thought of Solomon Idris being dragged through a lengthy trial after everything he'd been through made him sick.

'But it won't happen,' Noble said. 'Even if they did charge him, he'd get a psych review and walk on diminished responsibility. And the Met aren't keen on a trial either, what with the fact that he wasn't actually holding a gun when he was shot.'

'I can imagine,' said Harry. 'Anyway, I'd better go.'

He looked at his watch and got to his feet. Noble rose with him, and they headed outside, into the cold. He walked her to her car, and kissed her on the cheek. As he did so, her hair came back over her ear, and he saw what was behind it. A tattoo, seven capital letters in Celtic lettering, hidden from all but the most intimate observers. He'd noticed it before, the second time they'd had sex, but hadn't been able to see which word it was. Now he could.

'Courage,' Harry said.

Noble looked up at him and then immediately away, and he realised he'd put his foot in it.

'I'm sorry,' he said, 'I—'

'If I'd had a tough day, Jack would hold me,' she said, her eyes wet. 'From behind. And whisper that to me. Courage. After he went, I got that done. So he'd always be there.'

Harry nodded. It sounded like a good word to remember a man by.

'I'd best be off,' he said, turning towards the hospital.

'Wait.'

Noble unlocked the boot of her car, reaching in and pulling out a cardboard box stacked with the nondescript files common to every bureaucracy of the modern age. She hefted the box in her hands and passed it to Harry.

'I want you to have these.'

The file on top was marked 'KINSELLA, MARIE RACHEL. DOB: 19/03/1989'. Harry looked up at her in bemusement.

'I called in a favour,' she explained. 'They're all Caucasian women reported missing from central London in July and August 2011, aged seventeen to twenty-three. Just the top sheets, but it should be enough for you to rule a few out.'

Harry smiled. For some inexplicable reason, he felt like crying. Noble opened her car door and stood in front of it.

'Let's see each other soon,' she said.

'Sure.'

'Let's do something. I think it'd do you good.'

'What do you mean?' Harry said.

'As in, do something. Have a day out. Something that isn't work, or chasing ghosts and victims. Something you enjoy. Christ, Harry, there has to be something.'

Harry nodded, embarrassed. Started thinking. He saw the offer for what it was, but he still resented the accusation at its core. That now was the moment of intervention, where his life could depart on a number of trajectories, and she wanted to return him to the one as close to normality as possible.

'Football?' he suggested.

Noble laughed. 'Not on your life.'

'I'll think of something, then.'

'You do that,' she said. 'See you.'

Harry was early to work. He didn't need to pick up his bleep for an hour, so he dumped the missing-person files in his locker, changed into scrubs and refilled the empty aspirin bottle with white tablets. Maybe tonight would be a good night, and he wouldn't need to avail himself in the early hours. He headed out of the changing room and over to the surgical wing of the hospital, passing through the same lift alcove that George Traubert had been dragged through the previous weekend. It was perfectly clean, he thought as he looked around. That was the odd nature of hospitals: human beings gave birth, lived and died in these rooms, these corridors. But once they'd gone, the cleaners descended, and not a trace of them was left.

The lift arrived at the fourth floor and Harry followed the signs to the plastics ward, used his ID card to get in, and headed towards the burns high-dependency unit. As he did, he passed the consultant's office, the door open, and the name Simon Hart, FRCS, engraved on the plaque. The consultant was at his desk, answering emails at half seven on a Friday evening. There was a picture of his wife and two daughters next to his in-tray.

'Mr Hart, is it?'

The consultant turned around.

'Can I help you?'

'I wanted to ask about Charlie Ambrose.'

Hart slid his glasses down to the end of his nose.

'And who are you?'

'I'm the doctor who treated him at the scene,' Harry lied. 'I'm a colleague of his down in A&E, actually.'

'I thought you looked familiar,' Hart said. 'Close the door.'

Harry did so, and Hart offered him a seat. From the consultant's demeanour he worked out that the news wasn't good. The burns unit at the Ruskin wasn't big, and severe cases were usually moved to the specialist centre in Essex. The fact that Ambrose was still there suggested that they didn't feel there was anything to gain by transferring him.

'Mr Ambrose developed abdominal compartment syndrome,' Hart said. 'We performed a laparotomy to decompress it, but the CT scan shows an intra-abdominal catastrophe. I'm afraid that the prognosis is so poor that there's nothing to be gained by aggressive management. I'm sorry.'

Harry nodded. The burned skin across Ambrose's abdomen and the fluid from the tissue swelling had crushed his internal organs until they had necrosed, and even the operation to open up his belly and relieve the pressure had been too late. At the end of the day, it had always been a question of how and when Ambrose would die, not whether he would.

'Is he intubated?' Harry said.

'No,' said Hart. 'He's ventilating pretty well, actually. We woke him up after our initial debridement. We'll keep him comfortable.'

Harry thanked him and headed down into the high-dependency unit, which consisted of three separate rooms. One was empty. In the second was a young girl, no older than five, with dressings all down her right arm, and a gathered family in traditional East African dress, some clutching talismans, her mother kissing her hand. In the other room was Charlie Ambrose, asleep and alone.

Harry entered, closing the door quietly. Ambrose was sat up in the bed, oxygen tubes in his nose, fluid running into a vein in his arm, a syringe driver of morphine connected to a button, each press delivering another dose. Ambrose stirred as Harry came to his bedside and looked down at the leathery, charred skin, cracked like the stones of a lava flow, the yellow, swollen flesh glowing beneath.

'Harry,' said Ambrose. 'You're the first to come. Not even my wife's been, you know.'

Harry folded his arms over the railing.

'You know you're dying, don't you?'

'Yeah,' said Ambrose. He had to catch his breath with every word, and it made him sound like someone else Harry spoke to a lot. 'I'm ready.'

'You're ready?' Harry repeated.

'To be with God. I don't want to live. In sin. Like this.'

Harry found it difficult to disagree with that point of view, though he wondered what any God would think of the things which Ambrose had done.

'I've asked for forgiveness. And I'm ready to face my judgement,' Ambrose went on. 'And God. Will judge me.'

'Well, if you ask me, it's not him you need to ask for judgement,' said Harry. 'It's people like Solomon.'

Ambrose rocked his head slowly, and the oxygen tube got caught on his neck, so Harry shuffled it free. Then their eyes met. Ambrose's were pleading.

'I never touched them,' he said. 'I promise you. I just liked the pictures. I wanted to look at them. They were so beautiful. I never touched them. You have to believe me.'

'It doesn't matter if I believe you or not,' said Harry.

'Yes, it does.'

'George Traubert's been arrested,' said Harry. He had no idea whether the police had come to talk to Charlie Ambrose yet, though he suspected that there would be little point. He wasn't going to be put on trial, nor would he be around to testify against Traubert. Ambrose stirred a little, pressed his morphine button, and then met Harry's eyes again.

'All he wanted to do was hurt them,' Ambrose said. 'I hated him for that. He never loved them, like I did. But I couldn't stop him, because he said he'd kill me. I failed them. I'm so sorry.'

'You killed my friend,' Harry said.

'He told me I had to,' Ambrose said. 'I was scared. I didn't want to. I didn't want. Anybody to get hurt. The watchman. I just panicked. I saved his life, I didn't want him to die.'

Harry looked at Ambrose pitilessly. Here lay a man who'd been consumed by the choices he had made, the temptations he'd given in to. A man whose desires had eaten him up, and now he was facing the eternal, repentant in the shadow of inevitable death. Trying to justify the murder of one innocent man with the fact he'd saved another.

'What about Wyndham Road?' Harry said.

'George told me Solomon was going to go to the police. Told

me I had to deal with it,' Ambrose said. 'I followed him. From his house. I couldn't do it. There in the street. Or in the shop. There were too many people. But then he pulled his gun out. And the police turned up. And I just panicked. Hid. And . . .'

Ambrose didn't finish the story because he was crying, or in pain, Harry didn't know which. He didn't need to hear it, either.

'You believe in forgiveness, don't you, Charlie?' he said.

'Of course.'

'You believe in truth as well?'

Ambrose nodded slowly.

'OK,' said Harry. 'Tell me why you killed James.'

Ambrose's gaze turned upwards until he was staring, glassy eyed, at the ceiling, and Harry saw his lips tremble in prayer, like they had done when he'd been rolling around outside his burning house.

'Tell me,' Harry repeated. 'You owe me that, you sanctimonious prick.'

Ambrose finished his prayer and turned towards Harry.

'OK, but you need to,' Ambrose caught his breath, 'do something for me.'

Harry nodded.

'You know that infusion,' Ambrose went on. 'I can only press my button once every. Three minutes. To stop me from overdosing.'

'I understand,' said Harry.

'I just want it all,' said Ambrose, 'to go away. I don't want to live. With this filth in my head. Promise me.'

'OK. Why did you kill him?'

Outside, one of the nurses looked in through the small window by the door to see what was going on, but saw the pink of Harry's scrubs and turned back towards the main ward.

'James knew that something was going on,' Ambrose said. 'With Idris. He was worried. He thought it was more than. Just the drugs. He thought that someone within the project was up to something with Idris. That Duncan might be involved, so he came to me. Asking for advice.'

Harry looked up at the ceiling, a sick feeling rushing through his body, his hairs standing on end. Lahiri's final words, before the bullet had crushed his skull, asking Harry to wait, to calm down, because he thought he knew what was going on. He'd been right from the start, and just as Harry had, he'd suspected Duncan Whitacre. But Lahiri had trusted Ambrose, had gone to him, and the reward had been death.

'I knew if he told you the police would look into both of us,' Ambrose said. 'And George told me he'd set Lahiri up. That was the idea. To make it look like it was him and Duncan.'

And that explained the phone calls in the past weeks, and the days after Idris got shot.

Harry gripped the railing at the side of the bed, and thought of how everything might have changed if he'd just had two more minutes to speak to Lahiri on the night he'd died. Or if Lahiri had trusted him enough to tell him everything on the Monday. Or maybe the point of divergence was further back. Maybe, if Harry hadn't betrayed him, Lahiri would have come to him with his suspicions instead of to Ambrose. And maybe if Harry had walked into the Chicken Hut and persuaded Idris to walk out of there and into an ambulance, all of this would have been prevented. People were defined by the choices they made. He thought about that for a long while, until Ambrose pressed his button again.

'You know what I'm asking you to do,' Ambrose said quietly.

Harry looked across at the syringe driver. The infusion was set up so that it would only accept a low flow rate, therefore it would be difficult to overdose him without it taking hours, and by that time a nurse would notice for sure. There were other options. Injecting the morphine directly into his IV cannula, perhaps. But none of them was acceptable. Harry stood up straight and started washing his hands in the sink by the door.

'You promised me!' Ambrose protested, his pathetic voice as loud as it could go.

'You quoted the Bible at me, when we were in the taxi,' Harry said, turning back around. 'What was it again?'

He leaned closer. Ambrose's face scrunched up.

'A man reaps what he sows.'

Harry went to the handover meeting in the doctors' office on the ICU, but it had been a quiet evening and there were no urgent tasks waiting. He nodded as he half-listened to vignettes about sick patients on the wards who might need reviewing, his thoughts elsewhere. He stared at the date on the wall calendar. A month of the year was gone already. He finished the handover and headed away from the ICU, passing Idris's room as he did so.

Solomon Idris was sat up in his bed, still connected to a few wires and lines, but free of the breathing tube in his neck, a dark scar across his throat. His colour was good, though he still looked sick: the bones prominent, the hollows either side of them deep. Beside him, his mother was asleep, slumped over Idris's bed, while Junior sat on the other chair in the room, playing on a Nintendo DS.

Idris took off his oxygen mask, and looked up at Harry, who smiled back.

'Hello, Solomon,' he said.

Idris tried to form words, but he was too weak to talk, and Harry rested his hand on the teenager's arm.

'It's OK,' he said. 'You'll be talking soon, and you'll have plenty of time to talk if you want.'

That seemed to pacify him, and Harry leant against the side of the bed. The speech and language therapists had already started an intensive regimen of rehabilitation, as had the physiotherapists and the dieticians, the people who would really manage Idris's recovery now the doctors had done their bit.

'How are you feeling?' Harry asked. 'Good?'

Idris formed an expression that was close to a smile, and nodded. His movements were sluggish on account of the pain relief he still required, and it reminded Harry of what he had seen in the video. He tried to shake that thought, but maybe it was closer to the real truth – while it would take Idris months to recover from his physical injuries, his psychological wounds might need longer to heal. The first psychiatrist was going to visit on Monday, when hopefully they could start the journey to something resembling a normal life.

Idris had fallen asleep. Harry had a bizarre, almost selfish desire to be there when the psychologists told him that Traubert had been arrested, that the man who had hurt him and Keisha would be going to prison for a long, long time. But that wouldn't be for many weeks, not until he was psychologically ready. Likewise, Idris didn't yet know that he was HIV-positive. That revelation could come later, too.

Joy Idris had woken, and came to stand beside Harry.

'How is he, Doctor?' she said.

Harry considered everything he'd just thought about, how close Idris had come to slipping into the void, how far he had to climb towards normality. But perhaps all that mattered was that the gradient would be upwards now. He looked back at Solomon and smiled.

'He's doing well, Mrs Idris,' Harry said. 'All being well, he should go to the adolescent ward on Monday. I'll leave you in peace.'

He headed to the door and looked back as he shut it. They were a family close to being at peace, despite everything they had been through, and all the people who'd died, one way or another, because of what had happened to Solomon. Just like how the city outside his living-room window always carried on. Harry watched them for a while, then let them be.

It was that early part of the night shift when Harry felt he was waiting for someone's life to fall apart. There he sat, in his scrubs and running shoes, hunched over in a chair, elbow on his knees. He hated the doctors' mess at night, hated the nine or ten body clocks restlessly fidgeting around on uncomfortable sofas, none of them in time with each other. Which was why he was sitting in a side room on Tennyson instead, the bleep on his belt, the box of manila folders on the floor next to the chair.

He had started to truly grieve for James Lahiri, for a man he had hated for most of the last year of his existence, who had given his life to helping others. At least his death had been swift, and he hadn't suffered the ignominy of knowing that he was dying alone. There had to be others like Charlie Ambrose and George Traubert, Harry thought, whose lives were so solitary that even in crisis there was no one to provide a comforting hand, just an empty room.

There could be one right here, Harry thought as he looked at the girl. At Zara. Noble's words, her offers of a date, still stung his ears. *Chasing ghosts and victims.* It was a fairly true, if accidental, summary of his life. And after the previous weeks, there were even more ghosts for him to add to the list.

When she'd come in her hair had been shocking pink, the colour of fuchsias or bougainvillea, but as the autumn had progressed it had faded with the leaves. Her natural hair colour was that of straw, and in the months of her coma it had grown to past her shoulders, until Harry had suggested recolouring it that September. He had always thought that somewhere there must be a family who'd had a cavern struck into their lives, a vacuum that Zara had once filled. With every passing week, every on-call spent keeping her company, that possibility waned. It was like his relationship with alcohol or amphetamines, in the way that the precipice there hung over a chasm of addiction, but here over one of obsession.

He'd come to one decision in the five minutes he'd been in the chair. Fairweather and his loaded words aside, he had no other choice but to keep on working with the Met, be a thorn in their side until they either kicked him out or uncovered the identity of the girl in front of him. Noble seemed willing to help, which was a start.

Zara was not Marie Rachel Kinsella, who had been reported missing from her parents' house in West Lothian in July 2011 following an argument. The report listed the usual factors: familial strife, drug problems. A confirmed runaway, she had spent five days at a hostel in Soho before disappearing. Her last sighting was CCTV footage of her walking with her bags, somewhere near King's Cross, heading towards Farringdon, on 18 July. The photograph was old and the age would have fitted, but on the third page of the report was the detail. At the age of nine, Marie Kinsella had come off her bike and fractured her skull.

Harry hadn't even realised that he knew Zara's medical history by heart, but he didn't need to check any of her X-rays, CT scans or MRIs to know that there were no sutures in the skull, nor any previous fractures.

It was as he folded the file and put it to the bottom of the box that he saw it. The tremor wasn't massive, but her head twisted slowly, her face coming up towards Harry, and then back down again, like someone nodding on a jerky camera.

He was out of the chair, shouting. 'Hello? Hello?'

Vital signs stable, no increase in heart rate. He tried squeezing her hand. No response. He reached across to her wrist and pinched the muscle, willing her to react.

'Do that again, go on. Nod your head.'

He looked down at her quiet, pale face, willing it to move. Nodded slowly, just as she had, in case she couldn't understand him.

'Go on, do it again. If you did it on purpose, eyes right.'

Her eyes moved to the right, sluggishly, then left, then right again. Harry burst from the room and ran to the nurses' office, instructing them to call the neurology registrar, immediately.

The registrar arrived, tired looking and unimpressed. Harry had seen her around the ward before, working with Professor Niebaum, so he knew he didn't need to explain Zara's story.

'She moved?' the registrar asked. 'This is a patient in a minimally conscious state, you know that, right?'

'She nodded,' Harry said. 'Like she was trying to speak. She moved, alright! She moved!'

The registrar walked in calmly and began her examination. The girl was still minimally conscious, and when the neurologist repeated the tests Harry had done in more detail the hand remained motionless. Zara's eyes flickered from one side to the next in response to the usual set of questions, but she didn't respond to anything she hadn't responded to before. The registrar turned around, her expression showing nothing but pity.

'There's been no change in her condition,' she said.

'But she moved!'

'Probably just a myoclonic jerk.'

'It could have been voluntary. Means that she's recovered some cortical function?'

'It's a jerk. People in MCS jerk just as much as people who are asleep. As I said, there's been no change. I'll write in the notes, and we'll have Prof review it on Monday.'

A pager sounded, and Harry checked his belt before realising it was the neurologist's. She strolled calmly out of the room, leaving the door swinging. Harry stood for a while before returning to his chair. Slowly, he reached into the box and retrieved the next folder.

He opened it and began to read.